STRONGSTAND

MATTHEW JAMES MENDOZA

PublishAmerica
Baltimore

© 2009 by Matthew James Mendoza.
All rights reserved. No part of this book may be reproduced, stored in a retrieval system or transmitted in any form or by any means without the prior written permission of the publishers, except by a reviewer who may quote brief passages in a review to be printed in a newspaper, magazine or journal.

First printing

All characters in this book are fictitious, and any resemblance to real persons, living or dead, is coincidental.

PublishAmerica has allowed this work to remain exactly as the author intended, verbatim, without editorial input.

ISBN: 978-1-60749-127-9
PUBLISHED BY PUBLISHAMERICA, LLLP
www.publishamerica.com
Baltimore

Printed in the United States of America

CHAPTER ONE

"Wake up Andrew!" the young boy grabs his blanket made from animal skins and wool and rolls over to the sound of this faint whisper.

"Wake up Andrew"!, this time in a stronger firm tone yet still in a strange manner. It's as though the young boy hears his brother's thoughts in his head. Marcus, Andrews older brother lay in bed on the other side of the room trying not to giggle.

Andrew, opening his sleepy eyes kicks his feet throwing his blanket and yells**, "Stop doing that Marcus! I hate it when you do, that."**

Marcus says with a boyish smurk "Doing what? I'm just waking up myself."

Stumbling out of bed the ten year old boy, Andrew looks at his older brother with a frustrated look. His brown hair compliments his light brown eyes, the eyes of his mother. His features are smaller than Marcus's, however, holds himself in a solid manner. Andrews expressions are unique blending with a maturity yet characters that are very boyish. Its those eyes that glow and almost appear green in the right light that almost tell a story when gazed into. He resembles his mother very much but has the genes of his father, a strong man.

"I don't know what you're doing, just stop it or I will tell father."

"Tell father what!" Marcus replies, "I'm climbing into your dreams and telling you to wake up when its time to wake up. Go right ahead father will just laugh at you."

At that momemt the boys hear a loud strong voice coming from the large room of their home. It's their father, Marcus senior, hollering to them, "Time to get up, morning meal is ready, and Marcus, stop doing whatever you're doing!"

Both young boys out of bed already look at each other puzzled. Andrew asks Marcus, "How did he hear us?"

"I don't know but he does it all the time."

Marcus and Andrew could smell fresh cooked pork and eggs in the room. This was one of Marcus's favorite meals, Andrew didnt mind it from time to time.

Andrew say's to Marcus, "I wish we lived in a bigger home".

Marcus looks at his brother with his deep brown eyes and intense expression, "Don't let father hear you say that. He works hard to keep a roof over our heads and he is a very proud man, some say too proud." Marcus then gives his brother a curios look "What's wrong with our home anyhow?"

Andrew looks back at his brother, "Look around, its old, always cold with a damp smell, not to mention too small, don't you remember we share a bedroom."

"You're a brat!" Marcus says smiling at his younger brother. "If it rains are you wet? When it snow's are you cold? Father keeps us warm and dry and as we speak mother has a warm morning meal waiting for us. All you think about is a bigger home. Let's go eat, my stomach is rumbling."

The two boys enter the large room in their home where a hand carved table made of oak is set for four. Sitting in the middle are some plates with smoked pork, fresh-cut melon, eggs and fresh baked bread. Marcus shoots a look at Andrew, not a word just a look. Andrew knew and felt what it meant. Andrew not wanting to look at his brother looks out the window. The trees were full and flowers were blooming. Vines were hanging from the trees, it was a beautiful sight. He had only seen this scenary before in one particular place, his grandfathers. His mind drifts to his grandfathers home. The landscape there was unspeakable. It was one of the most spectacular places Andrew had ever seen. Vines and bushes accompanied with roses and shrubs so thick and full as far as the eye can see. It was like his Grandfather spent all day every day from dawn till dusk working on his landscape. At least that's what Andrew remembers, it's been more than four years since he's been there. Even though the landscape was beautiful, he did not enjoy going there. It was very irksome and boring for a young boy. It seemed as though all they did was talk when they were there.

Bringing his mind back to the table and away from Grandfathers, Andrew looks at his brother trying to think of a way to ask his father why they don't live in a bigger home. Marcus sits and looks sternly at his brother. Even only the age of thirteen, Marcus presents himself in a mature manner. His crisp dark hair reached down to his shoulders, with his bold stock chin and brown eyes that had a sparkle to them no matter what his mood. Marcus was a very handsome young boy. He stood five feet five inches and had broad shoulders and thick legs. It was clear that he was growing into a strong solid man with a quizitive mind and a heart of gold.

Andrew hears his brother's thoughts in his head, *"Don't ask, it will only upset him."*

Not understanding why he could hear his brother's voice in his head, an even more confusion thought, how did Marcus know what he was thinking.

Choosing his words carefully, he asks his father, "Why don't we live closer to the villages?"

"What do you mean?" his father says looking at him with a stern look. Marcus Sr. was surely the look of his oldest boy. His tall large frame and thick legs presented him with a confidence that made him bold and proud. His dark hair lay about shoulder length with a focal point on his face glistening from two sparkles represented by his dark eyes. All the men of the house were always kept clean and put together. Cleanliness was a priority within this family.

Andrew very nervous starts to stutter "W-well I-I think it w-would be easier for you if we lived closer to the villages."

"Why?" his father asks in a voice that sounded angry and concerned. Andrew now very uneasy and starting to sweat a little says "The traveling." he pauses and looks down at his food. "It two days of traveling to the big villages," he sighs a bit, " its just far."

"It's not that far Andrew," their mother Helen says. She is a fairly small women with long brown hair and light brown eyes, the eyes of her youngest son, so light that in the right light they look a greenish color. "My sister lives half way, we will travel for a day and visit her along the way. She always welcomes us and loves our company."

Marcus looks at his son "That's not it, is it? You think our home is too small, you think we should live better. I think we live just fine,"

Marcus Sr. pauses in his response and takes a bit of his food, "And no Marcus I'm not too proud I'm just proud enough. As to why we live so far from the villages, there are many reasons but the most important reason is so we can keep in touch with grandfather."

Marcus Jr. interrupts the conversation, "We haven't visited grandfathers in over four years."

His father looks at him with a reinsuring smile, "I am in contact with him a lot more than you think, and speaking of grandfather, I think its time we give him a visit."

That comment strikes concern on Helen's face. She does not think the young boys are ready to learn about their history.

At that moment miles away, an old man and his wife were cleaning up after their morning meal. The man looks at his wife with a smile and says, "The boys are coming!"

After breakfast, Marcus and Andrew both tend to their chores. Marcus restocks the firewood from the woodpile into their home while his brother feeds the animals. They then partner up on splitting and stacking the wood, making sure the supply stays plentiful. With every swing of the axe, Andrew begs his big brother for a turn. Marcus lets his brother take a few swings, however, the majority he does so the job gets done in a timely manner.

When they are done Marcus looks at Andrew, "I'll race you to the garden you little brat!" They both take off in a dead sprint, Andrew trying with all his might to keep up with his brother.

"Why do you always have to beat me, Marcus," Andrew says trying to catch his breath. "Someday I am going to be faster than you and you know what is feels like to be second all the time."

Marcus shakes his hand on Andrews head ruffling his hair, "Maybe you will beat me someday but you'll still be a brat! Come on lets finish these chores, check over the garden I will make sure the fence is in tack."

Andrew easily distracted starts to climb the fence instead of tending to the garden, Marcus yells at him to get down so he won't get hurt like the last time he decided to climb the fence.

Andrew jumps down, "I don't want to go to grandfathers, it takes too long to get there and it's always boring."

Marcus knowing his brother is right, "Try to think of it as an adventure, like were on a treasure hunt or something."

"A treasure hunt!" Andrew cries out, "We walk for three days, stay for two then walk home! That's a long boring treasure hunt to not find any treasure."

"Just try to be positive, and if you can't try to act it. Now lets go play the fence is fine and the garden looks good."

The two boys run off into the woods, Marcus well ahead of Andrew again keeps taunting him to catch up.

Andrew yells, **"Wait up! You're going to lose me."**

"You know where I'm going." Marcus yells back now far ahead of his brother.

After running for about fifteen minutes Andrew catches up with Marcus who is now sitting by a stream sipping water from his hands.

Marcus looks at Andrew "What took you so long? I though you had these big dreams of beating me!"

Marcus looks at his brothers knee and sees that it is bleeding. Andrew tells his brother he fell and scraped it.

Marcus grabs his brother by the lower leg and looks at his knee, "Lets clean it up with some of the stream water, its just a scrape the bleeding will stop soon enough."

Marcus reaches down to get some water and splashes his brother and says, "Grab a sip first you must be thirsty after trying to catch me!"

Andrew pushes Marcus on his shoulder and calls him a jerk. Andrew takes a minute drinking some water and washing his knee.

He yells at his brother **"Look!"** pointing down at the water.

Marcus, somewhat startled, yells back **"Look at what?"**

Andrew points into the water, "Look at the fish."

Marcus still a little startled, "A fish? Are you kidding me? A fish! We're at a stream, what did you expect, cows and goats? No! You made me jump out of my skin for a fish in a stream!"

Andrew, knowing he startled his brother and also knowing he is much slower, runs up and tags him, **"You're it,"** He yells as he runs into the woods.

Marcus still a little breathless from his brother scaring him realizes what his brother has done and gets up to chase. They both know the woods and have a lot of fun chasing each other.

After playing chase, they play hide and seek. It's a fun game for Andrew to play Marcus doesn't like it so much anymore, but he plays anyway. He knows their life is kind of boring living so far from the other villages so he tries to keep his younger brother as occupied as possible. Besides, it seems like no matter where his brother hides, or how long he gives him, he's always able to find him. It's like something tells him where he's hiding. But that's ridiculous, he tells himself. He just knows his brother really well and can find him easily.

After playing for several hours, Marcus finds his brother for the last time and they both head home.

"Did you have fun today?" Marcus asks his brother.

"Yes I did, why do you ask?"

"I'm not sure but I think were starting off to grandfathers tomorrow."

"Tomorrow," Andrew says in a whiney voice "I don't want to!"

"I know," Marcus says "I'm not sure but I think father wants to leave tomorrow morning, and I think it's more than just a visit"

"What do you mean more than a visit?"

"I'm not sure, I just have a feeling that something is bothering father, or at least something is on his mind," Marcus pauses before saying, "I think it's important so try to have a good time, or at least look like it"

At that very moment their grandfather miles away stands up with a concerned look on his face.

Sarah, his wife looks at him, she is much shorter than he is with dark hair starting to turn white with age, even though she's getting a little old, she has a glowing smile giving her a youthfull shine. "What's the matter?" she asks.

The old man with dark hair and dark eyes his hair also starting to turn white with age, Two deep scares on one side of his face, and one less noticeable on the other side, His hair long, yet very neat and a beard about one inch past his chin.

He takes a step and grabs hold of his staff or as he calls it his walking stick. "I don't think it's a social visit."

He stares deep and hard into the woods, when he does, there is an eerie feeling in the air.

His wife looks at him, although she knows his past it's still hard to believe. She tries to talk to him but he won't listen, he just looks deep into the woods.

This lasts for several long minutes, the wind is blowing strongly yet the entire time he stares into the thick forest not one vine, bushes or even the smallest leaf is moving. It's as though he has stopped nature while he was in thought.

Once again his wife says, "Calm down Andrew. What's wrong?"

"Marcus Jr. knows," the old man tells his wife.

"From what you have told me, that's impossible."

"Yes I know, but I just heard his thoughts and that means one of two things has happened, ether his father has opened his mind or its opening by itself which is extremely rear!"

He looks at his wife, "They will be leaving tomorrow."

"Will Helen be coming?"

"I don't think so. Who will take care of the animals and garden while they are away?"

"That's to bad. I would love to see her. It's been a long time."

The old man smile at his wife then says, "Maybe, and I'm not promising anything, but maybe after they visit we will go visit them."

She looks at him with amazement, it's been about ten years since they have been off their land and that was only to help with the birth of Andrew Jr. and before that it was to help with Marcus Jr. she can barely remember any time before that. They have always stayed on their land, Marcus and Helen have always come to visit them.

He looks back at her who now has a big smile on her face. "Once again, I said maybe"

They walk back into the home. Andrew Sr. walks with a very pronounced limp that he tries to hide but makes worse. So he leans on his stick for support.

Back in the woods, Andrew Jr. asks his brother, "Aren't we supposed to check on fathers fish trap.

Marcus looks at his brother then turns around, "Thanks for reminding me."

They both walk back in the opposite direction; they didn't want to tell their father they had forgotten. They walk back to the stream where their father has his fish trap. It's a small stream dug next to the big stream with a little pond dug out before connecting back into the big stream. The exit is blocked with a hand carved wood fence letting small fish escape but the big ones are caught. At the opening of the small stream before the pond there are two big stones, one on each side with a carved piece of wood on a swivel that will only let fish in.

There are five fish in the trap. Marcus tells Andrew to gather them. Andrew complains while he does it grumbling.

"Fish makes my hands smell."

Marcus agrees with his brother "But they taste good," he says.

They walk back to their home both carrying fish. *"It's a lot longer when you walk,"* Andrew is thinking.

Marcus says out loud, "I agree."

Once again there is a confused look on Andrew's face. Andrew thinks Marcus thought he said that out loud. He ponders about how his brother knew what he was thinking. He looks at his brother trying to figure it out.

As they see smoke from the fireplace at their home Marcus says, "Last one home feeds the animals!" and starts to run.

Andrew looks at him run, he is tired so he just keeps walking. He knows that their father will make them both feed the animals so he starts walking slower.

When Andrew gets home, Marcus is already feeding the animals, his father tells him to help.

They have a lot of animals for milk, eggs, wool and food so it's a lot of work. Marcus senior takes care of the animals most of the time.

When the two children are finished feeding the animals, their father pulls them aside in the food shed (which is made from stone and mud) just big enough to keep the animal's food dry and a place for the chickens to lye their eggs. On the back side is a pile of wood with a place to stack the split wood keeping it dry enough to burn, you never know when it may rain for a long period of time, Better safe than sorry. He tells them to make sure that there is plenty of food for the animals. He also tells them to look around and make sure that every thing is ready for their mother, because she will be taking care of the animals for at least a week.

Andrew sighs, "A week!"

His father looks at him, "I said at least a week. I think it maybe longer. Make sure your mother has what she needs for at least two weeks or more."

"Two week's or more!" Andrew cries.

Marcus Jr. interrupts and says, "Don't worry father, we will take care of it."

Andrew looking at his brother with disappointment as he starts to work, he knows it will take hours to do this.

Marcus Jr. looks back at Andrew without saying anything. Andrew knows to keep quiet so he looks down and continues working.

Marcus Jr. looks at his father and asks, "Father why two weeks?"

Marcus Sr. like his own father carries a walking stick that is always by his side.

"It's a long walk," he replies, "make sure your mother has what she needs and get some sleep. We leave at dawn."

Andrew looks at his brother once again wanting to complain but decides not to. He just keeps working.

Both Marcus and Andrew fill the food shed with plenty of food so their mother only has to put food in the animal's trough.

"I'm done," Andrew says.

Marcus looks at him, "We should go pick all the ripe vegetables from the garden for mother."

Andrew sighs, "I'm tired I want to go to bed."

Marcus looks at him with a long stare then says, "Mother takes care of us all the time this is the least we can do for her. We are going away for at least two weeks, let's try to make it easy for her while we are away."

They walk to the garden and pick all the ripe vegetables. Andrew not helping much but he does keep his brother company.

They made sure the fence is still strong so no animals can get into the garden then they walk around the animal's area and check that fence. They walk back into their home, have a quick bite to eat, tell their father everything is ready and go to sleep.

That night as Marcus Sr. and Helen lie in bed, Helen says, "I don't think the boys are ready. They are too young, especially Andrew."

Marcus Sr. says with great concern, "I don't have a choice."

She looks at him with a confused look, "What do you mean you don't have a choice?"

"Marcus already knows." He gives his wife a serious yet concerened look, "He's not sure what he knows, but he knows something and that felling is going to get stronger so he has to be told the truth."

"And what about Andrew?" Helen asks.

"I'm not sure," he says uneasy, "I'm going to let my father decide."

"He is a very wise man," Helen ensures her husband then adds, "I value his opinion."

They slowly fall to sleep. Helen stays awake a little longer hoping her children understand and except who they are.

The next morning they wake up both boys still tired from the work they had done the day prior. Their father ask them to check on the animals food and make sure things are set for their mother one last time before they leave.

Andrew still waking up and is not happy about going to their grandfathers asks, "Can I stay home and help mother?"

His father shaking his head, "I wish you could, but grandfather wants to talk with you also."

Andrew looks at his father, "What do you mean wants to talk to me! How do you know!?" Andrew awake now.

"Like I said," his father replies, "I talk to him more often than you think."

Marcus interrupts, "Is Mother still sleeping."

"Yes she is, so try not to wake her until we leave."

He looks back at his father, "I will make sure things are set for mother and take care of Andrew so you can get ready to leave."

"Thank you," his father says then tells them that some food will be ready when they are finished.

It takes about an hour to check on every thing and feed the animals. Most of the work was done the night before.

"I don't want to go," Andrew says to his brother as they walk back to the home.

Marcus gives him a sigh followed by a long stare, "It seems like something is bothering father," he gives his brother a half smile, "try to have a good time it will mean a lot to him if you did."

As they walk back to the house Andrew walks slower than usual.

"I hope your going to walk faster than that," Marcus Jr. says. "It will take a lot longer then two or three days to get there."

Andrew starts to walk faster, "I know, lets go eat I'm hungry."

When they get back to their home there is plenty of food ready. Helen who is now awake tells them to eat up. They have a long walk ahead of them.

"I don't want you to get hungry ten minutes into the walk," she smiles at Andrew.

They eat their food and begin to help clean.

"Stop," Helen says, "You three men need to get started," she smiles at them, "I will be fine"

Their horse is outside the home ready with a carry pack filled with the supplies they will need and a small cart trailing behind it with more supplies.

Marcus Sr. looks at his oldest son then the cart, "That's where Andrew will do most of his traveling." He smiles at Andrew, "his legs are too small to keep up."

"They are not," Andrew says already frustrated, "I will probably be ahead of you most of the way old man." Both boys giggle.

Their father look at them with an angry stare then starts to laugh also "You're probably right."

They kiss their mother goodbye and start on their journey. They head for the woods in the far corner of their home. The boys don't like playing in that area, the thorns and brier bushes are too thick there. The boys haven't noticed that the path they take to their grandfather's home is still there. The path is just wide enough for three men and a horse.

Marcus Jr. thinks this is very strange and the further they walk the thicker the thorns and briers around them become yet the path stays perfectly clear as they walk.

Marcus Jr. looks at his father after about an hour or so. "Father, when do you find the time to keep this path clear?"

Avoiding the question knowing it is impossible for him to be this far into the woods without them noticing, also impossible for nothing to grow in a single yet narrow path he points into the thick forest and yells **"Look, look at the deer!"**

Both boys look. Marcus Jr. knows his father was avoiding the question and decides not to ask again, He knew his father was hiding something and hoping this trip and the talk with his grandfather would help him understand what was on his fathers mind.

Andrew stays ahead of his father for about three hours then walks behind for about two more. He runs to catch up with his father and brother who are talking about all the different plants and flowers they have passed and what they can be used for. Their father seems to know about every plant, vine, bush or tree, Not only did he know the names of every plant, he also knows what they smell like, whether they are poisonous, if it can help heal a wound or if it tastes good in a stew.

When Andrew catches up he asks, "Can we stop to rest for a while."

His father looks at him, "We're not walking too fast for you? Are we?"

He then looks at his oldest son, "Are you tired Marcus?"

"Not really, But I do have to relieve myself."

His father smiles, "Well go do that then, but don't go too far and be careful. The thorns are sharp."

Marcus Jr. runs into the thick bushes, while he is gone his father pushes some stuff around in the horse cart. He tells Andrew, "Here, take a nap, we're going to keep walking."

He thinks to himself, *"I'm not such an old man after all."* He then looks at Andrew, "only take a short nap, I want you to sleep tonight."

When Marcus Jr. gets back they start walking again within minutes Andrew is sleeping.

Marcus Sr. looks at his oldest son, "Remind me to wake him up in about an hour."

They keep walking with Marcus Jr. looking around and noticing how tall the thorns and other bushes are. Still, the path they walk is perfectly clear. The trail they are walking runs close to a stream.

Marcus Jr. asks, "Is this the same stream near our home?"

"Yes it is."

"How far does it go?"

"At least two hundred miles."

"That's impossible," his son says.

"That's what I thought, but your grandfather will tell you differently."

"How would he know?"

"Your grandfather has traveled a lot further than you can imagine."

Marcus Sr. looks at his son, sighs than smiles, "And his stories will amaze you."

Realizing it's been more than two hours Marcus Jr. says "Its time to wake Andrew."

His father agrees as he looks at his young son sleeping, "Why don't you wake him."

"Me? Why me?" He says in a whiney tone. "You know how he is when you wake him."

"Yes I do," his father says with a smile, "that's why I want you to wake him." He pauses then says, "I don't want him angry at me." He stops and looks at his son, "He can be a brat sometimes."

Their father starts walking fast to put some distance between himself and his sons while Marcus Jr. wakes Andrew. Their father can hear some bickering between the two as they walk.

When the boys catch up to their father, Andrew says, "I'm thirsty."

His father looks at him, "You know where the water is."

Andrew walks to the back of the horse cart, takes a drink of water then tells his father his feet hurt.

His father with an angry glare, "Are you going to complain the entire way?"

Andrew looks at him with a smile, "Probably."

Marcus Sr. shakes his head and keeps walking.

They walk for a while longer and it starts to get dark, or at least it looks that way, buy now the bushes and thorns are so thick and full each side of the path almost touch high above their heads.

Marcus Jr. notices the path they walk is still perfectly clear and that most of the bushes are bent in the direction they are walking. This was very strange, he vaguely remembers the bushes and thorns doing this the last time on the way back from his grandfathers but it was a long time ago. He wanted to ask his father how and why but decides not too, he knows his father will avoid answering the question.

Suddenly his father holds up his hand to stop. Both boys stop where they stand. Andrew begins to ask what's wrong; his father quickly turns and puts one finger over his mouth, telling him to be quiet. He pulls his overcoat back, which is made from brown animal skins. Inside tucked in the side of his paints is his small wood ax. The ax has a hand-carved handle with strange symbols etched in it with a hard metal head. He has told his boys that the ax has been passed down from generation to generation for as long as he could remember and it was all you needed to catch food and cut wood for fire. The boys stood there holding very still not knowing what their father was hearing or seeing. They were both so frightened they didn't want to breathe. Their father stood very still holding the axe above his head. The boy's hearts were pounding so loud and hard they thought that anything in the forest could hear.

Their father takes a step forward and throws the ax as hard as he can. The boys hadn't seen anything. They stand motionless as they watch the ax fly. The ax twirls through the air for about thirty yards. The boys are now a little scared; they still have not seen anything except the ax, which is now about to hit the ground.

At that moment, a rabbit try's to scurry across the path. The ax strikes it dead.

Their father looks at the two boys "Looks like rabbit for our evening meal."

The boys both take a sigh of relief as they start to breathe easily again.

Their father starts walking, "I think our shelter hut is less than a mile from here."

They walk for about a mile and sure enough that's where it was.

Their shelter is made from vines, bushes and roots. It is shaped like an igloo and woven so tightly that the smallest bug couldn't get through.

Marcus Jr. is very confused, how has their shelter stayed the same.

His father knows he has questions. He looks at his son and says, "Start a fire."

Marcus Jr. then hears his father's thoughts the same way he does with his younger brother. *"This trip and the talk with your grandfather will explain everything and help you to understand."*

They both look at each other and smile.

"Now skin that rabbit and start a fire while I gather some more water."

Their father walks to the stream and fills their water pouches. On the way back he finds the vines that he uses for his heat lamps. The oily sap in this vine burns with a very dull, yet hot flame, the light won't keep you awake but it will keep a room warm. This is a secret passed down from their ancestors and cannot be done by just anybody.

Just by looking at the vine he makes it twist without breaking, beads of oil form on the surface that slowly roll down to the lowest point of the vine. It starts to drip in a steady stream that will be collected in a pouch that is used to fill the heat lamps as needed. He turns to make sure the boys have not seen him and returns to the hut where Marcus Jr. already has the rabbit skinned, a fire started with the meat already cooking.

His father looks at him and asks, "What did you do with the skin?"

His son points to a rock where the skin is stretched out to dry. He looks at his father. "I know we don't waist anything."

"That's my boy," his father says while filling his heat lamp.

After they eat some of the rabbit and berries they had gathered along the way they crawl into the shelter. Their father hangs the heat lamp in the center and they all quickly fall to sleep.

The next morning when the two boys wake, their father already has the supplies packed and ready to go. They eat some smoked fish and bread they brought with them. The rest of the rabbit will be saved for their evening meal unless another animal crosses their path.

That day they walk very fast. Their father tells the two boys they are making great time.

"I don't think we will reach your grandfather today but we will arrive early tomorrow."

Andrew looks at his father, "My feet hurt!"

Marcus Jr with agravation in his voice, "Would you stop complaining! It's making me crazy!"

Andrew gives his brother a big grin, "I know, that's what I'm trying to do," he runs ahead with his brother chasseing him.

"Don't get too far ahead!" their father shouts, **"There is more than just rabbits out there!"**

The boys slow down after hearing that, **"OK, we will stay in sight"** Marcus yells back to his father as he catches his brother. They both push and shove each other, they walk for a while longer before Andrew asks, "Can we rest for a while?"

Their father looks at Marcus "How are you feeling?"

"I'm fine," he replies.

"Take a nap in the horse cart" his father says with a big smile. "I guess your little legs can't keep up with an old man after all."

They all giggle.

They walk for about an hour more talking about different things while Andrew naps.

Marcus stops and looks at his father "What is this family secret? I know something is on your mind and its troubling you."

"Its not really troubling me," he takes a long pause and a deep breath, "I just hope you will understand," he looks at his son.

They both pause then Marcus Jr. asks, "Understand what?"

This time his father takes a long time to answer. "Our family history is very complicated and hard to believe. It is best if hear it from your grandfather."

"I already don't understand, why can't you just tell me?"

Marcus Sr. looks at his son with a sympathetic look, "I understand your frustration," once again he pauses then says, "If I tell you the story you wont believe me, I wasn't there." He pauses again before saying in a sincere tone, "Your grandfather on the other hand, well he's had a hard life."

He looks at his son like he wants to cry, "He has lost a lot and sacrificed everything for what we have."

"Is that where his scares come from?" Marcus Jr. asks his father.

"You will have to ask him that."

They walk for a while longer when Marcus Sr. says to his son "Do me a favor, I know you have a lot of questions for your grandfather, but your grandmother hasn't seen you in some time, try not to neglect her."

Marcus Jr. with a shocked look, "I would never."

His father smiles at him. "Go wake your brother."

"Do I have to?"

"Yes, unless you want him to be awake all night."

The young boy walks to the back of the horse cart to wake his younger brother, once again all you can hear is bickering.

Their father smiles as he keeps walking.

They walk for a couple more hours as day turns to dusk, they conveniently find the last shelter they use to sleep in. Marcus Jr. knows this is impossible he only smiles when his father says, "Just the way I left it."

They finish eating the rabbit they had saved with some more berries and go to sleep.

The next morning when the boys wake, once again their father is already packed and ready to go. He tells the boys to eat some bread and that they are very close they had traveled further then he thought the day prior. Andrew thought this was great; Marcus had other thoughts, if they traveled further than he had thought, how could the shelter be just the way he had left it. He wanted to say something but chose not to.

They walked for about two more hours talking about all sorts of stuff mostly plants, vines and the different bushes. That's when flowers started to appear, at first one here, one there then they started showing up all over the area before you knew it you were surrounded by flowers of all colors as far as the eye could see. They walk a little longer when they hear a voice from ahead.

"Is that my boys?"

Both young boys startled for a moment.

"What are you waiting for? Come give your grandfather a hug."

Both boys run and give their grandfather a big hug. They all start walking toward their grandfathers home talking about all that has happened to them over the past years.

Within an hour they come to the end of the path. At the end of the path is an open field with a home in the middle. The landscape is exactly how they remember maybe better. It almost seems impossible to have this many roses and flowers look so perfectly, but that's how it was, perfect.

They walk half way across the field when their grandmother comes running out of the home. She runs up to the boys and gives them both hugs and kisses.

"You boys are getting so big!" She starts to cry. "You have to come see us more often. I miss all of you." She wipes her tears and steps back. "How is your mother?"

Marcus Jr. answers, "She's well, she wanted to come with us but had to stay and take care of the animals and the garden."

"I sympathize," their grandmother says, then adds, "I hope you boys are hungry!"

They both look at her and say, "Yes we are," at the same time.

"Good, I've made enough to feed ten men."

They walk to the home and eat as much as they can, leaving plenty of food left for later. Their grandfather tells his wife to pack some food for the morning. He will be taking the boys for a walk.

The rest of the day is spent catching up on all that has happened the past years. The boys telling stories and their grandmother hugging them every chance she gets. Marcus Jr. spends as much time with her as possible; he knows most of the time would be spent with his grandfather. He also makes sure young Andrew spends some time with her.

Later that evening as they eat they talk some more and shortly after went to bed. It took some time for Marcus Jr. to go to sleep but finally does.

Chapter Two

The next morning young Marcus wakes up early yet very rested. He spent the night in his father's old room with his father and brother. He quietly walks into the big room trying not to wake the other two who are still sleeping. He notices his grandmother, already awake sitting at the table in the center of the room. There is a fire already crackling in the corner ready for cooking.

"I made sure I was up early to spend as much time with you as possible," she says smiling at her grandson, "You will spend much time with your grandfather this trip."

"I know," Marcus answers.

"Do you know why Marcus?" She looks at him with a concerned look on her face.

"No, I don't." Marcus says looking back at her trying to figure it all out. "Can you tell me what this big secret is Grandmother?"

"I wish I could," she says this with a long pause then continues.

"Your grandfather can explain it best." She smiles at him and touches his hand. "I can tell you one thing, it's good, it's hard to believe but mostly good."

Their grandfather walks into the room. "What are you two talking about?"

His wife Sarah looks at him, "None of your business." She looks back at Marcus and smiles then says to her husband, "If you wanted to know you should have woken up earlier."

He smiles, "What do you have cooking? We have a long day ahead of us."

She gives him a stern look, "Don't worry, I'm making sure you have plenty."

Marcus Sr. and Andrew walk into the room. The room is now much warmer from the cooking.

"Nice and warm in here," Marcus Sr. says, still a little chilled from the other room he slept in.

His father looks at him, "Are you afraid of the cold?"

"No I just keep my home a little warmer, I guess I'm used to being warm." He looks at his father smiling, "Lets eat I'm hungry."

While eating they talk a little more about the last couple of years. Their grandfather seems to know a lot of things that has happened since the last time they came to visit. Marcus Jr. thinks this is very strange, but he also knows what his brother is thinking without Andrew saying anything. He tries to convince himself that he is just close to his brother and he knows what he is about to say, but lately he is able to talk without speaking. He knows this is not normal, most people cannot hear others thoughts, but he suddenly seems to have this ability.

Their grandfather looks at Marcus Jr. *"Look at me boy."* Marcus Jr. hears his grandfather's thoughts. He turns to look at his grandfather who is staring directly into his eyes.

"It's not strange. It's a special gift. I talk with your father like this all the time." Marcus Jr. turns his head to look at his father who had talked to him like this on the way here and he thinks he is able to do the

same with his brother. Overwhelmed with confusion and a little scared he walks away from the table without saying a word.

"Where are you going?" Marcus Sr. asks. "Your grandmother has spent…" he was going to say, spent a lot of time making morning meal when Andrew Sr. interrupts, "Let the boy go." He looks at his son, "I will go talk with him." He gets up, grabs his walking stick and walks gingerly after him. The damp morning air always causes his leg to ache more. Outside he finds his grandson sitting on a log trying to absorb all that he is learning about himself.

"What's wrong with me?" Marcus Jr. very confused asks his grandfather.

"Nothing is wrong with you, you have a gift!" He pauses and sits next to his grandson, "We all have a special gift."

"Even Andrew?" Marcus asks his grandfather.

"Not as of yet, but he will when he reaches your age."

"So let me try to understand this, when you turn thirteen you are able to read each others minds?"

"Well, there's a lot more to it than that," his grandfather says. "When you reach a certain age, your father, grandfather or oldest brother opens your mind to this gift."

Marcus looks at his grandfather, "But father has not done anything to me."

"I know!" his grandfather answers, "You are very special. You have a very strong mind and it's starting to open on its own."

"So I can read minds?" Marcus asks with a confused look.

"No," his grandfather replies.

"Then what just happened?" he asks now even more confused.

"We are able to communicate with each other we can't read minds.

Our people can hear what the other is thinking," he pauses, "but only if you let him hear. Once you learn your gift, you will only let another one of us hear what you want him to." Still looking at his grandson. "But you must hear the whole story of our people before you can learn more."

"There's more?" Marcus asks already overwhelmed.

His grandfather looks at him with a big smile. "Well, we can also move trees with our minds."

Marcus laughs a little, "Stop joking grandfather."

His grandfather puts his hand on Marcus's shoulder, "Let's go finish eating." They walk back inside and sit down to finish eating.

"Everything all right?" Marcus Sr. asks, he already knows what was said outside.

"Yes, he's fine," their grandfather says. "He's looking forward to a long walk in the woods."

Young Andrew quickly asks, "Will I going also?"

At the same time their father says no, but their grandfather says yes.

"What do you mean yes?" Marcus Sr. asks. "He's only ten years old."

"I know how old the boy is." Their grandfather says in a strong stern voice.

Marcus Sr. then asks, "Do you think he's ready?"

Now young Andrew is thinking, *ready for what?* As their grandfather replies, "No!"

Marcus senior gives his father a confused look. "Then why is he going?"

There is a long pause followed by a sigh before their grandfather says, "Well the way I see it, is young Andrew can be quite the brat."

"**Hey!**" the young boy yells, "What do you mean brat?"

They all look at him with their eyebrows raised.

He gives a childish grin, "Ok, I guess you are right!"

Their grandfather continues, "Like I was saying, He knows I'm talking to Marcus about something." He then looks at young Andrew with his chin lowered and his eyebrows sunk very low. "He will keep bugging and bugging Marcus until he has no choice but to tell him."

"He's right!" young Andrew says with a smirk.

Their grandfather smiles as he says, "Let's save Marcus the aggravation and tell him the story also. Now let's finish eating." He turns to his wife Sarah. "Make sure you pack plenty of food we will be home late."

They finish eating and walk to the back of the home. Their grandfather looks at the two boys, "I noticed neither of you have a walking stick."

In a teasing voice Andrew Jr. says, "We don't need one our leg's work fine."

Their grandfather was not amused at this comment. A little angry he says, "It's more than a walking stick." He looks at Marcus Sr. "Our people have always had one at our side."

Just then their grandmother walks out of the home with three packs of food wrapped in woven pouches that are carried over their shoulder easily.

Their grandfather tells his son, "I have a list of things for you to do now that I am getting a little too old to do them. Your mother will tell you what they are."

Marcus Sr. looks back at his father, "Are you sure Andrew is ready."

Their grandfather tells his grandson Andrew to look at him; there is a long pause while their grandfather stares deep into his eyes.

"He will be fine." The old man says then looks at both boys. "Are you ready?"

"Yes" they both answer. So they start walking toward the thick woods in the back of his home. Both young boys are looking at each other each thinking the same thing. There is no path! It looked as though they were going to walk straight into thick thorns and bushes. They want to tell their grandfather to stop. He walks about five feet in front of them, a big smile appears on his face. Both boys stop and watch as their grandfather takes a step into the thorns and brier bushes, before his foot hits the ground the bushes separate and untangle like magic. Each vine and bush unwrapping and unraveling forming a path. Both boys stand breathless and amazed at what they have just seen. The boys stand still as they watch the path unravel as far as they can see.

Marcus Jr. thinks to himself "H*e can move trees? We can move trees!"*

"That wasn't a tree" he hears his grandfather's thoughts. "J*ust some bushes."* He yells back to the boys who are still looking at the path not sure what to do "**Lets go, we have a lot of walking to do, at least an hour."**

The boys move quickly to catch up still with the look of amazement on their faces.

Young Andrew looks at his older brother, "What's happening?"

"I'm not quite sure." He pauses, "But I think it is good."

Their grandfather stops and looks at them, young Andrew's face very scared. His grandfather walks over to him.

"Don't be frightened. We are very special people."

The young boy says back very nervously, "What do you mean we?"

Now their grandfather puts his hand on both boys' shoulders. "We all have this gift". He turns and starts walking again. "We will go see my parents grave first, then we will go to where my mother's village was. It is there that I will tell you the story of our people." He points to a vine, "That's where we get the oil for our heat lamps" and keeps walking.

The boys still in amazement follow and listen. Andrew was more confused than Marcus. Both boys can still see the path opening up in front of them as they walk. Marcus notices that it is closing up behind them, that's when he realizes his father does this every time they come visit their grandfather, which explains a lot of questions.

He asks his grandfather, "Is this why there is always a path to your home?"

"There is not always a path, your father makes it as he goes. He just won't let you see it happen. "Haven't you ever noticed that whenever you stop for the night, no matter how fast or slow you travel your hut seems to be there?"

They walk for a while longer following their grandfather thinking about everything that is happening. They come upon a big tree, its trunk is wider than the path.

Andrew looks at his grandfather, "Are you going to move this tree?" he asks.

His grandfather looks at him laughing out loud, "If I tried to move this tree it would crush us!"

The young boy takes a step back, "Don't try to move it then!" he steps further back. "I don't want to be crushed!"

His grandfather realizes he has scared the boy more than he already was. "I'm only kidding" he smiles, "There will be no crushing today."

The boy sighs with relief. His grandfather tells him he used to play in this very tree when he was about his age. "It was much smaller back then." He says with a smile. They walk around the tree with little room between it and the bushes.

Young Andrew asks, "Why don't you make the path wider around the tree?"

His grandfather looks at him, "I don't want to disturb the flowers. It's a very special place to me."

When they make it to the other side of this enormous tree, both boys have to stop. The landscape is so beautiful it takes their breath away. The roses were so full of color. There were so many flowers and color's words could never describe it. The two boys stood in one spot looking around, it takes a moment to take it all in. That's when Marcus noticed about fifteen big stones all with flowers surrounding them. He gives his brother an elbow to make sure he sees this. They were at the grave sight.

They stood watching their grandfather. He slowly walked to the middle and drops to one knee in front of two stones, as he does this, hundreds of flowers and roses followed him gathering around the two stones.

He looks at his grandson's, "Come meet my parents, your great grandparents." There are tears running down his face.

Andrew looks at his grandfather, "Why are you crying?"

He wipes his tears with the back of his hand.

"They were very peaceful and loving people." He pauses for a moment then sighs, "They died before their time." He looks at Marcus with a sad look on his face. "I was only a little older than you." One more single tear runs down the side of his face. "They were killed by an evil man." He stands up and wipes his eyes then looks at the boys.

"Come, its not far from here."

They start walking again further into the woods. Marcus realizes that the trees are very old and the vines and bushes are as high as he can see. They walk for a while longer when he notices a rock wall that was very old. He asks his grandfather what it was.

His grandfather looks back, "That was the boundary of our village."

They keep walking. There are fewer trees in this part of the woods and the rocks look like old ruins. There are stones piled like they used to be something, some close together others far apart. They walk past all the stones until they reach some stones that look as though it used to be a small home with a small fire pit in the middle. This one spot was well kept and the fire had recently been lit, it was set back from the others.

"This was the last place I saw my parents alive." He tells the boys. Once again his eyes tear up. He walks to the back wall and points into the thick forest. "Our people had a village about two days walk that way. It's been a long time since I've been there." He wipes his tears and tells the boys to eat a little something and to make themselves comfortable.

"You are about to learn about our people, and where you come from." He looks at Andrew, "I just hope you can pay attention long enough."

Andrew always having a wise crack to say, still trying to absorb all he has learned in the past few hours,

"I will" is his only response.

Chapter Three

Both the boys were now sitting on the ground leaning against the wall looking at their grandfather. He takes his hand and puts it to face. He begins to rub down his beard with his thumb and forefinger a couple of times.

"Where do I begin? Well I guess I'll start from your age Andrew. That's about as far back as I can remember with detail." He closes his eyes and pictures himself at Andrews's age. His mind drifts as he starts to tell the story, its as though he hears his mothers voice.

"Morning meal is ready. Time to get up Andrew." He is still tired and wants to stay in bed but knows the rules. He reluctantly gets out of bed and walks into the big room to eat. They lived in a large igloo shaped home with two rooms in the back to sleep and one big room for cooking and daily living. The entire home was made from roots and vines with a large entrance in the front and a smaller one in the back. Both are covered with several layers of animal skins to keep the elements out.

Each room has a man made heating lamp forged from metal. There is a large one in the big room and two smaller ones in the rooms they slept in. The lamps kept home fairly warm even in the winter. On the really cold days they would keep the fire burning continuously. They would always have extra animal skins lined with wool for the really cold nights. Andrews mother always made sure he ate well. She wasn't from their village but she was starting to learn the ways. She was a small woman with long light brown hair and dark brown eyes. Her features were petite from head to toe. With a cute button nose and big dimples when she smiled. Her hands looking so delicate yet posed so much strength. Even though she was the first outsider to join their village she adapted well always with a witty remark, making the people around her laugh. Andrews father met her one-day while he was hunting for food. He went a lot further into the woods that day than he usually goes. She was a young girl lost far from her grounds. He brought her back to make sure she was safe. The travel took about three days to get back to her village. He didn't use his power of moving the bushes, which was his main way of traveling, he didn't want to scare her.

After they met he would wonder to her village often to visit, against the advice from his friends and family. It took a lot of convincing to let her come and be a part of his village everyone told him that she would not understand their ways, they said it would frighten her. At first it was very overwhelming, she had never seen people so in touch with nature they could move any living plant as they pleased. She eventually accepted their ways and there was young Andrew ready to take on the world.

Andrews mother Rosemary had warmed some bread and fish for their morning feed; they didn't waist anything so they usually ate what they had the night before. After their morning meal they always cleaned themselves very well. At first Andrews mother didn't understand this, not that she's a dirty person, she was just brought differently. These people liked to be well groomed and very clean. They wash every morning and every night. It's been told most people only wash once a week, if that. Young Andrew didn't believe it. Just then Andrews father walks in. He had been up for hours already. All the men from the village wake up very early, before they even start their day they eat a little bread, some cheese, drink some water and go off to train. Andrew never understood this, they lived so far from anything that there was no one to fight, yet they trained several hours every morning and at least one more in the evening. Andrew's father Jonathan, about thirty-five years old, a tall, strong man with dark hair past his shoulders and eyes to match, he has a distinguished look about him, always very serious about everything. He scratches is short bread with his left hand and looks at his wife.

"What's to eat I'm starved" "Your uncle Julian almost beat me today." He says to his son.

Julian was his father's younger brother, a little shorter then Jonathan also with dark hair down to his shoulders and dark eyes. They resemble each other well, however Julian is never serious about anything and his facial expressions showed it, always with a smile or smirk ready to joke about anything.

"He's getting very strong."

Young Andrew decides this is the day he will ask. "Father?"

"Yes?" his father looks at him and notices he is very nervous.

Not sure how to ask he just asks, "Why do you train every day like your going into battle?"

His father looks at him and pauses for a long moment. He is thinking about how to answer this question.

"Well, there is a battle around every corner. We have to always be ready."

"What do you mean by that?"

Once again his father takes a long pause. " We are a very special people, others don't understand. Our people have had to fight throughout the times. That's why we live here."

"I thought we lived here because we like it here?"

His father looks at him with a smile. "We love living here. If we weren't here I would never have met your mother." A long pause as he looks at his wife then back at young Andrew. "We come from people who are great worriers and we keep up the tradition. Well over a hundred years ago a small handful of our people traveled to this place so they could stop fighting because of who and what we are."

Young Andrew thinks for a short moment, "Has anybody tried to go back?"

That's when Andrew's mother rolls her eyes. "Here we go! The bear story."

Jonathan looks back at her, "Its not a story! And it wasn't a bear, it was a man as strong as a bear with hair all over its body and knew our language."

She rolls her eyes again and goes back to cleaning up.

"When I was about nineteen and your grandfather was still alive, I used to travel a lot. He always told me, only go far enough so he could still ask were I was, I never listened. Most of the time I would travel about one week into the woods, just to roam around. I wanted to learn the woods as well as I could. I would walk around and listen trying to become one with the trees and bushes, as you know we can feel their energy and life. With deep concentration and training we can move them at will. This one time I decided to follow the way our ancestors came, I had told my father that I would be gone for a long time. I kept walking for days, which turned into weeks. I hadn't communicated with my father for a long time now I knew he must be worried. I had never seen the map of our ancestors but I was confident I was traveling in the right direction. I knew I would never travel the entire way, I wanted to see if any others had journeyed this way.

"Did you find any of our ancestors?" Andrew was awe stricken at the story.

"No, after about three weeks I was interrupted."

"Interrupted by what?"

His father looks at him with a serious look on his face then says, "At first it sounded like two ferocious bears fighting to their death. I wanted to keep my distance but also wanted to see the fight so I slowly moved closer trying not to bring attention too myself."

He smiles at his son, "I didn't want them both attacking me! I got close enough to watch from behind a big tree. That's when I noticed it wasn't two bears fighting." He looks at his wife Rosemary, waiting for her sly comment, there was none.

"It was a bear and a bear man!"

"What do you mean, bear man?" Andrew asks.

"A bear man, just what I said, a bear man!"

Rosemary with a big smile on her face tries not to giggle.

Jonathan glares at her, "Laugh if you want, but I tell you this man stood seven feet tall and had fur all over its body."

"Seven feet tall this time, the last time you told the story it was six feet tall, by the time our next child hears the story this monster will be twelve feet tall." Rosemary says with humor in her voice.

"Can I tell my story, and it's always been seven feet tall!" He says a little aggravated. "As I was saying, this beast was about eight feet tall!" his smile gets bigger as he glances at his wife, "All kidding aside, this thing was about seven feet tall and built like a bear but it had skin on its face and stood upright like a man. He or it carried a spare it was using to fight with. As they fought I could see this things face, it made expressions like a man. I tell you, no word of a lie! During the fight the creature pushed this bear that stood about three feet taller than it back several times but it didn't look like it wanted to fight with the bear. It looked like it was trying to get away rather than fight. That's when this bear like creature took a couple of steps back. I was close enough to see that it was sniffing like it could smell something. He took a couple more steps backing further away from the bear. It looked worried like it was going to be attacked from another direction. It kept looking for what it was smelling, that's when it turned around and looked directly at me. It looked me straight in the eyes. I realized it was me it smelled. There was no way this creature could know that I meant it no harm, so it turned toward me to defend itself. As it did the bear took several fast steps forward and struck this creature in the face knocking it to the ground. The bear viscously attacked it, lifting it up with its teeth and pounding this creature on the ground several times. I stood frozen watching as the bear threw the creature through the air it went about fifteen feet. The bear went to attack again, once again this creature looked at me, its eyes half closed breathing very heavy. I don't know why I did what I did but at that moment I used all the vines and bushes to entangle the bear and jumped between the two. Using the bushes to slow the bear I tried to push it back with my stick. This went on for about ten minutes. This bear was very strong even for a bear or at least

I think, it's the first time I'd ever fought one! I kept using the vines and bushes to tangle it while I hit it with my stick. This wasn't working. The other creature was trying to crawl out of the way but the bear was pushing me back. I knew it wouldn't be long before we were on top of this creature, so I decided to try something different. I wrapped some vines around the bears back and front legs. At the same time I pulled the back legs out and tightened the ones around its front legs and body. Every time I did this the bear landed on its face. As soon as it hit the ground I jammed my stick into it's nose as hard as I could. It took at least five times before the bear fled into the woods. I took a moment to get my breath back then looked at the creature, it was now unconscious. I wanted to leave but I also felt responsible, if I hadn't been there he may have been fine. Cautiously I looked at his wounds, some cuts were very bad, and his head and face had deep bite marks. I thought with a healing mix made from leaves and some proper wrapping the creature would make it. I rolled him over and made a fire to keep him warm. I started to gather certain leaves that I knew would help heal his wounds as well as some vines I could split in half to wrap the abrasions. It had injuries all over its body so I made sure the fire was warm and kept it close to the heat while I tended to his wounds. It took hours and as I wrapped the wounds it spoke words, words like stop, get back, go away but never opened its eyes. I wasn't sure if it was repeating words it heard me say or if it knew our language. It had a deep cut on its head and another on its face. I was very gentle wrapping its head but when I tried to cover the deep gash on its face it quickly sat up and looked at me. I wasn't sure what to do so I put both hands in the air to show I meant no harm. It looked at me then glared at the fire. Then it slowly focused back on its wounds that I had wrapped, then put its eyes back at me. Still not sure what to do I put the mix I made that would help heal the lesion in my hand and put my hand to my face were the gash was on his. Next I held out my hand to him with the mix in it. He felt the injury on his face patting lightly on his cheek were the wound was deepest, then took the healing mix from my hand and put it on his face. He or it, I still wasn't quite sure laid down and went back to sleep. The next day I woke up early, I didn't know what this creature ate so I gathered some berries and roots that were safe to eat. I had also caught a squirrel with my small ax and cooked it.

"When the creature woke, it was still unable to move very well. He looked at me not sure what to think, so I looked back at him and told him to eat. I then opened my arms to show him he could have whatever he wanted. At first he grabbed a handful of berries and ate them, I started to think, *"maybe I should have gotten more berries,"* then he grabbed the squirrel and just like that it was gone, he ate very fast I've never seen anything like it. I thought to myself, *that was for two,* but as soon as he finished he went back to sleep and slept for the rest of the day. I spent most of the day gathering wood and food, this time I made sure I had plenty for both of us and ate before I woke this creature. When I did wake him, I first showed him what leaves I used to wrap his wounds so he could do it on its own when we parted. He let me check and re-wrap his injuries. I could tell he was very cautious, so I went slowly. While I was tending to him, he ate, he ate everything even the roots. I think he may have swallowed a rock!"

"Did he choke or get sick at all?" Andrew asks with wide eyes.

"No he just continued until everything was gone. He then stood up like he wanted to leave but as he took a step he stumbled to one knee. I jumped up to help him, he just looked at me not sure what to do. I looked back at him shaking his head back and forth and told him to just sleep, I would keep the fire warm and he could travel the next day. He looked at me frustrated then sat back down next to the fire. He put his head down and went back to sleep. I stayed up most of the night keeping the fire going and finally went to sleep myself. When I woke up, to my surprise the creature was already awake. It had found the leaves and vines I used to wrap its wounds with and re-wrapped them the same way I did. It was smarter then I had originally thought. It started to walk through the bushes having some trouble because of his injuries, that's when I decided to help it home. He had seen me fight the bear so it knew what I could do. I stepped in front of him, as I did the vines, thorns and bushes pulled to the side forming a path. It looked at me with curiosity and started walking. It was strange, I kind of felt comfortable and safe with the creature. Not a word was said for several miles, all of the sudden he stopped and started sniffing the air. He held his hand up to my face then took about ten steps forward. I was pretty sure it wanted me to stay were I was. He took about ten more steps forward and sniffed the air again. All I can remember next is this awful, intense growling screech. I had to cover my ears so hard with my hands that they turned red. He stopped screeching and started sniffing again, that's when I heard another screech far off in the distance.

"Do you think it was his family calling him?" Andrew asks in a low tone.

"I wasn't sure but I knew where it was coming from so I opened a path as far as I could in that direction. He looked at me, so I put my hand to my chest and said 'Jonathan is my name'. He started to walk away then turned back and pointed at me using his growling voice said, 'Jonathan friend' then turned and proceeded down the path. I watched him walk until he was out of sight. I turned around and began to head home. On the entire journey I couldn't stop thinking about what I had experienced in the last few days."

"Weren't you afraid that no one was going to believe you?" Andrew said with deep concern in his voice.

"I certainly was!" He begins to speak again when Rosemary interrupts,

"That is just it Andrew we didn't believe your father, But it does makes a good story."

Jonathan looks at her, "It really did happen!"

"I've had some good dreams also dear." She says with sarcasm.

Once again agitated at her response he looked back at his son, "As I was saying, I was walking home and was further than I thought. It took at least three weeks before I was able to contact my father. When I finally did I could tell he was very upset that I was gone for so long. I knew he was just worried, that's what parents do. When I finally reached home I told my story, most people laughed at me, others said nothing."

"Well I believe you father."

"Of course you do Andrew." Rosemary says, "Your only ten years old."

Andrew looks at his mother, and then back at his father, "Did you ever contact the creature again?"

He looks at Andrew and sadly says, "I tried once but I did not travel as far. Maybe someday someone will see this creature and everyone will believe my story." He smiles at his son, "Now finish eating, you have a lot to do today."

They both finish eating and walk outside, the first thing Andrew does is restock the firewood his father had split the night before. He then walks to the stream and looks down it at the village, the homes are all oval shaped set back away from the stream and spread apart giving them privacy. About half way through the village, set back into the thick woods is a large open area with walls and a cover all formed from the vines and bushes in the area with a large fire place in the center, this place is where they would hold large gatherings, all drinking ale, some banging on drums made from hand carved wooden cylinders with animal skins pulled and tied tightly while others blew into carved wooden flutes, to create enjoyable music while others danced.

The plant life in the village is full of flowers and roses of all shapes and colors with tamed bushes through out the entire area tangled and wound together tightly, some formed into benches along the stream, others just pleasant to look at, the entire area was so beautifully arranged it almost seemed mystical. The stream is about twenty feet across with several arched bridges in various spot to cross, all formed from live bushes, vines and any plant life around. The stream supplies them with plenty of fish and water.

Downstream at the back end of the village is were they kept the animals, chickens, pigs, sheep, goats and cows all for milk, food and clothes. The fence is made from vines, roots and thorn bushes all woven so tight together no animal is able to get out; it also keeps any predator from getting in, it is a vast area running along the stream to provide the animals with water. One of Andrews's responsibilities was to feed the animals and tend to the fence making sure it was still held together tightly.

At the top end of the village is were the men of the village trained every day. Like all the structures in the village they have the bushes wound so tight together not even the wind could get in. When the winter comes they use the bushes and vines to cover overhead so they can still train without the elements affecting them. They would light a couple of fires one at each end to provide some warmth that way they could train all winter. Andrew never understood this.

Each home in the village was shaped like theirs; they were igloo shaped with rooms in the back for sleeping, one big door in the front and a smaller one in the back. There were about thirty homes fifteen on each side of the stream. All along the backside of the homes was a wall made from bushes and thorns about ten feet high. There was no end in sight it just kept going as far as the eye could see. Even beyond the wall the woods were thick and full, it would be hard for anybody without their gift to travel through, they felt safe. Andrew was finished stacking the wood so he started walking down the stream toward the animals. He liked playing with them. There wasn't anybody his age to play with. There were six other children in the village all much younger than Andrew but none his age, that was why he liked traveling to the village were his mother grew up. There were children his age to play with there, not many, but a few. Around here he played with the animals or his Uncle Julian. He was only a few years younger than his father but acted more Andrews's age. Then there was his uncle's best friend Jacob, he had a very bad temper but that's not why he scared Andrew. He talked to himself and the trees, not just a little, he did it all the time. He would sit on the ground and talk to trees and bushes around him. Anyway you looked at it, he was either strange or crazy, but he was Julian's best friend so Andrew acted as though he liked him.

About half way to the animals someone grabbed young Andrew from behind and pulled him behind one of the homes, it was his uncle.

He had Andrew's mouth covered so he could not speak, just then Jacob walked by, and Julian puts his finger over his lips telling Andrew to keep quiet. He waits a moment then says,

"I'm not feeling up for his company right now. Lets go for a walk."

Young Andrew was happy to have some company, "OK" he says.

The two walk into the wall of bushes behind the homes, as they do it separates in front of them and closes behind.

"What do you want to do?" Julian asks.

"I don't know? Anything will be fun." They walk for a while through the forest when Julian stops and looks at Andrew

"How much have you learned about your gift?"

Andrew looks back at him, "What do you mean?"

"Can you feel the life in the plants yet?"

"No" Andrew replies.

Then Julian says, "I know your using your gift, just a bit."

"I'm having a hard time."

"Your father doesn't think your ready. He needs to open your mind."

"What do you mean open my mind?"

"Well its hard to explain, you know how we can communicate with each other in our minds over a long distance and feel what the other is feeling if the other allows you to?"

Andrew looks at him, "Well I'm starting to understand but I really can't do it yet. I can only move a few small leaves at a time and it's very hard to do."

"That's what I mean by opening your mind." Julian says.

"I don't understand what you mean, open my mind?"

"When you turn thirteen or fourteen it is time to have your mind opened to nature, meaning your father or a close male relative lets you see and feel what he feels with nature, you can almost feel it breath. Its like you can talk with it, well not really it's hard to explain but once your father does this you will know what I mean. It's quite amazing but it's also extremely overwhelming at first. I didn't leave my home for about three days after." He smiles at Andrew before saying, "Look at Jacob, he never fully recovered, he actually talks out loud to trees and vines. He doesn't even realize that it doesn't work that way. The crazy thing is he moves them better than all of us. Sometimes I think he really is talking to them."

Andrew looks at him, "You said your father or a close male relative does it." Andrew pauses then asks, "Can you?"

"Your father would be very angry at me if I did, when he thinks you are ready he will. Just remember try to feel the root of the plant that's were they are the strongest."

Julian looks at Andrew with a big smile on his face "Lets go cause some mischief."

"What do you mean mischief?" Andrew looks back with a confused look on his face.

Julian still smiling says, "This is the time the women start filling their water buckets for cooking and cleaning."

"OK." Andrew says not knowing why he cares.

"I'm going to block the stream for a while, just long enough to make them wonder were the water has gone."

"You can be rotten sometimes," Andrew says now smiling also.

"Rotten maybe, funny yes!" He starts walking, "The stream is this way."

As they are walking toward the stream Andrew sees many different animals. The animals have never been afraid of them, they just go about there business. This sometimes upsets his mother, the animals always run away afraid of her. She once asked Jonathan why the other women of their village don't have their gift yet the animals don't run from them, only her. He told her that the women of the village do have this great power, they just don't exercise it. It takes great concentration to use this gift, that's one reason why they train so hard. They're not only learning how to fight but also learning how to concentrate so deep that they can feel the life in nature, that's why they are able to move it at, will.

He also told her he thinks at one time everyone alive could do this but thousands of years later, not doing any exercise has closed this part of the mind on most people for good. He thinks all people are the same with different ways of life. Most of our people think that we are entirely different from others. Andrew is really not sure what to think. He just knows that his father and mother come from two different ways of life and they are very happy.

Andrew kind of looses himself in thought thinking about this when his uncle says, "See the side of the hill over there?"

Andrew looks and realizes he's never been in this part of the woods, he also notices the side of the hill is shinning and sparkling, he turns to his uncle,

"Why does the sun make the hill sparkle?"

"That's were we get our metal to forge our pots, pans and heating lamps." Andrew remembers his father making a pot for his mother to cook with. He didn't pay much attention at the time he just knew it took a very long time in a very hot fire. He wasn't sure how his father did it but he now realizes it must have taken him a lot longer and much more work than he had thought. They walk a little further until they arrive at the stream.

"How are you going to stop it?"

"Step back and watch." Julian replies.

Andrew takes a couple of steps back. Julian starts to move a bunch of vines into the water. The vines start to tangle with each other forming a dam. He stops the flow of water for about ten minutes then untangles the vines so the water was flowing again like nothing had happened.

Julian smiles at Andrew, "Right about now the water should stop flowing through the village," they both start to laugh.

Julian was right, back at the village several women at the streams edge stop what they are doing and run to get their husbands, another screams out loud in a panic,

"The stream has stopped! What will we do?"

Jonathan at first looks a little worried then looks intensely into the woods in the direction of Julian and Andrew. He shakes his head back and fourth as he smiles,

"Don't worry, all will be fine soon." He stands at the streams edge and watched the water slowly come back, first at a trickle then in a steady flow like nothing had happened.

Julian puts his hand on Andrews back, "We should head back, your father wants you home." They start walking toward the village.

"Thank you for taking me with you today, I know you could be doing better things than entertaining a little kid."

"You think I'm entertaining you?" Julian asks in a surprised voice, "I enjoy your company, you may only ten going on eleven, but you act much older" Julian pauses then says " That works out great for me."

"What do you mean great for you?"

"Well, I act a lot younger than I am, so it works out great." They both laugh as they walk.

They arrive back at the village about an hour later. Jonathan is waiting for them sitting on a chair he has formed from bushes in front of his home.

Jonathan looks at the two, "You missed a big commotion today."

"Really?" Julian says. "We were deep in the woods taking a walk."

"I'm sure you were" he looks at both of them and smiles "You weren't anywhere near the stream by any chance were you?"

"I don't think so," Julian says as he looks at Andrew, both trying not to smile.

Jonathan shakes his head before saying, "Yeah, I didn't think so. You're a bad influence on him, thanks for keeping him company. "Before you went for your walk did you finish your work?"

Andrew with a boyish smile, "I did some."

"Some?" his father says, "All you did was stack the wood."

"It was my fault" Julian says, "I will help him finish."

"That would be great." He then asks Julian to come back for their evening meal when they are done.

"Sure, I hope its something I like."

Jonathan looks at Julian as though he was pushing his luck.

"Only kidding" Julian says. Andrew and Julian start walking down the stream.

Jonathan yells to the two as they are walking away,

"By the way, I already took care of his work, just make sure your work is done before your next walk."

Both Andrew and Julian say, "OK" as they turn around and sit by the fire next to Jonathan. Andrew gets up to help his mother prepare their evening meal.

Chapter Four

The next morning, Andrew wakes up with a bad feeling. He's not sure what it is, he just senses that something is wrong. He gets out of bed before his mother calls for him. He takes a look around and everything seems fine. His mother takes a long look at him, she can tell something is on his mind.

"What's wrong?" His mother says as she looks at his puzzled expression.

"Where is father?" He asks knowing his father was training but just wanted to hear her say it.

"He's fine. What's wrong Andrew?"

"I don't know. But I feel as though something is bad."

She looks at him very confused, "What do you mean bad?" She tries not to seem too worried, even though she is. "Well your father will be home soon and he will be with Julian." She starts to set the table, "He slept here last night so I told him to come back for his some food after they train."

That's when for no reason Andrew could mentally picture his mother's village for a moment.

"Your village is in trouble." Andrew says in a faint voice.

Her back is turned to him so she can hide her concern, "Well your father will be home soon and we will discuss this." She puts some pork and bread in front of him. She knows instinctively he is probably right but she keeps her fear to herself while she continues preparing the rest of the food. About a half hour later Jonathan and Julian walk in.

Julian says right away, "What's to eat?"

But Jonathan asks immediately, "What's wrong?"

Rosemary wants to say something, before she can Andrew states, "Something is wrong with mothers village!"

This strikes concern with Jonathan. He asks Julian to walk outside with him. Outside he looks at Julian with extreme concern in his voice and a worried look to his face.

"Andrew seems to have strange sense, its like he knows when something is wrong. He is usually right, if he thinks something is wrong we should probably travel and make sure they are all right."

Julian agrees "I will ask Jacob for help."

"Jacob? We don't need his help."

"I know you don't like him but he has a unique gift. He can feel someone walking in the bushes for miles, even days away."

"Its not that I don't like him, I just think he's crazy."

"He says the same about you."

"About me?" Jonathan says shocked.

"Well yes. You are all distinguished and proper, that's why he is afraid to talk to you."

"OK go and ask for his help, tell him the 'distinguished' asks of him." Julian runs off.

Jonathan walks back inside the home and looks at his son, "Why do you think something is wrong with your mothers village?"

"I don't know, I just see her village and my heart hurts like I want to cry."

"Well I'm sure its fine but we will go check. Its time we went for a visit anyway."

"All of us?"" Andrew asks.

"Yes, all of us even Julian."

This strikes great concern in Rosemary. She knows that if he wants Julian to go, he may need some help and he rarely if ever needs help. Julian returns from his visit with Jacob.

"Sit down, there is plenty to eat." Rosemary says,

Julian looks at Rosemary, and then Jonathan, "Can I talk to you outside for a moment?" The two walk outside.

"Jacob says he can only feel one person walking around and its not in a steady pace, he thinks something is wrong. He suggests we leave now to help."

"Really," Jonathan asks surprised. "Jacob wants to come along?"

"Jacob and I are ready to start traveling right away."

Jonathan puts his hand on his shoulder, "Why don't you do that, try to make good time. We will pack some food, supplies and follow."

Julian runs to get Jacob, who is sitting down still concentrating on the small village trying to figure out what's wrong and they both run off in the direction of the village.

Jonathan walks back into his home, "Julian and Jacob have already left."

Now Rosemary knows something is wrong. "Is everything all right?"

"I'm sure its nothing."

"Then why did Jacob and Julian already leave?"

"They know you are worried so they want to get there as soon as they can to let you know everything is fine."

She looks at the door then back at Jonathan, "They will tell me if something is wrong, wont they?"

"They will have no choice. We will be right behind them, they're not that fast."

Jonathan looks at her and smiles, "They will also have to find some food, Julian ran off without eating anything."

She smiles back at him then looks at Andrew, "Eat up so we can start on the way also."

"I was thinking the same thing," Jonathan says.

They finished eating and cleaned up. They quickly packed some things and proceeded out the front door. As they walk away, Andrew looks back to see the door close with vines and roots tangling with each other making a seal so tight that even a small bug could not get through.

Andrew thinks to himself, "*I can't wait to be able to do that!*"

His father looks at him and smiles. Andrew hears his thoughts "*You need to control your thoughts first, after that you can start moving vines and bushes.*"

Jonathan knows that they would be gone at least a week's time. As they walk past the women who lives next to them Jonathan stops and looks at her, her name is Sandra. She was a tall woman a little on the heavy side with long dark hair and eyes. She always has a smile on her face and a friendly tone to her voice with something nice to say about everybody.

"Tell your husband Daniel that we will be gone for some time. Can the two of keep watch on our home?"

Sandra lets him know that it will be no trouble.

They keep walking for several hours before they stopped for a rest. They have a quick bit to eat and drink plenty of water. Andrew was sitting looking at some small bushes, they moved ever so slightly, his father noticed.

"Very impressive, how long have you been practicing?"

"Not very long" Andrew replies, even though he has been trying for as long as he can remember.

"Well keep practicing, you will only get better."

Andrew takes a long pause before saying, "Father, why won't you show me how? I'm not sure what it means." He looks at his father now very serious, "Open my mind to nature."

"Your not ready."

"How do you know I'm not?"

"Trust me, I know!"

"Well I think I am!"

"I also know that, I know a lot more than you think I do. I have trained a long time and I know a lot more than even Julian thinks I know. The side of the hill that sparkles when the light hits the metal, its beautiful don't you think?"

Andrew looks at his father surprised, he had not told him were they had been. He thinks Julian must have told him.

His father looks at him again, "No, Julian didn't tell me. If he told me I would have known you were near the stream. By the way, was it fun stopping the water?"

Jonathan pauses while he looks at his son before saying, "I thought it was funny, you two caused quite a commotion. Now lets get walking." Once again the path opens up in front of them.

Many miles ahead of them, Julian and Jacob are still moving very quickly. They have stopped running but are moving on at a rapid pace.

"I need a rest." Julian says a bit out of breath.

"Its about time, I've needed a rest for about an hour."

"Why didn't you tell me?"

"I wasn't about to stop before you."

"That's just crazy."

"Are you calling me crazy Julian?"

"Well…yes I am!" They both laugh. Julian looks at his friend with an inquiring look on his face, "How can you tell only one person is moving from so far away?"

"You know how we feel the energy from the plants, trees and just about any living thing in nature?"

"Yes, that's something we can all do."

"It was you Julian that helped me realize I can feel people moving through the bushes."

"I did, what do you mean I did?" Julian now confused even more,

"One day when we where playing hide and seek as children, I already knew were you were and wanted to scare you with the small branch that was next to you. I was trying to slowly move just one small branch and touch your ear. I thought you would think it was a bug and make you jump trying not to get bit. Instead you grabbed the branch and broke it. I actually felt it break!"

"But Jacob, I can feel the branches break as well."

"Yes, but have you ever explored that?"

"What do you mean explore it?"

"I mean focus on one tiny branch or root, the tiniest vine in a big mess of vines, haven't you ever noticed that you can't hide from me?"

"I hide from you all the time."

"Do you? Like yesterday when you went behind that home with Andrew, then ran into the woods, you weren't hiding very well; I can take a hint."

"I'm sorry Jacob I didn't mean…" Jacob interrupts him,

"No need to apologize. We hang out every day, sometimes I get sick of you also. Why do you think I talk with the trees so often, do you think they talk back to me?"

Julian reluctantly says back, "To tell you the truth, I'm really not all that sure."

"Well they don't but I can tell you one thing, people leave you alone when you're talking to a tree." They both laugh. Jacob looks back at him,

"As I was saying, I focus on a bunch of branches far of in the forest. I follow their energy to the smallest edge. One day while I was doing this I felt an animal brush up against it. I felt some of the branches bend and others break, I could tell it was a small animal. With years of practice I have developed this gift so I can tell what is walking and how many. Right now there are two people walking back from the stream near Rosemary's village but they are walking very slow. I know were the village is, I have been there so many times with you and your brother so I focus on that area and feel the branches and grass bend and break as they walk through."

Julian thinks to himself, *"That makes a lot of sense, and he should start trying this."* But says, "I think your just crazy! Now lets get moving, rest over."

They had both been running for most of the day so they decide to walk. They will walk well into the night with only a little rest; maybe they will arrive there fairly early the next day. The other three have been walking much slower throughout the day, it's starting to get dark.

Jonathan looks around, "This is were we sleep tonight."

As he says this all the bushes around them form a circle entangling with each other.

"That will keep the animals away while we sleep."

It is a nice night so they will get a fire going and sleep under the stars.

Jonathan tells Andrew to gather some rocks and make a small fire pit while he looks for some wood. Within half an hour they have a nice fire going, they had no need to hunt for food, Rosemary brought the last of the fish, some bread and cheese. Sometimes it's boring to eat the same thing all the time but it's better than being hungry. Jonathan puts the last of the wood on the fire making sure it will burn all night. They all gather close together and cover themselves with their overcoats. Before they go to sleep Jonathan asks Andrew if he's scared.

"No I'm fine" but he really is a little frightened. They are deep in the forest and there are a lot of noises he doesn't normally hear near his village.

Much further ahead, Julian and Jacob are still moving quite quickly.

Julian stops and says, "We need to get some rest. "Go gather some wood, I will make a fire pit."

That's when they both look at each other and say at the same time, "**Food!**" realizing they haven't eaten all day and are very tired.

"Try to find something to eat while your gathering the wood"

When Jacob comes back with the wood, Julian is just finishing the fire pit. Within minutes the fire is going strong and Jacob goes to dig up some roots that he knows they can eat without getting sick. It's not much but if you heat them by the fire they get soft making them easy to chew. Neither one of them feels like hunting; so it's tasteless root or nothing. They quickly eat and go to sleep.

The next morning when Jacob wakes, Julian already has a squirrel cooking. Jacob slowly gets up, "Well that's better than root, I didn't even hear you get up."

"Its probably because you were snoring so loud!" They both laugh a little,

"I'm not kidding, you really snore loud!"

They finish cooking and eat the squirrel, they cover the fire with dirt. Before they start walking again Julian asks Jacob to see if anybody is walking around in the village they are heading for. Jacob sits down and a blank look comes over his face like he is in a trance.

Jacob is not a pleasant man to look at, his nose is incredibly crooked and one eye sits lower than the other. His head also has a funny shape to it. Like most of the men from their village he has dark hair about shoulder length and dark brown eyes. Julian was told from his father that there were problems when he was born. His mother passed shortly after giving birth and Jacob just made it. Jacob has always blamed himself even though there was nothing anybody could have done. His father was never the same after that. He opened Jacobs mind to nature when Jacob was only twelve years old. All the other men of the village were angry with him. They thought he was too young, even Julian's father who was his best friend said that he was too young and was angry for doing this. It wasn't until six months later when Jacobs father died from sickness, that people began to understand why he had done what he had done.

"There are people moving," Jacob says in a firm tone.

"What are they doing?"

"I'm not sure, it's like every time I check on them only two people are moving either toward or away from the stream."

"Why would they do that?"

"I'm not sure, my first guess would be water."

Julian gives him a friendly push as they both stand up and start running at a fairly quick pace.

"It should only take a few hours to get there." Jacob says.

Jonathan who has just finishing eating hears his brother's thoughts *"Some people are still moving to the stream, but only a few."*

Jonathan, not sure if this is good or bad replies *"Use caution when you get there. If there is trouble let me know before you do anything."* Jonathan turns to his wife and son, trying to show any concern in his voice. "Lets go, time is wasting." He looks at Andrew, "Cover the fire with dirt Andrew. I will help your mother pack so we can get going."

Rosemary looks into his eyes, "What have you heard?"

He tells her what Julian has just told her and she agrees they must start moving.

"Feeling strong son?"

"I'm always feeling strong."

"Good, I want to talk to your mother alone, so carry the bags when your done covering the fire, were going to walk ahead."

"Both of them?"

"Yes, both of them you said you were feeling strong. If it's to heavy leave your stuff behind."

Jonathan and Rosemary walk ahead in the direction of the village, they get far enough where Andrew can't hear them.

"If Julian and Jacob say there is a problem and they need my help I want you to turn around with Andrew and go home."

She looks at him with concern, "What do you know?"

"I don't know anything yet I just want you to be safe. I will have Daniel meet you on the way."

"OK…but everything will be fine, right?"

"I hope so."

They both look back at Andrew and his mother smiles "What's taking so long? Do you want me to carry them for you?"

Andrew catches up to his parents. His father takes one of the bags and they all start walking together.

Julian and Jacob have now been running for hours. They start walking when they come to the stream that runs fairly close to the village. They proceed with caution making sure to watch all their surroundings. Jacob puts his hand up telling Julian to stop, then waves it back and fourth telling him to hide. They both hide behind some trees and bushes waiting. Several moments pass, then a man appears in the distance, he is walking very slowly and carrying a bucket. Julian recognizes him, its Rosemary's brother. He is very pale and has lost a lot of weight. Julian looks around then asks Jacob if anyone else is nearby. Jacob says no.

Julian slowly approaches the man, "William, what's wrong?"

William is much shorter then both Julian and Jacob with short light brown hair and dark brown eyes. He has always been a thin man even though he has lost wait from being ill. He has a well defined scar on the side of his face along with the bottom piece of his ear is missing.

William falls to one knee and tells Julian to stay back. "We are all very sick, I think we are dying."

Julian runs over to him, helps him up and asks Jacob to fill the bucket with water.

"How many are sick?" Julian asks.

"All of us, you should leave before you grow ill."

"I'm not going anywhere." He helps him back toward the village.

Jacob starts gathering some leaves and roots that he will make into a drink. When the mixture is prepared you warm it and drink it hot, it helps with illness. He's not sure why they are sick but he hopes the drink will help. That's when he notices a small bush he had only heard about once, it had some leaves and berries picked from it. He knew what it was, his father had told him about this bush before he died. He also knew that this bush would make you sick, maybe even kill you if eaten. His father had also told him about a mix of plants that would treat this and how to administer it. People who have been struck ill would need to drink this antidote very hot. The home they were in also needed to be hot, the hotter the better, they needed to sweat the illness out. He stopped what he was doing, took a small piece of the plant and started running toward the village as fast as he could. When he got there he asked William if they had eaten or made anything with the plant.

William looked at it, "Yes it makes a tasty drink."

Jacob then tells Julian what he knew about this plant, so they decide to put all the sick people into one of the huts. Once in the hut they needed to get a fire going and keep it as warm as possible. After they did this Jacob runs off into the forest to gather the leaves he would need to make the drink his father had told him about. It takes about an hour to find and mix the drink. Both Julian and Jacob go into the hut, which was very hot by now, and make sure everybody drinks some of the mix. Before walking out they put another log on the fire making sure the air in the home would stay hot. Julian thinks for a moment and realizes he had not told his brother what was going on, so he stops to communicate with his brother who is still miles away.

"I already know, Jacob has already told me, I'm about to tell Rosemary."

Jonathan turns to his wife, "Your village is sick."

"What do you mean sick?"

"They made a drink from a poison plant."

She looks at him holding back her tears, "Are they going to die?"

"I don't think so, Julian and Jacob are taking care of them."

"Well let's hurry so I can help!" By now the tears are streaming down her face.

The three start to walk faster but they are still a long ways away.

Back at the village Jacob gives Julian a cup of the liquid mix he had made,

"Drink, my father told me that this plant is extremely poisonous, we can't help if we get sick also and we have both touched the plant." They both drink the mix.

"This stuff is horrible!" Julian spits it out as he is saying horrible.

"Yea, would you rather be sick or maybe die. Now shut up and drink!"

They finally get the drink down and go back into the home. It is very hot inside and they can see the people lying around dripping with sweat from their pale faces. There are twelve adults and three children, two boys Andrew's age and a girl much younger, they all drink a big cup of the mix. Julian puts some more wood on the fire and makes sure everybody is covered up to get them to sweat out the poison. William picks his head up and thanks them for their help. He is very weak but tries to explain his efforts.

"I have been trying to feed all of them but most won't eat. I have made sure all have drinking some water."

"Go to sleep William, there is nothing but rest and recovery to be had."

Julian and Jacob go back outside, both sweating.

Jacob turns to Julian, "We should see what they have for food, when they get up they will be hungry."

Julian agrees so they look in all the homes to see what they can gather together. There are about six homes made from dirt and rock with thatch filling the holes. They all slept in one damp uninviting room. Towards the back of each is a small rock fire pit that is occasionally used for cooking but mainly warmth. All the homes were in a circle with the opening facing the middle were there was a big fire pit. This is where they would eat most of the time, unless it was raining. The stream was about a mile away, maybe that's why they didn't wash Jacob was thinking. He could never live like this…and people think he is crazy!

They didn't find much and what they did find was old. It looked as though William and the other men that could still move took all the food they could find to feed the others. They would get some fish and hunt for some meat after a short rest. Both decided to get a roaring fire going in the middle of the village where they could gather back some energy to help the others. Julian falls asleep very quickly with Jacob not far behind him.

The next thing Julian remembers is Jonathan poking him with his stick in the arm, "Wake up."

Julian slowly gets up, he looks at his brother, "Where are Rosemary and Andrew?"

"They are right behind me."

"Don't let them go in the home we have her family in, it will only upset them."

"I've already told them not to."

Jonathan looks at Jacob still sleeping, "How did he know about this plant and more important, how did he know what to do?"

"His father taught him about his plant."

"His father was the best at knowing all the plants, some I've never heard of. If his father told him this will work it probably will."

"We need to gather some food, when they wake they will be hungry." He looks at Jacob who is still snoring louder than they are talking, " Should we wake him."

"I think we should let him sleep." They wait for Rosemary and Andrew to arrive. Jonathan tells her again not to go into the home were her family is. He also tells her that they will probably be all right and when Jacob wakes let him know were they are.

The two go back into the home and make sure the fire is going strong then walk into the woods to hunt for some food. A short while after Jacob wakes up, he realizes he has been sleeping for a long time and looks at Rosemary,

"Where is Julian?"

"Jonathan and Julian are gathering some food."

"I should be helping."

"You are a good friend and you've already done enough, now get some rest you look tired."

"Where's Andrew?" he asks.

"He's getting more water."

Jacob looks at Rosemary with a sad look to his face, "Have you gone to see your family?"

"No, Jonathan told me not to, but he says they will probably be all right thanks to you."

"Don't thank me, thank my father. He's the one who told me about the poisonous plant, and how to treat it."

"I have nobody to thank but you. You're the one who remembered and you're the one who is here helping, so once again I thank you."

He looks at her with a big smile, "I will go check on them and make sure they are healing."

He gets up, grabs the bucket that is about half full and walks into the home. He notices there is some color in some of their faces. He puts another log on the fire, its already very hot in there but he remembers his father saying, the hotter the better. He starts giving the drink to the children first. One of the young boys puts his hands to the cup he looks up to Jacobs's eyes,

"Thank you mister." Jacob finishes up and goes outside for some fresh air.

"Rosemary, I think they will be all right. Here comes Jonathan and Julian."

Jonathan and Julian walk out of the forest both carrying several small animals.

"Keep the fire hot, Julian killed a wild bore, and we were unable to carry it. Start cooking these while we retrieve it."

Jacob walks with them into the woods to help carry it.

Chapter Five

The next morning the three men wake but are still very tired. They have been taking turns checking on the sick people and keeping the fire hot. The wild bore they caught rests on a spit over the outside fire pit where the rest of the meat is already cooked. Rosemary starts to make a soup from the meat adding herbs and roots that she uses for flavor. Jonathan continues to help cure the sick with the special drink that Jacob made. Some of the villagers are talking softly to each other, which is a positive sign.

"Thank you Jonathan. You have helped our village from disaster" William says.

Jonathan notices the color is back in some of their faces.

"I'm hungry." Jonathan turns around to see a child trying to get his attention.

This brings a big smile to his face, finally a sense of ease overcomes him.

"Well I will go get you some food then." He finishes giving the drink Jacob has made to the others and walks out.

"Rosemary, is the soup ready, some are hungry."

She smiles back as she starts cutting some of the small animals that are already cooked into small pieces. Jonathan walks back into the home and gives a piece to the boy, then looks around to see if anyone else is up. There are two others awake so he gives them some meat and water as well. They keep the fire in the home hot and feed the villagers as they wake. By midday they all have eaten something, some only a little, but a little is better than nothing.

Julian and Jacob have spent most of the day hunting, which is very easy for Jacob, he always knows were the animals are. By this time most of the villagers have woken and begun gathering back their strength.

Jonathan is still making them drink the horribly tasting concoction. It is especially hard to get the children to drink the horribly tasting mix. Several of the people have come out for some fresh air, but they quickly go back inside for more rest. All day long Andrew has been helping his mother cook, gather water and firewood to keep the outside fire going as strong as possible.

"You look tired, get some rest. I will wake you in a short while."

He takes off his overcoat, puts it down under his head for a pillow and lies down right next to the fire where his mother is cooking.

"Wake me if you need anything."

He sleeps for about an hour, when he wakes he sees several people eating and sitting around the fire. Andrew sits up against a log where Julian and Jacob are having something to eat. Andrew rubs his sleepy eyes and asks his mother what he can do to help.

His mother gives him a smile, "Eat Andrew, you need your strength."

It's starting to get dark so Jonathan tells the villagers to get back inside, he knows it is uncomfortable but the heat will help them.

After all the villagers are in the home, the five of them sit by the outside fire until the sun sets, they are all very tired.

"Do we have to keep the fire going tonight like last night?"

"I don't know Julian. Jonathan what do you think?"

"I think they will be fine."

"I need a good nights sleep, I'm exhausted." Julian says this as he yawns.

Jonathan goes and puts some more wood on the fire in the home and returns back outside. He sees his son and wife with bags under their eyes. Julian and Jacob are looking out in a daze as if they haven't slept for days. Jonathan is concerned with their exhaustion, however, proud of the efforts put forth in saving Rosemary's village.

"We should all go to sleep, tomorrow will bring a fresh new start for our bodies."

The next morning Andrew wakes up and hears people talking, it's his uncle William and his wife Rachel; she is a fairly short women with reddish brown hair about shoulder length, her eyes an ice blue with a pointy nose. They are both sitting by the fire, he goes and joins them.

"I want to thank you. Andrew you are a very brave young man. Rachel and I can't express our gratitude for all you have done."

"You don't have to thank me, I mean what did I really do?"

"Helping use get better. I may have been sick, but I watched you run around, helping your mother cook and gather water."

He looks at his uncle with an innocent face and messy hair from sleeping,

"That's what family does, we help each other when we can."

"That's right" Jonathan says as he walks up from behind them.

"We help each other. Now help yourselves to some of that drink Jacob made."

They both get up and take a drink from the bucket. William tells Jonathan that he will give some to the others. Jonathan and Rosemary start cooking the food, they know that people will be waking soon and probably be hungry.

After a short while passes Julian and Jacob both wake and have some food then take a walk to the stream with Andrew to catch some fish and bath. When they get back, most of the villagers are up getting some soup or at least eating some small pieces of meat. All have been out for some fresh air and almost all of the color is back to their skin. The children are becoming more vibrant wanting to play, however, still feel a bit dragged down from the last couple of days.

Andrew walks over to three children and sits down with them.

"How are you feeling?"

"I want to play but I'm very tired." This said by a heavy set, tall boy named Thomas.

"Me too." A young girl named Teresa says looking at Thomas then Andrew.

She is much younger than the others only seven years in age, a tiny girl for her age with light brown hair down past her shoulders all messed up with big dark brown eyes. Even though she is still sick her smile is big and bright with a dimple on her chin.

"You are still recovering so lets play a game we can play sitting." He gets up and finds a bunch of small stones and one big on. He puts the big rock about fifteen feet away.

"We play up to twenty the closest small rock next to the big one gets a point." He throws one of the rocks, "I'll go first."

Everyone seems to be getting better around the village. Most have gone back to their own homes and falling into routine. William tells them stories about the big villages, which are getting closer. He says it used to be three weeks walk to the closest village, but now its only about one and a half weeks journey away. He tells them how dirty and rotten the people who live there are.

"There is one man who rules, they call him the Lord of the land. This man really scares me."

"Why does this man scare you?" Julian asks.

"He's a horrible man, he kills for fun. He claims to own the land and if you want to live on it you must give him half of what you own, or you die. And when he says die its told he kills in horrible ways."

"This can't be true! Its just tails and stories." Jacob cries out.

William turns to Jacob, there is a long pause as his face gets blank, as though he was scared to talk.

"This man puts fear deep into others. He has about five hundred men that will kill for him, anyway he asks."

"All stories that spread like fire and get fabricated as they pass from one to another, before you know it a harmless man is a killer." Jacob says this as he pokes a stick in the fire.

"Shut up! They are not stories!"

Jacob has never heard William yell before. "I'm sorry, it's just hard to believe that a man like this actually exists."

Several tears run down the side of Williams face "Its something I will never forget for as long as I live."

Jonathan interrupts. "You've seen this man kill?"

"It's the most horrible thing I've ever seen and promised myself I would never talk about it."

Jonathan looks at William and can tell it hurts to remember. "If you don't want to talk about it, you don't have to."

"I want to hear." Jacob says in his most serious voice glaring at William.

Jacob hears Jonathan's thoughts, *"SHUT UP!"*

William takes a deep breath and wipes his tears. "No, I want to tell you, I need to tell someone." He takes another long pause, "I had a friend who lived in one of the villages. Years ago I went to visit, my friend told me not to look at any of his men. I was told that I didn't want them to notice me, I wasn't sure why but I listened. We hadn't seen each other for many years so we went for a walk to one of the bigger villages to trade some skins for food. The people there were very dirty, they push and shove each other, I saw several men fighting. I didn't like it at all but we were two friends catching up on old times. That's when I saw a man trip on some rocks, but when he fell his hand hit another man in the face by accident. I didn't know that this was the man they called the Lord of the Land, neither did the man who fell into him. Three men grabbed him and held him up, another man hit him several times before saying,

"Apologies." then started to hit him again.

A women came running over crying, "Please don't kill my husband he does not know who you are."

The man they called Lord of the land gives her a long cold stare, "OK, I won't kill this man."

As she turns to her husband this man drove his sword into the middle of her back pushing it through the center of her chest.

Laughing in a deep evil voice he said, "You will be fine."

As the other man struggles to get free the Lords men through him to the ground, rolled him over so his head was facing up.

This evil man puts his knee on the man's throat and says, "That was the last thing you will ever see." he then pushed a small knife into each one of the man's eyes.

While his men held him down, the Lord of the Land yells to the others around that if he finds out anybody has helped him in any way the same would happen to them. The man lie there with no help, everyone was afraid even his friends.

The Lord of the Land walked away laughing about something else as though nothing had happened. I will never get that image out of my head."

William starts to cry again. No one has a word to say, Jonathan puts his hand on Williams back as he cries. Julian and Jacob can't believe what they have just heard. If William had not said he witnessed this they would not believe it.

"How can one be so cruel to another?" Jacob says in a weak yet still serious voice.

"I don't know, but I will never go back. It's been years and I have never seen my friend again."

They all sit for a while very quiet just looking into the fire.

William finally gets up and starts to walk away as he says in a faint exhausted voice, "I'm going to see if my wife needs me for anything."

Julian looks at Jacob who is looking back at him, they still can't believe what they have just heard, this horrible man so close to them. They both want to see for themselves but they also know that Jonathan will not allow it. It's not as though they need his permission, it's just that he has always been the most responsible of the three so they take his advice.

"I think you two should go for a walk."

Julian looks at his brother, "What do you mean, a walk?"

"I mean, if this man they call, Lord of the land is as bad as they say and getting closer we should check it out, and even keep an eye on him, that's what I mean!"

"When should we leave then?" Julian asks.

"Why don't you leave tomorrow. The people here should feel much better, Rosemary and myself can take care of them. I want to know about this man and if we should be worried?" Jonathan then tells them to try to blend in and not to bring attention to yourselves.

"Does this mean you don't want us to wash?" Julian asks.

"That's exactly what I mean. William says its only about two weeks walk, so try to get dirty, you both just blend with the others. William says these people are really dirty, and this is coming from him, so these people must be filthy."

They sit by the fire for a while longer watching dusk turn to dark.

Jonathan looks at the two men and stands up, "It's getting late, I'm going to settle in and get some sleep. You two should just get some sleep as well."

They all walk to the homes they are sleeping in and quickly fall to sleep. The next morning Julian is up early, he's getting some stuff ready. They don't need much, they live off the land very well. He gets some water, a little food to snack on and starts to put some extra clothes to change into when he hears Jonathan.

"What are you doing?"

"I'm getting ready to go?"

"Why are you packing clean cloths?"

Julian gazes at him with a blank look on his face, "So I can change?"

"You won't be changing, I said to blend in." That's when Jacob walks in, his hair is a mess, his face covered with soot from the fire, his hands filthy, and it looked as though he dragged his overcoat in dirt all morning.

"How do I look?"

"That's a good start." Jonathan can't help but laugh at him a bit.

Jacob sees the smug look on Julian's face, "What's with you?"

"I thought we would get there and make ourselves look dirty."

"No, we have to really be dirty so it's believable. If this man and his men are really that bad, I want to fit in, now get dirty!" Jacob throws some dirt a Julian.

"Your in charge Jacob. Let's go Julian you heard him, Get dirty!"

Jacob grabs Julian's hair with both hands, before Julian can pull away he messes it all up.

This aggravates Julian a little, as he pulls away he says, " You've always liked being dirty anyway."

"That's right, just like a child." Jacob says while he is still trying to mess Julian's hair. They all laugh.

Outside Rosemary has been up for some time cooking. Rachel and several other women have been helping. Almost everybody is feeling better, yet still very tired. Some of the men are at the stream catching some fish, others are hunting for meat and a handful are cutting wood. The four children are playing tag, they are all laughing and having a good time. Jonathan notices that Andrew always let's the young girl, Teresa, catch him allowing her to have fun also. This makes Jonathan happy to see his son care and show compassion for others feelings. He watches the children play for a while then calls William over who has been splitting wood.

"What do you want Jonathan?"

"I want you and everybody to rest, I'm watching everyone work to hard, you were all very sick, some almost died, so I want you all to take it easy."

"We will be fine, you have already done enough. You showed up at the right time, if you hadn't we would probably all be dead, so like I said, you've already done enough."

Jonathan looks to his son who is playing and laughing with the other children and says, "He doesn't have this kind of fun at home. If you feel as though you owe me something, that right there is enough. We have plenty of food and wood for the fire, the stream is only a short walk. Go tell all the men to rest, if I need their help I will ask. I want them to get better."

William continues to split wood as Jonathan persists for him to rest. It is clear that he is back to his strength and wants to provide for his village. Jonathan stands close by passing more wood to William as he continues on talking.

"Julian and Jacob will be going for a walk, a long walk so I will be here for at least three to four weeks."

"I didn't realize you would be staying for so long, but your more than welcome." William puts down his ax and begins to walk over to where the other men are working. He decides to take the advice of Jonathan and tells the others to slow down and rest.

Rosemary and the other women have cooked plenty of food and it's all lined up on a table letting anybody eat as they please. The men have all eaten quite a lot, the children eat quickly and run off into the woods to play. Rosemary loves it when Andrew is here, he plays well with the other children. Julian and Jacob walk up to the table and start eating.

Jacob looks at Rosemary, then the food on the table, which is still plentiful. Jacob grabs a piece of meat, takes a bite, and with a full mouth says,

"Is that all the food that is left? We will be walking for more than two weeks, you must feed us better than that!"

"You keep talking to my wife like that and you won't be eating anything you need to chew!" Jonathan says as he approaches them from behind.

"I was kidding."

"When you're done eating and before you and Julian leave I would like to have a word with you."

Jacob grabs a handful of food and stuffs his mouth full. "I can talk and eat at the same time so let's go for that walk."

They walk away from everybody to be alone.

"I want to thank you for helping us and for being such a good friend to Julian, your father would be very proud."

"Do you really think so Jonathan?"

"I know so, I know so because I'm proud of you, even if you are a little crazy!"

"I really don't remember my father very well."

"You were very young when he died."

"Do you remember him?"

"I remember him well, you were only twelve when he died, that made me seventeen almost eighteen, so I was already an adult and training. Your father was a very good man and could always make us laugh, kind of like you."

"You know I really don't talk to trees, I just like to feel their energy but talking to them is a good way to make people leave you alone for a while. This may sound crazy, but sometimes I feel as though I can hear or feel my parents in the energy."

"That's not as crazy as you think, it actually makes a lot of sense."

"What do you mean?"

"Well its said that when one of our people dies, we bury or burn their bodies letting their energy go into the life around, such as the plants, tree's and bushes. That's why when we die its really just the start of a new life."

"I've heard that before, yet never really knew what it meant."

"Well that's what it means and I believe it. So if you think you hear or feel your parent's energy in the trees and bushes, it's a good thing. I suggest you listen and try to feel their energy."

"Thank you" he says, then looks at Jonathan with a serious look,

"Can I ask you a question?"

"Yes, what would you like to ask me?"

"Why are you so proper all the time?"

"Do you want the long story or the short story?"

"We should get going so give me the short story."

"The short story, here it goes. When my father died, my mother was left all alone to take care of Julian and me. She also made sure you were provided for. Julian was always into everything and I was old enough to help take care of him, so I had no choice but become an adult. Believe me when I say having you around all the time was no burden, just having you there to play with him helped a lot. But as I was saying, I had to grow up fast and everyone around started to treat me as though I was older than I really was."

The two walk back both understanding each other a lot better and both feeling a little more like family. They return to where the others are gathered. Julian is picking at some food talking with Rosemary.

"Are you ready?" Jacob asks.

"I'm as ready as I will ever be."

"Well lets get moving."

William steps forward and asks, "Where are you going?"

"Don't worry about them, they will be fine."

William then looks in the direction of the villages he was talking about the night before.

"Their going that way, aren't they?"

Jonathan puts his hand on Williams shoulder and says with a serious tone, "As I said, don't worry about them, they will be fine."

"Please don't go, there is no need!"

"But there is!" Jonathan yells, and then says in a calm voice, "They are only going to see how close the other villages are and if we should be worried."

"Please be careful and don't draw attention to yourselves or you won't come back!"

Julian gives his brother a hug and Jacob shakes his hand.

"Thank you for the talk, it really meant a lot to me." Jacob says looking into Jonathan's eyes.

Jacob turns to Rosemary, gives her a kiss on the cheek, "I was only kidding earlier, you made plenty of food and it was delicious."

"They will be alright, won't they Jonathan?" Rosemary asks with concern in her voice.

"They will be fine. They are both smarter than most people think."

The two men disappear into the woods, they walk for several hours before stopping for a break and drink some water. They are walking close to the stream for that reason. It's easer than twisting water out of the vines like they do for the oil for their lamps.

Jacob with a smile says, "Maybe there will be some women of our age there."

"I think we should keep our minds on just checking things out and see if we need to be worried…but it would be nice."

They both laugh and start walking again.

After walking for about four and a half days, only stopping to sleep and eat, Julian stops and looks around. "Have you noticed that there is a different feeling to the trees?"

"Yes I have, I'm not sure how to describe it but it feels different."

They walk a short distance further when they come upon an old village that has been destroyed by weather. The bones of people are scattered all over the place, both men get a restless feeling.

"Julian, remember that feeling we had earlier, do you still have it?"

"It's even worse now, I have this intense sense of sad emotion but I don't know why."

"I want to try something." Jacob says with an intense look on his face.

"What are you talking about?"

"Something your brother told me. He said if I think I can feel my parent's energy in the trees and bushes, I should try listening to them."

"What!"

"He told me when we die our energy goes into the life around us. Just don't bother me for a short while, I want to talk to the trees."

"Now I know you're insane, but OK, I'm going to get some water and have a bite to eat." He walks toward the stream and finds some berries along the way. He sits down watching the water as he enjoys a short rest. When he returns he finds Jacob a pale white with tears running down his face.

Julian grabs Jacob by the shoulders and shakes him.

"Jacob! What's wrong?" he shakes Jacob a few times before he gets a response.

Jacob finally shakes his head back and fourth quickly then puts it down covering his eyes with one hand and the other on his knee.

"These people were brutally killed for no reason."

"How do you know that?"

"I don't know how I know, I just know."

"Well do you know what happened?"

"Not really, I just know some men came and killed them for no reason and had fun doing it. Its like some of the energy I felt is still dying and still feeling pain as though it will last forever." Jacob stands up quickly, "Lets go, I don't like this place."

Julian agrees so they walk away as fast as they can. Hours have now passed and they are starting to get tired and hungry.

"Are you all right Jacob?"

"I am not sure what I am."

"Do you want to rest?"

"Sure, I want to make camp and eat." He stops and sits on a rock. "I will get the fire going while you gather some food."

"Jacob, can you check ahead and see how far we are from the closest village?"

"I can't feel anybody walking yet, so I know we will be safe for the night."

Julian walks into the woods to look for some food while Jacob starts gathering rocks for the fire pit. When Julian comes back he is carrying a rabbit, Jacob already has the fire going. After the rabbit is skinned they put it on a spit and cook it over the fire. There will be enough so they can have some in the morning when they wake. Jacob looks at the sky, even the stars look different to him this far from home. After they eat they both slowly fall to sleep next to the fire, both wondering what they will find in the next couple of days. The next morning when they wake they realize another animal must have gotten the rest of their rabbit because it was gone.

Julian says with a grin "You pig, you ate all the food while I was sleeping." Jacob tells him that he's not very hungry anyway, they can find something to eat along the way. So they start walking toward the villages they are looking for. They walk for about half the day.

"Now I'm getting hungry." Julian says.

"Me too." Julian gathers some berries to eat while Jacob digs up the roots they eat and gets a small fire going. Julian comes back to see the roots warming by the fire, "You like those tasteless roots don't you."

"Yes I do, I think they have a nice taste to them.

"Yea, the taste of dirt."

"You don't have to eat them if you don't like them, but they do fill you up. Why don't you start twisting some vines to get some water we are far from the stream."

"Why don't you do it while I sit?"

"Because, I'm going to focus ahead to see how close we are to the villages." He looks at Julian, "Unless you want to do it. Oh that's right you can't, so start twisting."

Julian walks up to some vines, holds their water pouch under one and the vine starts to twist, small beads of water form on the surface and drip into the pouch. He goes back to the fire were Jacob is sitting, gets a handful of berries and one of the roots Jacob has warmed and starts eating.

"Anything ahead?" Jacob stops focusing on the forest and looks at

Julian eating the root. "I thought you didn't like root?"

"I don't but I'm hungry."

Jacob grabs one of the roots and takes a bite. "There is a small village about one day away, I really can't tell but it looks like much bigger ones further ahead."

They finish eating and cover the fire with dirt.

"People have traveled this way recently, some of the twigs are broken and it looks like there are small paths in the dirt." Jacob says looking around

"Yes, I've noticed this also."

They walk a little further when they come across the bones of two people lying next to a tree. They stop to look at them, one set lie intact, the other was scattered around.

"Look here Jacob, it looks like this person was beaten badly. The skull is cracked in several spots, most of the ribs are cracked or broken, and both arms and legs also have cracks and breaks in them. I think he was beat to death."

Jacob looks up to see a rope hanging from a tree above the scattered bones. "The other was hung."

"How far are we from the villages?"

Jacob looks at the rope, then the bones. "About half a days walk."

"Lets walk a little further and make camp, I want to be well rested when we meet these people."

They walk just far enough to get away from the bones, neither one of them wanted to sleep next to them. When they were far enough to feel comfortable they make camp, have something to eat and go to sleep for the night.

Chapter Six

When Julian wakes up the following morning, Jacob already has the fire going and a rabbit cooking, he was up early.

"Good morning, I thought you were going to sleep all day."

Julian rubs his eyes and takes a sip of water. "How long have you been up?"

"Long enough to get the fire going, catch and cook a rabbit." He smiles, "I know how much you like the roots we eat, but I thought we should eat a little more this morning. I think we will need our strength today so I went hunting for a bear and came back with a rabbit."

"This will be just fine." Julian stretches a little before he starts eating.

It's not long before they consume the food, cover the fire with dirt and are on their way walking again.

"How long do you think?" Julian asks.

"About three hours or so, we should be ready for anything."

They both keep walking with their walking sticks, ready to fight if they need to.

They walk for about two and a half hours when Julian puts his hand up telling Jacob to stop.

"I think I heard something. Can you tell if anyone is approaching?"

"No, these paths are warn in with no bushes or small vines to feel."

They walk a little further when two men come around a corner. These men were filthy, they could see they had minimal teeth, grimy knotted hair, clothes that appeared to have never been washed, and they smelt putrid.

The bigger of the two men step forward, "Who are you? You don't look like the Lords men."

"We are not."

The man takes a good look at them, "Well you don't look like you're from around here."

"We are not, we are simple woods men just traveling through." Julian says eying the man, ready to respond to any hostility.

The bigger of the two men looks at the other one then steps forward and pulls out a big knife, the smaller of the two also pulls out a knife.

"Well woodsmen, give me all your belongings and we will let you live."

Julian puts his stick in front of him and takes a small step back while Jacob takes a step forward so the two are standing side by side.

Julian looks into the mans eyes, "We wish no trouble, we just want to pass."

The larger of the two men holding knifes looks at his friend, laughs then turns back to Julian. "You're about to die and your still thinking about passing!"

Jacob then adds, "We have no desire to fight with you."

"Then don't fight!" the larger of the two men says as he lounges forward with his knife at Jacob.

Jacob calmly steps to the side and with his stick he pulls the man's front leg forward causing the man to fall backwards. As the man is falling Jacob hits the man in the head with his stick, before the man hits the ground Jacob swings his stick around and knocks the knife out of his hand so hard the knife sticks into a tree next to them. The moment he hits the ground Jacob put his stick on the man's throat and steps on the hand he can still move. At the same time Julian knocks the knife out of the other mans hand with his stick. Julian grabs the man's other hand quickly bringing him down to his knees crying out in pain, begging him to stop before he breaks his hand. The man lying on the ground opens his eyes to see Jacob standing above him with one foot on the hand he can still move and the end of his stick on his throat.

Jacob looks down at him, "As I said, we just want to pass with no trouble."

The larger of the two men lying on his back still a little cross-eyed says, "OK, no trouble."

Julian lets the other mans hand go, he gets up holding his hand close to his body still in pain.

Jacob steps off the hand of the man he is standing over and takes the stick off his neck. "Sorry about that but you gave me no choice." He helps the man up who is still shaken from the blow to his head.

"What's your name?" Jacob asks.

"My name is Charles and this is my brother Edward." Charles then says in a serious voice "thank you for not killing us."

"Kill you, I didn't even want to hit you."

"I can tell you're not from around here." Charles says rubbing the large lump on his head.

"Like my friend Julian said, we are just passing through, my name is Jacob."

"If you want you can walk with us, our village is not far from here."

"That might be a good idea, I gave you a nasty hit to the head. I want to make sure you get back without any problems."

Jacob hears Julian's thoughts, *"These men just tried to kill us, be ready. We don't want to be their friends, we just don't want them as our enemy."*

"I agree."

The four men start walking toward the village, some rain drops start to fall. As they walk the rain starts to get a little heavy.

Julian says to the men, "The rain is going to get really strong shortly."

"How do you know that?" Charles asks.

"See how the clouds are moving, dark clouds under the light ones. The dark clouds are moving quickly toward us and the light ones are mostly standing still."

"OK, I see this also." Charles replies in a confident tone.

"That means a storm is moving through." Just as Julian explains this there is a large flash of light followed by the crackling sound of thunder. Shortly after it starts to rain extremely hard.

Julian hears Jacobs's thoughts, *"This is probably the only time they wash."* Julian laughs out loud.

"What are you laughing at?" Charles asks.

"Nothing I just like a good storm."

The men keep walking through the rain, the storm quickly passes and the sun comes out. Edward looks at his brother,

"I hate the rain." Edward mutters under his breath.

Jacob, without looking at Edward says, "You should love the rain, without it everything alive would die."

Edward has no response he just keeps walking. They finally arrive at the edge of the village. Julian and Jacob both stop and look at the other two men.

Jacob gives Charles a look of concern, "Will we be welcome here, when we first met you we didn't receive a welcome feeling."

"If you're with us you will not be harmed, welcome I'm not sure."

As they walk into the village they can tell they are not welcome. Everyone they pass either stares or won't look at them at all. For dirty people things are put together quite well, the homes seem to be built better than the homes in Rosemary's village. They have some type of shelter over the middle of the village to protect them from rain, it looks like a mesh of vines tied from tree to tree with an assortment of leaves tangled in. It was built fairly well and the ground was dry underneath it, with several fires going. Julian also notices a few large buckets made of hand carved wood with metal rims. They looked like they were being used to collect the rainwater that would run off the mesh like shelter.

Jacob hears Julian's thoughts, *"For savage people they are well organized."*

An old man steps in front of them with two large men behind him. He is a short yet large man with long gray hair all knotted and dirty, He looks at Charles with an angry expression on his face.

"Who are these men and why are they here?"

"They are just passing through."

"And you're just going to let them pass through!"

"Believe me, we tried to stop them. They mean no harm, they just want to move on through."

The old man gets right in front of Jacob and the other two-step in front of Julian.

"How can we be sure they mean no harm?"

"If they meant harm Edward and I would already be dead. "These two men of yours will be no challenge for them."

The old man steps back still looking at Julian and Jacob, "Well pass through then and if you want to dry your belongings by our fires feel free to do so."

"Thank you, but we will just pass through." Julian says not wanting to stay there any longer then needed.

When they get to the opposite side of the village the two shake Charles and Edwards hands and keep walking.

"Well they weren't all that bad." Julian says with sarcasm in his voice.

"They seem to all fear this Lord of the land and his men. We must learn more about him."

They walk for another hour or so before stopping to rest, they start a small fire to help dry their clothing. They can both tell that this part of the forest is traveled often, the paths are all dirt with many roots showing at the surface. They also know that the closer they get to this so-called Lord of the land the more savage the people will become. Jacob catches a small squirrel and cooks it as their clothes dry. It wasn't much but they both wanted to start moving again, they were eager to find out about this man and head for home so they put out the fire and start walking. Jacob tells Julian that there are people all around the area but none very close. They walk for the rest of the day. Jacob tells Julian that they are getting fairly close to the larger villages. They both decide to find a good spot to make camp for the night; they know that they won't get much sleep this night, they must be ready to fight if need be. They find a spot that looks good to stop for the night and make a small fire. It's already dusk so they only have a little light left. Julian asks

Jacob if he can feel anybody around them.

"You have to teach me that skill Jacob. I want to be able to feel for myself."

"It takes a lot of practice."

"Yes, but its really handy."

"Yes it is, and no there is nobody around."

Julian stays seated by the fire as the bushes and thorns around them move and tangle together so they can sleep at ease. Jacob sees what he is doing and helps. It's not long before they are completely enclosed in thorn and brier bushes. When they have settled in they decide to catch some meat to eat, as they walk through the thorns a small path opens up for them and closes as they pass through. Jacob sees a rabbit off in the distance, before it can run some bushes wrap around it killing it. They also find some berries before walking back to the fire. The rabbit is put on a spit made from wood and slowly cooked. As the rabbit is cooking they talk about what's ahead of them. Neither one of them likes this place but they try to stay positive hoping that some of the people are friendly.

Once the rabbit is cooked they eat making sure to save some for the morning. The bushes are too thick for any large animals to get through, they are only worried about the small ones running off with the rest of the rabbit so they keep it close to them. It is very dark now, the fire is almost out and they both fall to sleep with an uneasy felling.

The next morning they wake to the sound of birds chirping, this sound is relaxing to both of them. They get up and eat the rest of the food before they start walking again.

About an hour has passed when they start to see the paths are more traveled in this area. They pass a small home deep in the woods of the trail, it's the first they have seen since the last village they passed through.

As they walk further into this area there are several more homes scattered around but everybody they pass seems to look the other way. They both think that these people are not very friendly but also know they are not here to make friends. There is a job to do so they just keep walking without saying anything to anybody. The more they walk the more homes they pass. Now people are looking at them but not in a friendly way. They see only a few animals in pens made from rock but not many, not to many bushes in this area either, just a lot of dirt and dust. All the low branches have been broken off the trees and the entire area smells bad, it seems as though no one cares about anybody but themselves. The two men keep walking with people watching them the entire way.

Julian turns to Jacob with a disturbed look on his face, "Its as though these people like to be dirty."

They walk up to a stream that crosses the beat in path they have been walking. Jacob takes a sip of water, "This place is dirty, but I see nothing to worry about."

"I agree, but these people seem to have no hope. I want to know why?"

"All right we better keep on walking."

They drink a little more from the stream, fill their water pouches and start walking again. They walk for about another hour, the further they walk the more organized the people seem to become. They both sense the fear these people have but they are not sure why yet. They are all afraid of something, the children all play behind the homes and when the parents notice Julian and Jacob they grab their children and bring them inside. The two men think this is very odd, they are just walking through. They walk until they reach another stream, this one is much larger then the other one they passed, it is about fifteen feet across. There is a stone path going through the middle in the direction they want to go, the rocks are slick on their feet as they cross.

As they turn the next corner a man runs into Jacob and falls to the ground. He is a small man and looks thin from hunger. Before Julian or Jacob can ask what's wrong this man gets up in a panic and starts running toward the water they have just crossed.

"What's that about?" Julian asks cautiously looking in the direction they are walking, wondering what this man was running from.

"I don't know, but lets get out of sight." They both step into the bushes and watch as about ten men run by, all dressed the same. One of them yells,

"I think he came this way!"

"O yes, we've got him now." Another says as the men run quickly by.

Julian and Jacob walk back through the woods quietly to see what was happening. When they reach the stream they had just crossed the ten men are holding the other man in the water, one holding his head below the surface until he stops kicking he then pulls him up.

"It's my turn." Another man in the group says as he slaps the man until he starts to cough out water. He grabs the man's hair and holds his head under water again until once again he stops kicking.

"Don't kill him yet," another yells as he grabs the man by the hair and pulls him out of the stream. "We want him alive so he can be hanged as an example for stealing!"

They tie the man's hands tightly behind his back putting a rope around his neck and start walking back the way they came. While they are walking they take turns hitting and tripping the man, dragging him until he gets up. Julian and Jacob both can't believe what they have seen, they decide to rest for a while and find a secluded place to sit.

"These people are horrible." Julian says with a look of disgust.

"Most are just scared." Jacob replies.

"I think those men were some of the Lords men."

"Why do you say that?"

"They were all dressed the same."

"So are we."

"Yes, but its different."

"What do you mean different?"

"I mean, they try to look the same all wearing black, we just wear the same skins and clothes."

There is a long pause as Julian looks down the path. "I think we should avoid them most of the way."

"That's a good idea. Lets travel through the woods instead of the path."

They start walking again in the same direction deep in the woods off the beat in path trying to avoid other people. They walk for a while longer when they find a rock wall about waist level. On the other side of the wall there are many homes all made from rock and dirt. They look very well built and a little bigger than the other homes they have passed along the way. All the people are going about their business, some men chopping wood, others working on the walls of their homes making sure it won't let weather in.

Most of the homes are lined up in a row all along a well beat in path. If you look into the woods you can see homes and huts scattered all around, some very well built others barely standing. Most of them have small fires going in front of them. Many of the women are cooking or skinning small animals to be cooked, they all seem to be busy.

"You know Jacob, besides them being dirty, this place doesn't look all that bad."

"I was thinking the same thing, this must be one of the bigger villages William talked about."

"Which way do you think we should travel?"

"I think we should travel down the path in the center of the village."

"Do you think that's a good idea?"

"I don't think these people care who we are."

They both start walking down the path keeping caution to their surroundings. The people don't seem to care who they are, they don't even look at them. If either of the two men looks at anybody they look down or turn away, so they just keep walking. A short while passes when a young boy a little younger than Andrew walks up to the two men, this boy is very short and thin. It looks as though he didn't eat very well and was very dirty with short dark hair and hazel eyes with a very curious yet innocent look on his face.

"Who are you?" the young boy asks.

Julian gives him a friendly smile, "We are just traveling through."

"Why?"

"We are woodsmen from far away and travel a lot."

The young boy then says with sad look on his face. "You should travel the other way, if you keep walking in that direction you might end up dead."

These words coming from such a young boy surprise Jacob, "Why would you say that?"

"Because, if his men don't like you they will kill you but first they beat you and take all of your stuff. They make you beg for your life, then hang you if your lucky. Some get dragged to the Lord himself, its been told if this happens it takes days, even weeks to die." The boy now has a blank look on his face as he looks down the path,

"They take what they want and kill whom they please."

The boy wants to say more but his father comes running over and grabs him by the arm pulling him off to the side of the trail,

"What have I told you about talking to strangers!" he yells.

Julian takes a step toward the man who quickly turns and puts his hand on a knife that is tucked under his coat. This man is tall and thin also with short dark hair and dark brown eyes. The tone of his voice and look in his eyes both showed anger toward his son for talking with the two.

Julian sees this and takes a step back, "The boy was not bothering us."

The man looks at Julian and then Jacob, he moves the boy behind him and firmly holds the handle of his knife,

"I'm not worried about him. It's you I'm worried about!"

As he says this both men take another step back, put both hands in the air,

"We mean no harm or wish to fight with anybody." Jacob states. Then Julian adds, "We are simple woodsmen just traveling through."

The man takes his hand off his knife, "Well OK then, I just worry about my boy, he talks to strangers often." The man shakes his head then looks at his son, "Some strangers will kill you for that reason alone! That's why I worry so much."

Jacob assures him, "As we said, we mean no harm, we just want to pass through."

"Just passing through, you should probably go around."

"Why would you say that?" Julian asks.

"You might have trouble getting through the way you are traveling." The man looks at Julian then Jacob, "How long have you been traveling?" he asks.

"Weeks" Julian tells the man.

"My mane is Richard" he holds his hand out to shake,

"You both look tired, would you like to rest for a while, we have some food if you would like."

Julian hears Jacobs's thoughts, *"I am tired, lets take the offer. We can take turns resting."*

Julian looks back at Richard, "A rest would be nice, we've been walking for hours."

They walk toward the home made from dirt and rocks and sit by the fire. Julian starts talking to Richard who has already told his wife to get some food ready. Jacob is sitting against a tree, within minutes he starts to snore.

Julian laughs out loud, "I guess he was tired."

Richards wife brings out a pot and sits it over the fire, she is a short thin women with long blondish hair, very dirty making it look darker than it really is, like her son she also has hazel eyes, unlike her son see has many freckles scattered about her face with a large birth mark on the side of her chin. Julian tells her that she doesn't have to cook for them.

She gives a friendly smile, "I don't want you to think that all the people around here are bad. Some of us try to treat others with kindness. Just because we live in a nasty place it doesn't mean we have to act that way."

Julian smiles back, "That's a nice way to think."

Richard puts his hand on Julian's shoulder, "I apologize, this is my wife Melanie and my son's name is Harold." Harold has already run off with another child into the woods.

"He is a little too friendly, some people around here only care about themselves." He sighs, "When I was his age it was different, the people cared about each other. We all helped with everything."

Julian with a somewhat confused look asks, "Why did it all change? This looks as though it could be a good place to live if the people were nice to each other."

Richard looks down and says softly, "The Lord of the land and his men, that's what happened."

Julian notices these words make Melanie very uncomfortable.

"Who is this man? I have heard this man mentioned before and everybody seems to be scared of him."

Richard looks around before saying, "If you don't know him you should turn around and leave before you do! This man just takes and takes, and if you don't give he kills you. The more time that goes by the more men follow him and the worse it gets."

"Why don't you just leave?"

"We want to but it's hard, I've lived here my entire life."

Melanie smiles at her husband then turns toward Julian, "We plan to leave and go to my sisters village. Its about three days that way." She says pointing into the woods, she tastes the soup with a large wooden ladle, "Good the soup is ready."

Julian throws a small stone at Jacob, "Wake up, these nice people are feeding us and all you can do is sleep." Julian winks at Melanie when he says this.

Jacob slowly gets up, stretches his back and walks over, "That smells good." Both Julian and Jacob only have a small bowl with a little piece of bread, they both know these people don't have much. Richard calls his son over who quickly eats a bowl of soup and some bread and starts to run off. Richard calls him back,

"Harold, what's in your hands?"

Harold looks at his father, "Some more bread."

"Did you not get enough to eat?"

"No, I ate plenty."

"Then why are you taking bread with you? We don't have any to waste."

"My friend is hungry, he has not eaten today. He's waiting for his father to come home with some food."

"Give the boy some bread and have him come over for some soup."

Julian hears Jacobs thoughts, *"I would call these people friends."*

Julian and Jacob both stand up Julian looks at Richard, "Thank you for the food, I hope we see you again."

"That would be nice."

Julian turns to Melanie, "Three days that way, maybe we will travel back that way and see her village."

"Her name is Pauline," she says.

The two men start walking in the direction of the Lord and his men. They walk for about two more hours, the people seem to become less friendly the further they walk. They walk past a large garden with several men standing at the front of a rock wall.

Julian hears Jacobs's thoughts, *"These men are all dressed the same way the men were that beat the man in the stream."*

Jacob then hears Julian's thoughts, *"Look at the tree above the men."*

Jacob had not noticed but there was the man hung by the neck, his clothes had been striped off and they could tell that he was dragged and beaten the entire way. This sight makes them both a little sick, they walk by trying not to look at the men or the tree.

"Nobody deserves that," Julian says softly with an appalled look on his face.

As they pass the garden they both looked in, it is very well kept, big trees of fruit, many berry bushes and vegetables of all sorts. There were men in the garden taken care of it and others standing out side, they were all wearing the same black clothes. They just walked by not looking at any of the men, once they passed and were sure none of the men could hear them, Julian asked a man sitting on a log on the side of the path,

"What did that man do to be hanged?"

"What man?" The man says with a glazed look as though he was in shock.

Julian thinks for a moment, "The man hanging in front of the garden."

"Oh that man, I told him it was a bad idea but he didn't listen."

"Did you know him?"

"Yes, he was my friend," the man pauses and looks like he's holding back tears, "I told him it was a bad idea, but he still tried to sneak into the back of the garden and steel some berries."

"They hanged him for that?" Jacob says with a shocked look.

"Of course they did, that's a crime against the Lord, and any crime against the Lord is punished by death or worse!"

The man looks at Julian and Jacob then back at the ground and begins to cry, "I thought he was dead before they hanged him but they made sure he woke first, they waited for a while throwing water on his face, making sure he was awake before they hung him. They let us know that this is what would happen if we were caught stealing from the Lord."

The two men walk away watching the sun get lower in the sky, they decide to find a place to sleep for the night. They walk until they find a spot where they can walk into the woods without anybody noticing. They walk for at least an hour picking up wood along the way. They find a good spot to start a small fire. As they sit around the fire they use their gift to bring as many bushes and thorns as they can to surround them. They completely cover the area, they use as many roots, vines and bushes as they can. There is no way anybody would stumble upon them.

After what they have seen they are not very hungry, Jacob warms up some of the roots he likes, and they both agree to stay clear of the Lords men as much as possible but still need to see how many men he has. They put the last of the wood on the fire and go to sleep.

Chapter Seven

The next morning they wake up hungry. Julian gets a fire going while Jacob goes to gather some food. He finds a bunch of berries he knows are eatable and to his surprise, a fairly large snake. Snakes have been scarce for a long time, normally they leave them alone when seen, but they are hungry and it was there. Plus Jacob thinks it would be a nice change.

When he gets back Julian sees the snake, "I thought we didn't eat snake?"

"We do when were hungry and we don't want to spend a lot of time hunting."

"Snake it is then." Julian takes the snake from Jacobs's hands and starts cutting it into small pieces and asks Jacob, "Do you know what it tastes like?"

"No I don't but its food." He puts a piece on the end of a stick and holds it over the fire. "Only one way to find out."

Julian cooks the piece and takes a bite, "it doesn't taste that bad."

They sit around the fire for a while and watch it go out, talking about the day prior. They also decide to get as close as they can to the Lords grounds and see how many men he has. They begin walking with caution.

"I tell you one thing," Julian says smiling, " the next time I see a snake, its food!"

"I have no problem with that."

They walk back to the path that leads to the Lords grounds, if they walk in the wood it looks as though they are hiding something, so they will walk the path and try to blend in the best they can.

When they get back to the trail and start walking toward the Lord's grounds, they see a lot more of his men. They are easy to spot, all carry a sword and wear black clothes with a metal cover over their chest. Some wear metal hats while others just cover their heads with black cloth. One thing is certain, everybody fears them, people won't even look at them.

Julian hears Jacobs's thoughts, *"I can beat any one of these men."*

"So can I but its not just one."

"OK, I can beat any five or ten of these men.

"I know you can but let's not that would bring attention to us."

Jacob looks at Julian and says out loud in a sarcastic voice," You really think so?" Julian just shakes his head at him. They pass another garden with guards in front of it. Jacob looks at Julian in disgust, "All this food and people are still hungry. I don't understand why one man would do this to others."

"He must be very cruel and hateful."

As they walk past the garden, they see a man being beat by three of the Lord's men. Once they pass Julian asks a man on the side of the trail,

"What did that man do to get beat?"

"Nothing at all. One of the Lords men doesn't like him. They beat him often."

Julian and Jacob both shake their heads.

The man looks at the two with a sad look on his face, "One day they will kill him, I told him he should leave this place, but he has no place to go."

As they walk they feel this blanket of eeriness consume them.

Julian trying to hide the disgust he is feeling "This place gets worse the further we travel."

"At least we have met some nice people."

Julian with a dismal tone in his voice says, "Yes, but they want to leave."

"To a village they say is a nice place to live." Jacob stops for a moment looking at two men fighting on the side of the trail, "I think we should walk back that way to see this village."

The larger of the two men fighting starts to kick the other man who is now on the ground, it looks as though he wants to kill him.

"I don't want to come back this way." Jacob says still looking at the man continue to kick the other who is now unconscious.

They keep walking until the homes become scarcer with very few people walking around. When they do see someone they are looking at the ground and won't make any eye contact. They all seem very scared, so scared they won't even look at a stranger. They continue walking and observe the horror.

"I haven't seen a home or any person in a while." Julian says with concern.

"Neither have I, but I have noticed the trail is well kept."

"I think we should walk in the woods the rest of the way. We must be getting close to his grounds."

"I think that would be a good idea."

They quickly walk off the path and into the woods making as little noise as possible. They also decide to stop talking out loud and use their gift to communicate. Communicating like this takes a lot more energy but it will be safer. They keep walking until Jacob holds up his hand.

What's wrong?"

Jacob can feel that there are no trees or bushes ahead in the distance, just open land.

"If you want to learn how to use the tree to see what's ahead this would be the best time to do so. Try to focus on the trees in the distance."

"OK, what do I do?"

"Feel the energy of the plants"

"I know to do that, how can you feel things moving through it?"

"Well you know how to use their energy to move them, that is easy. You need to feel the energy to the smallest point so if the smallest twig breaks off a branch you feel it."

Julian looks at Jacob then stares in the direction they are traveling. He gazes into the woods for about five minutes then turns back at Jacob,

"I'm not feeling anything, I can feel the energy close but when I focus off in the distance I can't feel anything its like the energy is gone."

"That because there is no energy to feel"

"What do you mean?"

"You can not feel what's not there."

"I have no idea what you mean?"

"Let me try to explain it, you can move bushes and vines at will, the more that are there the easier it is, its something you do and comes easy to you."

"OK, I'm still trying to understand."

"What if there were no bushes to move? Could you still move them?"

"Of course not. You can't move what's not there."

"That's what I'm saying, you can't feel what's not there."

"Are you saying there are no trees or bushes ahead?"

"That's exactly what I'm saying. We must be close to his grounds."

Both men walk in the direction they have been traveling, but they walk very cautiously making sure they are not seen by anyone. They are fairly sure no one is around but some of the paths are well beat in, there could be men on them without Jacob knowing.

They walk to the edge of the forest were there is a huge open field. In the middle far in the distance they can see a large stone home, bigger than any they have seen. It stood very high in the air and looked about three levels high with small windows on each side. There is a small wall on the top rim were men were sitting with bows and arrows at the ready. Around the perimeter of was another stone wall about ten feet high with another walkway on the top of it. On each corner of this wall there were small huts with windows. More men all with bows and arrows stood along the top of this wall. Julian surveys all this, looks around making sure no one is around before saying, "This man protects himself well."

"I was thinking the same thing. It looks like men stay on the wall surrounding his home at all times."

Jacob examines the rock huts at the corners of the wall, "Even in bad weather."

They decide to walk the outer edge of the woods for a while and observe the grounds and his men. Outside the wall, which surrounds his home in the open field, were hundreds of small huts for his men to sleep. It looks as though they practice fighting on the open ground, they can tell this by the lack of grass and bushes, its mostly dirt. As they walk a little further they see some of his men training with swords, others practicing with bows and arrows. They walk a little further and see others on horseback fighting that way.

Julian hears Jacobs's thoughts *"These men are very well trained. And there are many of them. I think we should study as much as we can while we are here."*

Julian looks at Jacob with an uneasy look, *"I don't want to spend the night anywhere near here!"*

Both men keep walking the edge of the woods near the open field that separates them from the men. They walk for a few miles and it's the same thing, the Lords men seen to have whatever they need. Some are cooking, some training with swords, others doing nothing at all.

They cluster together close to the Lords wall and get more scarce as they go out toward the woods with a big open space all the way around. In the large open field are towers made from stone in various spots, on the top of each tower sits a man just staring into the forest. As they walk around his grounds they have seen many well beat in paths leading away from the grounds.

"These must be the paths to the villages, they are well taken care of and often traveled." Julian says looking down one of the paths.

They both take cover in the thick bushes when they hear voices in the distance,

One of the voices says, "Get up scum, push the cart or die."

They then hear the scuffle of feet like someone was being kicked as they plead for their life.

"Please, don't kill me. I'm just hungry!"

Julian and Jacob stay hidden while the men pass, one skinny man pushing a large cart using two handles in the back with two large wheels made from wood on each side of the cart. This cart was filled with fruits and vegetables. In front of the cart walked two men with four more behind all dressed like the Lords men and carried swords.

The man pushing the cart falls to the ground, one of the lord's men behind pulls out his sword, "This man is useless! Can I kill him?"

"He's not useless, he can still push the cart." Another says as he kicks the man, "Get up or die!"

The man slowly gets up and starts pushing the cart.

"See he's not useless, unless you want to push the cart."

They keep walking with the man struggling and stumbling, but he keeps pushing the cart with the other men laughing and making jokes. Julian and Jacob decide to follow to see what will happen. They keep their distance but are able to keep an eye.

Its not long before they are at the open field were they are greeted by more of the Lords men. The man, who had said he wanted to kill him, then hits him in the back of his legs with his sword causing him to instantly fall. The man grabs his legs, which are now bleeding badly. One of the men they have just met at the paths opening asks,

"What did he do?"

"He didn't think we were looking and took a piece of fruit from the cart."

The man on the ground looks up at the men, still trying to stop his legs from bleeding says, "I was just hungry, if I knew it was the Lords food I would never have taken it.

The Lord's man who was talking to the man then throws him a piece of fruit, "Eat up."

The man on the ground starts to eat, while still trying to stop the bleeding.

The Lord's man who threw him the fruit then smiles at the man,

"It will be the last piece of fruit you ever eat!" he turns to the other men,

"Hang him!"

Two of the men grab the man by the hair and drag him away with him screaming and begging for his life.

Julian turns to Jacob with a disgusted look on his face, *"I've seen enough."*

"I agree, lets go home, but lets travel a different way. I want to see the village Richard was talking about, it sounds nice, and maybe we can make some friends."

"Sounds like a good idea."

They both start walking in the direction they think Pauline's village is. They walk through the woods for a while, the entire time they walk they talk about the men they have seen and how they train, some were very good with bows and arrows and others with swords. They also felt sad for all the people living in fear of this man and his men.

"I think we should keep an eye on this man." Jacob says in a serious tone.

"I think we should keep an eye on all of his men. I want to keep them far away from us."

"It's like they have fun killing and hurting other people."

"That man who was pushing the cart, that was horrible, he was just hungry. He might have a wife, children and all their lives are ruined. All for a piece of fruit, its just very sad."

"I feel the same way, but there was nothing we could have done, unless you wanted to fight all of his men. Then hundreds would have died."

"I know, between the two of us we can beat about thirty of them, that's including the two or three you could take, but we still would be outnumbered by hundreds more."

Jacob laughs at the joke. "Please, I can take as many of them as you can."

"OK, but we would still be in trouble. Now lets find some food, it's going to be dark soon."

They keep walking, the thick vines and bushes moving out of their way as they travel, with the trail closing in behind then making sure no one will follow. While they are walking a rabbit runs out in front of them, when Julian sees it he uses the bushes to catch and quickly kill it.

"Well that was easy. I would still like to be further away before we stop and make a fire for the night."

"We can gather wood as we walk, I would like to get it started before dark."

They walk for about another hour, dusk is setting in, it will be getting dark soon. The woods are starting to get very thick, plenty of vines and bushes to make a shelter.

"This looks like a good spot." Jacob says.

Both men drop the wood they are carrying and gather some rocks for a fire pit.

"I got the food you can get the fire going."

"You got the food! It's more like the food came to you." They both stack some wood in the fire pit and gather some small twigs and dry brush to put under the wood.

Jacob takes a small stone out of his overcoat. He starts scraping his small knife across the stone creating sparks. It's not long before the fire is going and the rabbit is cooking.

Off in the distance they see a flash of light, moments later they hear a slight rumble in the sky.

"Sounds like rain." Julian says looking up into the sky.

Then another flash followed by a louder rumble.

"Sounds more like a storm." Jacob says, "we should make a strong shelter for the night."

"I agree."

Both men look at the woods surrounding them, without getting up the bushes and vines start to move closer to them, the vines are interweaving with the bushes, and some of the bushes are moving on top of the vines. It all forms an oval shape around the men and the fire, the vines and bushes inside the small hut ravel together forming two beds so the men can sleep up off the ground. The fire is going between the two men making it very warm, they eat the rabbit and watch the smoke from the fire escape through small holes above. The storm brings extremely heavy rain and wind that keeps both men awake for a while. They finally fall to sleep untouched by the weather, the fire keeps the shelter warm all night. Julian keeps waking up through out the night, more from Jacobs snoring then the storm.

The next morning it's still raining a little, they finish eating what's left of the rabbit and start walking using the vines and bushes to cover them as they walk. It was as if they were walking through a tunnel.

Julian looks back at the shelter, "We can't leave it like that, if one of those men find it they will look for who built it, maybe kill innocent people."

"I agree."

They watch as the shelter's vines and bushes untangle without any of the branches or small twigs breaking off. Within minutes it looks as though no one was there except for the small fire pit, which would be normal for travel of these people.

The two walk off into the woods with the bushes and vines staying over their heads, stopping the rain from hitting them, as they walk the vines and bushes go back to the way they were before they passed. This continues until the rain stops.

Back at Rosemary's village Jonathan, Andrew and Rosemary are sitting in Williams home eating as they seek refuge from the rain all laughing and joking.

Jonathan smiles at his wife, "Julian and Jacob are probably getting drenched as we sit nice and warm."

Rosemary says with a smirk, just loud enough for the others to hear, "Maybe it will wash away some of their childish behavior, the two have a lot of growing up to do."

All laugh at the remark then continue to talk.

Julian and Jacob are now in very thick woods, so thick other people would have a hard time passing, they would have to cut their way through just to move forward. These men walk through with ease as a path forms in front of them and fills in behind them.

"We have been walking for hours, lets stop to rest." Julian says breathing a little heavy.

"I don't think we have to worry about any of his men out this way." Jacob says.

"I don't think we have to worry about anything in these woods, they are to thick."

The men rest for a short while, before starting to walk again. They walk for the rest of the day without taking much, they are drained of energy, not only from walking but also from what they have seen. They slowly watch the sun get lower in the sky.

"We should stop and look for some food." Julian says looking back at Jacob, who looks very tired, "Why are you so tired?" He asks.

Jacob sits leaning against a tree, "I'm trying to feel ahead for anybody walking around, I've been doing this for a while in all directions. This takes a lot of my strength and energy. This looks like a good spot to spend the night." He stretches his legs out even further and puts his hands on his stomach. "I'm hungry, go gather some food while I get the fire going."

"Why don't you get the food while I start a fire."

"OK, I hope you like root because that's all I'm looking for."

"I'll get the food, just have a good fire going when I return."

Julian disappears into the woods seeking some food. He gathers berries along the way. Hunting in woods this thick is very easy for these men, they just use the bushes to capture small animals. Within ten minutes Julian spots a few large pheasants perched on a tree full with vines. Before the birds can fly away the vines wrap around then, they has no chance. He walks back to Jacob with the food who is pleased to see it is something rather than small rodent like animals. Both men are very tired and fall to sleep shortly after eating.

The two men sleep late into the morning, much later than they usually sleep. When they awake they finish what's left of the pheasants and start walking. They are fairly sure they are traveling in the right direction, they use the sun as a guide.

They walk for about two hours when Jacob stops, "People"

"What?"

"There are people ahead, quite a few of them. I think it's a village."

"Good I was starting to think we were traveling in the wrong direction, how much further?"

"A couple of hours."

"We should rest before we get there, we have no idea if these are the people we want to find and even if they are they may try to protect themselves before we can tell them we mean no harm. All the people in this area are very scared with good reason."

"I agree, if we have to fight I would like to do so with out hurting anybody unless left no choice. We should walk for about an hour then rest."

They start walking again, as they are walking they start to notice some small paths.

"It looks like people travel this way." Julian says.

"Probably to hunt and gather berries."

"I think we should rest here," Julian says as he sits down leaning against a tree, they both eat some berries they had gathered along the way. Both men were more tired then they had thought, they fall to sleep as they're sitting resting. They are woken when a deer scurries past them followed by voices in the distance.

"It went that way."

Then another voice, "Are you sure?"

"Yes, don't let it get away."

Julian and Jacob quickly jump to their feet and hide in the thick bushes.

Julian hears Jacobs thoughts, *"Why did you fall to sleep?"*

"Me! What about you?"

Two men slowly walk into sight, both with bows and arrows at the ready looking back and fourth.

One of the men says, "It's around here somewhere, keep your eyes open."

Julian trying not to be seen, knowing these men are looking into the wood for deer which is long gone by now will probably see them. He decides to make some of the bushes ahead of the men move, both men let their arrows lose.

"Did you hit it?"

"I don't think so." The two run in the direction they think the deer went.

This gives Julian and Jacob a chance to think.

"We should talk to these men when they come back this way." Julian says.

"Why?"

"If we talk to these men and they are not friendly, we fight only two, we can put then down with little harm. If we go to the village first it may not be so easy."

"Good thinking."

Both men stand in the trail and wait. About ten minutes go by before they hear the men walking back toward them.

One says, "I told you it ran the other way."

"You should have gone that way then!" the other says. Then adds, "It doesn't really matter which way it ran, once a deer starts to run its gone within seconds."

As they turn the corner they see Julian and Jacob standing in the trail, both raise their bows and arrows and point them at the two, Julian and Jacob are ready to move quickly.

"Who are you? What do you want?" The larger of the two says.

Julian steps forward, both men now point their arrows at him.

"Don't move any closer! We don't want to harm you, but we will if we must."

Julian steps back and puts his hands in the air, "We are friendly, we are looking for a village and a women named Pauline."

"What do you want with this women?"

"We are harmless woodsmen, we have traveled a long way and in our travels we met her sister and her sisters family. They told us that Pauline's village was a nice place with friendly people."

One of the men lowers his arrow, "What's her sisters name?"

"Her name is Melanie and her husbands name is Richard, their little boys name is Harold." There is a pause, and then Jacob says,

"They are very nice people, they fed us with what little food they had, I'm happy to call them friends."

The other of the two lowers his arrow, the older of the two smiles and says,

"If your friends with them your welcome in our village. My name is Phillip."

He is a large framed heavyset man with short dark hair and dark eyes to match, he presented himself in a strong manor standing strait with a look of confidence in his eyes. "This is my friend Samuel."

Samuel is shorter than Phillip and very thin with light brown hair about shoulder length with light brown eyes. Phillip looked less confident not looking into ether mans eyes seeming to be very uneasy.

"We were trying to catch some food but Samuel took us the wrong way. Your names are?"

"My name is Julian and this is my friend Jacob. We are very well at hunting, and there are four of us, we can probably catch quite a few animals in a short time."

"Sounds good to me." Phillip says,

"Lets go."

Julian hears Jacobs's thoughts, *"I will go into the woods and make some animals run this way."*

"We will stand here and Jacob will go deep into the woods and make some noise, the animals will run this way, just try to stay still and at the ready."

Jacob walks down the path for a short while then walks into the thick forest.

The other three men stand still waiting. After about fifteen minutes Samuel whispers to Phillip, "This is a waist of time."

Julian looks at him, puts his finger over his mouth telling him to be quiet, then pulls his small ax from inside of his overcoat and throws it into the woods. The two other men haven't seen anything. Julian quietly walks into the woods and picks up the rabbit he has killed. He can't help smirking a bit but puts his hand to his mouth again signaling for silence. The two other men are now looking into the woods for anything, one of the men sees a deer running and lets his arrow lose hitting it. The other hits a rabbit. Within half an hour they have three rabbits, two squirrels and a deer that still needs to be found.

Jacob emerges from the thick woods, "How did you do?"

"Better than we've ever done before." Samuel says, and then asks, "What did you do?"

"I simply walked a good distance around the area as quiet as I could be, then walked in a straight line back toward you making a lot of noise, the animals, scared from the noise run away, right into you waiting for them."

"Well it works. "Samuel says as he looks at the animals they have killed.

"We have plenty now, follow us to our village. You will be welcome there and Pauline would love to hear how her sister is doing.

Before heading to the village they track the deer that ran off with a arrow in it, the arrow hit it in the center of the chest so it was only able to run a short distance before dying. The four men start walking in the direction of the village taking turns dragging the deer.

Chapter Eight

As they walk toward the village the woods look more traveled and the paths are well kept. They notice several fruit trees along the walk, as they reach the village there is a large garden with all kinds of vegetables. On one side of the garden is a rock wall about three feet high. Inside this wall are many cows, pigs, goats, and chickens as well as a hut for the chickens to lay their eggs. On the other side of the garden Jacob notices two carts and a well-kept path leading away from the village as far as the eye can see. He points it out to Julian then asks Phillip,

"Why does it lead out as if you travel away from the village with vegetables?"

"It keeps the Lords men from coming here and taking them. If his men come here they will take a lot more then we give. So we bring then half of what we grow."

"That's not fair!" Jacob says with anger in his voice.

"Fair no, but if his men come here, they may kill some of us and destroy it all." They walk by the garden and into the village. The village has another rock wall built around it.

Samuel notices Jacob looking at the wall, "It keeps the small children from wandering into the thick forest."

"Good idea, children will wonder."

They walk into the village there are homes built from rock and dirt scattered all around, but very neat and organized. There are animal skins hanging from several trees drying. Some of the homes have fire pits with food cooking in the front of them making the air smell of burning wood and various meats cooking. It looks as though all of the homes have some sort of fire pit on the inside. All the homes are built with only one large room.

Another man from the village walks up to them, "Who are these men Philip?"

"They are travelers, don't worry they are friendly."

"Well if they are friendly they are welcome here." Two small children run by, it looks like they are playing tag.

Julian looking around says to Jacob, "This village reminds me of Williams village."

"There is another village like ours?" Samuel surprised at the remark.

"Yes, but it is a long travel from here."

"That's good to hear. I was starting to think we were the only good people left."

They walk through the middle of the village, Philip and Samuel saying hello to everybody they pass, they finally stop at one of the homes.

"**Come out here Pauline.**" Philip yells into the opening.

"I'm right in the middle of getting soup ready, is it important?" Just then a little girl runs out and gives Samuel a big hug.

"This is young Sarah." She is a small girl about Andrews's age with dark brown hair hanging about three inches past her shoulders with big brown eyes. Her eyes so big and brown they give a sparkling shy innocence to her smile. Samuel rubs the top of her head messing up her hair.

"She's a handful!"

Philip then tells them that Sarah is Pauline and Aaron's little girl, and that Samuel is Aaron's little brother.

"Well, put some extra soup on, Philip yells back into the home, we have guest."

"How many?" she calls back.

"Two, they have seen your sister."

Within seconds Pauline walks out with a big smile on her face. Like young Sarah she is a fairly short thin women with the same hair and eyes of her daughter also with a big bright smile.

"You've seen Melanie? How is she?"

Julian also with a smile, "She's doing well, Richard and young Harold are fine also."

This makes the smile on her face even brighter, she then asks, "Who are you and how do you know them?"

"We are just woodsmen traveling through the area. We met them the same way we are meeting you."

"She lives days away, why did you come this way?"

"We traveled the path in their village and met them, they fed us even though they had little and told us they wanted to come here to live. We walked a little further and came to, as you call him, The Lord of the lands grounds. We didn't want to travel any further so we decided to travel home and thought it would be a good idea to travel this way and tell you we had seen her and she's doing fine."

"Is that the only reason you come this way?" Pauline asks with somewhat of a baffled look.

Jacob gives her a serious look, "To tell you the truth we thought it would be nice to meet some friendly people, most we have met are dreadful to each other. Back home we all treat each other nicely."

She now has a bright warm smile, "Well we are all nice here, we all try to help each other. We are all like family."

"These two men showed us how to hunt better," Philip says as he points to the animals they have killed. "It took us less than an hour to kill these."

Samuel then asks Pauline, "Where is my brother?"

"He went to catch some fish and gather some wood, we are almost out."

Julian looks at Jacob then says, "If your cooking soup for us we will gather some wood."

Both men get up and walk into the woods, the other two follow. It's not long before the men come back with arms full of wood, Julian tells them that they will help gather more if needed.

Pauline looks at the wood, "That's plenty, and the soup is almost ready. I wonder what's taken Aaron so long? He should be back by now!"

Jacob hears Julian's thoughts, *"Can you feel were he is?"*

"I will try." Jacob becomes very quiet as he looks into the woods.

Several minutes pass with Jacob just staring into the woods.

Samuel notices this "Is their something wrong?"

Jacob looks away from the woods and looks at Samuel, "I think we should take a walk and see if we can find him."

"Do you want me to come?" Julian asks.

"No, Samuel and I will be fine."

Julian hears Jacobs thoughts, *"There is a man walking very slowly dragging one leg, I think he's hurt but he's less than one mile away. Two men will be fine."*

The two men start walking toward the thick forest, its still light but will be getting dark soon. The two walk for about ten minutes when Samuel turns down a different path.

Jacob Stands at the fork in the paths for a moment, then calls out to Samuel, "I don't think this is the way we should go."

"My brother always catches fish this way."

Samuel continues walking down the path. Jacob runs down the path and catches up with Samuel he stops him by putting his hand on his on the back of his shoulder,

"I wish you would follow me the other way, I have a strong feeling he's that way."

"I told you already, he always catches fish this way."

Jacob turns and starts walking the other way, "I'm going this way, I'm never wrong about my feelings and I have a strong feeling he needs help, so when you get to where he catches fish and he's not there hurry back this way, OK."

"Your never wrong?"

"Never! I have a very good sense for things in the woods and I truly think he's this way."

Samuel turns and starts walking the way Jacob wants to go. As they walk Samuel keeps calling out his brothers name. They walk for about ten minutes when they hear Aaron.

"Samuel is that you?"

Samuel hears this and starts to run with Jacob right behind him.

When the two men turn a corner around a big oak tree, there is Aaron sitting on a rock with his leg stretched out in front of him. Aaron is a little taller than his brother with short light brown hair and eyes that match, he looks like a strong man with broad shoulders and solid look to his face. Although he is Samuel's brother he seems more mature with a serious look in his eyes that showed leadership.

"What's wrong Aaron?" Samuel asks.

Aaron turns his leg and shows them the side of his foot. It is bruised and badly swollen, the side of his leg has a nasty wound on it and it looks as though his knee is swollen as well.

"What did you do?" Samuel looking at his brother's leg, clenching his teeth tightly together.

"I didn't catch any fish today so I was walking through the woods gathering some berries, I wanted to come back with something. As I was walking I saw a rabbit out of the corner of my eye, I spun to throw my ax at it but my foot was between two rocks, and this is what happened. I fell landed on my knee, twisted my ankle, and apparently the rock I landed on was extremely sharp, I've been trying to stop the bleeding with little success. I don't think I'll be walking for a while."

"Do you mind if I take a look at it?"

"Who are you?"

"He's a friend." Samuel says.

"My name is Jacob." Jacob examines the wounds very carefully.

"Are you sure he's a friend? It seems like he's trying to hurt me."

"I'm just checking the bones making sure none are broken, they feel fine, but we should keep him off the leg anyway."

"Lets get moving, we can both help him back to the village."

"Not just yet we need to stop the bleeding." Jacob then tells the men he will be right back. He is gone for about ten minutes, when he gets back he is carrying some thick vines and a bunch of assorted leaves. He puts the leaves on a flat rock and pours a little water on them then starts crushing them with another small rock. He pours a little more water and continues crushing them until they are a mud like pasty mix. He then takes his small knife and carefully cuts the thick vines into thin slices. He rubs the pasty mix into the wound and wraps it with the vines. Jacob looks at Samuel this will stop the bleeding, relieve some of the pain and keep out infection. Samuel and Jacob both help Aaron to his feet. Aaron puts his arms around their backs while Jacob holds his stick in the other hand for support. They start walking back to the village, its not very far but the walk is slow going.

Aaron thanks Jacob for his help then asks, "How did you meet my brother?"

"My friend Julian and I were traveling through the villages miles away and we met Melanie and her family."

Aaron stops walking and looks at Jacob, "You've seen Melanie? How is she doing?"

"She is fine, her son and husband are well also."

"That's good to hear, I wish they would come live over this way."

"I think they will soon." They start walking again.

"As I was saying, we met Melanie and her family, they warned us not to travel in the direction we were traveling, we did not listen."

"Did you see any of the Lords men?"

"We walked right up to his grounds."

Aaron looks at him with a stunned look on his face, "Your lucky to be alive!"

"We were not seen, but we did see how horrible they are."

"We don't even like to talk about it here. Sadly we just bring him half of our food, it keeps them from coming here."

"If that is what it takes to keep them away it's a good idea," Jacob says with a sigh, "But its still not right, anyway, Melanie said her sister lived in a nice village, and we were going to travel back kind of this way so we decided to travel back this way hoping to find some people we can call friends."

They come to the edge of the village. Samuel calls to Pauline who comes running. Julian and two other men come to help. They get him to his home and sit him on a rock near the fire.

"What happened?" Pauline asks overwhelmed with the excitement.

"I just fell that's all."

She looks at the leg, "Does it hurt?"

"I will be fine."

One of the other men named Roy takes a look at the leg, "It seems to be wrapped well."

Roy is a small man with short light hair and blue eyes, his eyesight is poor making him lean forward and squint as he talks to you.

Aaron tells him that Jacob stopped the bleeding with some leaves mixed with water,

"It works well. Will you show us what you have done?"

Aaron turns back toward Roy, "It stops the bleeding and some of the pain."

"Its very easy, three kinds of leafs and something to wrap it with, I will show you tomorrow when we re-wrap it."

"Put new wrapping on it? I should leave it covered until it heals!"

"Leave it until it heals! That could kill you! You need to clean it every day to keep out infection."

Aaron and Roy both look at each other.

Roy looking at Jacob with a stern look says, "Around here we leave it wrapped to keep out the dirt, that's how it's always been."

"Where we come from we clean and put a new wrap on a wound every day." Jacob looks at Aaron's leg before saying, "Very few wounds get worse, and they are the really bad ones."

"Only a few?" Roy asks.

"Hardly any." Julian joins the conversation with confidence in his voice

Roy turns toward Aaron, "Lets try it there way this time."

"We don't even know these men."

"What harm can it do? It's your leg anyway."

"OK, but if I lose my leg, I'm taken yours."

Pauline then joins the discussion, "I'll take both of your legs if Aaron doesn't start eating. He needs his strength." She puts her hand on Jacobs shoulder. "Thank you for your help carrying him back."

"It was no trouble, you seem like nice people and I'm happy I could be some help."

Young Sarah comes running over and goes to jump on her father. Julian catches her before she lands on his legs.

"Be careful." Aaron says as he pulls his leg back.

"What's wrong father?"

"I've hurt my leg but don't worry I will be fine."

"Will you still teach me how to fish tomorrow?"

"I don't think so." He sees the disappointment in her eyes, "We will go as soon as I get better, OK."

"OK, when your better we will go, right?"

"I'm looking forward to it."

Julian looks at Aaron and can tell he is feeling badly and wants to change the conversation, "How old are you?"

"I'm ten, I will be eleven soon."

Julian looks at Aaron, gives him a wink, "Your smart for your age, do you have any friends to play with?"

"Yes." She says in a quite shy voice.

"My brother Jonathan has a son your age, you two would get along great. The next time we come to visit we will bring him."

Julian hears Jacob's thoughts, *"Next time we visit?"*

Julian replies, *"These people are nice."*

"I agree, but come back?"

"I want friends our age, we've met five people here our age so far. And it's not far from Williams's village, about seven days travel if we move quickly, and I think Sarah and Andrew will get along well.

"OK, but before we start planning to come back we should talk to your brother, especially if you want to bring Andrew."

None of the other people sitting around realize they just had this conversation, they thought they were just quiet for the moment.

"I noticed a lot of animals when we walked into the village." Julian says looking at the others.

Aaron answers, "We try to keep a lot, we eat the pigs, but not many we try to keep the same amount, we use the old ones for meat and keep the young ones alive to bread. The cows are used for milk but it's the same way with them. When they get old they become food, it's the same with all the animals, we try to keep an even balance. Sometimes in the cold days of winter we have trouble hunting so we eat more than we like." Aaron gives Julian a somber stare, he knows the cold days are coming and his leg is hurt which will make it hard to hunt.

Julian puts his hand on Aaron's back, "My friend and I are very good hunters, even in the coldest days of winter. We will teach you and Samuel everything we know." He then turns to Pauline, "You wont have to worry about food."

Aaron looks at his wife she then tells the two men that they are welcome to stay inside their home for the night.

Julian smiles at the generous offer, "It's a nice night and there is a good fire going, I think we will sleep outside tonight. Besides if we sleep in your home his snoring will keep you awake all night."

They all laugh, even Jacob.

"OK, but if you get cold or it gets damp outside your welcome."

Pauline and Sarah go inside their home for the night, the other men sit a little longer before they walk to their homes, leaving Aaron, Julian and Jacob sitting by the fire talking well into the night. Aaron explains to them that Samuel has no wife and that's why Pauline takes care of him when it comes to cooking. They all hunt and fish making sure everybody in the village has food, all the people also help in the garden making sure there are plenty of vegetables for all.

Aaron stares at the two men for a moment and with much hesitation in his voice asks, "It's starting to get late, Can one of you help me inside?" Aaron is a proud man, asking for help is a very hard request for him. Julian and Jacob both stand up to help him into his home.

Julian can tell that he does not like asking for help, "Tomorrow I will find you a walking stick, you will be able to get around without asking for help."

"That would be nice."

They help him into his bed and tell Pauline if she needs any help, feel free to ask and let Aaron know he needs to stay off his leg.

The two men walk back outside and put some more wood on the fire and find a good spot to lie down.

"I like these people." Julian says.

"Yes, they are nice."

Then Julian hears Jacobs's thoughts so no one can hear, *"They just need to bathe, or at least wash."*

It's a nice cool night, winter will be coming soon, both men fall to sleep looking at the stares. The next morning the two men wake well rested, they both agree that it was a good nights sleep. The fire is still smoldering so Jacob puts a small log on to start the flames, it is a little chilly.

Pauline walks out of her home carrying two bowls of warm soup, she hands them to the two men, "I want to thank you once again for all your help."

"That's what friends do." Julian says as he takes a bowl of soup.

She smiles back at the two men and walks back inside of her home. About ten minutes later Aaron walks out with Pauline helping, he is able to walk a little but still needs help. Julian quickly gets up to help.

Aaron reluctantly asks, "Can I use your walking stick for a moment?"

Julian looks at Aaron then Jacob and turns back toward Aaron; there is an uncomfortable pause. Their walking stick is like a part of them, it never leaves their side and none of their people would ever ask that question. Julian hesitates for a long moment before handing him his stick letting him walk to the fire with it.

Julian hears Jacob's thoughts, *"You had to let him use it, if you said no they would think we were strange."*

Jacob then hears Julian's thoughts, *"We are strange if you think about it,* "he raises his eyebrows, *"it is only a stick."*

Aaron sits down next to the fire and hands him his stick back; he could tell that Julian did not want to let him use it,

"I will get my own stick as soon as I can."

Samuel then walks over from his home,

"Anything to eat?" he asks

"Warm soup" Pauline says.

"Soup sounds good, I'll have a bowl."

Aaron says in a stern voice, "You know were it is, get it yourself."

Samuel looks at Aaron, "I thought you would get it for me. O, that's right; you cant!" he laughs.

Aaron does not think it's very funny.

Jacob looks at Samuel, "Eat up, when your done I want to take you and Pauline to gather the leaves we need to re-wrap the wound."

Pauline looks at Jacob, "You want to take me along?"

Jacob then gives Aaron a smile and a wink, "I have to take you along, there are three leaves and one vine." He then turns and looks at Samuel,

"You will never remember all that!" he gives him a friendly nudge with his elbow.

Jacob turns to Aaron, "You will look at them before I crush them into the mix and then we will wrap the wound fresh."

Julian helps him take off the wrap so they can clean it and let some air into the injury for a while. Jacob leads the others into the woods. He tells Samuel to look for a good solid stick for his brother. He also tells him that his brother will need help for a couple of weeks and he should stay with them. He stops and looks at Samuel,

"Your brother likes to be self reliant, he won't ask for help, so you should just be there to give it to him."

Jacob can tell that Samuel is not very smart and might have to be told this. Samuel tells him that he will give him all the help he can and walks ahead.

Pauline thanks Jacob for his foresight and they keep walking. It doesn't take long before they find the leaves they are looking for. Samuel comes back with a stick that looks a lot like Jacobs.

Jacob looks at it, "Very nice but not what I'm looking for."

As Samuel goes to toss it aside, Jacob stops him,

"He will need that later, right now I'm looking for something with a handle."

They walk for a little longer when Jacob stops and points to the top of a tall tree, "That's what I'm looking for."

Jacob stands at the bottom of the tree and looks up for a moment. He then takes off his overcoat and climbs the tree so quickly Pauline and Samuel cannot believe their eyes. He cuts the branch with his small ax and climbs down as quickly as he went up.

At the bottom he picks up the stick, "This is what I was looking for, it has a handle about waist level and when I'm done it will have a nice soft top edge to support his wait."

They start walking back to the village all talking about different vines and trees. Jacob seems to know a lot more than the other two.

He points to the top of a tree and asks Samuel, "Do you know what that is?"

Samuel looks at it, "It's a bunch of leaves, that's what it is."

"It's a squirrels nest." Jacob shakes his head back and fourth,

"The most important thing about hunting in winter is knowing you're prey." They walk a little further and a rabbit crosses their path, Samuel goes to throw his ax at it.

Jacob stops him. "Why kill it? We have plenty of food for days."

Samuel puts his ax back in his overcoat,

"You sure know a lot about the land Jacob."

"My people and I have lived deep in the forest away from any villages for many years, we survive off the land and try to waist none."

Pauline amazed with Jacobs knowledge, "Were do you live?"

Jacob looks at her, "We live very far and deep into the thick forest."

Wanting to change the subject he grabs Samuel by the shoulder and points to a rabbit going into its hole,

"See that? In the coldest days of winter that would be a nice catch."

Samuel looks at him with a puzzled look, "We can almost never catch rabbit in the winter, it's too cold to wait for them to come out and they hide very well and are too fast."

"You have to be smarter then them, not faster."

"What do you mean smarter?"

"You make a trap and just check on it periodically." Jacob has not used a rabbit trap since he was a little boy, but he remembers how to make them.

"I will show you and your brother how to make one when we get back to the village."

They walk for a while longer, its not long before they reach the stonewall that surrounds the village. Some of the homes have fires burning in front of them. Pauline walks a little faster than the two, she is anxious to check on Aaron's leg. The two others catch up with her at the home, she is sitting next to her husband both looking at the wound. The cut is deep with a lot of swelling and dark black bruising all around the ankle and half way up the leg to the knee, which is also swollen and bruised.

Samuel with a surprised expression of his face, "That's bad brother!"

Julian looking at the leg, "It looks worse than it is. I think the bones are fine, but the gash is deep so it must be kept clean. It must be cleaned and re-wrapped every day until the cut is healed."

Julian then looks at Aaron smiling as he takes out his ax and puts it on the rock next to him, "Or we can just take off the leg now!"

Aaron looks at the big smile on Julian's face, then at the axe once again back at Julian.

He turns to his wife, "Make sure to watch closely as they mix the leaves and wrap it,"

Jacob has started to carve out the stick he has found to help Aaron get around, it doesn't take very long to carve out a notch at the top of the stick.

He looks at Pauline "Pauline, do you have any extra animal skins I can use for this?"

She gets up and walks into her home, minutes later she walks out with a large deerskin, "Will this do?"

"That will be fine, do you mind if I cut it?"

"Do what you want, we can get another skin if we need to."

Jacob stats cutting the skin into different sized strips, he leaves quiet a few in big pieces. He then tightly ties another piece of wood he has carved into the notch at the top of the stick. He wraps some of the big pieces around the small stick in the notch, then ties some more small strips around that, he keeps doing this until all the skin is used up. When he has finished he stands up, puts the part with the skins under his arm and grabs the handle part which is waist level and walks around the fire, checking out his work.

He stops in front of Aaron, "This will help you stay off that leg."

The entire time Jacob was making the stick Julian was showing Pauline and Samuel how to mix the leaves and wrap the wound.

Aaron takes the stick, slowly gets up and walks a little with it, "This will work great. Thank you."

Jacob tells Aaron that it is only to get around if he needs to, but the more he stays off the leg the better it will heal. Aaron agrees then tells Samuel that he will have to do all his work until the leg heals.

"Not a problem." Samuel replies.

Young Sarah then runs up and stands in front of Julian. There is a long pause.

Julian finally asks, "Do you want to say something child."

She gives a bashful smile and looks at the ground, "When is Andrew coming to visit us?"

"I have to make sure its ok with his father first, but even if it is it will be a long time before we come back."

"Run along and play." Aaron tells his daughter. She runs off toward the middle of the village were the children usually play. The rest of the day Samuel takes them around to see the rest of the village, most of the people are nice. When they get back to Aaron's home Julian and Jacob tell them all they know about hunting in the winter, except the fact that they really don't have to hunt, they just tangle their pray with vines and bushes. Pauline has cooked a large evening feast, she knows they will be leaving first thing in the morning and its already starting to get dark. After they eat Jacob shows them how to make the rabbit trap he was talking about with Samuel. He tells him its good in the winter because it doesn't kill the rabbit so it won't spoil and they can eat it when they want. Everybody goes back to their homes except Aaron and Pauline they stay up a little longer.

Aaron looks at the two men, "I want to thank you again for your help."

Julian smiles, "It wasn't help, it was the start of a new friendship."

Pauline looks at the two, "I hope to see you again."

"You can count on it" Jacob says.

"The sooner the better." Aaron says then slowly gets up using the stick Jacob has made him, "It works great."

He walks toward his home, stops and turns to the two men sitting by the fire, "Will you be here when we wake?"

Julian answers, "It depends on how early you get up."

Aaron slowly walks to his home and Julian and Jacob go to sleep shortly after.

Chapter Nine

The next morning when the two men wake Pauline and Aaron are already up to see them off, Pauline gives them some bread and dried meat to take with them. Julian thanks her and asks if she remembers how to wrap the wound. She lets them know that it will be easy for her to do. She also tells them that she will make him stay off the leg until its better. Young Sarah comes outside and gives the two a big hug, they all say goodbye and the two men walk into the woods.

"How far do you think it is to Williams village?" Julian asks.

"I'm not sure, I was thinking about five to seven days walk if we walk fast."

"My brother must be worried about us by now, we've been gone along time."

"I was thinking the same thing, I know it's too far but we should keep trying to contact him. As soon as we are close enough we should let him know what we have found."

Jacob turns to Julian with a grave look, "I don't like this Lord man and I think Jonathan will be worried. He likes the suffering of others, these people have little hope."

"I feel the same way.

They walk for about an hour, Julian stops and looks back, "I think we are far enough, can you tell if anybody has followed?"

Jacob takes a long stare in the direction they have just trekked, "No one has followed."

"Good I'm tired of walking through these bushes."

The two men start walking again, this time the bushes and vines pull apart opening a path for them. They form a wall on each side of the men and as they pass the path goes back to the way it was, closing behind them. The woods are very thick so they only open a path about ten feet in front of them as they walk.

They walk for about two days only stopping to sleep, eat and rest. On the third day they walk through the remains of another small village, only about ten homes all destroyed by weather. Not much to see except the bones of several people who have been killed by arrows.

"How old do you think this place is?" Julian asks looking around.

"I'm not sure, it looks very old. It looks as though the homes were burned before the weather destroyed them."

Julian looks at Jacob not a word said just a long sad look. He then turns and walks toward one of the homes that was burned, when he looks inside he feels like crying. He sees the bones of several people all in the far corner.

He turns and looks at Jacob with anger in his eyes, "Who would do such a thing?"

Jacob sadly looks at him, he has a feeling what Julian has seen inside the burned home. "Do you have to ask that question? You know the answer."

Julian now has a pale color to his face, "Lets keep walking before I become sick."

The two start walking again, they walk well into the dark, they want to be far away from the ruins before stopping for the night. The Forest is extremely overgrown making it easy to catch several small animals for food. When the sun starts to grow low and dusk sets in they decide to stop and build a fire, it doesn't take long to get the small animals cooking.

Jacob puts his hand on Julian's back, "You haven't said a word all day, what's wrong?"

Julian with tears in his eyes and the look of anger on his face, "I have been brought up to believe that every living thing has a purpose, even the animals we kill for food keeps life going. We believe their energy stays alive in the surroundings so it lives on, our people believe that we don't die, our life's energy just starts over, it's a new beginning."

He looks at Jacob tears still in his eyes, "This man deserves to die! And his energy die with him! He should exist no longer."

He looks into the fire for a long moment then back at Jacob, "There were the bones of a family in that home I looked in, even a small child."

He now has tears of anger streaming down his face; **"I want this man to die and his energy die with him!** He deserves no new beginning." Julian wipes the tears with his arm and looks back at Jacob. "I have never felt this way about anybody or anything and I don't like feeling this way."

"You are the best friend a man could ask for, and when I tell you I feel the same way I mean it, this man should die and if we're lucky when he dies his energy dies with him."

As the rest of the evening passes the two talk for a while, trying to remember some fun child memories keeping their minds off the horror they have seen. They both go to sleep feeling a little better knowing they are on their way home.

When they wake the next morning they finish what's left of the food and start walking again.

"Have you had any luck contacting your brother?"

"Not yet but I have been trying."

They walk for a while longer. Jacob looking around, "Have you noticed that this part of the forest is very damp?"

They stop for a rest, Julian sits on a rock, "The ground is very mushy and there are a lot more bugs."

They sit for about ten minutes looking around while they rest. Jacob concentrates deep into the woods ahead of them,

"It's going to get a lot worse, the ground is covered with water up ahead."

"Should we find another way around?"

"No, the water is not deep, it just covers the ground. There are still many trees. We can walk on the roots."

They start walking again, when they reach the water, they don't stop, they keep walking, and as they do the roots from the trees emerge from under the water to form a strait path. As they walk across, the roots submerge back into the water. This goes on for most of the day, some spots are very deep, yet the roots keep forming a path for them. They walk across as though the water didn't exist. While they are walking Julian stops and sits down for no reason. Jacob turns back and sees his eyes closed and a smile on his face, he knows that he can hear his brother's thoughts, Jacob sits down also.

"Are you both Ok?" Jonathan asks.

"We are both fine," he replies.

"What did you find out?"

"I will tell you everything when we get back, talking like this takes too much energy and I have little left, but we are both OK."

"I will make sure Rosemary has a big meal and a clean bed to sleep in waiting for you when you get back."

"That would be nice." Julian replies before opening his eyes to see Jacob looking at him. "It looks like we are going the right way."

"Did you contact your brother?"

"Yes I did."

"Did you tell him everything?"

Julian gives him a look as though he was crazy for asking, "If I told him everything I would be sleeping before I finished!"

Both men start walking again, there is little dry wood to be found so they gather what they can find before stopping for the night. They find a spot of ground above the water just big enough to make a small shelter, they have very little dry wood so making a small shelter will help the wood last for heat most of the night.

The two men stand in the middle of this small patch of land as the vines from the nearby trees as will as the roots from the surrounding water slowly creep closer to them.

They start to tangle with each other, vines over roots, roots over vines. The more they tangle the tighter they become until it's a small igloo shaped hut with a small door to crawl through and another small hole at the top for smoke to escape.

When they are done they build a small rock fire pit in the middle of the hut but don't light it. They walk around gathering what little dry wood they can find, breaking the dried branches off the surrounding trees. Between the two men they gather a small pile of wood, enough to burn through the night.

Once the shelter is built and the wood is gathered Jacob looks at Julian, "What would you like to eat? I'm thinking fish!"

Jacob turns to the water, and raises both of his arms over his head. As he does this, all the roots and vines under the water rise to the surface bringing with them many fish and some black snake like things they have never seen, they decide not to eat them.

Julian carefully walks across some of the slick roots gathering some fish that are flopping around looking for water. As he starts to walk back toward Jacob, he stops and looks at him, "Why did you raise your hands over your head? I know our hands have nothing to do with moving the roots!"

Jacob smiles at him and puts his hands down. The roots and vines stay were they are, "I know, I just thought it would look good."

Julian shakes his head back and fourth. It was only dusk but making a path over the water takes a lot more of their energy then just moving vines and bushes out of the way, so both men are very tired.

They go back to the shelter they have made, start the fire, clean and cook the fish. They go to sleep shortly after eating.

When the wake the next morning the sun is already above the trees, they have slept a lot longer then they wanted to, yet they needed it.

"How much further do you think?" Julian asks.

"How much further until what? Were out of this water filled part of the forest, or back at Williams village?"

"Both I'm tired of this water, and I want a warm clean bed to sleep in!"

Jacob stares into the woods for a moment, looks back at Julian, "A couple of hours until were out of this wet land and we should be back at Williams village by dusk tomorrow."

There walk is interrupted by a loud growling screeching sound which make both men stop and put their walking sticks at the ready to fight! They stand silent and motionless until they hear another screeching sound on the other side of them further away. Both men are in an anxious like state, ready to fight at any moment. They stand completely still for about five minutes.

"Can you feel any bushes or branches move?"

Jacob looks at Julian and puts his finger over his lips telling him to be silent.

Julian hears Jacobs's thoughts, *"There is a man running, but this man is very big and very heavy!"*

"Will we fight?"

"I don't think so. It's running toward the other noise we heard."

Julian takes a small step back breaking a small twig, Jacob puts his hand on his shoulder stopping him from moving any further.

"What's wrong?"

"I think he or it heard that twig break!"

Julian puts his walking stick ready to strike at any moment, *"Is it that close?"*

"No it's about twenty minutes walk away but it heard that twig break?"

"What do you mean it heard that twig break?"

"I don't know, but as soon as the twig broke it stopped running and stood still for a moment, before it started to run again."

"That's impossible!" Julian says with his mouth.

Jacob looks into the woods for a long moment before saying, "That's what I thought, but as you just spoke out loud the two creatures have stopped and are now walking this way. I think they know were here."

"Why did you say creatures this time?"

Jacob gives him a troubled look, "They are too big to be man!"

"What should we do?"

"I'm not sure, they know were here and we know their there and they are walking toward to us."

Julian starts to walk, "I think we should keep walking maybe they will turn and walk the other way."

"Sounds like a plan, not a good plan, but it's better than my plan, which is no plan."

The two men start walking forward, not trying to be quiet any longer. They keep walking on the path over the water made from roots and vines.

About an hour passes before Julian asks, "Are they still walking toward us?"

"No, they have been walking along side of us for a while now, I'm surprised we haven't seen them."

"Are they that close?"

"No, but they can hear every word we say and are watching us very closely."

"What should we do?"

"I think we should do what we have been doing, just keep walking."

The two men keep walking, Jacob can tell that the two men, or creatures are walking along side of them. This goes on until they reach the end of the wetland, they walk for about ten minutes on the dry land when Jacob stops,

"I think they have stopped watching us. Whatever they are must live in the wetlands."

The two men give a sigh of relief and walk further away from the swamp.

They walk well into the dark before stopping for the night. The next day they walk until they are close to William's village, they stop making a path and walk through the bushes until the find a beat in path that heads toward the village. As the village comes into sight, young Andrew runs up to them. He wants to know all about their journey, "Did you meet anybody? How many? Were they nice? Any children my age?" He was always excited about new things.

"Calm down!" Julian says, "I will tell you all about it after I see your father."

He picks the boy up and puts him on his shoulders, "You're getting to heavy for this." Julian says as they walk into the village.

Jonathan and Rosemary are the first to greet them as they walk into the village, Jonathan tells his son to get down, "Your uncle has walked for weeks, he must be very tired." Jonathan looks at the two men smiling, "And very dirty!"

He pulls Andrew off Julian's shoulders and rubs his head,

"Run along and play, I want to talk to your uncle and Jacob alone for a while."

He turns to Rosemary, "Why don't you go start warming up some food, these travelers must be very hungry." She walks away.

The three men walk slowly as they talk. Julian tells his brother about the Lord and his men. He lets him know how cruel they are and how they like other people to suffer.

Julian sadly looks at his brother, "It's like other peoples anguish makes them happy!"

Jacob in an angry yet sad voice, "It makes me sick!"

"How far did you travel before you came to the first village?"

Jacob gives a gloomy look, "A village with life or a village that was destroyed years ago?"

"Your first encounter with other men."

"The first man I put on the ground was about five days from here."

Jonathan with a concerned look, "Put on the ground?"

"He swung a knife at me, I had no choice!"

"Is there anything closer we have to worry about?"

Jacob hesitates before saying, "The creatures in the wetland, I would be concerned about them."

Jonathan turns toward Jacob giving him his full attention, "What creatures in the wetland?"

Jacob points in the direction they have just walked, "About one and a half days travel that way is a big swamp."

Yes, I know all about the wetland, what about the creatures we should be worried about?"

"I'm not sure if they are creatures or some sort of man." Jacob tells him what had happened."

"Were these creatures big?"

"Yes, they were very big." Jacob answers.

"The noise you heard, what did it sound like?"

"It was a growling screech."

"I don't think we have to worry about those creatures, they mean us no harm."

Julian shakes his head, "You think it was one of those bear men in the tale you tell."

"Its not a tale! What else could it be?"

"He has a very good argument." Jacob says smiling at Julian.

"I would rather pretend that nothing happened in the wetland then believe his story…OK it's a bear man or a man bear, whatever you call it." He turns and walks toward the home he is staying in with the other two following him.

"I hope it remembers the story as well as you do. They are very big, and can hear the smallest sound from a long distance." Jacob says looking at Jonathan with a smug yet friendly look.

When they arrive at the home they are staying in Rosemary has a large meal warming for them, before they eat both men want to wash. It doesn't take very long there is a bucket of water and a washcloth waiting for them.

"Before I go to sleep, I'm walking to the stream to bathe myself well!" Julian says.

"I'm kind of used to being dirty." Jacob says with a big smirk.

Jonathan, Julian even Rosemary all stop what they are doing and look at him with disgust.

"I'm only kidding." Jacob responds quickly.

They all go back to what they are doing. Julian starts telling his brother about the people they have met, some nice most awful! Before he can continue Andrew walks in with a boy his age, they get along very will.

Andrew looks at his uncle, "Tell me about the girl my age."

Julian looks at Jacob who looks back at him, both with a confused look on their faces.

Jonathan notices the look, "Was there a girl his age?"

"Yes but we haven't told you, neither have we told Andrew yet?" Julian says still with a confused look.

Jonathan looks at his son then Julian, "This is not the first time he's done that, sometimes he knows things you are about to say before they are said. I think his gift will be powerful like his great, great grandfather."

They know the man they are talking about was one the greatest worriers of all time and had the most powerful gift of all their people. He was also the man who led a small group away from the fighting to live in piece were they live know. Jonathan is worried that this Lord of the land may change all of that. Julian continues telling him about the people they have met and the little girl Andrews age.

"They sound very nice, I would like to meet them."

Jacob adds, "It will be a long walk for Andrew."

Jonathan turns to his son, "He will lead the way. We will travel there before the cold days of winter."

Both men look at him as though he was crazy, they both know winter is close.

"Do you think you can travel that far?" Jonathan says looking at Andrew.

Andrew hesitates before saying, "Not a problem!"

"Good it will start your training." Jonathan turns toward Julian and Jacob,

"He starts training with the men in the winter."

Jonathan hears Julian's thoughts, *"Do you think he is ready?"*

"Yes, but I want him to train with us before his mind is opened so he can see how powerful our gift can be, I don't want it to overwhelm him."

Julian pushes Andrew off the log he is sitting on, "You get to fight me now."

Jonathan smiles at his son, "Who has never beaten me!"

After eating Julian and Jacob walk to the stream, while washing, Jacob looks at Julian, "Does Jonathan think Andrew is ready?"

"I don't think so, I think he is worried about this Lord of the land more than he lets on. I think he wants Andrew ready to fight if need be."

Jacob, in a somber tone, "I think he'd rather have him run then fight."

"You may be right, with the proper training of moving the vines and bushes out of the way you can run much quicker!"

They finish washing and put clean cloths on, both men are happy to feel clean. They start walking toward the village. By the time they get there its already dark. Andrew and the other children are quietly playing by the light of the fire. Rosemary tells the children that it's late and they should go home, Jonathan tells Andrew to wash his face and hands before going to sleep. It's not long before he's sleeping. Rosemary, Jonathan, Julian and Jacob sit by the fire after all the adults go to sleep talking about all they have seen and all the details. It takes about an hour or so, Rosemary and Jonathan can't believe their ears, some of the stuff was just unbelievable.

Julian decides to end the conversation talking about Aaron's village. He thinks it would be a good idea to talk about a nice thing before going to sleep. He finishes telling them about everything he can think of.

"These people sound very nice, I am eager to meet them but first we must travel home." Jonathan says then looks at Rosemary, "I think we should leave tomorrow."

Rosemary looks back at her husband, "You can tell Andrew!" They both know Andrew likes it here more, there are children his age to play with.

"Don't worry, he will be fine, he has a lot to look forward to."

They all get up and walk to the home they are staying in.

The following morning when Julian wakes he can hear Andrew whining about going home, he wants to stay longer and play with the children his age.

"The only children in our village are much younger then me or Julian who acts my age!"

This makes Julian laugh as he gets out of bed. He puts his overcoat on and walks out, "What do we have for our morning meal, I'm hungry!"

Jonathan answers, "We have what we ate last night, we also have a long walk ahead of us." He looks at Andrew, "Start saying goodbye to your friends and get ready!"

"OK" he starts walking toward his friend's homes.

"We will come back soon, I promise." Jonathan says as Andrew walks away.

Julian then adds, "When we are at home I will try to act more your age OK!"

Andrew looks back at him with a big smile; he didn't realize Julian had heard him say that. He was a little embarrassed. All of them can still hear Jacob snore!

"Wow! He really sleeps loud." Jonathan says.

"If you only knew." Julian says under his breath.

They wash in a bucket of water and start eating the food Rosemary has warmed. By the time they are done eating Jacob has awaken and has started to eat. When they have all finished eating, they clean up. They make sure that no food is left in the small huts they sleep in. Rosemary and Jonathan come to visit often, sometimes with others so William has built two small huts set of on the backside of the village. William makes sure they are kept clean for them.

"Everything is ready to go. We are just waiting for Andrew to get back." Jonathan says.

Rosemary says with a stern look. "Let him say goodbye to his friends!"

They wait no longer than ten minutes before Andrew comes back with his Uncle William, who says, "I didn't think you would be leaving this early?"

"We want to get an early start. "Jonathan replies.

"I can't thank you enough for all you have done."

Jonathan looks at his wife then William,

"We are family, that's what family does, we help each other."

William puts his hand out to shake Jonathan's hand, while shaking he puts his other hand on Jonathan's shoulder and says, "When you first met my sister I did not approve, I thought you were strange." He looks Jonathan in the eyes,

"Now that I know you, I'm proud to call you brother." He let's Jonathan's hand go, "You have a safe trip home."

They walk through the village to say goodbye to the villagers before walking down the path that leads away. The further they walk down the path the more it becomes overgrown with bushes, they walk for a while stomping through them.

"Is anybody following us?" Julian says looking at Jacob.

"No, there is nobody close to us."

The moment Jacob says no, the path opens up in front of them, all the vines, bushes and thorns pull away right from under their feet and as far as the eye can see. Rosemary takes hold of her husbands hand, it doesn't matter how many times she sees this she will never get used to it. Every time Andrew sees it he wishes he could do it. He keeps telling himself he will train harder than anyone has ever trained before. They all start walking down the path, which fills in behind them as though it was never there. They walk all day only stopping to eat. They walk well into the night before stopping to sleep. Julian and Jacob get a big fire going while Jonathan makes the shelters. He makes two igloo shaped huts out of the bushes and vines, it doesn't look like it will rain so they are not wound together very tight but they will keep the wind out and the warmth in. They still have some food they have brought with them so they don't have to hunt, they just warm the food by the fire.

Julian looks at his brother, "Why two small huts and not one big one?"

"I've heard him sleep, if he sleeps in the same hut as me, I wont!" They all laugh.

Andrew who is now very tired asks, "What did you mean when you said my gift might be as strong as my great, great grandfathers? How do you know his power was strong and not just stories told through the years?"

Jonathan looks at Julian, who yawns, "I'm getting tired, how about you Jacob?"

"Not really."

Julian gives him an elbow in the side. Jacob then says,

"Now that you mention it I'm having a hard time keeping my eyes open."

Both men walk into their shelter, at the same time Rosemary gets up,

"Good night" she says and gives her son and husband a kiss and walks into her shelter leaving Andrew and his father to talk.

Jonathan looks at his son, "Come over here, your not to old to sit next to your father are you?"

Andrew who was sitting on the other side of the fire gets up and sits next to his father.

"There is something you must know." Jonathan says.

Andrew now looking anxiously at his father who puts his hand on his sons shoulder. Jonathan now looking into Andrew eyes,

"You have heard of your mind being opened to nature, It's much more than that. It's always done from father to son for a reason, unless the father has passed on before his time, then it's the closest male in the family who does it."

There is a pause while Jonathan puts another log on the fire.

"The reason for that is when your mind is opened you also receive a lot of the memories from the person doing it as well as our ancestors. As your mind is opened you will receive some of the strongest memories as far back as our people have lived."

Jonathan looks at his son, "Some of these memories are so strong its as though you are there. All of your great, great grandfathers memories are of a worriers memories, some good some horrible, most of battle and fighting."

Jonathan looks at the fire, "That's why I want you to learn more of our gift before I open your mind." He rubs his sons head, "It's getting late, we should get some sleep, when we wake I will tell you a story of a great battle, the one that made your great, great grandfather leave the city of our ancestors and settle in our village with the hope for peace.

Chapter Ten

When Jonathan wakes Andrew is already up sitting by the fire, the fire is going strong and some food is warming, he was very excited to hear the story.

Jonathan sits next to his son, puts his hand on his shoulder, "I didn't hear you get up."

"I tried to be quiet so you could get as much sleep as possible."

"Thank you," Jonathan proudly looks at his son, "That was very thoughtful."

Julian and Jacob have now come out, Rosemary is already packing things to travel. Jonathan tells her to sit and rest, they are in no rush. He looks at his son, then his wife.

"I want you to walk ahead with Julian and Jacob, Andrew and I have some talking to do."

She looks at him with concern, curious to know what they were going to talk about. Jonathan tells her not to worry, he was only going to tell him the story of his great, great grandfather. He gives her a smile and a wink. Julian, Jacob and Rosemary finish packing and start walking, leaving the two sitting by the fire.

"Where should I begin?" he pauses, "I should start with the city of our ancestors, it has always been under constant attack from the outside. They had no choice but to build two separate walls from wood with about thirty feet of brier and thorn bushes between the two walls. Both walls have walk ways on them, the walkway on the inner wall is much higher to see far in the distance letting them see any attack approaching.

On the top of these two walls, worriers from the city would take turns walking around making sure no enemy was trying to attack. The city was the largest village you can imagine, homes as far as the eye can see with paths between them, some of the homes had two even three levels, all made from roots, vines and bushes, that's why we called it a city, it was quite spectacular. Along the paths there were slanted walls leaning against the homes made from carved wood, every ten to twenty feet there was an opening, if a horn sounded it didn't matter where you were or what you were doing you stopped and hid behind one of these slanted walls. There was enough room to get back to your home, you would have to be careful passing through the openings. On the outskirts of the city where the homes were spread apart there were various shelters scattered through out the paths for shelter,"

Jonathan gives his son a very serious look,

"When the horns sounded it meant they were under attack and arrows would be flying in. The people who lived outside the city were savage and wanted to do nothing but kill our people because they thought we were different. We did not like to fight but they left us no choice. The defense around our city was strong and we were always able to keep them out. One day while your great, great grandfather was standing guard on top of the wall he saw a great force approaching, he sounded the horn letting people of the village know to take cover from the arrows. He sounded the horn two more times letting the worriers of the village know that the force was big and they would have a large battle that day. After he sounded the horns he started communicating with his close friends and the strong worriers of the village with his mind, letting them know that this was one of the largest attacks that he'd ever seen! The worriers were now rushing to the wall, Robert started to see arrows flying in, within seconds there were so many arrows the sun went dim.

He gave the city worriers another long hard blow letting the worriers know to take cover behind the slanted walls and move to the battle under cover. The arrows started falling like a heavy rain into the city. Robert looked over the wall, he was looking at it least one thousand men rushing the wall, he started using the thorns and briers, roots and vines to tangle and kill the approaching force. When the other city worriers reached the wall they knew they would have no choice but go outside the city and fight. These men, about six hundred strong went into battle with about one hundred more men standing on the wall, using the roots, vines and thorns to entangle the enemy while the other men in battle used their swords and staffs to strike down this savage force trying to push their way forward. This battle went on for most of the day, the enemy was slowly being pushed back. Robert was looking at the battle, it seemed as though they were winning but for some reason he had a bad feeling. It wasn't until he looked behind him that he knew something was wrong. He wasn't sure why but he knew he had to go to the back of the village and check on the few worriers standing guard on the wall there. He left the battle and started to run toward the back wall. When he arrived at the wall he could see nothing wrong but he knew he was there for a reason. He looked deep into the woods, he was puzzled, he started asking himself what to do, he knew something was wrong so he decided to sit and feel the bushes in the distance. That's when he felt a small force moving through the bushes. They were far away, what could they be doing?

He finally saw a man disappear behind a tree far in the distance, he closed his eyes to feel his movement. He could feel the man moving closer but it felt as though this man was walking directly on the roots. When he opened his eyes the man was no where to be found. He thought about this for a moment, that's when he realized they were digging a tunnel under the wall and the attack was only a decoy to let them into the city. If they were able to get in, innocent people would be killed! He told another one of the men on the wall to sound the horn letting the other worriers know that the back side of the wall was in danger. He walked the ground using his gift to feel the roots and where the tunnel was. It was dug deep behind the wall into the city. He waited for the first man to show his head when the hole opened in the ground, to the man's surprise Robert was waiting for him when he burrowed through and poked his head out of the tunnel.

With a single blow from his walking stick he killed the men. That was only the beginning, when the first man fell into the hole many more men came pushing through, one after another. Robert fought the men, they just kept coming out of the tunnel. While Robert was fighting he was using the roots to seal the tunnel, he could hear the remaining men in the tunnel scream as the roots started to crush them and the dirt was pulled into the tunnel from above filling it in. About twenty men had already gotten through and he was fighting all of them with his stick as he used bushes to tangle them. The men tried to surround him but Robert moved around not letting them, he tangled a few of their legs with some vines knocking them to the ground and quickly ran over and struck them with his stick killing some leaving others unconscious.

The biggest of the men lunged forward trying to stab him, he stepped to the side grabbed the man by the wrist and pulled it in the opposite direction breaking the bone. Still holding the wrist he stomped on the lower part of the mans leg cracking it in half, the man cried out in pain with both his arm and leg broken, he was no longer a threat. At the same time he did this he pulled the man's knife out of his hand throwing it into the neck of another man trying to attack, killing him instantly. Three more men tried to attack all at the same time. Robert stepped forward and drove his stick into the knee of one of the men, swinging the stick around crushing his throat. With another step he strikes another directly in the face dropping him, in the same step he swings his stick striking another man in the side of the head killing him. He then turned to face the remaining few of the men in a strong fighting stance. They dropped their weapons and fell to their knees with their hands in the air. Robert wanted to kill them as well but it was against his beliefs, so he waited for the other worriers to come to his aid. When the other worriers arrived he looked at the men he had just killed, even though he had no choice he felt badly, he slowly walked home. That night he told his wife he wanted to leave and start a new life far away from all the fighting. He talked to some of his close friends about how he felt and a handful felt the same way. They were tired of all the fighting and wanted to start a new live as well. That's why we live were we live now"

Jonathan looks at his son, "We should start walking, I've been talking longer than I thought."

"That story makes me proud to be who I am!" They get up and start walking,

Jonathan asks his son, "How strong do you feel?"

"Why do you ask father?"

"I think we can quickly catch up to the others!"

"I will be first" he says as he starts running. Jonathan watches his son run down the trail, he smiles

"Don't forget!" he yells, **"you can only run as far as I open the path!"** and starts running after his son. It only takes a minute or two before Jonathan catches up with his son, Andrew is already breathing heavy.

Jonathan runs along side, "Slow down" he says, "don't use all of your energy, keep yourself at a pace that you can run for a long time."

They both slow down a little.

Jonathan then says, "Running full speed is only good for a short distance, or if you have no choice!"

The two keep running at a steady pace for about an hour before they catch up with the others. Jonathan starts walking as though he has not used any extra energy. He looks at his wife, "Have you rested at all?"

"No, why do you ask?"

Jonathan raises his eyebrows and turns to his son, Rosemary also turns and looks at Andrew who is holding his side and breathing so heavy he can barely talk, he is still trying to catch his breath and walk at the same time.

Rosemary smiling says with sarcasm, "What's wrong Andrew, did the old man wear you out?"

They all chuckle a little, all except Andrew.

Julian asks his brother, "How long did you run for?"

"About an hour."

"Did you stop at all to rest?"

"Not once, and he stayed ahead of me most of the way."

Julian looks at Andrew, "You're a strong boy, that's a long time to run with no rest."

Andrew who is now sitting down on the path still trying to catch his breath looks at his uncle, gasping as he says,

"Thank you." He then lies flat on his back with his arms spread out; he slowly catches his breath.

Jonathan says to the two men, "He will be fine to train in the winter."

Julian adds, "I will start running with him every day after he does his work." He turns to Jacob, "You are welcome to come."

Jacob pokes young Andrew with his stick in the ribs, "I do like the boy, if I can help I will." He then takes a knee next to Andrew, "Besides, I can't wait to smack him around while we are training." He keeps a serious look for a moment then smiles and messes up Andrew's hair.

Andrew jumps to his feet, "I'm done resting, we can start moving again."

They all start walking at a steady pace. They walk a good portion of the day.

Julian turns to Andrew, "Lets go hunting for dinner."

Andrew is happy about this, he is finally being treated like an adult, even though he is still very young.

Julian looks at Jonathan, "As long as you don't mind."

"Not at all, its time he learns to hunt for himself."

Julian and Andrew silently walk into the woods away from the path and the others. Andrew can tell Julian is looking for something, but he's not sure what.

He then hears Julian's thoughts, *"Be very quiet, we are looking for a spot to sit and wait."*

Andrew not sure what he is doing, he just follows him as silent as possible. They come to a small clearing in the woods and sit with their backs against a tree. Andrew has a puzzled look on his face until he hears Julian's thoughts again,

"See those bushes over there" as he points, *"It's a perfect spot to trap a small animal, such as a rabbit or a squirrel. All we have to do is get them there."*

Andrew not sure what his uncle is talking about, sits and watches his uncle stare into the forest. After several minutes the bushes far off in the distance start to move, it's quite a stunning sight. It looks like a small wave of bushes moving to where they are sitting. As Andrew watches the bushes and to his surprise he sees a large deer running through them, Andrew is shocked when his uncle lets it pass, it would have made a nice meal.

Andrew now realizes his uncle is making the animals move right into a spot he can easily catch them with the bushes. It's not long before several squirrels and rabbits are tangled in the bushes so tightly they are killed.

Julian picks up the rabbits and lets Andrew gather the squirrels. Julian looks at the squirrels, "Not much meat on squirrel, but with the rabbits we will have plenty for all of us." Andrew now realizes how easy hunting can be once you can move the vines and bushes with your mind.

He looks at his uncle with a confused look, "Why did you let the deer pass and settle for rabbits and squirrels?"

"It was a large deer and we would have wasted a lot of meat or had to carry it back with us. When we travel we usually hunt for the smaller animals so there is little waist." He smiles at Andrew, "The deer would have made a nice catch if we were home."

They quickly walk back to the trail and catch up with the others who already have a fire going. They eat a good meal with the meat and some berries they have gathered. They sit around the fire for a while talking until they all go to sleep. There is only about five hours of walking left until they reach their village but they are in no rush so they decide not to walk any further.

The next day they walk the rest of the way, the people of their village are all happy to see them back. Daniel is the first to greet them, he is a large framed man a little on the heavy side with dark hair a little past his shoulders and a beard about one inch long. Like most of the men in the village he has dark eyes. Daniel, like Andrews father carried himself in a confident manor always standing strong, when he spoke it seemed as though he was looking through you, not at you.

Jonathan shakes his hand, "After we get settled I want to talk to the old men, there is something we should discuss."

Daniel looks at his friend with great concern. Daniel and Jonathan grew up together, even though Daniel was older they became great friends. They spent most of their child years playing together causing mischief like all young boys do, if there is trouble to find they will find it.

"Should I be worried?" Daniel asks.

"I wouldn't worry just yet, maybe a little concerned." Jonathan tells him then says, "After we eat we will talk, I will tell you all about it."

Daniel hears Jonathan's thoughts, *"I don't want to scare Andrew."* Then adds, *"He will start training with us in the cold days of winter."*

Daniel looks at Andrew with a smile, then takes the stuff Rosemary is carrying, "I will carry this for you."

She thanks him and they walk down the streams edge toward their home. When they arrive Daniel's wife Sandra already has a fire going and some meat cooking, she also has vegetables cut and ready to eat.

She smiles at Rosemary, "I know how it is when you travel with these men, no time for fruit and vegetables, just meat!" She looks at the men as they put down their stuff, "I know you can find some fruit with a little effort, they just prefer meat!"

Rosemary tells Andrew to eat some of the vegetables Sandra has cut up, then eats some herself. Julian, Jacob and Andrew sit by the fire while Jonathan and Daniel take the rest of the stuff inside as Rosemary finishes cooking.

They all eat and talk for a while before heading home, Daniel and Sandra live right next to Jonathan. Julian and Jacob live in small homes down the stream. It's still early in the afternoon but Jonathan and Rosemary are very tired so they decide to lie down. Andrew is also tired but he wants to go thank Daniel for taking care of his responsibilities while he was away so he walks toward his home to find him. Rosemary and Jonathan clean up a little and walk inside their home, nobody has been there for several weeks so it smells a little musty.

Rosemary looks at her husband, "I think we need some fresh air in here."

He smiles at her then looks at their home which is made from vines, roots and bushes tangled together keeping the weather out even in the strongest storm. Jonathan turns and looks at the walls. As he is turning various spots in the walls on each side of their home untangle and unravel from each other, pulling away forming holes for air to flow through their home.

"How is that?"

"That will be fine, now lets lie down, I'm exhausted!"

They both lie down and quickly fall to sleep. Andrew has walked over to Daniel's home where he finds him splitting some wood.

"Would you like me to help you with that?" Andrew asks.

"No I will be fine."

"I want to thank you for taking care of my work while I was away, if there is anything I can help with just let me know."

Daniel can see the that Andrew wants to help, "You know what, my hands are a little tired. I can use a short rest."

Andrew jumps up and takes the ax from Daniels hands. He steps up to the wood Daniel is splitting and takes a big swing at one of the logs only hitting it on the very edge.

A little embarrassed he says, "Sorry the next swing I will hit it perfectly."

Daniel smiles, "If you want to hit it perfectly try swinging a little softer." Andrew swings the ax a little softer yet still very hard and hits the log directly in the center, the ax only goes half way through.

Daniel sees a look of disappointment on Andrew, "That was perfect. When I was your age I could barely hit a log, you went half way through! One more swing like that and the log will be split."

Andrew hits it the same way splitting it. He splits a few more the same way trying as hard as he can. When he starts having a little trouble Daniel gets up and takes the ax, "Thank you for the help I really needed a rest."

"If there is anything else I can do to help just let me know."

Daniel steps next to Andrew and puts his hand on his shoulder, "Your father has raised a fine young man, and I won't hesitate to ask but right now I am fine." Daniel starts splitting the wood again and Andrew walks away.

Daniel yells to him, **"Tell your father I will be by shortly."**

"OK" Andrew yells back then walks to the stream to get some water.

As Andrew walks down the stream he talks to several people along the way, he wants to check on the animals and their fence. The village is fairly small so it doesn't take very long to get there. He finds that the animals have been will taken care of. Andrew likes to make sure that they are fed and the fence is fully intact, keeping any predators out. Andrew knows this let's the older men of the village take care of the more important things. He stays with the animals for a while, petting some and chasing others around, he makes sure they have food for the night and starts to walk home. Most of the day has passes as he walks around the small village talking to several people and he is now starting to feel hungry. He stops in front of a small one-room home. He is trying to peak inside until a voice from behind startles him,

"Can I help you with something?" It's his uncle Julian.

"I was trying to see if you were home."

"I am now, I was out gathering some fruit and vegetables earlier."

"Why don't you come to our home to eat?"

"I'm there all the time, I want to give your mother a break. She is a good women and always feeds me."

"I think both her and my father are laying down, it would be nice if we got the food ready for them so all they have to do when they wake is eat."

Julian tilts his head to the side and gives Andrew a half smile, "Are you bored."

"How can you tell?"

"I know you well Andrew, all the other children are younger yet you still play with them. I see none around and you have already played with the animals for a while." He pauses then says, "That's how I know!"

He puts his hand on Andrew's shoulder and they start walking up the stream toward Andrews home. "It will be nice to get things ready for your mother."

Andrew looks at his uncle, "I wish there were some children my age to play with."

"I wish the same thing sometimes but if there were, the only person I would have to hang out with would be Jacob, that would make me insane."

Andrew knows Julian is kidding, Jacob has always been his best friend, he also knows that Jacob's strange ways can be very aggravating sometimes.

Julian looks at Andrew, "Next time you get bored come find me, you keep me feeling young!"

They walk past Jacobs small home, who is sitting behind his home staring into the forest, they can hear him mumbling something. They both giggle a little as they pass trying not to disturb him, Julian knows he just wants to be alone.

A smile appears on Jacobs face as they pass, he gets up and goes to the front of his home and starts the fire. He was about to start it before they passed but he was in no mood to talk. When the two arrive at Andrews home they can hear Jonathan and Rosemary talking inside. They are very quiet starting the fire. When Rosemary comes out to start cooking she is pleasantly surprised to see fish already cooking and fruit and vegetables ready to eat.

When Jonathan walks out he looks at Julian, "This was a nice thing to do."

"It was your son's idea."

Jonathan sits down, takes a piece of fruit and starts eating.

Julian gets up and pulls the fish away from the fire, "We should let it cool before we eat."

They all talk for a while before eating.

Shortly after they eat Daniel shows up. "I talked with some of the older men from the village, they are ready to hear what you have to say." Daniel says then grabs a piece of fruit and takes a bite, "We will talk where we train, the old men will be there."

Most of the older men in the village only trained in the morning, they have no need to train twice a day anymore but tonight they would be there. When Jacob shows up at Jonathan's home all the men start walking up the stream to where they train, Andrew is left behind with his mother. He helps her clean up the mess and sits across from her by the fire. They talk a little about her village and how Andrew plays with the children his age.

His mother sadly looks at him, "I'm sorry there are no children your age here."

"All the children here are much younger than I am. I like playing with then but it's more like they play with each other while I watch." He looks at his mother with sad eyes, "If it wasn't for Uncle Julian trying to act my age I would have no one to play with."

He slowly looks away from his mother and back at the fire. "Sometimes I wish we lived at your village."

Rosemary wants to cry but holds her tears back, "Come sit next to your mother, that is if you're not to old."

Andrew walks around the fire and sits by her side. She puts her arm around him and pulls him closer to her. "Your father and I have talked about moving to my village but there is a problem."

Andrew gets excited at the thought of moving to his mother's village, then he realizes the problem, "I'm starting my training with father in the cold days."

Rosemary sadly looks at him then gives a small smile, "That's the problem, if we live there you will not learn your fathers ways."

Andrew has a sad and confused look on his face, he is not sure what he wants more.

Rosemary pulls her son closer, "Don't worry, we will figure something out." She then smiles at him, "You're not starting your training in the winter, you're starting to learn how to fight in the winter, you're starting your training first thing tomorrow morning. You will be running while they train, your father, uncle and Jacob will take turns running with you every morning while the others train." She looks at him with a serious look, "They say your lungs have to be strong, they want you ready. So you'd better get a good nights sleep tonight."

"What are the men talking about tonight? It seems important."

His mother looks at him trying to hide her concern, "I don't know."

She knows it about the things Julian and Jacob have seen and the evil man that causes a threat to their way of life.

"Its probably nothing." She says with a smile.

Andrew now wants to get to sleep early. He puts another log on the fire and tilts his head back looking at the stars, it's a nice night but a little chilly. His mother goes inside getting things ready for the morning.

After about fifteen minutes Andrew decides to go to bed, he lets the fire burn knowing his father will be home late tonight. He gets up, walks into his home and gives his mother a kiss on the cheek.

She smiles at him, "You want to be well rested for the morning, don't you."

Andrew gives her a boyish smile, "I just want to be able to keep up!"

With humorous tone, "Don't worry it's your fist day, I'm sure your father will go easy."

Andrew starts walking into his room, he turns to his mother, "I don't want to let him down."

This time in a serious tone, "Don't worry you will be fine."

Andrew turns and continues walking into his room.

Chapter Eleven

All the men of the village were at the training area waiting to hear what Jonathan has to say. The men from the village all spend a lot of time there. The walls are made from the thick bushes and vines wound so tightly. In the summertime they cove the top, only to keep out the rain, they use the abundant supply of vines hanging from the numerous amounts of trees that surround the area. This leaves a large opening between the walls and the roof letting cool air to flow through.

In the cold days of winter they use bushes and vines to fill in the space leaving only a few openings for smoke to escape from their fires and heat lamps, which they hang in various spots. The area is fairly large and they don't want to warm it up too much. When they train they need little heat, only on the extremely cold days do they get the fires going strong most of the cold days the fires are kept small, only to break the chill. All the men of the village are there, forty-three of them, they all train together every morning and are very close with each other, so close they treat each other like family.

Jonathan walks up to the oldest man in the village named Joseph, he is about Jonathan's height with hair well past his shoulders and a long beard reaching down to about mid chest. Both are mostly white with age and well groomed. The skin on his face shows his age with deep wrinkles in the corners of his eyes and when he smiles. He presents himself in a positive manor, so confident that when you looked into his dark brown eyes you can almost see his wisdom. Most men are a little nervous in his presence. Jonathan shakes his hand and looks at Joseph's brother Nathaniel who is close to Joseph in age, also with long whitish hair but kept his beard close to his face and carried himself in a less serious manor.

"Its good to see everyone here."

"It's not often someone wants to talk with all of us, something must be bothering you so I thought we should all be here to listen."

Jonathan bows his head to Joseph showing his respect. Even though Joseph is the oldest, not one man in the village can beat him at any of the training exercises. When it comes to fighting, he teaches all and all respect his word!

Nathaniel standing next to Joseph, "What on your mind Jonathan?"

Jonathan looks at him then Joseph, "We should be concerned with a man." He looks at all the men gathering around to listen.

"This man is evil and has hundreds of men that will kill for him."

Joseph looks at Jonathan, "How far away from here are they, and why should we be concerned?"

Julian steps forward, "I have seen how these men kill for fun. They do not know we are here but if they did there are too many to fight!"

Joseph ponders these words before asking Jonathan "Is your wife's village in any danger?"

"I don't think anybody is in danger yet, but we do have to watch out and keep our guard up."

"I agree." Joseph says, he looks at his brother,

"Tomorrow after we train, take Jonathan and a few good men into the woods and make sure the bushes and thorns are so thick no one wants to come our way." He turns and looks at Jonathan,

"You are my friend and I love your wife as though she was family, we should do the same for her village."

Nathaniel steps forward, "I will help, and I'm sure any man here will help also."

A short and thin man named Terence steps forward, he is the youngest of the old men and one of the friendliest in the village. He is also one of the only men in the village to keep his hair short to his head and his face clean from any hair.

"I will go with you, it will be nice to take a long walk."

Most of the old men start walking home, training in the morning is enough for them.

Jonathan looks at Terence, "I thought you would go home with them. We do more than play at night, I don't think you can handle it old man."

As he says this all the other men back up leaving the two men standing in the center of the training area. Both men look at each other as they slowly walk around. While they are circling each other a vine slowly creeps up and wraps around Terence's foot pulling it back. At the same time Jonathan charges forward with his stick in the striking position. As Terence's foot is pulled back he uses his stick to throw his body into the air doing a complete flip landing directly in front of Jonathan bringing his stick down at his head who blocks it with his stick. All the men watching step further back making sure they are completely out of the way. The two men are now swinging their sticks at each other making a loud cracking sound every time the sticks meet.

While they are swinging the sticks, vines, bushes and roots are reaching out at them from every direction, each man moving out of the way trying not to be grabbed and brought to the ground as they fight. This goes on for about ten minutes before both men stop and look at each other and shake hands.

"You have learned all you can be taught" Terence looks at Jonathan and smiles, "Now you will just get better!"

All the other men pair off and start fighting.

Jonathan and Terence walk over to the back wall.

"I want Andrew to start training with us soon."

"Do you think he's ready?" Terence asks.

"Yes, I do"

Terence then gets a serious look to him, "Are you going to open his mind?"

"I want him to train a little first." Jonathan thinking about his father says with sadness in his voice, "The way our father did it with us."

Most of there people have their minds opened before they start training. Jonathan's father had him and Julian train for a while first letting them understand how powerful their gift really was before opening their minds to the nature.

"Andrew is a smart strong young man, and it will be a pleasure training with him." Terrance says with a smile.

"How do you think the older men will feel about this?"

"I think they will be pleased, it's always nice to start training a young man and teaching him our fighting skills."

The two men walk back toward the middle of the training area where the other men are fighting, some of them are tangled in the vines that are hanging from the top, others are on the ground wrapped with bushes. Most of the men are starting to get a little winded.

The vines and bushes that are tangled around some of the men unravel letting them free. The men start to slowly leave the training area washing in the stream before heading home. Terence walks with Jonathan until Jonathan is home, he walks with Julian and Jacob further down the stream, he lives close to them.

The next morning when Andrew wakes he is excited and a little nervous, he knows that his father will be insistent that he keeps up while they are running. Andrew knows that all the men are very serious about their training. When he walks out of his room, he sees that Julian, Jacob and Daniel are all there. Andrew sits at the table and his mother gives him some warm bread to eat, his father tells him not to eat too much but drink plenty of water. All the men sit talking as they eat.

Jonathan looks at his son, "The men sitting here will all take turns running with you, we will run for at least an hour maybe more then we will teach you how to stretch properly keeping your muscles loose, the stretching is very intense but is necessary. After a good amount of stretching you will learn some basic fighting defense moves. Where taking turns for two reasons, if I do it all myself I will fall behind on my training, but the more important reason is that we all fight very differently. It is a good idea to learn the basics from different people, nobody fights the same and its good to start learning that early in your training." He pauses before asking, "Do you think you're ready?"

Andrew looks at him not very sure and extremely nervous, afraid of letting his father down, "Of course I'm ready."

"Good. Julian will go with you today."

This makes Andrew a little less nervous, he knows his father will push him very hard, he is glad that his uncle will run with him first.

"After today you will have two days rest."

"Why two days rest, don't we train every day?"

The four men all laugh a little, knowing that the intense stretching will make him extremely sore for the next couple of days.

"Tomorrow you will know why. After your two days rest, Jacob and Daniel will each do the same with only one days rest between, then its my turn." He looks at his son with a serious look, "We will all push you very hard, doing your best is all I ask."

Julian hears his brothers thoughts, *"Don't push him to hard today, I don't want to discourage him."*

"I was planning on going easy today."

Jonathan still looking at his son, "We will give you a days rest until you think you are ready to train every day. Just remember one thing, the harder you push yourself, the quicker you will learn!"

Jacob stands up, "You are becoming a man, now lets get going!"

All the men walk outside, Rosemary watches them exit her home. She feels like crying, her little boy is growing up.

As they are walking to the training area Jonathan looks at his son, "Remember to keep your breathing steady while you are trying to keep up, don't push yourself too much, and stay at a steady pace."

Julian turns to Andrew, "What are you waiting for? Lets go!"

Julian starts running off into the woods at a quick steady pace with Andrew following, they run for about a half an hour with Julian talking very little to Andrew, he knows it will only make him lose his wind. The entire time Julian stays ahead but just far enough to make Andrew push himself. After a while he slows down to let Andrew catch up. It takes a few minutes, when he does they run side by side for a while. Julian has taken him to run in a very rocky part of the forest, they are not just running, they have to work with the rocks to avoid falling.

"Do you want to rest?" Julian has noticed Andrew starting to stumble a little and doesn't want him to get hurt.

Andrew says in a heavy breath, "Just a short one, I'm really trying to push myself."

Julian slows to a quick walk, Andrew does the same, walking at his side.

"Don't push yourself too much, if you break your leg I'm in trouble."

They both laugh and walk for about ten minutes sipping some water.

Julian stops for a moment, "After this hill most of the rocks are gone, we will head back a different way on flat ground with no rocks to trip on."

Andrew likes the sound of that, and they both start running again. They run for about twenty more minutes then slow down to a walk. Andrew now knows where they are, it's not far from the village.

"Now we stretch."

They spend a good twenty minutes stretching. Julian shows Andrew how to stretch in ways he didn't think was possible, by now Andrew's body feels like mush, he can barely move his arms or legs.

Julian can see that Andrew is exhausted, he tells him that they will go over some easy defense moves. Julian shows him how to block a straight punch, stepping to the side with his arms and legs in striking position. Andrew is trying very hard but his arms are so tired he is having a hard time.

Julian puts his hand on Andrews back, "I think we are done for the day. You should be proud of your self, you've done better than I thought you would for the first day."

They walk back to the village at a slow steady pace. As they walk Julian says, "Just to let you know, I was a little tough on you today. I was going to go easy but changed my mind when you kept up so well. You will be soar tomorrow!"

Andrew looking at his uncle laughs, "I'm sore now!"

"Tomorrow and the next day will be fun for you."

"What do you mean by that?"

"You will know what I mean when you wake in the morning!"

They keep talking while they walk back to the village. When they arrive home Rosemary has some food ready. Jonathan, Daniel and Jacob are already there, sitting by the outside fire waiting for them.

"How did he do?" Jonathan asks.

"He did better than I thought he would. I didn't even take it easy on him, he kept right up."

Jonathan looks at his son, "You should rest for a while after we eat, I will take care of your work for today and tomorrow."

"You don't have to father, I can do it."

"I know you can, but I think you should rest, besides tomorrow you might think differently."

"You should eat and listen to your father, he knows what he is talking about." Rosemary says then looks at all the men, "You should all eat, I've made plenty."

She looks at Daniel, "Where's Sandra? There is plenty for her also."

"She's coming, but you know her; she's always late."

Rosemary smiles when she realizes Sandra is already walking over and is close enough to hear him, she gives Daniel a wink as she says, "Don't let her hear you say that."

Daniel now knows his wife is right behind him and has heard what he has said, "My beautiful wife would know I was only kidding."

Sandra now close enough to give him a friendly push in the back of the head, "Nice try" she says and sits down next to him.

They all laugh a little and spend some time talking. After a short while the men get up and start their daily work around the village, gathering wood, hunting, checking the fish traps and making sure no one needs any help doing anything. Andrew spends the rest of the day helping his mother, but feeling tired all day. When his father gets home he restarts the fire that is almost out and Rosemary reheats what was left from earlier, they all sit down to eat.

While they are eating Jonathan asks his son, "How did you like today?"

"I liked it a lot. When I can run without getting tired I will like it much more."

"I remember that feeling, it won't take long."

After they eat they sit outside by the fire talking for a while, Jonathan notices his sons eyes starting to get heavy even though its only dusk.

"Why don't you go get some sleep Andrew, you've had a busy day and you need a good nights rest."

Andrew gets up, says good night to his parents as he walks past them and quickly falls to sleep. Rosemary and Jonathan talk for a while discussing how Andrew has no one his age to play with, Jonathan feels the same as his wife. He expresses the importance of his son to train with the men of his village so he can learn the old ways and how to defend himself. Not sure what to do Jonathan puts another piece of wood on the fire and his arm around his wife. They sit back leaning against a backrest Jonathan has made, its two thick roots arching out of the ground slanted back with bushes wrapped around them creating a comfortable place to sit and watch the fire burn with their legs stretched out. Jonathan has fallen to sleep many of nights there looking into the fire.

As they are sitting, looking at the stars Jonathan sits up, "I have an idea!"

"I'm listening." Rosemary says still looking at the stars.

"Children play much more in the summer, there is little to do in the winter."

Jonathan looks at his wife who is still looking at the stars. "Do you agree?"

She now sits up and looks at him, "Yes I agree, it's too cold to play outside for a long period of time in the winter and there is less daylight. That's not and idea, it's common knowledge," she gives him a friendly smile, "what's your idea?"

"We can live at your village in the summer when the weather is nice, I can still train him in the mornings and he can play with kids in the daytime. When the days get short and its too cold to play outside we can travel back here and he can train with the men from this village all winter."

Rosemary looks at him with a big smile, "That's a great idea!"

She gives him a big hug. They both sit back and fall to sleep looking at the stars. When the flames from the fire get low Jonathan wakes up, it's a little chilly so he wakes his wife and they walk inside. Rosemary makes sure there is plenty of oil in the heat lamps as she lights them, she is very quiet as she goes into Andrew's room to light his heat lamp trying not to wake him.

As she is leaving Andrew's room he quietly says. "Love you mother."

She smiles, "Love you to son."

The next morning when Andrew wakes up he can smell that his mother has been cooking, he also knows that his father has already left, he cannot hear his voice. When he rolls to get out of bed he can just about move his legs. He now knows what his uncle meant when he said tomorrow would be fun. He slowly gets up and walks into the big room of their home. When his mother sees him walking like an old man she turns away as she smiles, she does not want him to see her smiling at the way he is walking.

Rosemary tells Andrew to sit while she gets him some food; he gingerly sits. Rosemary puts some vegetables, left over fish, bread and a bowl of soup in front of him, she tells him to eat up.

"Your father wanted me to tell you to try and stretch a little, it will keep your muscles from getting tight and help you heal quicker but that is up to you."

"I had a hard time getting out of bed and you want me to stretch!"

"I don't want you to do anything, I'm telling you what your father said."

Andrew finishes eating and walks outside for a moment. The days are getting cooler, he remembers his father saying before winter they will go to the other village, which is a long travel. He slowly walks back inside and tries to stretch his muscles a little. He tries to stretch all the ways his uncle has showed him, his legs are very soar so he can only stretch a little.

After stretching he walks outside to the front of his home and sits next to the fire pit. It still has some hot ember in it so he puts a log on top. He wants to relax so he just watches as the log heats up and slowly catches fire, he watches the log burn as his eyes start to feel heavy. The next thing he remembers is waking up to his fathers voice talking to his uncle.

When he opens his eyes Jacob says, "Lets go Andrew, time to get up and train with me today."

Andrew sits up with a confused look as he rubs his eyes.

"You've been sleeping for two days," Jacob says, "Its time to train with me now."

Andrew not sure what to think starts to get up when his father says, "Sit down son, he's just teasing you, you've only been sleeping for an hour or so, sit and rest."

Jacob rubs the top of Andrew's head, " Got ya! You train with me next, your muscles will still be very soar so we will take it slow and easy."

Julian smiles at Andrew, "After my first day I had trouble walking for two days."

"Its not the running," Jonathan says, "Its stretching the muscles and the way we push ourselves to stretch, it helps in our fighting. Don't worry, after the first week or so the pain will go away, then its just keeping your breath and learning how to fight."

These words are a relive to Andrew but right now he wants to stay sitting. His legs hurt so much he knows if he walks the other men will tease him so he stays sitting and listens to them talk. It's not long before they go about their business leaving Andrew alone sitting by the fire. He watches it burn for a while before going inside to help his mother getting things ready to cook for the evening and brings their clothes to the stream for washing. He spends the rest of the day sitting around doing nothing.

When his father comes home they eat and talk for a while about the day, Andrew goes to bed early leaving his parents sitting by the fire. The next morning when Andrew gets out of bed his legs are still very sore but not as bad as the day prior. He decides to stretch before doing anything. When he walks into the big room his mother has some bread and cheese waiting, he takes a small piece of bread and eats some cheese. His mother asks him how he is feeling.

"Better than yesterday."

"You should rest for today, tomorrow you will go with Jacob."

Andrew thinks he will be fine the next day, "I'm going for a walk, I want to get my legs working again. They are still fairly sore." Andrew has a strong heart and a lot of determination.

He gives his mother a kiss on he cheek and walks outside. He walks down the stream toward the animals, as he walks he picks up a stick to walk with. He wants to be like his father. He likes walking with a stick but this one doesn't feel right. When he arrives at the animals he sees that they have not been fed yet, his father and Daniel were probably going to do it after they train. Andrew decides to feed them while he was there. He fills their feeding troughs with grain and puts plenty of hay and bushes in their area. When he is done with that he walks around checking the fence making sure there are no holes in it.

After petting and playing with the animals for a while he starts to walk home, along the way he sees Joseph walking by carrying some wood. Andrew knows that if Joseph is home his father must also be done training. He wants to go home but he has also noticed that Joseph is carrying a lot of wood and has dropped a few pieces. Andrew quickly runs and picks up the wood Joseph has dropped.

"Let me help."

"I was told you were to sore to walk and here you are offering help. I always liked you and yes I could use some help."

Joseph gives Andrew some more of the wood to carry and they start walking back to his home. When they get there they both drop the wood.

"I can finish."

"Are you sure, I can stay and help if you need any."

"No, I will be fine, you should go home and rest."

Andrew smiles as he walks away, Joseph watches Andrew walk toward his home. Andrew knows that Joseph is the oldest and wisest man in the village, if there is a question, you can ask him, he will know the answer.

Joseph turns back to stack his wood, he is now smiling, he can tell that Andrew's gift, or power you may call it, will be a great. Andrew walks home stopping several times talking with people in the village. When he gets home his father is already there eating.

"If you are feeling strong enough to walk around, you can feed the animals."

"I've already done it father."

Jonathan takes another bite of bread before saying, "Tomorrow you run and train with Jacob, That should be interesting."

"I'm ready for anything."

"Good, with Jacob you never know what's next."

They both laugh as they finish eating. The rest of the day Andrew did very little except rest. After eating Andrew goes to bed making sure he is well rested for the next day.

The next morning Andrew wakes to his father's voice, "Time to get up."

Andrew gets out of his bed and grabs the stick he was walking with.

When he walks into the room his father asks, "I've noticed you've been walking with a stick, how does it feel?"

"I'm not sure yet, I want to use it for today and see."

"Its too small."

"What do you mean, too small."

Jonathan takes his stick and hands it to Andrew, "I've had this stick since I was your age. Notice how it has no chips or scratches on it."

Andrew looks at it turning in his hands he then asks his father, "How is that? I've seen you and Julian playing around many of times, hitting them together." He turns the stick some more, "There are no marks!"

His father takes his stick back, puts it at his side, "When you find your stick, you find one this size." He puts his stick in front of him, "It takes a long time to make it strong."

"What do you mean make it strong?"

His father grasps his stick tightly "It takes quite some time to make a stick like this. First you find a stick that will last your growing, making sure it is not to short when you are taller. Then you rub certain tree saps on it every night before bed, you also soak it in oils from another tree over night for several months. After doing this and your stick dries it becomes light, yet so hard not even an ax can make a mark on it."

Andrew looks at the stick he has been using and realizes it is too small, "I'm going to start looking for a good stick."

His father smiles "Make sure you find one you are comfortable with, it takes a lot of time to make it strong; make sure its worth the time."

Andrew now knows why the men of their village don't like anybody touching their walking sticks, its as though it's a part of them. Julian and Jacob walk in, each takes a piece of bread.

Jacob looks at Andrew, "Hope you ate well, I'm going to work you hard today." He then laughs, "Just kidding."

Andrew takes a bit of bread before looking at Jacob with a confident smile, "I just hope you can keep up with me."

He continues smiling as he finishes his bread and cheese. All the men walk outside toward the training area eating some bread and talking.

When Jacob finishes his bread he looks at Andrew, "Are you ready?"

Andrew takes a sip of water and replies, "Are you ready?" he says as he starts running.

Before Jacob takes off Jonathan puts his hand on his shoulder, "Do you remember what we talked about yesterday?"

"Yes I do."

Jacob then takes off after Andrew. They run side by side for a while until Jacob starts' running very fast, Andrew has a hard time keeping up but tries his best.

They run for an hour or so in a big circle, Andrew now breathing very heavy. When Jacob finally stops Andrew catches him and slowly walks back and fourth catching his breath. It takes a few moments. They stretch for a while mostly doing the same stretches his uncle has showed him. After they stretch they start walking back toward the village.

Andrew asks, "Why are we not training?"

Jacob walks a little further then stops, "This looks like a good spot. Your father asked me to train you differently." He asks Andrew to sit and listen.

"When I was a young boy about your age my father died, your grandfather treated me as though I was family." He turns and looks at Andrew with a serious face, "But I still spent a lot of time alone."

Andrew has a hard time taking Jacob seriously, only because he never is, but the tone of his voice is different so he sits and listens without interruption.

"Your father wants me to teach you how to focus on the small branches, the very tips, the ones that don't break, just bend."

"Why, is it not more important to learn how to fight?"

"Its easier to fight when you know how many, how far and where they are!" Andrew gives him a look of understanding, "OK, I'm listening.

"Your father tells me that you can already move some small vines and bushes, this is a good thing, when your mind is opened it will come easy to you."

"He thinks I'm to young and won't understand."

"Your father is a smart man, you should listen to him, our gift is a strong power."

He pauses then says with sadness in his voice, "If you don't understand it first it can be very scary, or make you lose touch with reality for a while."

Andrew can tell Jacob is talking from his own experience.

After a pause Jacob says, "Wait until your father thinks you're ready, its not just the gift you receive you also receive memories from the past." Jacob stares at Andrew with a long deep sad stare, "Some of these memories are not good."

Jacob looks away and is very silent for a moment, then says, "Back to training. I want you to look at the small branch I'm moving over there." Jacob points, "Can you see it?"

It takes a short minute, "OK, I see it." Andrew says.

"Now focus on it as hard as you can, as though you were trying to move it, but don't, just try to feel it move."

About ten minutes goes by Andrew can not feel anything, he looks at Jacob, "I don't think its working."

"You're not focusing hard enough. I can see you looking at other things, now look at the branch and don't think about anything else just the small branch."

This time Andrew stares as hard as he can at the branch, about five more minutes go by, "I think I can feel it but I'm not sure?"

"OK Andrew, while you are looking at the branch slowly close your eyes but keep focusing on the branch, when you feel it change tell me."

Andrew closes his eyes as Jacob keeps bending the branch back and fourth. Jacob watches Andrew for a moment and the branch suddenly breaks.

At the same time Andrew says, "I think I felt something!"

Jacob gets up, "I think that's enough for the day."

Andrew opens his eyes to realize the branch was broken and he had felt it break, "Did I do good?" he asks.

"I don't know? I've never tried to teach anybody before." He puts his hand on Andrews shoulder, "Lets go home, I'm hungry.

They walk back to the village.

Chapter Twelve

That night after eating Andrew lie in bed still amazed at how he felt the branch break, he was starting to realize how much of a power their gift really was. He lies in bed trying to feel the branches outside move with the wind, he does this until he falls to sleep.

That night his dreams were very strange. He dreamed he was walking through the woods, as he walked the trees were talking to him. Every time he took a wrong turn trees blocked his path telling him to go a different way, they kept telling him to call for help. If he didn't listen to them and walked the wrong way arrows would shoot out of the woods at him until he got back on the path the trees wanted him to travel, they kept telling him to call for help. At one point in his dream he saw the people from his mothers village calling out for help and the next moment he was there but as an old man. When he awoke he was sweating and a little scared, the dream burned in his mind. The last thing he remembers was himself with all women and children from his village walking down a strange path as the trees continue telling him to call for help. Andrew did not want to let his father know about the dream, he thought a dream about trees talking to him would discourage his father from opening his mind to the nature. He knew Jacob would understand so he would wait and talk with him.

The next couple of days went by quick, Daniel and his fathers training are very similar, both work very hard on blocking and striking moving around trying to make your enemy move the wrong way then striking back. Julian on the other hand came right at you, you either blocked or you were hit, one thing he noticed was the more he trained the easier it was to keep up. His legs were not sore in the morning and he was able to keep his wind. The next time he trained with Jacob he told him about his dream, Jacob didn't know what to think.

"Sometimes dreams are what you were thinking about that day. You have a lot on your mind, your mothers village was sick, starting to train, knowing your mind will be opened soon and you think that I talk to trees."

Andrew asks timidly, "Don't you?"

"Sometimes I do, lately I listen more than talk, most of the time I just want to be alone." He gives Andrew a look telling him not to tell anybody he wants to be alone and not really talking to the trees.

"Dreams can be funny, most dreams are just energy trying to get out. It builds and builds, it has to go some place. You have a lot going on lately, I'm not surprised you've had a strange dream, keep it in the back of your mind. Don't let it overwhelm you, it's just a dream until it's not a dream."

"What do you mean until its not a dream?"

"Well if you're walking down a path and the trees start talking to you, it's not a dream, and the first thing I would do is call for help! If you have this dream over and over, you should talk with your father about it, until then I wouldn't worry."

They continue training, Andrew has worked hard on focusing on the small branches, every one Jacob breaks Andrew feels, they run back to the village at a quick steady pace.

About two weeks go by after that with Andrew training every day, he has no problem keeping up, sometimes he is ahead. He is also learning how to fight and defend himself, he is getting better and his father lets him know. After one day of training with his father and they return home, Julian and Jacob are there already eating.

Andrew notices some bags packed, "Are you going somewhere?"

"We all are" his father replies.

"Mother also."

"No, your mother would not keep up, it will be the four of us."

"Are we going to the village Julian talked about?" Andrew asks with excitement in his voice.

"Don't get to excited. Its about an eight day walk, I plan on making it in five or less."

"Do you think I'm ready father?"

"You have impressed me so far, I might have a hard time keeping up with you at times."

Julian says under breath his but loud enough for everybody to hear, "I will surprised if the old man makes it."

"Old man! I'm not that much older than you."

They all laugh a little as they eat what's on the table. When Jonathan finishes his food he sits back and tells Andrew to drink plenty of water. After Andrew finishes with his work he spends the rest of the day playing with the younger children from the village. Before he goes home that evening he walks to the animals checking on them one more time before they leave.

He walks home and sees Daniel sitting by his fire cooking some meat, his wife is cutting some fruit.

"Is there anything I can do to help?" Andrew asks.

"Were really not doing much of anything right now." Daniel replies. He can tell something is on Andrews mind.

"If you really want to help you can finish cooking while I put some more wood on the fire." Daniel walks to the woodpile, gets a few small pieces and puts them on the fire. Andrew walks to the fire and turns the small deer cooking over it.

"What's on your mind?" Daniel asks.

"How do you think I'm doing?"

"What do you mean?"

Andrew looks back at him with a serious look, "How is my training going? And I want the truth, you have always been very honest with me and have told me the truth with little concern about how it had me feel. I want that now more than ever." He gives Daniel an unsure, somewhat sad look, "I'm not sure if the others are telling me I'm doing good only so they wont hurt my feelings."

Daniel looks at Andrew with the most serious look he has ever given Andrew, "You want the truth?"

Daniels wife Sandra walks over and sits beside Daniel. Daniel looks at his wife, then Andrew, "Someday we want a child, we have tried, it just has not happened. When we do we hope the child is as strong and smart as you, and as far as your training, you couldn't be doing any better. You make us both proud to be a part of your life."

Daniel gets up and puts his hand on Andrews shoulder, "Nobody is lying to you, you really are doing well."

These words put a smile on Andrews face, "Thank you." He says and gets up and starts walking toward his home, he turns back and asks Daniel if he can feed the animals while he is gone.

"Not a problem," Daniel answers.

Andrew walks to the stream before walking home to eat.

When he gets home, Julian and Jacob are there, his mother has made a large meal. She tells him to eat as much as he can, he knows in the morning he starts a long journey. He wants to eat and go to sleep. After eating he sits by the fire listening to the men talk while drinking ale.

He looks at his uncle, "Do you think I will like them? They are different from us."

"Different yes, but they are very friendly. I think you will like them just fine."

Andrew sits back and stares into the fire,

He wakes to his father's voice, "Go to bed, its getting late."

Andrew walks inside, gets in bed, quickly falling to sleep.

The next morning when he wakes he hears Julian and Jacobs voice, he quickly gets out of bed to help get ready for the trip. He sees that everything is already packed ready to go. They will only carry one bag of supplies each letting them travel more miles in less time. Andrew starts eating.

"Don't eat too much, it will slow you down, but drink plenty of water." His father says.

Andrew takes several big gulps of water and walks over to his mother. She hands a pouch filled with water, its made from a dry animal skin soaked in a certain tree oil then stretched in the center to form a pouch, tied at the top keeping the water in. The tree oil they use to soak it in keeps the water from seeping through the skin.

She gives him a kiss, "Don't over do it, if you get tired rest!"

She looks at her husband, then the other two men, "If you hurt my boy you have to answer to me." She gives them a strong look, "Understand!"

The three men all say, "Understand" at the same time.

Jonathan puts his hand on Andrew's head and messes up his hair, "Lets get going, you lead the way."

The four leave the home and start running at a slow pace. They run for about an hour when Jonathan says "Its time to speed it up"

After about ten minutes Andrew starts to breathe heavy but quickly gets his wind back.

Jonathan notices this, "Are you OK son, or do you want a rest already?"

"I'm fine father, I just lost my breath for a moment, I feel good now."

"OK, but don't be afraid to stop for a rest, its your first long journey."

They travel for more than half the day, with the bushes forming a path in front of them and closing behind them. Jonathan slows down and starts to walk, he is surprised that Andrew has kept up with them, never falling behind.

"We should stop for a rest and a bite to eat." He says.

They each pull a piece of dried meat cured with smoke out of their bags and drink some water, they sit for about ten minutes and rest.

Jonathan gets up, "Are you ready Andrew?"

"I feel fine father."

The four men start running at a steady pace again.

"Once the sun starts to go down and dusk is upon us we should start looking for some food." Jonathan says as he leads the group.

They run for the rest of the day, the three men are talking as they go, Andrew is just trying to keep his wind. They have stopped several times to rest along the way, Andrew is about to ask his father for another rest when Jacob puts his hand in the air and stops running. He looks into the thick bushes in the distance, they quickly tangle around two rabbits killing them before they can run.

Jacob walks into the bushes and brings them out, "That was easy."

Jonathan can see Andrew is breathing heavy and looks exhausted,

"We will walk for a while until we find a good spot to spend the night."

"I can run a while longer if you want me to."

"You have nothing to prove, you have already done better than I thought you would, I don't want you to over do it."

They walk until it starts to get dark, the entire time Jonathan is telling Andrew about the different leaves, roots and vines, what you can eat, what is poison, what oils can be extracted from different trees and vines and what it is used for. Andrew has heard this over and over but he listens, he knows his father likes to tell him.

His father points to a thick vine hanging from a tree, "See that vine Andrew?"

"That thick ugly looking vine?"

"Yes, the ugly one. Remember what it looks like, someday it might save your life."

"How can it save my life father?"

"That vine their holds water in it, even in the hottest days with no rain and no water to be found, that vine will have water in it. We can't survive without water."

They walk a little longer,

"This is the spot I was looking for."

Andrew looks at his father, "It's a little overgrown to spend the night, isn't it?" Seconds after Andrew says that the vines and bushes start to pull away creating a circular wall around them.

Jonathan looks at his son, "Don't worry, I know what I'm doing, now lets get a fire going."

It's not long before there is a hot fire going with the rabbits cooking over it.

"We should get our shelters made" Jonathan says, as he says this; vines and bushes start to move around and tangle with each other forming a small igloo shaped shelter.

"Andrew and I will sleep in this one."

Jonathan takes out his small heat lamp and walks into the woods to find some of the vines he gets the oil from. When he returns he hangs the lamp in the center of the shelter.

"This will keep us warm."

"Which shelter are you sleeping in?" he asks Jacob.

"That one." Jacob says as he points to one of the shelters, and then asks

"Why?"

"Can you go inside for a moment?"

"OK" Not sure what Jonathan is doing.

Once inside Jonathan asks, "Can you hear me?"

"Yes I can." Now Jacob very confused.

Jonathan gives his brother a wink, "I can also hear you Jacob, you can come out."

Once outside of the shelter Jacob asks, "What was that all about?"

"There is no way I'm letting your snoring keep us awake all night!"

As Jonathan says this, another layer of bushes forms over the top of Jacob's shelter.

"Good idea!" Julian says.

And yet another layer of bushes pulls away from the surrounding wall and form another layer over Jacob's shelter making it almost sound proof. They all laugh except Jacob. After that they sit by the fire and eat saving some of the meat for the morning.

Andrew falls to sleep sitting next to the fire. Jonathan doesn't wake him, he just carries him to the shelter and lights the heat lamp, the other three men go to sleep shortly after. Andrew sleeps well that night, he has never been so tired. He wakes to hear his father's voice.

"Let him sleep a while longer, he needs his rest."

Andrew gets up and walks out of the shelter, he can tell it's still early from where the sun is. "I didn't sleep too late, did I?

"You slept fine, its still early, how do your legs feel?" his father asks.

Andrew's legs are sore, but not too bad. "They are fine."

His father gives him a piece of meat from the night before and his water pouch,

"Drink all your water, you will need it. When you are finished I will fill it from some vines."

Andrew sits and eats a little more while his father replenishes their water pouches. Julian and Jacob cover the fire with some dirt, wrap what's left of the meat with some leaves and put it in their bags.

Jonathan gets back with the pouches full of water and puts his hand on Andrews back. "Are you ready."

"I am."

They start running at a slow pace, when they start running the vines and bushes of their shelters untangle and move back to where they were. Andrew is now able to talk as he runs, as long as they run at a steady pace, his wind is getting better.

They run for days stopping only to rest, sleep and eat, they talked the entire time about all sorts of things. As they travel through the wetlands Andrew was amazed at how his father used the roots from under the water to move up and form a path letting them cross like there was no water beneath, he had no idea there was such a large mass of water so close to them.

After passing through the wetlands Julian runs ahead and changes the path they are running.

"Why are you changing the path?" Jonathan asks.

He hears Julian's thoughts, *"There is a burned village with the remains of people ahead, and the remaining bones have arrows in them, so you can tell they were killed. I don't want Andrew to see that."*

Jonathan nods his head agreeing with Julian and follows him in the direction he is leading. Julian's emotions must have been stronger than he realized, Andrew heard every thought but says nothing, he has no desire to see anything like that. They have now run for many days at a steady pace. Andrew has been very tired at the end of each day but has no problem keeping up. On the fifth day when they stop for the night and are sitting by the fire Jacob says, "We will be there tomorrow."

"How far away are we?" Jonathan asks.

"If we keep at a steady pace tomorrow we should be there when the sun is highest in the sky."

"Has anyone thought about shelter when we arrive there?" Jonathan asks.

"Not really" Julian replies.

"Well we just cant turn bushes into huts when we get there, they might think we are different!"

"Do you have a plan?" Jacob asks.

"Yes, tonight we make our shelters with our hands."

"Have you ever done this before?" Julian asks.

"No, but it can't be to hard, we just use sticks and bushes making two small walls, angle them the right way and tie them together. Tie another small wall on the back to keep the wind out and face the front toward the fire for heat."

"That sounds like a lot of work." Julian says.

"Well you better get started." Jonathan says as he starts gathering the sticks he needs to make the walls. It takes about one hour and all three men have a small shelter, two walls covered with leaves and bushes wrapped with vines then covered with another layer of bushes, if it rains it should keep them reasonably dry.

"That wasn't so hard, was it?" Jonathan says.

"No, but if it rains and the fire goes out we will be very cold." Julian says in a sarcastic tone.

"I've already thought of that. We build another small wall or hang animal skins in the front, if it rains you cover the front, hang your heat lamp and stay warm."

"Sounds good to me." Julian says.

They sit by the fire eating what's left of the food they have saved before going to sleep. That night Andrew is awoken by the wind several times, he can hear a lot more outside noise in this shelter but it keeps them warm.

When he wakes in the morning he notices the ground is very damp, it must have rained a little and the hand made shelters kept then dry. Julian was up early using the wood from the shelter to make a fire, Jacob has caught a wild turkey and gathered some berries to eat. After the meat is cooked and all have eaten they start moving toward the village, this time they move at a slow pace.

A few hours pass and Jacob starts to walk, "We are very close, we should walk the rest of the way."

They walk for about a half hour or so when Jacob stops, "There is someone walking over that way." He points his finger.

The path they have been traveling fills in with bushes and they start pushing their way through them.

When they are able to see the man Julian smiles, "Its Roy."

"What is he doing?" Jonathan asks.

"It looks like he is hunting." Jacob says. "There is another man about a half mile away moving toward him making noise, just like we showed then."

Roy is now standing very still pointing his arrow into the woods. The four men stay where they are trying not to distract him as he hunts. Roy lets his arrow lose hitting a deer, before he can get another arrow ready two more run past him. As the deer with an arrow in it run close to the four men, Julian and Jacob both throw their small ax killing it, they start dragging it toward Roy.

"This almost got away," Jacob, says when he is close enough for Roy to hear.

Roy jumps and turns quickly, sees that it is Julian and Jacob, "Don't do that! You startled me." He puts his hand out to shake, "Good to see you."

Jacob shakes his hand, "How have you been?"

"I've been fine," Roy looks at Julian then Jonathan, "This must be your brother, he looks a lot like you."

"Pleased to meet you." Jonathan says as he puts his hand out to shake, "My brother says your village is a nice place, this is my son Andrew."

A voice from the woods can be heard, "**Did you catch anything?**"

Roy yells back, "**I caught a couple of big ones, come see.**"

A few moments pass and Samuel emerges from the woods, he smiles when he sees Julian and Jacob. "I wasn't sure if I would ever see you again?"

"I told you we would be back. How is Aaron's leg?"

"He is fine, the wound healed quicker than I've ever seen."

"I told you it would."

Roy then says to Samuel in a low voice, "Maybe they can help with Richard?"

"Melanie's husband Richard?" Julian asks.

"Yes" Roy says with a sad look, "We don't think he will make it."

"What's wrong with him?" Jonathan asks.

"He was beaten badly by the Lords men, after that he traveled to our village with his family, now he's sick, and we don't know why?"

"If we can help we will." Jonathan says.

They walk toward the village. When they get there Melanie and Pauline are sitting by the fire talking, Aaron is splitting some wood, they all stop what they are doing to great the men.

Young Sarah runs out of her home, sees Andrew "Hi, my name is Sarah, What's yours?"

"Hello my name is Andrew"

"Do you want to go play with some of the other children?"

Andrew looks at his father, "That's fine, just don't go far."

Andrew and Sarah walk toward the middle of the village.

Melanie's son Harold walks up and sits on his mothers lap, he has a very sad look, "My father is sick."

"I'm sorry to hear that." Jonathan says then looks at Melanie, "What's happened, why is he sick?"

She tells her son to go play with the other children, he gets up and runs to catch up with Andrew and Sarah.

Melanie looks at Jonathan, "Up until a few weeks ago we lived near the Lords grounds, it is a nasty place."

Melanie looks at Julian and Jacob knowing they have seen it. "Richard would not leave, his family had lived there for generations. A few weeks ago our son Harold walked up to some of the Lord's men, just to be friendly. It was too late to stop him, he said hi my name is Harold what's yours. That's when one of the men pushed him to the ground by his face, he started to cry as any young boy would.

Another one of the men picked him up by the hair, told him to stop crying and slapped his face a few times before throwing him to the ground again. Richard quickly ran over and said,

"Please don't hurt him, he's only a child, he means no harm." He picked Harold up and started walking back toward me. One of the five men ran behind Richard, hitting him in the back of the leg with his sword just below his knee dropping him to the ground.

Harold ran to me as one of the men said;

"Now you will take your sons beaten."

Melanie starts to cry, Pauline gives her a hug, she stops crying and takes a deep breath, "They viciously beat him until he was unconscious and kept beating him for a while after, I thought he was dead!"

Once again tears stream down her face, "He woke about two hours later, I wrapped his wound and we walked here leaving everything behind. Only now he's sick and getting worse."

Jonathan looks at Aaron, "Will you take me to see him?"

"Yes, but I don't think there is much more we can do, we keep cleaning and wrapping the wound the way your brother has showed us."

"I would still like to take a look."

Aaron and Jonathan walk to where Richard is. The moment Jonathan looks at him he can tell he is extremely ill. His face is still brushed and swollen from the beating but his skin looks very pale.

"We think the beating he took to the head is making him sick?" Aaron says with an unsure look.

"Not if he walked for days after the beaten." Jonathan puts his hand on Richard's head. "His head is very hot, he has infection, let me see the wound."

"OK," Aaron says,

"But it has a bad smell to it" Aaron unwraps the wound.

"That's what I was afraid of" Jonathan says in a discouraging voice.

The wound has a dark gray, almost black color to it and has a very bad smell. The rest of the leg below the knee is swollen with a purple color to it. They walk outside and back to the fire.

"The wound is infected, the infection has spread throughout his body." Jonathan looks at Jacob, "The mix you made for Rosemary's village make some and take Melanie with you and show her how. I don't know if it will help but it can't hurt."

Jacob and Melanie walk away to make as much of the mix as they can.

Aaron looks at Jonathan, "What can I do to help?"

"Go find me the sharpest knife you can find, some cloth and a bucket of water."

Aaron looks at him with a confused look, "What are you going to do?"

"Infection has set into the wound and poisoned his body." Jonathan gives him a grim look, "First we must get rid of the infection."

Aaron in a somber tone, "That's what the knife is for isn't it?"

"It's the only way, we must cut out the meat that has the dark color to it, or any bad smell."

"Is there any other way? That is a lot of his leg!"

"I know but if we don't he will not live. He may still die even if we do, but he will have a better chance." Jonathan pauses before saying, "If we do this, we must do it now! The longer the leg has infection the more poison enters his body."

"I will tell Melanie the moment she gets back." Aaron says then goes off to gather the stuff Jonathan asked for. Julian is already mixing the leaves with water into the pasty mix they need to put into the wound to help heal it. When Jacob returns with Melanie Jonathan tells him to mix some of the drink right away and have Melanie make Richard drink some.

Aaron comes back with the stuff Jonathan asked for and asks Melanie to take a short walk with him, she starts to cry when Aaron tells her what needs to be done. They walk back to the fire.

Melanie stops crying and looks at Jonathan, "If you think you can save my husband, do whatever is necessary." She starts crying again, "I have already excepted the fact that he will die." Pauline hugs her as she cries.

Jonathan has finished sharpening the knife on a stone, "It will take all of us to keep him steady."

He looks at Pauline, "If he cries out in pain, do not let Melanie or

Harold enter, they should not see this!"

Pauline nods her head then looks at Melanie, "Let's get Harold, we are going for a walk." They walk off into the distance to find Harold.

Inside the home Jonathan gives Aaron a piece of cloth that is folded and rolled up tight, "Put this in his mouth so he won't chip his teeth."

Aaron puts the cloth in Richards mouth and tells him what they are about to do and why. Richard barely conscious nods his head and softly says OK, then closes his eyes. Aaron puts his hands on Richards shoulders, Roy and Phillip each hold an arm. Samuel holds the leg that is not hurt to keep it from kicking and getting in the way. Julian and Jacob both hold the leg with the wound that Jonathan will be cutting.

Jonathan takes a good look at the infected area, he wants to know where to start and where to finish. When he starts to cut he wants to be quick and accurate, he also wants to be sure he gets all the decaying flesh out. He decides to cut out more than he thinks he needs making sure he gets it all.

He looks at the other men, "Are we ready?"

They all take a firm grip and hold Richard down as tight as they can. When Jonathan starts to cut Richard tries to move but is unable to, he bits down on the cloth and tears fill his eyes, within minutes he is completely unconscious. Jonathan cuts for a couple more minutes before he stops and wipes the blood away letting him take a better look. He cuts a little more, "I don't see any infection on the bone."

"The bone? You cut that much out?" Samuel asks.

"I had no choice, I cut all the infected meat out, if he lives he will have a hard time walking, but with time he will be able to." He pauses as he looks at the wound, "That is if he lives? There is a lot of poison in his body, we have stopped the cause of the poison, now its up to his body to fight the rest of it." He looks at Julian, "Get the healing mix, fill and wrap the wound."

Jonathan turns to Aaron, "It must be cleaned and cleanly wrapped twice a day until skin starts to form." He then tells Jacob to get the drink he has made,

"This drink helps the body when you are sick. I have no idea if it will work on poison from infection, but it can't hurt. He must drink as much as you can make him."

When Julian finishes wrapping the leg they wake Richard and give him some of the drink, he takes a large sip and falls back to sleep.

Jonathan looks around, "I think we are done here, lets clean the mess and let him sleep."

"You have already done enough, we will clean up." Aaron says.

The three men walk to the fire where there is a bucket of water and some cloth to wash with. The other men clean the mess and join them by the fire. Andrew and Sarah come running up, they have been playing all day and have no idea what's been going on.

Andrew can tell by looking at his father something was wrong,

"What's wrong?" he asks.

"Nothing, now go play, I want you to have a good time."

Andrew looks at his father, "OK, but you will tell me later, wont you?"

"Yes I will, but right now I want you to have fun."

Andrew and Sarah both take a piece of bread and run off to play with the other children. A short time passes when Melanie, Pauline and Harold come back and sit next to the fire. There is a long moment of silence as they all stare into the fire.

Jonathan says to Harold, "Why don't you run off and play with the other children for a while."

Harold looks at his mother, who nods her head, "Go play but take some bread with you. When you get hungry come back, some food will be waiting."

Andrew hears his fathers thoughts, *"Harold is coming to play, try to make him laugh."*

Andrew stops and looks at Sarah, "Harold is coming to play with us." The two walk back to meet him.

Back at the fire Jonathan explains to Melanie what they have done. He tells her that even if he lives he will never walk the same again.

"I don't care if he walks at all, I just want him to live." Melanie says with tears in her eyes.

Jonathan stands up and puts his hand on Melanie's shoulder, "Lets go see him, it might make him feel better."

They walk toward the home where he is. When inside Melanie sits next to her husband and quietly weeps. She can see where the leg is wrapped and his head is still very hot. Richard opens his eyes to see Melanie sitting there, he says nothing, just squeezes her hand and closes his eyes again.

Jonathan quietly says, "You should give him some of that drink." He points to a jug.

She pours some into a small cup, tilts his head forward and pours some into his mouth making him drink. She kisses him on the cheek, covers him up, "I will be back in a while to check on you but for now get some rest."

The two walk out and sit by the fire.

"We can't thank you enough, "Aaron looks at the three men, "Every time you come here you help us."

"I told you before," Julian says, "That's what friends do."

Pauline stands up and puts her hand on Melanie's back, "Lets get some food cooking it's starting to get late."

Jacob stands up and looks at Melanie, "Stay seated, I will help cook, you get some rest, you have a lot on your mind." Jacob and Pauline walk away to gather some food.

Jonathan stands up and pokes Julian with his stick, "Lets make our shelter's for the night."

Roy asks if they need any help.

"That wont be necessary." Julian replies.

The two men walk into the woods and gather the stickers they need to make the walls and lay them on the ground, vines and bushes tangle and wrap around them as they watch, within seconds the walls are made and they start dragging them out of the woods. When they get them close to the fire they angle them just right and tie the tops with some vines and ask Aaron for some skins to cover the front to keep the weather out. Aaron amazed at how quickly they have built the shelters gathers some skins for them. When he gets back they tie the skins to the front draping it over the top. If it gets cold they can pull it down covering the front and light their heat lamp. The children have all come back and are now eating. Andrew is sitting next to Sarah.

Jonathan hears Julian's thoughts, *"Have you noticed they haven't left each others side."*

"How can you not notice?"

They sit by the fire a while longer before going to sleep.

Chapter Thirteen

The next morning Jonathan is surprised to see Andrew has woken before him. When he hears Sarah's voice, he looks over to see the two are sitting by the fire. They have started to warm some soup and bread. Jonathan lies in his shelter listening to the two talk and giggle for a while.

He finally gets up and tells his son, "Don't eat to much, we have a morning run to do."

"I'm ready whenever you are." He turns to Sarah, "We run, stretch and learn how to protect ourselves everyday, it keeps us strong."

Julian starts to wake up, Jacob is still snoring, he wont be up for a while.

When Julian makes his way to the fire, Jonathan asks him, "Will you take Andrew for a run? I want to check on Richard."

"That's fine, just let me wake and have a small bite to eat."

Jonathan gets up and walks to the home where Richard is sleeping. When he walks in he sees Melanie lying on the ground holding Richards hand, her eyes are barely open but she's still awake.

Jonathan takes her hand, "Go get some sleep, I will change the wrap and stay with him for a while."

She walks over to the other side of the home, covers herself with a large animal skin and falls to sleep. Jonathan feels Richards head, it still very hot, he then takes off the wrap and looks at the wound, it still looks clean with no infection so he put more of the healing mix on it and wraps it up clean. He then sits Richard up and pours some of the drink into his mouth Richard swallows some but spills most. After that Jonathan puts some more wood in the fireplace keeping the home warm and walks back outside to join the others by the fire.

Pauline and Aaron are now awake talking with Jacob.

Jonathan looks at Pauline, "Melanie needs some rest, she is going to make herself sick."

"What can I do?" she asks.

"Sit with her in the home so she knows someone is watching Richard while she sleeps. Don't bother her know, I think she is sleeping."

"I will wait until she wakes and bring her some soup."

"You should also try to feed Richard a little something, even if he eats a small amount it will help."

Julian and Andrew have been running for a while, when Julian says, "You like that girl, don't you?"

"I don't play with kids my age often, she's just fun to talk to."

"I see," Julian says, "Fun to talk to. You know what I think?"

"What do you think?"

Julian turns his head toward Andrew and with a big grin, in a teasing voice says.

"Andrew has a girlfriend!" as he starts to run faster leaving Andrew behind.

"I do not!" Andrew yells as he speeds up to catch his uncle.

They run for about an hour then stretch a little before going over some blocks and counter strikes. As they walk back toward the village Julian tells Andrew that he should start looking for a walking stick.

"You never know where you will find the perfect stick."

"I have already started to look."

On the way back to Aaron's home they walk through the center of the village, some people greet Julian, they recognize him from the last time he was there. Andrew sees some of the children playing a game they showed him the day prior.

There are four big baskets surrounding a small one. Ten stones are what you start with and stand a long distance away from the baskets. Each person takes turns throwing the stones trying to get them in the baskets, the first person with no stones wins. If you get a stone in the small basket the person with the least stones has to take the stones from the bucket with the most, it was fun for the children to pass time.

"If you want to stay here and play that would be fine." Julian says.

"I think I will go eat first, I'm a little hungry."

They walk back toward Aaron's home, when they arrive there Andrew has a bowl of soup and some bread.

Sarah sits on a rock next to him, "I waited for you to go play."

Andrew looks at his uncle who is smiling at him, his cheeks turn red.

Pauline turns and looks at Sarah, "Don't forget about helping gather some vegetables."

Andrew smiles at Sarah then turns toward Pauline, "I will help her, that way you can stay and help with Richard."

"You people have already done enough," Pauline says.

"It will be fun for me." Andrew answers.

Jonathan adds, "The boy is right, your help is needed here."

Pauline looks at Sarah, "Fill the wagons first, Phillip and Roy will be bringing some food to the Lords men, they leave in the morning."

"OK mother"

Andrew has finished eating so the two walk off toward the garden.

As they are walking Andrew asks, "Why are they traveling in the morning with food?"

"If we don't bring the food to them, they will come here and take it, if they come here they will probably destroy everything and kill most of us, so we bring them the food."

"That's not right!" Andrew says with anger, "You should say no and when they come, fight!"

Sarah stops walking and looks at Andrew, "Don't let anyone hear you talk like that! There are too many, if anybody says no they die! They will kill everyone in a village and have fun doing it."

Sarah now has tears in her eyes, "We give them what they want so they stay away."

Andrew is saddened that a young girl only ten years of age knows so much about people killing others just because they want to. He stops talking about it and tries to make her laugh by pretending to trip and fall, but when he does this he rolls all the way over and lands on his butt with his legs straight out.

"I'm OK." He says.

She laughs and puts her hand out to help him up.

"Your funny" she says.

Andrew takes her hand and gets up, "After we pick the vegetables lets go play with the other children."

"That sounds like fun."

They walk into the garden and start picking vegetables, there are other people also gathering some. It's not long before they fill both wagons. After they are filled Sarah grabs a bucket from the front entrance of the garden, they are left there for anybody to use and everybody brings them back.

"Once this is full we are done," Sarah says, "All we have to do is bring it home and we can go play."

"Lets hurry and fill it then."

The two start picking all sorts of vegetables to fill the bucket. When its filled Andrew asks her to let him carry it back. The two walk back toward Sarah's home. On the way they pass the place where the children gather to play, it's in the center of the village, the older children can play keeping watch on the younger ones. The adults can go about their business with little worry. As they pass one of the other children, a boy a little older than Andrew, Paul yells,

"Are you coming back to play?"

Sarah yells back, **"After we bring the vegetables home."**

"Good" Paul replies, **"Andrew is fun to play against, he beat me yesterday, but not today!"**

Paul is the oldest of the young children and always wins the games. When the two get back Andrew asks his father if there is anything else he can help with.

"That will be all for now, go have some have fun."

Both children run off to meet the other children, they spend most of the day playing all sorts of games, Andrew wants to remember all of them so when he is at home and at his mothers village he can show the other children how to play. Close to the end of the day all the children, fourteen all together from the ages five to thirteen have a big game of hide and seek. Andrew has a lot of fun just running and laughing, he tries to stay with Sarah hiding in the same spots most of the time, he really likes her company and enjoys talking with her. There are some older kids in the village but they run off into the thick forest and find other ways to play and pass time. As the daylight starts to fade away the children decide its time to go to their homes and get some food. Andrew and Sarah race back to her home, Andrew let's her win, but not by much.

"I win," Sarah cries out.

"I would have won, but I had to stop and catch my breath."

Jonathan smiles at Andrew, he knows his son can run for a long distance without loosing wind. The two children sit next to Harold, he wanted to be near his father so he came home earlier and sat with him for a while.

Sarah takes a look around, "Where's mother?" she asks her father.

"She's sitting with Richard letting Melanie get some sleep."

Andrew gets up to get some soup, he takes two bowls and gives one to Sarah, he is about to sit when he hears his father's thoughts,

"Give the other bowl to Harold, he hasn't eaten much today."

Andrew looks at the sad look on Harold's face and put the soup in front of him, "This is for you."

"I'm not very hungry."

"You should eat anyway, at least a little, it will keep you strong so you can help your father when he gets better."

Harold takes the soup and looks at Andrew, "Thank you." He says and starts eating.

Andrew goes to get himself another bowl of soup. They sit by the fire talking for a while, it is now dark outside and you can hear all the night animals over the crackle of fire. Everyone stops talking when they see Pauline walk up to Aaron and whisper in his ear.

Aaron looks at Jonathan, "Can you come with me?"

Pauline and the two men walk into the home, everybody by the fire is extremely quiet. About five minutes pass and Pauline quickly walks out, takes a bowl of soup and walks back in without saying anything. At least ten more minutes pass, the three walk out and sit next to the fire.

Jonathan looks at young Harold, "You should go talk to your father while he's awake."

Harold smiles and quickly gets up and runs into the home.

Julian asks his brother, "How is he?"

"He's awake and eating, but is still very sick."

"Do you think he will live?" Jacob asks.

"I think he is getting better." Jonathan looks at Aaron and Pauline, "Even after we leave that wound must be cleaned and rewrapped twice a day or he will die."

Aaron looks at Jonathan with a serious look, "I will make sure it's done."

"When Harold comes out I will show you what you need to do and tell you what flesh you will need to cut out if need be."

About twenty minutes pass, both Harold and Melanie walk out. Jonathan stands up and asks Melanie if he's sleeping, she tells him he is.

"You should also see this." He says looking at Melanie.

Aaron gets up and the three walk back inside. Inside Jonathan cuts the wrap of the wound. Melanie's legs wobble a little and her face turns pale when she sees how much of the meat has been cut out. Most of the meat from the back of the knee all the way to the ankle is missing.

Jonathan looks into her eyes, "It had to be done or he would already be dead." He then shows Aaron and Melanie what to look for and how to keep the wound clean. He explains that if any bad smell or the meat turns dark gray or black, all you will be able to do is take the leg off and try to keep that wound clean; that's why its important to keep it clean now. He puts a thick layer of the pasty mix on the wound covering any exposed meat and wraps the wound tightly. He tells them not to wrap the leg to tight, blood has to flow through. Wrap it just tight enough so the dirt and dust will stay out. Jonathan then puts his hand on Richards's head to feel how hot it is.

"His head feels a little cooler, that is all we can do for tonight, tomorrow we will know."

They walk back out to the fire, Melanie asks Harold if he wants to sleep with her that night, he quickly gets up and says yes. The two walk back inside the home where Richard is and go to sleep. The rest sit by the fire well into the night talking and laughing as they drink ale.

That night Andrew wakes to another bad dream, this time it is very vague. All he can remember is a large tree, it's the same big tree he saw in his last dream. He tries to walk past it and the branches stop him and push him in the other direction, as he walked in the direction he can hear the tree telling him to call for help. The tree said it several times before Andrew wakes up to see his father sleeping next to him. He lie there for several minutes trying to figure out what it meant, if anything, then falls back to sleep.

The next morning he wakes to hear his father and uncle talking by the fire. As he sits up he remembers the dream but doesn't think much about it. He thinks it was just a strange dream, all he can really remember was a big ugly tree. He gets up and sits by the fire.

"Its still early son, if you want you can rest a while longer." His father looks at him, "Or would you like to talk about the dream you had last night?"

Andrew with a surprised look asks, "How did you know?"

"You were talking in your sleep, you were also tossing and turning, I had no choice but listen."

"It was just a bad dream." Andrew says.

"Well if you want to talk about it my ears are open." His father does not want to tell him that Jacob has told him about his other bad dream so he doesn't pry any further.

Andrew still a little tired, "I think I will rest for a while longer, but don't let me sleep to long, I have my training to do."

Andrew walks back into his shelter and falls back to sleep. Jonathan and Julian get the fire going strong and heat up the soup and start warming some bread.

Melanie walks up to the fire, "Good, your awake."

"Is everything alright?" Jonathan asks.

"Richard is awake and hungry, I'm not sure what to do?"

"Feed him!" Jacob cries out from his shelter.

Jonathan and Julian try not to smile until they see the smile on Melanie's face.

"I know that!" She says looking at Jonathan, "When he's done eating I want you to watch me change the wrapping on his wound, making sure I do it right."

"I will go with you. Is Harold still sleeping?"

"Yes, he woke up throughout the night, but he's sleeping now." Jonathan takes a glance at Julian, "Why don't you pick up Harold and lie him next to Andrew, he shouldn't see his fathers wound until we know he will get better."

They all walk into the home, Julian quietly and carefully picks up Harold and walks him into Jonathan's shelter. As he puts him down

Andrew opens his eyes, Julian puts his finger over his lips telling him to be quiet, Andrew closes his eyes and goes back to sleep. Julian walks back into Melanie's home.

When Richard sees him he smiles, "I'm glad I offered you food and rest when you were passing through, Melanie has told me you and your brother saved my life."

"Try not to talk, just eat and rest."

Julian then looks at Jonathan, "Is his head still hot?"

"It's a little warm, but I think he will live"

Richard interrupts, "Just not walking for a while but a least alive!"

"Don't worry about walking right now, just rest." Jonathan gives him a serious stare, and then turns toward Julian. "While you are resting we will make you some sticks that will help you walk, don't worry when you are better you will get around."

Jonathan gives Melanie some of the drink and tells Melanie to make sure he drinks it all. The two men start walking out of the home.

"This stuff tastes awful!" Richard cries.

"Then drink it quickly." Julian says, "It will help you get better."

The two men exit the home leaving Melanie and Richard alone. Back at the fire Andrew and Jacob are now sitting with Aaron, Pauline and some of the other men from the village, they are eagerly waiting to hear how Richard is. Jonathan takes seat by the fire, grabs a piece of bread and looks at all the faces waiting to hear now Richard is,

"I think he will be fine." He takes a bite from the bread then looks at the men sitting by the fire, "He will not walk for a long time and when he can walk it won't be very good. He will need all your help providing for his family."

"Everybody in this village will be happy to help." Aaron says, "We just can't thank you enough."

"No need to thank us, we're friends. "Julian says.

Andrew then asks his father, "Are we going for a run this morning,"

If they were he wants to get going so he can get back and play with the other children.

Jacob stands up, "I want to take him today, I'm in the mood for a morning run."

"That will be fine," Jonathan says.

The two run off toward the woods, they run for about half an hour and stop, Jacob tells Andrew to stretch for a while, and does some stretching himself. When they are done Jacob asks Andrew to sit and focus into the woods and points,

"That way," he says, "Try to feel anything moving."

Andrew stares in a deep concentration for about ten minutes then looks at Jacob.

"I think I feel something, but it feels strange? It doesn't feel like an animal or a person walking."

"That's fine, try to describe to me what it feels like." Jacob says with a serious look.

Andrew looks back into the woods he stares for a moment longer, "This may sound crazy, but it feels like an enormous snake!"

"That doesn't sound crazy at all, I wanted to bring you here for a reason."

"What reason is that?"

"You do not know this area, you have no idea what's over there." Jacob stands up, "Try to keep focusing on it as we walk closer."

Andrew stands up and follows Jacob focusing so intense he has a hard time walking without stumbling as he walks.

As they get closer to what Andrew is feeling, he is amazed when he realizes it's a stream. He is feeling the water moving through the bushes on its edge.

"There is not much more I can teach you about how I do this, all you can do now is practice and get better."

"I will practice every day." Andrew still amazed, looking at the stream.

"Lets go back to the village so you can play with the other children," Jacob smiles at Andrew, "Or should I say spend some more time with young Sarah!"

Andrew gives him a friendly push, "Shut up!!" he says and starts running toward the village, Jacob follows.

When they arrive back at the village they both have some soup and bread. Harold has already run off to play with the other children. Most of the men have gone about their business, Andrews father, uncle and Aaron are the only ones sitting by the fire.

"Has Sarah gone off to play?" Andrew asks.

"No, she's inside helping her mother getting things ready to cook for tonight." Aaron yells for his daughter to come out. She comes to the opening of the home and sees Andrew, she looks back at her mother,

"Can I go play?"

"That will be fine."

Sarah runs to her father, "Can I show Andrew where the two streams meet?"

Aaron looks at her with a long stare, "Do you promise to stay off the slippery rocks?"

"I promise."

Aaron tells Jonathan that the rocks are very slippery and the water is very deep and fast.

He looks back at his daughter, "I mean it! Do you promise to stay off the rocks?"

"Yes father, I promise."

"If its OK with Andrews father, and you promise to stay off the rocks I guess it will be OK."

Jonathan looks at Andrew, You heard him; stay off the rocks!"

Sarah smiles at Andrew, "Take some bread with you, it's a long walk."

The two children each take some bread and walk past the wall that surrounds the village and into the thick forest. They walk until they find the stream the men from the village fish in, its about twenty feet across and the water moves very quickly.

Andrew thinks to himself, *"This is not the stream I saw earlier."*

The two children follow the stream through the woods, they see many animals drinking from it, and all sorts of fish swimming in it.

"With all these fish in the water why don't you eat more fish?" Andrew asks.

"Fish are hard to catch, my father gets some with a sharp stick, but it's never enough."

Andrew stops, "A sharp stick? We make fish traps letting the fish catch themselves, all we have to do is walk to the stream and gather them. I will have my father show yours how to make them and you can have fish more often."

The two keep walking on the path near the stream, Andrew can see its walked often by the dirt on the ground and how the bushes are pushed away from the trail.

They walk a while longer when they start to hear the water roar in the distance.

Sarah looks at Andrew, "This is the place I wanted to show you."

She runs ahead following the stream until it turns and joins with another stream, the two streams form into a rapidly moving river with enormous rocks on each side. The rocks have been worn smooth by the water rushing through them. The water between the rocks moves at a rough intense pace. The sides of the rocks shine with water, and the angle down is rather steep, the water looks very deep. The sight almost takes Andrews breath away.

"It's really amazing," He says as he stands and looks at it for a while.

"Beautiful isn't it?" Sarah says.

"Yes" as he sits on the edge of the dirt looking down at the violently moving water.

Sarah continues walking toward the rocks on the streams edge.

"Remember your promise to your father!" Andrew yells loud so she can hear him over the roar of the water.

Sarah walks back to Andrew and sits beside him, "My father takes me hear often, usually when he tries to catch fish, sometimes I think he just wants to get away from the village for a while. He doesn't really try very hard to catch fish most of the time we end up here just talking."

"Maybe he wants to spend the day with you," Andrew smiles at Sarah, "It is very peaceful here and you make good company."

Sarah smiles back, "So do you." She pauses then says, "I'm glad I brought you here."

They both sit silent for several moments while they look and listen to the water.

"My father never lets me get close," Sarah says as she stands up and walks onto the rocks.

"I'm sure he has a good reason, its probably very slippery near the edge."

"Don't worry, I'm not even close to the edge, I just want to see some fish rush through."

Andrew now stands up, "Sarah, I'm not kidding! Your on the wet part of the rocks, come back here!"

She turns and looks at Andrew, "I'll be fine, I just want to."

Before she can finish her sentence both feet slip out from under her, she screams as she lands flat on her back and slides into the rapidly moving water. The violent water twisting and turning her body as she tries to keep her head above, the water quickly pushes her off into the distance. The very instant Sarah's feet slide Andrew stands up and runs to the waters edge and without hesitation dives in head first, he swims as hard and as fast as he can watching her head go above and below the water.

He tries yelling to her, **"Calm down and keep her head above the water!"**

The sound of the water is to loud for her to hear him so he just swims as hard as he can! It takes several long minutes but he finally catches up to her, she is kicking and screaming. Andrew can see she is in a panic choking and swallowing the water. He gets behind her and puts his arms under hers holding her head above the water and uses his feet to keep them both afloat.

"Calm down! Calm down!" Andrew yells he keep saying it until she realizes Andrew is holding her above the water and she can breath without choking, she stops screaming and starts crying.

"Don't cry yet, we still need to get to the edge and out of the water."

The water is moving extremely fast and they have to avoid hitting rocks. Andrew uses his feet to direct them toward the edge, it takes some time but he is finally able to grab a branch and pull himself and Sarah to the edge where they are able to climb out of the water. Sarah puts her arms around Andrew and starts crying hysterically.

Andrew hugs her back, "Its OK we're safe now." She stops crying.

Andrew realizes she is now shivering from the cold. "Let me start a fire." He says.

They both gather some wood and Andrew gets a fire going, he makes it fairly large so they can dry their cloths. They sit for a moment to warm up then Andrew gets up to gather some sticks and vines. He drives the sticks into the ground close to the fire and ties the vines from one stick to another as tight as he can.

Andrew looks at Sarah, who is still shivering a little, "Don't worry, its OK we are near a warm fire now?" he pulls his shirt off and gives it to her, "I know its wet, but you can cover yourself with this while you hang your cloths on the vines by the fire, they will dry quickly there, I'm going to find some food."

Sarah still sobbing a little but the warmth from the fire has taken the chill away.

"Don't leave me." She says and starts to cry again.

"You will be able to see me, I'm just going to dig up some roots."

Sarah gives him a strange look, "Roots?"

"Their not very tasty, but you can eat them."

Andrew walks around, finds and digs up four of the roots he wants. They are long brown roots with a somewhat round shape to them. He walks to the stream and washes the dirt off them, he then walks back to the fire and sits down.

Sarah looks at the roots with a disgusted look, "You eat that?"

"We sit it next to the fire for a while and it gets soft so you can bite and chew it easily. There's really not much taste at all."

"I will try it, but don't think I will like it!"

They both giggle as Andrew puts the roots as close to the fire as he can. They sit for a while letting the fire take the chill out of their bones.

Sarah is very quiet staring into the fire, "You saved my life,"

"I just did what another would do."

"No, most would have let me die." She starts to cry a little, "You could have died trying to save me because I was doing something stupid."

"You weren't being stupid, you just went onto the rocks you promised your father you would not go no. Then you ignored me telling you to stop and fell into a viciously flowing river." He smiles at her then laughs a little, "OK you were being a little stupid." She laughs back at him.

Andrew reaches out and feels her clothes hanging, "I think they are dry."

Sarah puts her cloths back on and gives Andrew his shirt back, which he hangs over the vine.

He then pulls the roots away from the fire, "You have to let them cool for a while, they are very hot!"

"How far down stream do you think we traveled?" Sarah asks.

"I'm not sure, the water is moving really fast so we probably went quite far."

"Are we lost?"

"No, we can just follow the stream back to where we were," He gives her a big smile before saying, "Just stay off the rocks!"

After a short while he picks up the roots, "Here you go, but be careful they are still a little hot."

She takes a look at the root, then back at Andrew, "You first."

Andrew takes a bite, "See it's not that bad."

Sarah takes a bite, "It really doesn't taste like anything." She continues to eat it.

After they both eat Andrew puts his shirt back on, "We should start back.

He gets up and puts the fire out by covering it with dirt. The two start walking following the stream.

As they are walking Sarah stops and looks at Andrew, "Please don't tell my father about this."

"That's up to you, but I will tell my father." Andrew replies.

"If you tell your father he will tell mine."

"Yes, there's a good chance of that."

"Then why tell him?"

"Because, if I don't tell him and he finds out, he will be mad."

"How will he find out if we don't tell him?" Sarah asks knowing her father will be furious at her for not listening.

"My father finds out everything."

The two keep walking, it takes an hour or so before they get back to where Sarah fell into the water. They take another look at how stunning it is before they start walking back to the village.

They talk the entire way about different things, Andrew keeps pointing out different types of plants and what they can be used for. He realizes he sounds a lot like his father. Sarah asks him several times along the way for him not to tell his father. Each time she asks Andrew tells her that he will know something is wrong or has happened.

Andrew thinks to himself, "*He probably already knows, this was too much excitement to hide my thoughts.*"

When they arrive back at the village they sit by the fire with the others.

Sarah's father looks at the two, "You two were gone for a long time, did you have fun?"

The very instant Jonathan looks at his son he asks, "What happened?" in a stern voice.

Sarah not giving Andrew a chance to answer, "I fell in the water and Andrew pulled me out, it was really no big deal."

Jonathan knowing there was a lot more to the story than that, "Well OK then, as long as you're both alright." He looks at the two children and smiles.

"Why are you not wet?" Aaron asks his daughter.

"Andrew made a fire so I could dry my clothes." Sarah tells her father. She then asks, "How is Richard?" Wanting to quickly change the subject.

"Richard will be fine."

Jonathan adds, "His head is cool and he is eating. It will be a long time before he is out of bed. You should try to keep young Harold occupied while he heals."

Sarah smiles, "I will do my best."

Jonathan then tells her that after the winter they will come back to visit.

"When are we going home?" Andrew asks

"We will stay tomorrow, we head home the first thing the next day." He looks at Andrew, "There will be no running for you tomorrow morning, OK."

Aaron tells Sarah to go get Harold who was playing with the other children in the center of the village. "Your mother has cooked a lot, so hurry back."

The two children run off to get Harold. It's not long before they come back with Harold, Melanie and Pauline are both sitting by the fire eating.

Harold sits next to his mother. "Will father be OK?" he asks.

She looks at him with a big smile, "We think he will be fine."

Harold hugs his mother, then runs over to Jonathan and gives him a big hug,

"Thank you for saving my father. Thank all of you!"

Jonathan puts his hand on Harold's shoulder, looks him in the eyes, "Your father will be extremely sore for a long time, Even when he is healed he will have a hard time walking. You must be a strong boy and help him as much as you can."

Aaron adds, "Don't be afraid to ask for help, there are many of us here that will be happy to."

Harold looks at Jonathan, "I will do my best."

He then sits down next to his mother and starts eating. The rest of the early evening is spent sitting around the fire talking about a lot of different things.

Jonathan tells Aaron he will show him how to make fish traps when they wake so they can eat fish more often. Andrew and Sarah are both very tired and go to bed very early. As Andrew lie in his shelter he can hear the adults talking, he falls to sleep thinking about how much he is going to miss Sarah and is already looking forward to the next time he will see her.

The next day goes by quickly, Andrew spends most of the day in the middle of the village playing with all the children. After they eat that night Andrew and Sarah walk around the village, they are both happy they have met, but they also know that it will be a long time before they see each other again. Andrew promises that he will come to visit as much as possible. They spend the rest of the night sitting by the fire side-by-side listing to the adults talk until its time to go to sleep. They give each other a hug, Andrew walks to his shelter and Sarah walks into her home.

Jonathan says to Aaron, "It looks like we will come visit often."

Aaron smiles, "I don't think you will have a choice."

Jonathan, Julian and Jacob all go to bed shortly after Andrew, they will start their journey home early.

Chapter Fourteen

Jonathan is up early the next morning, he wants everything ready so when the other three wake they can have a bite to eat and go. He quietly walks into Richards home trying not to wake anybody, he smiles when he feels Richard's head, it feels cool. Jonathan is sure that as long as they keep the wound clean he will live. Before he can take his hand away, Richard reaches up and grabs his hand,

"Thank you," he says.

"I'm just thankful I could help." Jonathan quietly says.

"Will I ever see you again?"

"Yes, we will travel here often."

Jonathan puts his finger over his mouth telling Richard to be quiet. They don't want to wake Melanie and Harold who are sleeping next to him. When he turns to walk out he sees that Melanie's eyes are open, she doesn't say a word, just a smile as he walks out. When he gets back to the shelter Julian and Jacob are already awake and eating some bread and cheese, Andrew is just opening his eyes.

"Time to get up, we are getting ready to head for home." Jonathan says to his son.

Andrew wants to stay longer but he also wants to start training with the other men from his village learning how to fight, he gets up and sits next to the other men, eats some bread and drinks at much water as he can. After he eats he helps his father break down the shelters they have made. The last thing they do is fill their water pouches before running into the woods in the direction of their village. They run for about half an hour, Jonathan asks Jacob if there is anybody around them.

Jacob stops for a moment, looks around, "No, there is nobody around for miles."

"Good. Running through these bushes is a lot of work!"

As he says this all the bushes and vines they are pushing their way through pull out of their way off to the side making a clear path for them to travel. They start running again this time at a faster pace. They travel the same way they traveled on the way there. Andrew has no problem keeping up with the older men, they stop several times each day for food and rest, he tries to drink a lot of water each day. As they travel over the wetlands Andrew is still amazed at how his father can bring the roots to the surface creating a path for them to run on.

They run a little faster on the way home, they arrive on the fifth night of running. By the time they get there it is late but Rosemary has warm food waiting for them. Andrew gives his mother a big hug and starts eating.

"How was the trip?" She asks her husband.

"The best way to describe it would be interesting." He smiles at her.

"Are they nice people?"

"They are very nice, and happy to have us stay with them."

"Did you have fun Andrew?"

"Yes mother, I had a lot of fun."

"Were there any children your age to play with?"

Before Andrew can answer Julian And Jacob both say at the same time, in a teasing voice, "Andrew has a girlfriend."

Andrew's cheeks turn red, "She's just a girl my age!"

"Stop teasing the boy." Rosemary says, then looks at her husband, "What are they talking about?"

Jonathan looks at his son, then Julian and Jacob and back at Rosemary,

"I have to agree with Julian and Jacob." He turns to his son and in the same teasing voice, "Andrew has a girlfriend."

Rosemary looks at her son and smiles, "I want to know all about her tomorrow, but now its too late."

They finish eating and Andrew goes to bed. He can hear the adults talking as he lies there, they tell his mother about Richards leg and are still talking about the village when he finally falls to sleep.

The next morning his father wakes him early, "Have a bite to eat and lets get going."

"I thought I was going to start tomorrow?" Andrew says like a question.

"You are but I think it would be a good idea for you to sit and watch for today. We do a lot of fast paced training, it will be hard for you to keep up if you've never seen it before."

Andrew is happy to hear that he will only be watching today, he is still a little tired and his legs are still a little sore from the run home. He quickly eats a piece of bread and drinks some water. He takes another piece of bread for the walk, before leaving with his father he gives his mother a kiss on the cheek and the two walk out the opening of their home.

As they walk his father tells him to be very quiet while the men are training but to pay close attention. Andrew is a little nervous but very eager wanting to learn.

"Try to relax, you will make mistakes, that is why we practice." Jonathan puts his hand on Andrews shoulder before they walk in, "Just remember one thing, we have all been training from the time we were your age every day, most of us twice a day, we make things look easy that will be hard for you, give it time, you will learn."

"I will try my hardest."

"That is all I ask of you." The two walk inside the training area.

Once inside Andrew looks around, he has been here before but has never taken a good look around. He looks at all the men, about forty of them, they all have a very serious looks on their faces.

Jonathan turns to his son, "Everybody is treated with the up most respect while we are in here, nobody is better or less than the other, we are all treated like worriers going into battle. That's the way it is, and has always been."

Andrew takes a look at Julian and Jacob and the serious look on their faces, then looks back at his father. He now realizes how serious these men take their training and the ways of their ancestors.

"I understand." He says as he backs up against the wall to stay out of the way.

Joseph walks up to the two, he puts one of his hands in a fist out in front of his chest and wraps the other hand around it, tilts at the waist keeping his eyes on Jonathan, who does the same thing back.

"I thought Andrew was going to start training tomorrow?" Joseph asks.

"He is but I thought it would be a good idea for him to watch today."

"It can not hurt." Joseph says as he turns toward Andrew, "Are you sure your ready?"

"I think so," Andrew says hesitant, "I will do my best."

"You will do fine." Joseph says, and then adds, "The air is cold today. It would be nice if you kept the fires hot."

Andrew looks at the two fires that are burning at each end of the training area,

"I can do that."

Joseph still looking at Andrew, "We will stay on some simple basic stuff for a while, it will be easy for you to learn." He tilts his body at him the same way he did toward his father. Andrew not sure what it meant does the same thing back. Joseph turns and walks away.

Jonathan looks at his son knowing what he is about to ask, "It's a sign of respect, you do it the first time you talk to someone in here, before you fight anybody and before you leave. It comes from our ancestors and is an important part of our culture, it is called a bow."

Andrew watches as his father walks toward the center of the training area, and lines up with all the other men. The men line up in two separate rows facing each other, each man has about ten paces on each side. The men stretch the entire length of the center area, the training area is divided into two sections. The middle that is clear from any bushes and vines and the area surrounding the center. That part is full with bushes all over the area and vines that hang down from the top.

Andrew watches as all the men bow to each other.

Joseph yells, **"Readyyy"** all the men take a fighting stance,

"Fight!" He yells in a strong stern voice.

This is surprising to Andrew, Joseph is a very quiet man who keeps to himself most of the time but when he yells fight all the men start fighting at the same time. Andrew watches, he notices the way the men are lined up, one man is punching and kicking at the other who is just trying to block himself from getting hit. They do this for a couple of minutes until Joseph yells stop. All the men step to his side facing another man, this time the man who was punching and kicking is now blocking. The two men on each end walks to the other side, this goes on until every men has faced each other.

Andrew can see that all the men are sweating and breathing heavy. They are now on the ground stretching their muscles keeping them lose letting them kick high and hard without hurting themselves. While they are stretching Andrew puts some more wood on the fire at each end keeping the chill out. When they are done stretching Andrew watches all the men pair up again, this time they practice moves that can easily break bones or kill a men if need be. They also practice some moves that will bring a man to the ground and beg for mercy. His father, Julian, and Jacob have all told him that they fight only to defend themselves killing only if left no other choice, Andrew likes that rule! He watches trying to absorb all he sees but they are doing so much. All of them know so many different ways to take a man down, break bones or kill, it's very overwhelming. He sits and watches until it seems as though they are done or at least taking a rest, some drinking water others stretching a little more.

Jonathan walks over to his son, "Are you sure your ready?"

"As ready as I will ever be."

Jonathan picks up his walking stick that is next to Andrew, "The next part of our training you won't be doing for a long time."

Andrew gives his father a look of disappointment, "Am I not ready?"

"Not one man here was ready at your age, just watch and you will understand."

Jonathan walks back to the men who are all lined up again waiting for him all holding their walking sticks.

Once again Joseph yells in a loud voice, **"Readyyy!"**

All the men take a fighting stance, holding their sticks with their hands shoulder length apart slightly in front of them. It's as though all the noise has stopped while the men are waiting to hear the word fight. Andrew wants to watch his father who is facing Joseph's brother Nathaniel, he is one on the strongest fighters in the village.

Joseph yells **"Fight!"**

When the men hear this they start fighting with their sticks, the speed and accuracy of them swinging their sticks at each other is incredible. Andrew steps back until he is against the wall of vines and bushes, he tries to watch all the men but mostly keeps his eyes on his father who is battling with Nathaniel, they fight like it's a real fight. The sticks are moving so fast that if you miss a block you will be hit, and hit hard. Each man is trying to win.

Andrew watches his father fight but the sound of the sticks hitting has a very loud cracking sound, the sound is coming from every direction making him look around at all the men fighting. He notices that when the fights enter the outer area with the bushes and vines, they become weapons. The men are now trying to block the sticks coming at them while bushes try to tangle and trip them. The vines from above are trying to strike their faces, wrap around their arms and legs or pull their sticks from their hands.

Andrew stands back and watches, now all the men are fighting in the outer part of the area with all the bushes, vines and roots, its as though the entire training area is alive. The roots are trying to wrap around their legs but is stopped with the stick the man is fighting with or another root wraps around it and pulls it away. The bushes try to pull the sticks out of their hands but the fighters just twirl their sticks not letting this happen. As the bushes wrap around their stick they use another bush to tangle with the bush trying to pull the stick away. Vines are shooting down from the top trying to hit the faces of the men fighting or tangle around arms and legs.

Andrew watches all this going on around the men fighting, not one man takes his eyes off his opponent. He puts his focus on his father who is fighting on the other side.

Nathaniel uses his stick to pull Jonathan's leg forward then quickly swings his stick around to strike his upper body pushing him back. As Jonathan leans back to avoid being struck a vine wraps around his leg pulling him off his feet and into the air. Jonathan now with his feet over his head swings his stick knocking the vine off his leg, he swings it so hard that it hits the ground before he falls and uses it to flip himself backwards landing on his feet ready to fight. The moment he lands he has to block Nathaniel's stick with his, he uses his foot to pull Nathaniel's leg forward knocking him off balance. In the same motion he puts his stick behind him to push himself forward striking with his elbow, stopping just before his elbow hits Nathaniel's throat. They both know the strike would have ended the fight. As they look around they see that most men are now watching them. They show their respect with a bow and shake hands.

The men all line up again facing the man they started with, they bow showing their respect looking at the man in front and start walking around, some taking sips of water others stretching. Jonathan walks back to Andrew who is still in the same spot trying to absorb all that he has seen.

"Still think your ready?" Jonathan says breathing heavy sipping some water.

"I'm not ready to fight with sticks but I'm ready to start learning how."

"That's good. You don't have a stick to fight with yet."

"It wont be much of a fight then, Will it?"

Jonathan puts his hand on Andrew's head and laughs as he says, "Your probably right. You should start looking for a good stick but now let's head for home, I'm getting hungry."

They walk out of the training area down the stream toward their home. When they get there Rosemary has warm food waiting for them, they all sit and eat.

Rosemary looks at her son, "Do you want to tell me about your girlfriend now?"

"She's just a girl my age I was playing with, that's all." He says with red cheeks.

Jonathan speaks up "That's true but he played with her from the time he woke until the time he went to sleep." He continues to eat.

"Really!" Rosemary says with a big grin.

"Lets not forget about the big hug you gave her the last night we were there." His father adds.

Rosemary still smiling, "My son does have a girlfriend."

Andrew looks at his father with an angry look for teasing him, then his mother, "She's not my girlfriend!"

He smiles at both of them, "Not yet," he says in a quiet voice and quickly looks down at his food with red cheeks.

Jonathan tells his wife that he plans on traveling there often, probably twice a year. Hearing this makes Andrew happy, he finishes his food and goes outside for a walk. He wants to feed the animals and gather some fruit and berries for his mother. After that he will see if any children are around to play with. As he walks toward the animals he stops by Jacobs home. Jacob is sitting outside by the fire heating some meat. Andrew sits by the fire opposite of Jacob says hi and gazes into the fire.

"What's on your mind Andrew?"

"I'm nervous about tomorrow."

"You should be," Jacob, says, "You're starting something new."

"Were you nervous when you started?"

"I was terrified, don't worry every man you saw today, no matter how good they are now started just like you, and everyone was scared."

"Do you think I'm ready?"

"You've already been training every morning for weeks, you have the energy, I think you have been ready for some time now, just remember, when you make a mistake or do something wrong, we all have, and still do."

Andrew stands up, "Thank you, that makes me feel a little better."

"Glad to help."

Andrew starts walking toward the animals again. After they are fed he walks into the woods to pick some fruit and berries, he brings them home he decides to take a small run and stretch a little to keep his legs loose. He spends some of the day playing with some of the younger children, he wants to keep himself busy so he doesn't think too much about his first day of training.

That night he eats a lot of food and drinks plenty of water. He goes to bed early knowing he will have a hard time getting to sleep so he gives himself plenty of time for a good nights rest, he knows he will need it.

Andrew wakes early the next morning, his father is just getting up. Andrew has an uneasy feeling in his stomach but ready for his first day of training. His mother has warmed some bread for them and puts a big jug of water on the table.

"Eat only a little bread, but drink as much of the water as you can." Jonathan says.

They both eat a couple of pieces of bread and have some big sips of water. As they walk toward the exit Rosemary runs over and gives her son a hug.

"Good luck today, try to have fun." She turns toward her husband, "Don't be too hard on him." She pauses…"Please."

"We will let him learn at his own pace."

The two men walk out of their home. Not much is said on the walk to the training area. When they walk inside most of the men are there, some stretching others talking to one another. Joseph walks up to Jonathan and Andrew, bows to them, they both bow back.

He then turns toward Andrew, "Don't be nervous and don't try too hard, work at your own pace. If you do too much too soon you will hurt yourself, we want you to enjoy this. As you get better it becomes more fun, it won't be long before you're as good as all of us."

Joseph turns to Jonathan, "He can stand between the two of us so we can both correct him."

All the men walk to the center of the training area and line up in two rows facing each other. Julian and Jacob line up so they will be the first two that will face Andrew.

Joseph says in a loud voice, "This is Andrews first day. When you face him fight at his pace. Do so until he's comfortable." He then yells, **"Readyyy"**

The men all take a fighting stance. When Joseph yells fight all the men start punching or blocking, all except Andrew. He is waiting for Julian to start punching at him so he can block.

Julian smiles, "Its your turn to strike, I have to block you."

Andrew realizes that he is the one who should be striking and quickly starts to punch at Julian, who has no problem blocking every punch. When Joseph yells stop, all the men stop and walk to the next person they will face. This time Andrew is blocking the punch and kicks. When they start to fight Jacob punches and kicks, if Andrew misses a block, Jacob lightly touches him letting him know that he would have been hit.

"We will do this for a while until your ready, after that if you miss a block you will really get hit."

"Or if you miss a block I will hit you."

Jacob smiles back at Andrew, he is happy to see that he is enjoying himself. By the time Andrew has faced everybody his arms and legs feel very heavy, he can just about move them. His father and Joseph have been correcting his stance and showing him the proper way to either strike or block every time they see him doing something wrong. Andrew is relieved when they go to the ground to stretch, he follows the way the others are stretching. Joseph is sitting next to him along with his father making sure he is stretching properly.

When they are done with the stretching and stand up. Joseph says, "I can tell you have been working hard with your father and uncle."

Andrew adds, "Daniel and Jacob have helped also."

All the men start to pair up again, Joseph looks around, "Terrance!" He calls out.

Terrance turns and walks over toward them. "Do you want something Joseph?"

"I want you to work with Andrew while I watch and correct him."

Joseph explains to Andrew that most of the men fight very similar, hard kicks and punches.

"Terrance has a very unique way of fighting that I think will help you. He makes you make a mistake and when you do he uses your weight against you. Most of the time he does this by grabbing your arm and moving it in the opposite direction until the bone breaks." Joseph looks at both men, "Once you break someone's bone, you probably will win the fight!"

He looks at Terrance, "I want you to teach him this."

"Ok, but I want to show him how quick and effective it can be, throw a punch at my face."

Terrance looks at Andrew, "Watch closely.

Both Jonathan and Andrew take a step back as the two men stand ready to fight. Joseph throws a punch at the face of Terrence who blocks it, as he blocks he takes a step back using his forearm to push the punch in the air. As he does this one of his hands hits the wrist of Joseph and the other hand grabs the hand turning his palm toward the sky. He twists his body so his back is now facing Joseph and drops to one knee pulling Joseph's arm out in front of him dropping his elbow onto his shoulder, stopping to show Andrew.

"If I go any further, I break the arm; Fight over!"

The two men stand up, "You have to be careful practicing this, you can easily break the arm of a friend training, we will start slow and easy."

Joseph and Jonathan step away as Terrance starts to show Andrew different ways to grab and twist a man's arm in a fight.

"I will start showing you how to bring a man down with little damage, when you are good at this I will teach you how to break bones."

They do this for a while until its time to rest. Andrew walks over to the side to drink some water, Julian is already there, drinking and talking with some of the other men. Jonathan and Joseph walk up, both have some water.

"You need to get yourself a good walking stick." Joseph says as he looks at Andrew.

"I've been looking, but I haven't found one I like yet."

"Give it time, but until you find a stick to make yours, just get a stick about this size." Joseph puts his stick in Andrew's hands, "That way we can start teaching you how to fight with a stick, until then watch us closely, how we stand and block with the stick. It is a great weapon in battle."

Andrew walks to the side as all the men line up to fight with the sticks. He watches as they fight into the outer edge of the training area using all the bushes and vines as weapons.

Andrew tries to imagine what it will be like when he can do this as he watches. Joseph fights with one of the other men using all the nature around him like its part of his body, moving vines and bushes at will. They fight for about twenty minutes then all line back up and bow to each other, they are done for the morning. Jonathan walks toward Andrew who already wants to get going so he can finish his work in the village and start looking for a stick to make his own, or at least find one he can start practicing with. Andrew and Jonathan start walking, they are with Daniel, Jacob and Julian.

Rosemary has planed on all the men stopping at their home to eat and talk about how Andrew has done his first day. When they arrive, Rosemary and Sandra have freshly cut vegetables and fruit on the table with some warm meat and cheese. Rosemary is eager to hear how her son handled his first day.

"How did my son do?" Are the first words out of her mouth.

"He has done well for his first day, he kept up with all the men and made few mistakes." Jonathan answers.

She turns to her son who is washing his hands in a bucket of water getting ready to eat, he has worked up quite a hunger.

"Did you have fun?" she asks.

"Yes I did mother, I really think I'm going to enjoy training with the older men."

While they are eating Andrew listens to his father tell his mother about his first day, he seems to think Andrew has done very well and is proud of him. This makes Andrew feel good about himself. After they are done eating Andrew asks if he can start his work so he can finish it early.

"What's the rush?" his father asks.

"I want to find a stick I can train with until I find the stick that will be mine!"

Jonathan tells him to run off, but to do his work right before he runs off into the woods. Andrew stacks the wood his father has split the previous day, picks some vegetables from the garden and brings them back to his mother then starts walking down the stream to the animals to feed and to check their fence. On his way there he passes Josephs home who calls him over.

"You were very impressive today."

"Thank you, I'm relieved you think so, I was very nervous when the day began."

"I could tell you were, but I think in no time you will be a great fighter."

Andrew thanks him again and starts walking toward the animals. When he gets there he quickly feeds them, checks the wall of bushes, making sure it is fine and walks into the woods to find a stick to train with.

Chapter Fifteen

Andrew walks deep into the woods past the animals, he is not familiar with this part of the forest. He stays close to the stream that way he can follow it back and will not get lost. He picks up almost every stick along the way, most of them break easily the others are either too big or small. He can't seem to find a stick comfortable to fight with so he keeps walking deeper into the woods, the further he walks the thicker the woods become. It's not often anybody travels this part of the forest. The brier and thorn bushes are extremely over grown and the ground is very mushy, it's hard to travel in these conditions without their gift.

He pushes through a little further, he stops when he comes across a half broken branch hanging off a tree, he twists and turns it until it breaks off. He grabs it in the middle, it feels thick enough but its to long. It's not the stick he will make his own but he can definitely start training with it until he finds the right stick for himself. He starts walking back to the village using the stick for walking like his father. He has traveled further then he realized, it takes quite some time to get back to the village and is getting very hungry.

As he passes Josephs home he is called over, "Found a stick have you?"

"I will still look for a better stick but I can start training with this."

Andrew hands the stick to Joseph who turns it in his hands looking at it.

"This will be fine to start with." He hands it back to Andrew. "When you find your stick their well be no question, it will just feel good in your hands and comfortable to work with."

Andrew starts walking again, when he gets home food is already waiting for him so he puts the stick down, washes his hands and eats.

After eating he goes back outside to see his father holding the stick, "It's a little long for you."

"I was going to ask you to cut it for me?" His father hands him the small ax that he carries, "Your stick, you cut it."

Andrew takes the ax and starts cutting the stick to the length he wants.

His father sits down beside him, "You walked deep into the woods past the animals to find it, didn't you?"

Andrew looks at his father with a puzzled look, "How did you know that?"

"I can tell by the type of wood it is, that kind of tree only grows in very damp wet ground."

"I'm going back that way to look for a better stick." Andrew says as he hands the ax back to his father.

"Keep the ax until you find the stick that is for you, that way you can cut it down easily but don't lose it, its very old and has been in our family for a long time." His father pauses then says, "Someday it will be yours."

Andrew puts the small ax down next to him, "I will take good care of it father."

"I'm not worried." Jonathan gets up and walks inside their home.

Andrew starts peeling the bark off the stick with the small knife he carries. When all the bark is off he uses a stone to grind each end so they are nice and smooth, he's ready to fight with a stick.

When his father walks back outside Andrew asks if he can go to the training area with him that night just to watch the men fight with their sticks. His father tells him that it would be fine but all they do in the evening workout is fight with sticks so he will only be watching.

"I just wanted to observe, that's all. The more I watch the easier it will be for me to learn."

Jonathan takes an armful of wood and brings it inside their home. Andrew follows with his arms full as well. Its been getting very cold at night and their heat lamps can only do so much. On the really cold nights they keep the fire going keeping the chill out. A short time later Jonathan and Andrew walk to the training area, most of the younger men are there already. They're either talking to each other or stretching their muscles. Andrew stands near one of the fires watching as all the men pair up with one another and start fighting with their sticks. They are going a little slower than they were earlier and are correcting any mistakes they may be making.

Andrew is quietly watching, paying close attention when a hand on his shoulder startles him, making him jump and turn quickly to see Joseph standing there.

"I didn't mean to scare you," Joseph says with laughter in his voice, "But I thought I would find you here."

"I wanted to watch them fight with their sticks helping me learn the basics by watching."

"That's one way to learn." Joseph looks at the stick Andrew has found, the bark is pealed off and the ends smooth. "You've done a good job with that stick Andrew, now pick it up. Here's a better way to learn."

Joseph starts showing Andrew the proper way to hold and stand while fighting with his stick. Joseph then picks up his stick and stands opposite of Andrew making him block as he slowly swings his stick at him,

"You have to properly block first, you can't strike very well from your back side on the ground looking up!"

Andrew gives him a boyish grin, "I think I should learn how to block first."

Jonathan is pleased to see Joseph working with Andrew. When the young men of the village are done training for the night, they walk back to the fire were Andrew and Joseph are training. Andrew is blocking fairly well for someone who has just started, he does not notice that the other men are watching until Terrance says,

"He's already ready to start fighting with us."

Andrew takes a step back, twirls his stick a few times and puts it down next to his side, "You first."

All the men laugh a little, Joseph look at him with a serious look on his face,

"You are catching on rather quickly." Joseph smiles at Jonathan, "He will be ready to fight with sticks sooner than we think."

Joseph looks back at Andrew, "Anytime you want to work on your stick fighting I will be more than happy to help."

"I was going to come here every night to watch and try to learn on my own." Andrew replies.

"I am a little old for every night but I will be here as much as I can."

Joseph looks at Jonathan then the rest of the men, "The nights I'm not here I'm sure these men will take turns fighting with you."

He gives Andrew a smile and a pat on the back "It won't be long before you can beat most of them anyway."

They put out the fires and start walking home, as they are walk Andrew asks his father if he is upset that Joseph offered to train him with the stick.

"Not at all, I just hope you know what your in for!"

Andrew gives his father a puzzled look, "What do you mean by that?"

"Will just say that Joseph can be kind of tough, he is a lot better than he shows and he expects the same from the people he is training." Jonathan smiles at his son as he messes his hair, "Don't worry, he's getting old, I'm sure he's not as tough as he used to be."

"All I can do is my best." Andrew says with an innocent smile.

Jonathan under his breath barely loud enough for Andrew to hear says, "I just hope your best is good enough."

"What did you say father?"

"I said your best will be fine."

When they arrive home Andrew is very tired, he washes his hands, has a small bite to eat as he sits by the fire. He goes to bed very early leaving his father talking with his uncle and some of the other men from the village, there was going to be a gathering that evening but Andrew decided he needed the rest instead, he was very tired.

Andrew lies in bed for a while trying to sleep, he starts to hear the sound of music off in the distance along with the laughter of several villagers, the gatherings seem to grow louder the more ale they drink. He starts thinking about young Sarah, he is looking forward to the next time they will be together. That thought is broken by the thought of his mind being opened to nature and the amazing things he will be able to do with his power once he gets it. He is really exhausted and falls to sleep shortly after with a smile on his face.

The next morning when he wakes he is excited about training, until he rolls over and stands up, his legs are a little sore but his arms and wrists are so sore he can hardly move them. He walks out into the big room, sits at the table and takes a small piece of bread.

His father notices how slow his arms are moving, he gives his wife a nudge with his elbow so she looks.

"I think your mother needs some help this morning."

"I can help when we are done training," He turns to his mother, "Will that be OK?"

"That will be fine." Rosemary turns giving her husband a sympathetic look.

Jonathan turns to Andrew, "I can tell you're really sore, there is no shame in missing a day."

"I'm really looking forward to training and I'm sure if I tell the other men how sore I am they will understand and let me go easy."

His father smiles knowing how tough some of the older men can be, "I'm sure you will be fine." He takes a bite of his bread looking at his wife.

Rosemary with the look of concern on her face says, "Will Andrew be OK?"

"He will be fine." Jonathan looks back at his son, "But if he wants to stay home today that would be alright."

"I'm just a little sore, I will be fine."

He finishes his bread and drinks as much water as he can, the two walk out toward the training area. Jacob is the first person to see how sore Andrew is, he pokes him in the chest with his finger.

Andrew steps back looking at him "Stop that!"

Jacob then pulls Andrew aside, "Don't let anyone know how sore you are unless you want a lot of that."

"I thought I would tell them so they will take it easy on me."

Jacob gives him a friendly smack on the back of the head, "For a smart kid, your not that smart. If you ask them to go easy on you, the older men will go harder, the young men will just hit the spots that are sore."

Andrew now a little concerned, "What should I do?"

"Just train like a worrier and hopefully if you can't block they will go easy because you're here like a worrier and not asking them to go easy on you."

Andrew and Jacob walk back toward the other men. Jacob hears Jonathan's thoughts, *"Thank you."*

Jacob smiles at Jonathan and walks into the center of the training area lining up in front of another man, as the men line up, Andrew stands in front of his father. Joseph yells the words readyyy—fight! And that's what they do, Andrew trying to block his father's punches. He is relived to hear stop, but now he has to punch and kick the next time Joseph yells fight.

Andrew has done his best to keep up, most of the men have noticed he was having a hard time. All of the men give him some respect for being there and trying his hardest, he is relieved when they are done for the day.

The rest of the day Andrew doesn't do much of anything except his work in the village and gather some wood. All the men of the village gather wood every day until its too cold or the snow comes, that way they have plenty to last a long cold winter.

The next day he is feeling even sorer than the day before. He works his way through the morning training the best he can. As the day goes on he starts to feel a little better. While walking home from feeding the animals he sees Joseph sitting by the water just staring into it, he goes and sits beside him. A long moment of silence passes before Andrew asks,

"What's on your mind?"

Joseph turns to Andrew with a sad look on his face, "Just thinking about the past and how it would have been nice to have a child of my own."

Andrew knowing Joseph's wife died shortly after he was born asks, "Why didn't you have any children?"

Joseph is a little surprised at the question from such a young boy, "It just never happened, we both wanted a child but it was not meant to be."

Andrew puts his hand on Josephs shoulder, "All the men of the village look to you for guidance," Andrew pauses then smiles at Joseph, "It's like they are all your children."

The sad look on Joseph's face goes away as he thinks about what Andrew has said, "For a young boy your very smart. You know what to say to make a man feel better, Thank you."

Andrew stands up, "Why don't you come to our home for some food, I'm on my way there and I'm sure my mother won't mind."

"That would be nice." Joseph stands up and they both start walking.

As the two approach Andrews home Jonathan says to his wife, "I think our son has made a friend."

Rosemary knows Joseph has been alone for many years and keeps to himself except for training, "I think it will be good for him,"

She starts cooking a little more food making sure there is enough. After they eat they sit by the fire talking about all sorts of things, mostly listening to stories of the past, Josephs eyes get a little watery when he talks about his wife. It's a side of him that no one has seen in many years but it's also good to see him laugh a little.

Jonathan stands up, "It's about time to go train," he looks at his son, "Are you coming with me or would you like to stay here?"

Andrew looks at Joseph, who says, "If you want me to come and help I will go slow and easy. We can work on your stance and form. I can tell that you're still very sore."

Andrew answers his father, "I'm coming with you."

The three men walk up the stream to the training area. Joseph and Andrew work just as Joseph has said, slow and easy, all they really do is correct the way Andrew stands, blocks and holds his stick. When they are finished for the night, Joseph walks back with Jonathan, Andrew, Jacob and Julian. They all sit by the fire where they are joined by Daniel and his wife, all-laughing as they drink ale. They are still sitting by the fire when Andrew goes off to bed, he falls to sleep listening to others outside.

The next morning his father awakes him, "Are you coming today?"

Andrew sits up realizing that his muscles are not that sore, "Yes, he says with enthusiasm, let me get ready."

That day Andrew does fairly well and is confident he will get better. As the day's pass that is exactly what happens, he finds himself blocking most of the men's punches and is able to hit some of them. He knows that he is not as strong as the other men but he is getting rather quick. His strength will come with age.

Several weeks have now passed and every day after he finishes his work in the village he walks into the woods in different directions looking for the stick he will make his own. One particular day he walks the streams edge past the animals, the same way he went the day he found the stick he is working with now. He doesn't really like the way it feels but he does like the wood. He continues his walk further into the forest past the spot where he found the stick he is using. He knows from what his father has told him that this wood only grows in very wet soil that is back into the thick overgrown forest.

As he walks he starts to notice that the wind is getting a little strong but pays little attention to it. He walks as far as he can making sure he has time to get home with no one worrying about him. As he walks he looks up at every tree and picks up every branch that has fallen. When he starts walking home, the wind starts to blow with a great force and is getting stronger. As he walks he starts hearing the trees crack and branches are starting to fall all around him.

He hears his fathers thoughts, *"hurry home, there is a strong storm upon us!"*

Andrew continues walking as fast as he can. Even though the forest is overgrown he can feel that the wind is getting stronger. He pushes forward with the wind now blowing steady in his face. He is starting to get tired, struggling with the bushes that are blowing all around him so he stops to catch his breath.

While he is resting a loud crack at the top of a large tree makes him look up, he sees a half broken branch at the top of this large tree. For some strange reason it catches his attention. He sits for a short moment thinking, then starts to climb the tree. The strong gusts of wind make it hard to climb, he almost falls several times. When he finally reaches the branch that has caught his eye he takes his fathers small ax and chops at it until it breaks free and falls to the ground. The tree he has climbed is very tall so he can see far in the distance, that's what makes him nervous. Off in the far distance, are the darkest black clouds he has ever seen with continuous flashes of light and long deep rumbles of thunder. When he looks down at the stream, its water is moving at a much more rapid pace than normal and is starting to overflow its banks. Andrew is not sure what to think all he knows now is he must get home as fast as possible. As he climbs back down the tree the wind gets stronger and stronger, he is almost blown off several times.

When he finally gets to the ground he thinks to himself, 'that *was stupid!*

Until he picks up the branch he has cut down, the moment he picks it up he knows it is his stick, it just feels good in his hands! He also knows he has no time to make it the right size. He uses the ax to cut it making it bigger than he wants it, just so he can easily carry it.

As he runs through the bushes, the freezing rain is falling so hard he can hardly see, his body is now fatigued, his legs are so tired he can hardly run anymore. He stops for a short rest, the freezing rain has made him so cold his feet are numb, and his fingers and body ache. He is so scared he wants to cry. That fear turns to joy as he sees the bushes and vines open up in front of him forming a path with Jacob running through it.

"Are you OK?" Jacob asks as a complete shelter forms around the two out of the thick bushes.

"Yes I'm fine, I just need a short rest."

"You look wet and cold." Jacob lights his small heat lamp. "We will let you warm a little first, we are not far."

Jonathan hears Jacobs thoughts, *"I found him and he's OK, were going to warm up a little before we head back."*

Jacob picks up the branch Andrew has found, twirls it a little then hands it back to Andrew, "Now that is a stick to call yours! And it comes with a story!"

They sit for about twenty minutes warming before heading home. As they walk the bushes and vines cover their heads keeping them dry as they travel. It takes a short while before they reach the village, when they arrive Andrew sees that the stream is very high and the rain is still falling extremely hard, the thunder and lightening is so rapid it's astonishing. Andrew is worried that the stream will overflow flooding the village but none of the other men are out so they can't be too concerned.

When Jacob and Andrew walk up to Andrews home it is completely sealed, the front entrance quickly untangles and forms an opening just big enough for the two to walk through. The very instant they are in it closes up behind them keeping the rain and wind out. Andrew is happy to see Julian sitting with his mother and father.

His father looks at him, "You had us worried son"

"I'm sorry."

"Nothing to be sorry for, the storm came on very quickly, there was no way of knowing until is was right over us."

Andrew puts both of his sticks down and walks into his room to put on some dry clothes. When he walks back out his father is holding the new stick he has found.

"It's a little long, but this is a good stick!"

"I had to climb to the top of a very tall tree in heavy wind to get it."

His mother stops what she is doing and quickly turns looking very angry, **"You what?"**

Jonathan looks at his wife, "Calm down." He says, and then turns to Andrew,

"There are some things your mother will never understand."

"Understand! What's there to understand? The same tree with the same branch would be there tomorrow. What I don't understand is why you didn't just wait until the storm was over and go back for the stick, that's what I don't understand!"

Julian and Jacob decide that right now would be a good time to keep their mouths shut and stay out of their business. They walk to the wall that faces the stream, as they do a small opening appears so they can check on how high the water is.

At the same time Jonathan smiles at Andrew, "Your mother does make a good point, you probably should have gone back tomorrow."

"I was thinking the same thing once I got down."

Rosemary lets out a big sigh and walks back to the fire where she is cooking soup.

"Father. What happens if the stream starts to flood the village?"

"It has only happened once before. If it happens we use the bushes and roots to build the banks higher."

"What if that's not enough?"

"That has never happened but if it does some of us will walk up stream and divert the water around the village. Others will stay here and use the roots and bushes to keep it flowing on the outer edge until it passes the village, but it has never happened and lets hope it never does."

Andrew picks up the new stick he has found, stands up with it and finds the spot that feels best in his hands. He starts cutting it to the size he wants. He is very careful with it trying to make it just right, he starts to peel of the bark,

"Be very careful peeling off the bark, you don't want to chip the wood." Jacob says, and then adds, "It would be better if you use your hands, that way you won't chip or scratch the wood."

Andrew starts peeling the bark with his fingers. It takes quite some time and is very hard to do. When he is done he stands up and holds it in a fighting stance with a big grin on his face. He really likes the feel of his new stick but also knows it will be some time before he can use it. He has to soak it in the tree oil and let it dry and harden, until then he will use his other stick to train with. He puts the new stick down and smiles, even though his fingers hurt a little.

They all eat some soup and bread, the heavy rain has now turned to a light drizzle, most of the wind has stopped and the thunder and lightning is in the far distance. Andrew's eyes are very heavy and he starts to fall to sleep sitting in his chair. His father tells him to go to bed. As he is walking into his room his father tells him that tomorrow they will start soaking his stick. Andrew lies down and quickly falls to sleep.

He wakes the next morning and hears his mother say, "Do you think he is ready?"

"I'm sure of it" His father replies and then says in a soft voice, "He's awake." The two stop talking, whatever they were talking about. Andrew walks into the room, sits at the table and takes some bread.

As he sips water and eat some bread Andrew asks, "Are we going to train this morning?"

"Why wouldn't we?"

"I thought with such a strong storm we would spend most of the day cleaning the village."

"It's already done, all the men were up early to clean Julian and Jacob are checking on the animals as we speak,"

"Why didn't you wake me to help?"

"I wanted you to sleep, you had a rough day yesterday and you needed the rest."

"Are we going to start soaking my stick today?"

"Yes, but not until after your work in the village is finished, then I will show you the right sap and oil to use and how to do it."

The two finish eating their bread, Andrew gives his mother a kiss on the cheek and they start walking toward the training area. Andrew takes his old stick with him. When they get there all the men are already in line, Andrew and Jonathan line up quickly with no time to talk. Andrew has been training long enough that all the other men treat him as though he was an adult, he finds himself getting hit quite often, however, he gets some jabs in as well.

When they finish training and are walking home Andrew turns to his father, "Why did all the men treat me differently today?"

"They didn't treat you different, they are starting to treat you like an adult and giving you the respect that comes with it."

Andrew smiles when he hears this, he likes being considered an adult. When they get home Andrew quickly eats the soup his mother has warmed and runs off to start his work in the village. He is anxious to finish and learn how to soak his walking stick, he can hardly wait until its ready to fight with. He makes sure he does everything properly but works as fast as he can. After he is done he rushes home where his father is waiting for him.

"I had a feeling you would be back early."

His father says holding the stick he has found, then stands up and takes a fighting stanch. He twirls the stick so fast Andrew can hardly see it, suddenly stopping it inches in front of Andrew,

"You have found yourself a good stick, maybe better than mine, you should be proud." Andrew takes the stick,

"Now lets show you how to make it as strong as mine."

Jonathan tells Andrew to go inside and get the pail they use to gather the oil for their heating lamps. Andrew runs inside and quickly comes outside with the pail, the two walk up the stream past the training area into the woods.

As they walk Jonathan asks Andrew lots of questions about the training and how he liked it.

He stops for a moment and faces Andrew, "But most important, I want to know if you've been watching use move the roots, vines and bushes in our fighting, do you think you understand how powerful this gift is?"

"I have been watching," Andrew now with a serious look, "I think I understand."

"I'm asking you because soon I will be opening your mind, I want to make sure your ready. Remember you don't just receive the power to move the plant life, you also receive many memories of our families ancestors, some good, some bad, some so horrific it will make you cry even when you're an old man like myself." He continues to look at his son, with a low sad voice, "Our people have had to fight for as long as we have existed because others think we are different. With all that fighting is a lot of death and horrible things that go with battle. You will remember these memories, they will become yours, some so strong it's as though you are there. You need to realize that they are just memories of the past,"

Andrew now has a serious look, "I think I am ready, or as ready as I will ever be."

His father nods, "First we have to show you how to get your walking stick ready."

They stop in front of a tree.

"That's what I was looking for." Jonathan says looking up into a tree. As he says this three thick vines slowly creep down like snakes stalking prey. Andrew watches as his father brings the vines down so they are directly in front of them. His father then tells him to hold the pail under one of the vines. Once the pail is there the vine starts to twist, squeezing its oil to the surface dripping down into the pail. Between the three vines they collect enough oil for what they need.

They walk back Andrew carries the bucket of oil trying not to spill any.

"Don't we need tree sap? I remember you telling me about a certain tree sap."

"The tree sap we need is in a tree right next to our home."

As they walk down the stream toward their home all the men they pass ask to see the stick he has found. All agree that it is a very good find and when it is ready it will make a fine weapon and be very good to walk with. When they get inside Jonathan sits at the table and asks Andrew to put the stick on it. Jonathan then rubs his finger on the top and bottom edge. He then hands Andrew a very smooth stone,

"Use this to make the edge as smooth as the stone, once you start soaking it in the oil it will be impossible to smooth it out." Jonathan gets up,

"When you are done come get me, I will be outside splitting wood."

Andrew spends about an hour getting it as smooth as possible then brings it to show his father.

Jonathan picks it up, feels both edges, "Nice Job!" he says and walks to a tree behind their home.

When he gets there he takes a long sharp stone and taps it into the tree with a bigger stone making a small hole, within seconds sap starts oozing out of the hole.

He looks at his son, "Cover the stick with this sap and make sure the entire surface is covered."

Andrew starts to rub the sap all over his stick, the sap is a little thicker than water and quickly soaks into the wood. He goes over the surface several times making sure to cover it all. When Andrew is finished he follows his father into the room where he sleeps. Jonathan looks around to find the wall with the most surface, Andrew watches as this wall made from tightly wound vines and bushes starts to unravel and move around until it forms a ledge with a grove just deep enough to submerge Andrews stick in.

Andrew can see that the grove is wound together so tightly that he can pour the oil in without any seeping through.

"Place your stick in the grove." Jonathan tells his son.

"How will I keep it from floating?" Andrew asks.

"Don't worry, just place it down and watch."

Andrew puts the stick down lying flat in the grove, as he pulls his hands away several small vines wrap around it holding it on the bottom.

"Now fill it with the oil, tomorrow we take it out for the day letting the air at it, we do this until the wood is completely dry, then we let the oil harden and your stick is done. It will take some time for the oil to dry."

Andrew has a sad look on his face, "Shouldn't I be doing this?"

Jonathan gives him a half smile, "You will be soon, now lets go get some food, I'm hungry."

They both walk out into the big room where Rosemary has some warm food waiting.

Chapter Sixteen

After they eat they sit and talk for a while, Rosemary is always interested about new things they do. They talk about Andrew's stick and what has to be done to make it a fighting weapon that will stop a sword without a single chip.

Jonathan takes a look outside, "It's time to go to the training area."

It's a little early, isn't it?" Andrew asks.

"Its just the right time, we have some work to do first."

As they walk up the stream Andrew notices every man they pass gives him a strange smile and turns away. He says nothing and just keeps walking. When they arrive, Daniel walks past them and gives Andrew a bow then says to Jonathan,

"The heat lamps are lit." He bows to Jonathan and walks away.

Once inside Andrew sees that only Julian and Jacob are there, both sitting by the fires, one at each side. No one else just the two of them sitting by the roaring fires.

"If you want them to leave it will be fine but you are very close to the both of them and I want to keep it warm in here."

Andrew now realizes that his mind was going to be opened and starts to get a strong restless feeling, "No, I would like them to stay."

The two walk into the center of the training area. Jonathan tells his son to sit, then sits right in front of him.

"Close your eyes." Jonathan says.

Andrew closes his eyes.

"Try not to think about anything, just let your mind rest."

This is hard to do but he tries his best, they sit for a moment in silence as Jonathan concentrates hard, trying to get deep into his own mind while letting Andrew mind enter his thoughts. Andrew quickly jumps up when the vision of a sword striking a man down enters his mind.

Jonathan stands up, puts his hand on his sons shoulder, "That is to be expected, but you must relax and let it all in."

"It was like I was there," Andrew pauses, "It feels like my best friend was killed, yet I've never met this man?"

"That's how your going to feel, even though you weren't there, it was one of our ancestors memories of battle. It was his best friend being killed in battle, that's a memory you will live with now, as though it's yours. You will receive some happy memories also."

The two sit back down and Andrew closes his eyes again. Once again Andrews mind joins with his fathers, this time he sees the battle as though he is there. He is in the middle of many men fighting, he sees men striking men down with sticks, watching others be killed by sword. He can see hundreds of men fighting in front of a large wall made from trees. These trees are very tall with a walkway at the top and many men standing on it. That's when he notices the bushes and vines moving, pulling and grabbing the men trying to fight against them. It's horrible, vines wrapping around the necks of the men, roots piercing through the bodies of others and the bushes pulling the swords and arms down letting the staffs strike the heads of the force trying to attack their grounds.

This memory is so strong he even smells the sent of battle in the air. Andrew realizes this is the city of his ancestors and they have no choice but fight and kill the men attacking their home or all inside will die. It makes him sad that a man can be left with no choice but kill or be killed, so sad that he wants to cry. It seems like hours have passed in this one battle, many have died others are wounded. Finally the men attacking start moving back.

The last memory Andrew has of this battle was carrying his best friend off to the side. He lie the body with the other worriers from the city that have fallen, their bodies would latter be burned. Andrew knows that this man is not his best friend but he feels the loss as though it was. That memory is pushed back by the memory of his father meeting his mother. Jonathan was walking through the forest exploring like he usually does, this time in a different direction, he stops when he hears a quiet sobbing in the distance. He walks toward it and sees Rosemary, a young girl sad and lost. As he approaches her she is startled, grabbing a rock and throwing it at him.

"**Stay away!**" she yells as she picks up a stick and swings it at him.

Jonathan backs up, "I mean you no harm, I just want to help." He takes another step back, "Why are you crying? Can I help?"

She takes a step back, "I don't need any help! Go away!" she says not knowing him.

Jonathan takes a big step back, "OK, but if your lost I can probably help, I'm really good in the forest."

She looks at him as though she is examining his every inch. Jonathan can tell she is lost and has been for some time. He can also see that she is exhausted.

She starts to cry hysterically, "I'm lost, I'm so lost I don't know which way to go, I'm probably going to die out here!"

"First put the stick down." Jonathan says, he then walks up to her, "You look cold and hungry,"

He gives her a piece of dried meat and some bread, "Eat this while I get a fire going to warm you." As Jonathan starts a fire he asks, "How long have you been lost?"

"I left early this morning and walked for some time, when I realized I was lost I started to run in a panic, I spent most of the day running, and here I am."

Looking at the position of the sun Jonathan says, "There is little light left, we should stay here for the night, I will get some food and keep the fire going for warmth."

"No, I have to get home, my parents will be worried!"

"OK, if you say so, but we will travel in circles all night getting nowhere, or we can stay here, eat some food and stay warm. Tomorrow we can find your home, it's hard to track a trail in the dark."

She gives him a long hard look, "Will you help me in the morning?"

"I promise, but now you look hungry so let me catch some food and gather some wood for the fire."

That memory is interrupted by the memory of the bear man story his father tells, its as though he is the man helping this beast. Memory after memory floods his mind, he sees birth after birth, death after death, some just from old age, others in battle, some just bad luck. Hundreds of memories flow through his mind, some of the old memories deep into the past are so horrendous he realizes why they live in seclusion. Somehow he remembers the way back to the city of their ancestors, his father has told him he didn't remember the way.

As all these memories fill his head he slowly starts to hear a faint swishing sound in the back of his head. It slowly starts to get louder and louder until all he can hear is this loud swishing sound. It's very strange, he can actually feel it from his fingers to his toes. It keeps getting stronger until there are no more memories filling his head just this laud swishing sound, so loud it actually hurts his head and makes his body ache.

Andrew hears his father's thoughts, *"That's the sound of all the life that's around you, its very overwhelming and hurts at first,"*

"How can you sleep or do anything with this loud noise and this painful feeling in your body?" Andrew realizes he has talked without moving his mouth.

"It will pass in a few days, until then you can stay home and get used to it."

Andrew now knows that the feeling he is experiencing is the life of all the bushes, vines and all the life that is around him. He opens his eyes to see all the bushes and vines around his moving around in a frantic motion.

Jonathan is smiling at his son, "Your doing that! Now you have to learn to control it."

Andrew closes his eyes again and concentrates hard trying to stop it all from moving, when he opens his eyes all has stopped.

His father still looking at him, "Very good!"

Andrew stands up to see Julian and Jacob walking over to him.

"How do you feel?" Julian asks.

"I'm not sure?" Andrew replies with a loud swishing noise in his head, "How long before the pain goes away?"

Julian chuckles, "The pain will be gone tomorrow, the noise will take several days."

Jacob says with laughter in his voice, "Don't plan on sleeping well tonight!"

They start walking down the stream toward their home, Andrew doesn't say much. His mind is occupied by hundreds of memories, some so old there was no metal they used stone to chop wood. The noise in his head is making him feel nauseous. As they walk every men they pass gives Andrew a bow of respect, they say nothing, just a simple bow. Andrew realizes they have all done this and know how it feels.

When they are back inside their home Rosemary has a big meal waiting for them, Daniel and Sandra are both there. Rosemary gives Andrew a big hug and a kiss on the cheek, she notices he has a pale look to him.

"Are you OK?" she asks.

"Father was right, it is extremely overwhelming," he pauses, "I will be fine."

Daniel smiles, "I was unable to keep food down when my mind was opened." He gives Andrew a funny but serious look, "If your stomach wants to come up try to go outside."

"Don't worry" Andrew says, "I don't feel that sick, but my head sure does hurt a lot!"

"That is normal," Jonathan says, "You've just received hundreds of years of memories and the power to feel all the life in the plant around you in less than two hours. Some men go unconscious when their minds are opened, he smiles at his son, "Your doing fine."

Andrew hears Daniels thoughts, *"You're doing better than your father did, he came home and went to sleep without talking to anybody."*

Andrew looks at his father and smiles as he starts to eat but he doesn't eat much, his stomach is a little uneasy. After eating he stays up for a short while, his head is throbbing so he goes to bed early, all the men understand why he is so tired. As he lies in bed he hears his mother ask his father,

"Will he be OK?"

"He won't sleep much for the next couple of days but he will be fine."

Rosemary walks into Andrew's room and sits down next to him and rubs his head, "Try to get some sleep." She gets up quietly and walks out.

Andrew lies awake most of the night listening to the noise in his head. As the night passes the pain in his body starts to go away and the noise is slowly getting quieter. Every time he closes his eyes another memory enters his mind keeping him awake until he has no choice but sleep.

When he wakes the next morning he is extremely tired, the pain in his body is gone and the noise is much more quiet, but his head still hurts quite a bit. He slowly gets up, the first thing he does is take his stick out of the oil to let it dry for a while. When he walks into the big room he notices that his father has already left.

"How did you sleep?" his mother asks.

He sits at the table, "I don't think I really got any sleep, I kept waking up all night."

"Your father wants you to rest for the day, he said he will take care of your work and check on the animals." She says as she puts some food in front of him.

He eats most of it but still feels a little uneasy. He wants some fresh air so he walks outside and gets the fire going to sit by. As he sits by the fire he looks at all the bushes around their home, he wants to see what he can do, if anything. He stares at one of the bushes and tries to focus on it, he's not sure what to do so he just thinks to himself,

"Get on the ground. The moment he thinks this the bush he is looking at drops and lies flat on the ground!

He thinks to himself, *"That was easy.*

Looking at the same bush, which is across from him fairly close to the fire, focusing on it, he thinks. *"A seat would be nice,"*

As he thinks this, the bush starts to tangle with its self and before his eyes forms into a seat. He walks over and sits in it, being so tired he quickly falls to sleep. When he wakes his father and uncle are sitting by the fire.

"I see your starting to learn your new power." His father says.

"Its really not that hard once you understand and get a feel for how it works." Andrew says. Then adds, "I just wish the pain in my head would go away."

Julian laughs, "Your already doing better than both me and your father, we didn't try to move any bushes for days, you've already made a seat to sit in."

Andrew sits upright, "I've watched all of you older men closely the entire time we were training trying to understand, I really think it has helped."

Jonathan interrupts, "No, I think Joseph is right, your gift is very strong and will develop into a great power!" He gives his son a big smile and raises his eyebrows, "That's a good thing!"

Andrew now wanting to see if he can communicate through thought,

"Joseph are you there?" Andrew thinks.

A moment passes then he hears Joseph's thoughts, *"Learning your new gift are you?"*

"Yes and no, I wanted to see if you could hear me. I also wanted to talk with you later, you're the oldest and wisest man in the village. I was just hoping you could help me understand some of the memories I have seen?"

"I would be happy to, stop by my home anytime you want but for now remember using your thoughts to communicate takes a lot of your energy away."

When Andrew is done communicating with Joseph he realizes what Joseph has meant, he is ready to sleep. He stands up to go see how his stick feels.

As he walks away he thinks to himself, *"The bush should be back the way it was."*

As he thinks this, the bush he was sitting in untangles and is exactly the way it was earlier.

Julian looks at Jonathan, "He has already learned how to control his gift, that's amazing!"

"Yes it is," Jonathan replies.

"It took us quite some time to move the smallest vine or bush, he was already moving small vines before his mind was opened and I was always told that was impossible."

Both men jump when Jacob sneaks up behind them and yells, **"What are you talking about?"**

Jonathan sits back down, Julian yells, **"Don't do that!"** as he gives a friendly shove.

"We were talking about how quickly Andrew is learning his gift." Jonathan says

Jacob looks at the two, "You do realize that his mind was opening by its self, he can already feel things moving through the bushes the way I do. As far as I know I'm the only one who can do this, yet he was doing it before his mind was opened!"

"Yes, I know. Somehow his mind was opening on its own." Jonathan says with a confused look.

Andrew walks back outside holding his stick, it has now dried for a while.

Julian stands up, "May I see it?"

Andrew gives him a strong look already not wanting anybody to touch it but hands it to his uncle, "Be careful, it has only soaked for one day and I don't want any chips in it."

"I will treat it as if it was my own."

"That's what I'm worried about, your stick has several chips in it, and from what I'm told that can only happen before you soak it properly."

Jonathan and Jacob both look away trying not to laugh.

"OK, I will treat it like your stick that you really care about."

Julian takes several steps back and starts to spin the stick in front of him, then takes a fighting stance. He starts doing an exercise that Andrew has never seen, he is moving around using the stick to strike as though he is being attacked from all directions. The stick is moving so fast Andrew only sees it when it is used to strike. He does this for a few minutes then takes several steps toward Andrew who is just watching.

He spins the stick around his back grabbing it with the other hand swinging it down so fast you can hear it cut through the air stopping it inches in front on Andrews face.

"This may be the best staff I've ever held."

Andrew takes the stick back, "Can you teach me how to use it like that?"

"All it takes is practice, and you will be getting plenty of that!"

Andrew sits back down next to the fire leaning against the wood his father has split, still tired and heavy eyed he hears his fathers thoughts,

"You look tired, why don't you get some rest."

Andrew looks at his father, *"I think I will, if you need anything wake me."*

He gets up and walks into his home carrying his stick. He lies in bed and slowly falls to sleep, while sleeping he has another strange dream like the one he has had before. This time he only hears the trees telling him to call for help. He sleeps for about an hour and once again the last thing he remembers from the dream is the same big tree blocking his path telling him to call for help. When he walks into the big room of their home his mother is mending some clothes. He takes a piece of bread and gives his mother a kiss before telling her he is going for a walk.

He walks outside up the stream past their training area into the thick forest. He finds a peaceful place to sit and just stares deep into the woods. He tries to relax and feel the life all around him, at first it makes his head hurt a little more, but it starts to feel better after a short while and just feels strange. He looks at a bush and can feel where the roots end in the earth. If he looks at a vine he can feel it from the beginning to its end, even if its intertwined with hundreds of other vines, he knows exactly which one he has started with and can move it at will. He spends some time feeling the life all around him, moving some, and trying to understand how it works. He knows how the other men can move the vines and bushes, what he is trying to understand is how they can feel them coming at them when they fight each other. He spends some time just trying to grasp it all.

After a short while he decides to try and feel his mother's village, he focuses the way Jacob has taught him. As he does this all he can feel is hundreds maybe thousands of animals scurrying around. He knows it will take some time before he can tell if it's a man or animal moving through the forest, and how far away it is. He decides to just move some of the vines and bushes around, he has a thick vine creep down low enough so he can take hold of it and pulls himself high into the trees, he looks around at the tops of the trees for a while before bringing himself down. He wants to form a shelter so he finds a thick spot full with bushes and concentrates on them, they form a hut but its not tangled as tight as the older men make it. If it rains water will get in, he will keep trying until he gets it right. He spends a good portion of the day just learning his new gift, the noise comes and goes but his head does not hurt anymore. As he walks back to the village he tries to move the bushes out of the way which he is able to do but not as fast as his father.

When he gets to the village he walks past his home and heads toward Josephs. He hopes that he can explain some of the bad memories he has received and why his people have had to fight their entire existence. Joseph seems to always know the answers to all the questions. Whenever his father has a question he asks Joseph, he decides to do the same. When he gets to Joseph's home, Joseph has just finished splitting wood.

He sees Andrew, "Good, I'm glad you're here, you can help me stack this." Andrew starts gathering the wood with Joseph and carries it to the fire pit.

"You wanted to talk with me?" Joseph asks.

"You seem to have all the answers to all the questions. I've noticed all the men from the village come to you for advice or seek your wisdom."

"With age comes knowledge, and I'm really old, how can I help you?"

"Why do our people have to hide in the woods, or behind walls? What's wrong with us that makes others want to kill us?"

Joseph gives Andrew a somber look, "You've received many memories of battle when your mind was opened, haven't you?"

"I remember battle after battle, generations of families fighting and being killed. I don't understand why every memory I have of battle is just to defend ourselves from being killed. All the memories I received tell me that all we want and have ever wanted is to live in peace but we have to keep fighting and killing just to stay alive, I just don't understand why?"

"There is nothing wrong with us, we have a gift. Others think its some find of evil power, it scares them so instead of trying to understand it's easier to hate. Once you hate something long enough the next thing to do is to just get rid of it."

Joseph looks at the fire then Andrew, he sighs before saying, "That's why they try to kill us, they just don't understand. That's why your great, great grandfather moved deep into the woods with our families. We have lived here in peace ever since,"

Joseph looks into the fire with a look of concern on his face he says, "I just hope it lasts!"

"The men of the village are right for coming to you." Andrew says, "You do have a lot of wisdom and you explain things so they can be understood."

"Someday you will have more wisdom than I do" Joseph says then asks, "Will you be training tonight or will you rest some more?"

"I've spent most of the day in the forest learning how my gift works and trying to understand it which has really made me tired, I think I will rest tonight but I will be there in the morning."

Andrew gets up and starts walking away, he stops and turns, "Thank you this talk has really helped."

Joseph smiles as Andrew walks away, he thinks to himself, *"He really is a smart young man."*

He starts cooking some fish on the on the fire that is going fairly strong for warmth. The days are very cold now and they are expecting a long winter. When Andrew gets home Rosemary has some warm food waiting for him, his father has already eaten and is sitting by the fire.

"How are you feeling son?"

"I'm feeling a lot better, it will take a long time to get used to the new memories I received. I have more good than bad, some I'm not sure what to think."

He looks at his father then around the village, "I'm happy to be here with people who love me, even though the city of our ancestors seems like an fascinating place to live."

Jonathan laughs, "Have you seen any memories of all the men sitting together laughing and talking very loud all drinking a drink made from purple berries."

Andrew looks at his father, "Yes I did, what where they drinking?"

"I'm not sure?" his father answers, "Its a drink made from berries called grapes I've looked for this berry many of times, there are none to be found. But the drink is similar to the ale we drink."

Andrew looks at his father giving him an innocent yet disappointed smile, he also wanted to try this drink made from grapes, but if his father has looked there are none.

"Maybe someday we will visit our ancestors." Andrew says.

"That walk would take a long time, we would see several seasons change during the journey," He pauses and gives his son a serious look, "Our home is here now, our families left for a reason and they knew there was no turning back," he smiles at his son, "But we do have some good memories of our ancestors home."

Andrew smiles back, "That we do."

Jonathan gets up and puts some more wood on the fire, "The really cold days will be here soon, we need to start gathering a lot of wood to last through the coldest days of winter, this year you will help."

Andrew looks at his father with a puzzled look, like he wants to ask something.

"What's on your mind son?"

"I can feel the life in the bushes and all the trees that are around us, yet we always have wood for the fire. Isn't that killing life? What I mean is I can feel the life in the tree also."

"I asked my father the same question, and he told me that he asked his father the same thing. The answer I was given made a lot of sense, we don't just cut down any tree, we find trees that are dying or are already dead."

"How does that make it right? We are still killing trees."

"Yes we are, we are also giving life to the smaller trees around that will die without the sun or water the older trees take."

"How do you know if a tree is dying?"

"We can usually tell by looking at it, if the branches are dry and look lifeless it will probably die soon. Those are the trees we take down, they are usually very tall and block the sun from the smaller ones."

"That makes it seem a little better, it allows the smaller trees to grow and the wood helps us for cooking food and warmth."

Jonathan gives his son a smile, "The main reason is to survive, it's like hunting and fishing, without the fish and meat for food we would die."

"I do understand. I just don't like to kill anything, I also know we need to survive."

Wanting to change the subject, Jonathan asks his son. "Are you going to train with us tonight?"

"I think I will rest tonight, tomorrow I will be ready."

"Before I leave for the training area your mother and I have something to talk to you about." Jonathan hands his son a bucket, "Go fill this at the stream, were out of water. When you are done come inside to talk."

Andrew walks to the stream a little puzzled, trying to think if he's done something wrong. What could they want to talk with him about and why did his father seem so serious when he said he wanted to talk to him. These questions were all filling his mind as he filled the bucket and walked back to their home. When he walks inside, his mother and father are both sitting at the table with serious looks on their faces. Andrew puts the bucket down and sits at the table across from them,

"Have I done something wrong?"

"No" his mother ensures him, "we just have to discuss something with you."

His father looking into his eyes, "Every choice we make effects you, we wanted to hear your thoughts before making a big decision like this."

Andrew now confused about this conversation asks, "What are we talking about? What decision?"

Rosemary looks at Jonathan who says, "We know there are no children your age to play with here, we thought you would like to live in your mothers village in the warm days of summer and come back here in the cold days of winter."

Jonathan looks at his son waiting for a response, then adds, "Its really your choice, if you want to go we will, if you want to stay here that's fine also."

Andrew smiles at the thought of living with other children his age, the smile goes away when he asks, "What of my training?"

"You will train in the winter here, in the summer we will find a nice spot to train over there. Your uncle and Jacob will travel there often to help with your training. I'm sure some of the other men will visit, training will be no problem."

Jonathan then smiles before saying, "We will also visit your girlfriend Sarah several times a year."

"She's not my girlfriend! She's just a friend!"

Andrew looks at his mother with red cheeks. "It would be nice to play with children my own age," Andrew says then asks, "Who will take care of the animals?"

"That won't be a problem, there are men here capable of that. Any one of them can feed the animals or they can take turns, I assure you someone will tend to the animals."

Andrew looks at his mother then his father, "Are you sure you want me to make this decision?"

"Son, we want to do this for you, we want you to have children your own age to play with. Your mother and I really don't care were we live as long as you're happy, besides it's only a two days walk."

Andrew says with a big smile, "If that's how you both feel it would be great to play in the warmth of summer with kids my own age."

Jonathan stands up, "How is your walking stick drying?"

Andrew gets up and they both walk into his room. The stick is standing in the corner, Jonathan picks it up and rolls it back and forth in his hands.

"This stick will be perfect when it dries, you should be proud!"

"How long before I can use it to train with?"

"Well that depends."

"What does that mean?"

"Do you want chips and dents in your stick, if you do you can use it tomorrow but if you want it to stay perfect you need to be patient. It will take some time, several months."

Jonathan hands the stick back to Andrew who puts it back in the oil on the ledge. He pours the rest of the oil into the grove and makes several small vines wrap around it submerging it into the oil.

"Very good, you're learning your gift quickly. Get some rest tonight, you look tired."

They both walk out of Andrews's room. Andrew sits by the fire and watches his father put on his overcoat and walk out through the front wall, which opens up just long enough for him to pass through and quickly closes. After he passes its as though the opening was never there. Most of the time it is left open covered with animal skins but when it gets really cold it is sealed. That's the way the wind hits their home and leaving it open makes it hard to keep the home warm. Rosemary and Andrew use the small opening in the back when Jonathan is out. Andrew sits by the fire for a while watching the wood burn. After a short time he gets up and gives his mother a kiss on the cheek,

"Good night" he says and walks into his room.

The next couple of months are as they have expected, very cold with a lot of snow. The men from the village use the thick briers and bushes to form tunnels just big enough to walk through behind all the homes sheltering them from the snow and wind letting them walk from home to home. The tunnels run from the training area all the way to the animals on both sides of the village, the stream already has several bridges that they also cover in the cold days using bushes and vines. Andrew now being old enough to help with the wood understands why they gather so much before the cold days arrive, as he watches the woodpile get smaller.

A lot of his time is spent in the training area. He trains every morning with the men and most nights he works with Joseph who is teaching him how to fight patient, letting his mind fight for him.

As the days start to get warmer and the snow melts, Joseph starts to really work hard with Andrew on stick fighting, he knows Andrew will be leaving for the summer and wants him to learn as much as he can teach. Joseph now looks at Andrew as though he was a grandson and wants him to be a great fighter.

One evening while working with Andrew Joseph asks, "Where's that stick of yours?"

"Right now it's drying, it will be soaking tonight."

"Its been several months, I'm sure you can use it now."

"I want to check with my father first, but I think it is ready."

"I'm sure your father will say its fine but it's a good idea to ask him."

They spend the rest of the night going over some basic stick moves. All the men start leaving the training area, Andrew starts walking toward the exit with his father and uncle.

"Don't leave yet," Joseph says to Jonathan. "I think Andrews stick is probably ready to fight with."

Jonathan and Julian both take a big step back when Joseph turns toward Andrew, "I know that's not the stick that will be yours, but lets see if you're ready to fight with a stick anyway," Joseph takes a strong fighting stance.

Andrew takes a stance to defend himself, "Give me your best."

Joseph takes a quick step forward lunging his stick at him in a straight line into Andrews face. Andrew takes a quick step to the side blocking Joseph's stick spinning him a little. Andrew uses his foot to drag Joseph's foot forward causing him to put his stick behind him to keep him from falling. Joseph pushes off as hard as he can arching his back in the air landing on one foot and the other hitting Andrew in the center of his chest knocking him to the ground. Andrew rolls back using his hands to spring himself up landing on his feet putting his stick over his head with enough time to block the hit coming at him. Andrew's left hand holds his stick high keeping Josephs stick away from his head, he rolls his right hand underneath pulling Josephs stick past his head making him take a step forward. Andrew continues pulling the stick until he is able to strike Josephs in the chest with his elbow pushing him back several steps. Andrew takes a step forward using his stick like a spear right at Josephs chin. Joseph blocks the strike using the inside of his forearm wrapping his wrist and palm over the top of Andrews stick twisting it. He jars it loose from Andrews's hands, then takes a big step to the side pushing Andrew and his stick into some bushes. Andrew still ready to fight tries to take a step forward. Joseph smiles as some bushes and vines wrap around Andrews feet and legs causing him to fall to the ground. Andrew quickly untangles himself and stands up,

Joseph can tell that Andrew is a little frustrated says, "I would say that you're more than ready to fight with the men, and your stick will add more speed to your step."

Joseph now standing next to Andrew puts his hand on his shoulder, "You just have to use the vines and bushes and even more important you have to feel them coming at you so you can block them while you fight."

They all walk home together.

The rest of the winter goes by quickly, Andrew is now fighting with all the men. They all understand that he is still learning and help him with the vines and bushes in their fights. They move them slowly letting Andrew feel, that way he can learn to block them using the other bushes or just stop them as they come at him. He spends a lot of time in the thick of the forest learning and using his gift to move the bushes and vines, sometimes just feeling the life flow through them. He can't wait to play with kids his own age and is very eager to see Sarah again.

Chapter Seventeen

One early spring morning Andrew wakes to the sound of birds chirping, he gets out of bed with a big smile on his face. He knows that birds chirping means the warm days of summer will be here soon, this means he will be able to play with kids his own age. He also knows that he will travel to Sarah's village soon, which makes his smile even bigger. He takes his stick out of the oil, wipes it down and walks out to see his father.

"Did you sleep well?"

"I slept fine." He says while he stretches.

Rosemary already has food ready on the table so they all sit and eat.

"We will be leaving for your mothers village soon, think about what you want to take with you." his father then asks, "May I see your stick"

Andrew has been practicing with his stick when it's him and Joseph doing slow basic moves but when he fights with the other men he uses the other stick. He wants this stick to dry perfectly without any marks or dents on it.

Andrew hands the stick to his father who looks at it rolling it in his hands, he taps it on the side of the table and looks at it again.

He hands it back to Andrew, "Hold it with a good grip over your head."

Andrew stands up holding the stick over his head with both hands.

Jonathan takes his stick, "Hold it strong" he says as he swings his stick very hard hitting it in the center.

"Let me see it again." Jonathan takes the stick and looks at the spot he has hit.

"Not even the smallest mark on it."

He hands it back to Andrew. "You won't have to soak it anymore, just let it dry and as it does it will become harder yet lighter."

They both sit back down and finish eating before they head off to train. Andrew is now training at full speed with his stick. The other men are stronger than he is but his speed and agility makes it an even match. Some of the other men have a hard time fighting with him because he is so quick, that is until they start using the vines and bushes. Andrew still has a hard time moving them while he is fighting, whenever he tries in a fight, the man he is fighting with can easily strike him. He continues to try, and every time he does he takes a hit from the man he is fighting but he is determined to learn.

The morning before they will leave for his mother's village every man he faced went extremely hard with him. When their training was over all the man there walks up to Andrew, bows with respect, with something nice to say. Most telling him how quickly he has improved others telling him how he was going to be a great worrier some day. This makes Andrew feel good about his progress and feel respected as though he was becoming a man.

The rest of the day is spent getting ready to travel and clean up, making sure there was no food or water left inside. Daniel has told them that he will watch their home while they were away making sure no animals find their way inside. Julian and Jacob have decided to travel with them to Rosemary's village for a stay, after that they would travel to Aaron's village and visit. Andrew was excited about everything, he was eager to start on their way. He goes to bed shortly after eating that evening, he has a hard time getting to sleep but eventually does. The next morning Andrew is awake before his father, his mother has already started to warm what food was left over from the evening prier. She used the outside fire pit so when she was finished cooking she could just cover it with dirt and they are ready to go.

When she brings the food in, Andrew asks, "Would you like me to cover the fire?"

"That's a good idea. That way when were done eating we can just leave." She smiles at him, "That is if your father ever wakes up."

Jonathan has been up early for as long as he can remember and wanted to relax for a while before they are on their way. A few minutes later he is awake and ready to travel. Julian and Jacob have also arrived and are ready to go. They are each carrying several small bags over their shoulder, they all start walking up the stream into the thick forest.

Several hours pass before they stop to rest, they all have a small bite to eat. When they are ready to start walking again, Julian who has been leading, moving the bushes and thorns out of the way asks Andrew,

"Do you want to lead the way for a while?"

"I can try, I'm not sure if I can move the bushes as fast as we walk."

"We will walk a little slower, that way you can keep up." Jonathan says.

Andrew looks at his father with a boyish grin.

Jonathan adds, "It will be good practice for you," he pauses before saying, "Where in no rush."

They all stand up, ready to travel, Andrew starts walking first, concentrating hard on the bushes as they start to move out of the way forming a path, the others follow his lead.

They walk for about another hour, Jonathan looks at his son, "You've done enough."

Andrew is relieved, concentrating so hard has taken a lot of his energy, he's not sure if he could keep a clear path much longer. He wants to walk with his mother for a while so he lets Julian and Jacob pass.

"You look tired?"

"I will be fine mother." He says as he walks along side of her.

They walk for most of the day at a steady pace.

Jonathan finally stops, "This looks like a good spot to stay the night."

"There is still plenty of daylight left to travel" Julian says looking at the sun.

"Yes, there is." Jonathan looks at his son, "But Andrew needs time to build his first shelter."

"My what?" Andrew says a little surprised.

"Your shelter, you will use the vines and bushes to make a place to sleep keeping you warm and dry."

"I don't think I can make a shelter that can keep out the rain yet."

Jonathan gives a small wink to the others then turns back to his son, "You'd better hope it doesn't rain then. That's why we've stopped early, when you think you're done I will check it for you making sure rain will stay out."

Jonathan points to an area with many vines and bushes, "Sit and concentrate, close your eyes and visualize a small hut like our home, try to see the vines and bushes tangle with each other forming walls."

Andrew sits for a long while looking at the spot he wants his hut to be, feeling the life in the bushes. He then closes his eyes trying not to listen to the others talk. The vines and bushes move and tangle with each other, he keeps his eyes closed and continues to visualize the hut. When he opens his eyes, there is a hut, but there are many spots where water or wind can get in.

His father walks up behind him, "Not bad son, you can fill the holes with some bushes, or I can finish it for you. I had planed on making a hut right next to it for your mother and me with a small opening between the two so you won't feel alone."

Andrew looks at his father feeling exhausted, "I could finish with some bushes," he pauses, "If your going to make yours that close, you can finish for me."

Andrew sits and watches as all the holes in his shelter close and within minutes his fathers shelter forms, it's a perfect oval shape and the bushes are wrapped tightly together, just as he had said there was a small opening between the two. Andrew is fascinated at how easy this is for his father to do. The two go sit by the fire where Julian and Jacob have already caught and cleaned some small animals to cook.

Before Rosemary start cooking the meat she looks at Andrew, "Why don't you gather some nuts and berries to add to the meal?"

Andrew gets up and walks into the woods, as he enters the thick bushes they separate forming a path for him to walk along.

His mother yells, **"Try to gather enough for the morning also!"**

She continues cooking as Andrew walks down the path. After a short walk he finds a small tree with some purple berries on it. He knows they are not poison so he starts to gather them putting them in a pouch his mother has given him, he fills it quickly and starts to walk back. He stops when he hears a rustle in the bushes next to him, he is curious what it is so he stands still and waits. Within moments a small baby bear crosses his path, about fifteen feet in front of him. At first he thinks its harmless until he remembers something his father has told him years ago, never cross between a mother bear and its cub! Andrew uses his gift and the ability Jacob has taught him to see if any other movement is coming his way.

What he feels terrifies him, an enormous mass is moving through the bushes straight at him, he is not sure what to do so he closes his eyes and tries to contact his father, *"Father I need your help."*

"What is the problem son?"

"I've crossed between a mother bear and its cub, this bear is huge and heading toward me, what should I do?"

"I'm on my way, don't move until I arrive, if you've gathered any berries throw them in front of you as far as possible and don't move even if the bear knocks you to the ground!"

Jonathan quickly grabs Julian by the shoulder as he stands, "Lets go, Andrew is in trouble." Jacob also jumps to his feet.

Rosemary turns her head quickly, "What! What's wrong?"

"No time to explain we have to go now!" The three men run in the direction of Andrew, Jonathan explains what wrong while they are running. Jacob now leads the way heading toward the bear; he can feel that the bear is heading toward Andrew they run for a few minutes.

"The bear has stopped moving!" Jacob says.

"How far are we from it?" Jonathan asks.

"Its right ahead, we should slow down for a moment and think about what we are going to do."

The three men spread out, Jonathan in the middle walking slowly straight at the bear and the two others walk toward the sides of the bear. Jonathan walks until he finds Andrews pouch which is torn open and all the berries gone, as he walks a little further being very cautious he sees a large brown bear standing right in front of his son sniffing Andrew, the bears nose is within inches of Andrews face. Jonathan can see the tears of fear streaming down Andrews cheeks, but he remains still.

Each of the other men is about fifteen feet away from the bear on each side, Jonathan thinks for a moment.

Julian hears Jonathan's thoughts; *"I'm going to throw a rock at the bear, the moment it hits use the bushes to pull Andrew away as fast and as hard as you can."*

Jacob hears Jonathan's thoughts, *"The instant Julian pulls Andrew away I'm going to rush the bear, when I do tangle it with as many bushes as you can, I will do the same, while it untangles itself we can get away.*

Andrew hears his father, *"Julian is going pull you away with the bushes, let him do so. Be prepared for a strong hard pull, it will be quick enough that if the bear tries to strike you won't be there!"* Andrew gets himself ready.

Julian watches as Jonathan picks up a rock and throws it at the bear, he times it so the moment the rock hits the bear he grabs Andrew with the bushes and as quick as he possibly can he pulls him away straight into his arms. He throws him over his shoulder and starts running away in the opposite direction.

As soon as Andrew is pulled away Jonathan runs at the bear yelling, causing the bear to turn and charge at him, Jacob uses as many vines and bushes to wrap and tangle around the bear slowing it down, Jonathan does the same thing leaving only a path toward the bears cub. The large brown bear tries to fight its way toward Jonathan for a short while, but eventually stops trying to attack and runs down the path toward its baby.

Jonathan and Jacob start off in the direction Julian and Andrew have run. When they catch up with them Jacob looks at Andrew and sarcastically says,

"Did you give the bear all the berries?"

Jonathan nudges Jacob's shoulder with his fist, looks at his son and can tell he is still a little startled.

"Are you OK son?"

"I'm fine, but the bear did get all the berries," he smiles at Jacob, "Its OK, there is a large tree up ahead with plenty."

The three men walk to the tree Andrew is talking about and pick as many berries as they can carry then walk back to their shelters. Rosemary has the meat cooked and ready to eat, the men sit and start eating. Jonathan tells Rosemary what has happened, when he is done telling the story she gets up and gives her son a big hug and kiss on the forehead.

"I'm fine mother, you can stop squeezing me."

She gives him another kiss on the cheek and sits down. After eating dusk slowly turns to dark, Jacob looks deep into the woods.

"The bear is many miles away moving in the other direction."

He wants to ensure Andrew that the bear will not be back. Jonathan knowing his son is still a little spooked from the whole experience looks at the other two men then all three stare into the woods. As they do the bushes and vines start moving, thorns tangle with vines and bushes overlap everything making the area around them very thick and full.

Andrew looks at the three men with some relief. "Thank you. Now I can get some sleep tonight."

The next morning Andrew is the first to wake, he quietly gets out of his shelter and walks into the woods to look for some food, shortly after he returns with a rabbit and squirrel. When the rest wake he already has them cleaned and cooked ready to eat with the berries from the day before.

Rosemary is pleased to see this, she can just sit and eat for once instead of cooking first. After eating they cover the fire with dirt and start walking again. That day is spent the same as the day before, Andrew leading the way for a short while for practice then his father taking over to make up more time. As they get within a mile from the village Jonathan begins to really scope out the area.

"This will be a good spot for our training area." He says.

Andrew looks around, the area has flat ground with plenty of bushes and vines, the trees are spread through out the area leaving plenty of room to move around, yet providing more than enough of vines to form shelter over them keeping the weather out.

Jonathan looks at the three men, "With a little work we can make this spot like our area back home."

Andrew agrees and they start walking until they reach the village. Its about mid morning when they arrive at the small village, Williams wife Rachel is the first to see them, she runs over and gives Rosemary a big hug. She notices that they are carrying more than they usually bring with them, "Why so much this time?"

Rosemary smiles, "We will be staying for the summer."

"That's wonderful," Rachel says, then looks at Andrew, "Thomas, Michael and young Teresa have all asked about you, they like playing with you."

"Where are they now? I can't wait to tell them that I will be staying."

"I think they went to the stream to get some water, but I'm not certain."

Andrew looks at his mother then father who says, "Go on, have fun."

As Andrew is running toward the stream his father yells, **"Be back soon, we have to settle in."**

The rest of the group put the sack's they are carrying down in front of Williams home and sit by the fire in the center of the village. William joins them hugging his sister and shaking the hands of the men,

"Always good to see you, how long will you be staying?"

"We will be here until the days start to get cold." Jonathan says.

A little surprised William says, "That's good to hear. If your going to be staying that long I'm sure you will be building a bigger home than the small hut you have here now, I will be happy to help."

The adults sit by the fire for a while, they discuss where they will build their home. Jonathan wants it near some thick bushes set away from the others. William thinks it should be close to the others but Jonathan is very firm about where he wants it.

Andrew and the other children are now back in the village all running around laughing. Andrew has young Teresa on his back, her legs and arms wrapped around him so tightly he is having trouble breathing at times. William shakes his head when he sees this. Patrick, Teresa's father laughs a bit as he sees his daughter squeezing the life out of Andrew.

He yells at his daughter, **"Get off him! You have your own legs."**

"Its no trouble," Andrew replies, "She was having a hard time keeping up with us, it was my idea."

Teresa laughing to hard to speak jumps off Andrew, "I like you, your fun to play with." She puts her hand on Andrews hip, "Tag, your it." She says and starts running away.

Andrew looks at his father then the other two boys before he starts chasing, letting her stay just a little ahead of him, she is giggling so hard she finally stumbles over her own feet. Now laughing on the ground, Andrew standing over her,

"Your it." He says as he touches her shoulder and slowly runs off. The four children play for quite some time until Andrew hears his father's thoughts, *"Time to come back, so you can help settle in."*

Andrew walks over to where they will build their home, Julian and Jacob have most of their shelters built.

"Andrew, why don't you take William and Patrick to gather some animal skins."

Andrew looks up, he knows his father only wants the two men to leave for a while.

Andrew looks at the two men, "They will use them to cover the front and back exits, we will need quite a few."

It's already warm so there are plenty of skins not being used for warmth at night. The three walk toward the rest of the homes to gather what they need.

While Andrew is gathering the skins with the other two Jonathan, Julian and Jacob take the walls they have built and set them down in some thick bushes, the bushes entangle the walls making them waterproof. They cut the bushes at the edge of the walls and lean them against each other tying them at the top using vines to wrap them tightly. They then place them on the higher ground of the area so if it does rain it will wash away from them keeping them dry. When Andrew and the other two men return with the skins, William and Patrick are amazed at how will the shelters are built. They spend little time hanging the skins and are soon sitting back at the fire eating and drinking ale.

Jonathan wants to tell the people of this village about their gift and who they really are but he is worried how the other children will treat Andrew knowing the truth. He decides to keep it a secret, he goes to sleep that night thinking about the best way to build his home. In this village they all share one room, Jonathan likes his privacy and will make his home have several rooms.

The next morning the four men are up early and walk to the place they want their training area to be. Julian and Jacob stand at one end and Jonathan and Andrew at the other, they have already talked about how it should look.

They all stand silent as bushes and vines move around, thorns and briers entangle forming walls as vines hanging from the trees wrap around tree branches along with the thick thorn bushes to form a cover sheltering them from any rain. It only takes a short while until they have a training area similar to the one at their home. They spend about an hour going over some basic moves and practice a little with their sticks.

As they walk back to the village Andrew asks, "What do we say if someone finds it and they ask questions?"

His father looks at him, "No one will find it."

As he says this bushes and thorns around the area gather together so thick and tight it will be impossible for anybody to pass. When they get back Rosemary has a large piece from a deer warming over the fire, that William has provided for them. They have already made a nice fire pit near their shelters. As they sit by the fire eating Jonathan explains how he wants the home built, it will be done mostly by hand so it will take some time. After he finishes explaining what needs to be done and how they will do it Andrew asks, "When can we visit Sarah again?"

"Our home is more important right now, we will travel to their village the moment we are done."

Andrew gives his father a big smile and continues to eat. When he is finished eating he sees Thomas off in the distance.

"Can I go play?" he asks his father.

"It will be fine for a short while but were starting to build our home today and the more help the sooner it will be finished."

Andrew runs off to play with the other children.

The next several days are spent building, Andrew helps as much as he can but the older men do most of the work. They build it one wall at a time using cut wood, dirt, and rocks. They use dirt and crushed stone mixed with water to fill in any holes where water might seep through. This is the way the homes in William's village are built. It would have taken minutes to build it the way Jonathan wanted to and be much more weather resistant but he decides to build it this way so there are no questions.

After about five or six days it was complete. Andrew and his parents each have their own rooms to sleep in and one big room to eat and talk. Not another word was said about visiting Sarah's village but Andrew was eager to go and his father knew this. That night while eating Rosemary puts more food in front of Andrew without him asking.

"Eat up son, you have a long walk tomorrow," She looks at Jonathan, "What is it five days?"

Andrew smiles as he eats the rest of the food his mother has given him. Little is said for the moment until Jacob says,

"Good for you Andrew, you get to see your girlfriend."

Rosemary, Jonathan and Julian keep eating as they look down trying not to laugh. Andrews's cheeks turn red but he says nothing, he has already told them that she is just a friend, he doesn't want to say it again. Andrew just sits and finishes eating with red cheeks and thinks to himself, *"Not yet.*

The nights are still fairly cold so they keep the outside fire going strong as they sit and talk. William and Rachel have now joined them along with Patrick and his wife Josephine, Josephine is a petite women, like her daughter has brown hair and eyes, even though she is a very quiet women she always seems to have a smile on her face. Teresa is sleeping in her arms. They talk for quite some time all laughing as they drink ale watching the fire burn out before heading to their homes. Andrew is in bed shortly after they have left, he is awake staring at his heat lamp, the dull warm flame is soothing to him. He watches it flicker until he falls to sleep.

He wakes to his fathers voice talking with his uncle, as he walks into the big room of the home he sees that food is already cooked and Julian and Jacob are ready to travel.

"We didn't want to wake you, we could tell you were having bad dreams last night and weren't sure if you slept well."

"If I had bad dreams I don't remember them."

Jonathan surprised to hear this, "You were talking and yelling in your sleep, not making any sense just yelling"

"Well I'm fine," he sits down to eat, "When will we be leaving?" He asks.

"We are all ready to travel, we are waiting for you," his father looks at him, "No rush, whenever you're ready."

Andrew starts eating and drinks as much water as he can, he knows they will be moving at a fast pace all day. When he is done eating he gathers the stuff he will be carrying, they don't take much, just their water pouch, another small pouch with some dried meat, a pair of extra cloths and a warm overcoat made from animal skins to keep them warm if it should get cold. All of this is packed tight in a small sack they carry over their shoulder with the two small pouches are attached to their sides. They plan on moving quickly spending no more than five days traveling.

Andrew hugs his mother, who gives him a big kiss on the cheek, "Behave yourself." she says.

He picks up his walking stick and follows the other men out the opening and into the woods toward young Sarah's village.

They travel for about two days and are now deep into the wetlands. Andrew has tried several times to bring small roots to the surface, he has failed each time. His father seems to do it effortlessly, he knows someday he will be able to do the same.

After passing through the wetlands it's about two or three days travel. Jonathan looks at the sky, the sun is starting to fade behind the trees, dusk is setting in. He asks Julian and Jacob to gather some fish. Jonathan and Andrew would stay there and make a fire pit and gather some wood to burn. After they have a nice fire going with plenty of wood for the night, Julian and Jacob return with enough fish to eat.

Jonathan puts his hand on Andrews's back, "While they are getting the fish cooked why don't you make our shelter."

Jonathan has made their shelter traveling through the wetlands. Andrew sits down near some bushes looks at them for a long moment then closes his eyes. The bushes start to tangle with each other, it only takes a short while making his shelter this time. When he opens his eyes he is happy to see a shelter that looks complete. The bushes have intertwined with some vines forming a small oval shaped hut with an opening in front, no visible holes where water or wind might get in.

Jonathan looks at his son with confidence, "I told you with some time and patience you will learn."

"Will it keep water out if it rains?" Andrew asks his father.

"We won't know unless it rains, the sky looks clear tonight."

They walk back and sit by the fire eating some fish.

The next several days is spent mostly with Andrew leading the way. When they arrive at the village and emerge from the thick forest the first thing they see is young Harold. As they walk over the stone wall that surrounds the village they are all happy to see a man walking using two sticks under his arms to support his wait, its Richard, he has lived and is getting around. Richard starts walking toward them when he sees them, as fast as his legs will allow him too.

"Harold," he yells to his son, **"Go bring back your mother, Aaron and Pauline!"**

Harold turns to see why, he sees the men that have saved his father and runs off to get his mother. Richard greets the men and shakes their hands.

He looks at Jonathan, "I never had a chance to thank you properly."

"There's no need to thank me, I just helped a friend."

Richard smiles, "Well friend, Melanie will cook you a nice meal tonight, how long will you be staying?"

"About five days." Jonathan replies.

"If you need anything while you are here just ask, what's mine is yours."

"We will be fine." Jonathan says.

They start walking back toward Aaron's home. Aaron, Pauline and Melanie soon greet them.

Melanie walks up to them, gives them a big hug. "I want to thank you all for saving Richards life. Because of you Harold still has a father and I a husband, words cant explain how grateful we are." She says with tears in her eyes.

She is interrupted by young Sarah running past them wrapping her arms around Andrew almost knocking him to the ground.

"I'm happy to see you, I didn't think you were coming back."

Andrews's cheeks are now red, he doesn't know what to do so he hugs her back,

"I said I would be back, I just wasn't sure when."

The adults look the other way trying not to embarrass Andrew any further.

As they approach Aaron's home Jonathan turns to Julian, "First thing we need to do is build some shelters."

Richard interrupts him, "That won't be necessary."

"Why not?" Jacob asks.

"It's already done for you."

When they arrive at Aaron's home they see three shelters built off to the side with a fire pit between them. The shelters are big enough to have small fire pits on the back wall for warmth if need be.

"You said you would be back, we wanted to make it easy for you when you arrived." Richard says.

Jonathan says with a proud look. "You did not have to go through all that trouble for us, we would be fine."

"It was no trouble. Most of the men in the village helped." He smiles at all three men still looking at the shelters, "You once said to me, that's what friends do, we help each other."

Andrew, Sarah and Harold have already run off to play, the adults walk back and sit by the fire in front of Aaron's home. Pauline and Melanie start cooking, they want to make sure there is with plenty of food for all.

"I see you have an ample amount of fish." Jonathan notices that fish is a big potion of the food the women are cooking, along with a stew made from rabbit and some vegetables from the garden.

"Yes the fish traps you showed us how to build work great. And thanks to you there is always fresh rabbit and deer." Aaron says smiling at the three men.

They talk for a while longer while the food is cooking.

"I will go get the children." Richard says as he stands up. Julian and Jacob both stand up,

"We will walk with you." Julian says.

As they walk toward the center of the village Jacob looks at Richard, "You are getting around fairly well with those sticks we made for you."

"It took some time getting used to and under the arms hurt every now and then but it's better than not walking at all."

They continue walking until they reach the spot where the children play, they watch for a short while as the children run around.

Jacob shakes his head back and fourth, "It looks like Andrew and

Sarah are playing their own game, they seek each other out as though they are the only two playing."

Richard notices the same thing, "The other children have to run into them to get tagged or they would be the only two playing."

Julian smiles, "They are young now, but as they get older we should keep a close eye on them."

They all let out a little laugh, Richard yells, **"Harold, Sarah, Andrew the food is ready!"**

The children stop playing and they all start walking back.

They stay in Aaron's village for about five days, each day Andrew spends a lot of time with Sarah but he always includes Harold with them so he doesn't feel left out. Every now and then Andrew and Sarah go off for a walk alone in the woods, they just walk and talk about all sorts of things. Sarah has told Andrew just about everything there is to know about herself, Andrew is a little more secretive about himself. He tells her little about his village but none of his gift, he is worried that she won't like him if she thinks he is different. He is also worried about how his father would feel if she found out but sometimes he wants to tell her everything.

The day they leave Aaron's village Sarah gives Andrew a big hug and kiss on the cheek. "I wish you could stay longer, I'm going to miss you."

He hugs her back, "I will miss you also."

"Promise me you will return before the cold days are here."

Andrew hesitates and looks at his father before answering. He hears his father's thoughts, *"You can promise her that, we will return another time before the cold days arrive."*

Andrew looks back at Sarah who is waiting for his answer.

"I will do my best." He says and the four men walk into the woods toward William's village.

The rest of the summer passes quickly, Andrew spends most of his time playing with Thomas, Michael and Teresa. He is still training every morning with his father. Julian and Jacob travel back and fourth between his mothers village and their own. Every time they are there they help with his training. Joseph, Terrance and Daniel have each traveled there several times which was nice. Before winter arrives they travel back to Aaron's village and stay for several days. Once again Andrew and Sarah spend the entire time together.

Chapter Eighteen

The next several years is spent the same way. In the winter Andrew stays at his fathers village training very hard twice a day. He has excelled quite well, now being able to use the vines and bushes while he fights, he is now an even match for most of the men, some he can beat easily. Most of the older men are able to win the match, but they have to give it their all to do so.

The summers are spent at his mother's village. He enjoys having children his own age to play with and always includes young Teresa in all the games they play, even if they go hunting the three boys let her tag along. Andrew knows how lonely it can be having no kids your own age to play with, he wants her to feel welcome to play with them, he sometimes has to remind the other two.

But most of all the past several years Andrew has traveled to Sarah's village twice a year. Terrance and Daniel have each traveled with them once just to meet Sarah and her parents, Andrew talks about her so often they wanted to meet her. Andrew is now willing to call her his girlfriend without turning red in the face. He is now fourteen going on fifteen years of age and starting to act more like an adult.

The warm days have just arrived, Andrew and his father have traveled to Sarah's village and are on their way back to their mother's village, they have just passed through the wetlands.

Andrew stops and looks in the direction to the side of them, he just stares into the woods.

"What's wrong son?"

"I'm not sure." He continues to stare into the woods then says with a puzzled look, "There is a man running," He points, "That way."

"Just one man?" His father asks.

"I'm not sure, there is a man running and there are five large animals some distance behind him. The animals keep stopping a man gets off the animal and feels some bushes then they start moving in the direction of the man again," he looks at his father, "Its really strange?"

Jonathan thinks for a moment, "They are probably tracking the man."

This is very concerning to Jonathan because they are so close to Rosemary's village,

"Lets go and check it out, you lead the way." Jonathan then adds, "Let me know when we are close, we don't want them to see or hear us."

The two start walking toward the men. Andrew has really perfected the ability to feel others walking in the wood, how far, how big and how many, he practices every day. Jonathan has tried numerous times and is still unable to feel anything moving through the bushes, even though he has done everything Andrew and Jacob has showed him, he is starting to think that only a handful of his people have this ability.

Andrew stops, "The man is running back and fourth."

He looks at his father, "I don't think he knows where he is, and he keeps falling down."

"How far are we from them?" Jonathan asks.

"Not far at all, far enough so they won't see or hear us, but we are close."

Jonathan looks around, they are very close to the village, so close there are some beat in paths used for hunting, this brings great concern to him.

Once again Andrew stops, "We have to move back, quickly! He has turned and is running straight toward us!"

Andrew and Jonathan both step back into the thick bushes, using them to form a wall around them.

"Be very quiet." Jonathan says as he hears the man running through the bushes.

The man is franticly screaming, **"Help! Somebody please help me! They are going to kill me!"**

As he runs past the two hiding in the bushes, they notice that most of his cloths are torn off, his skin is ripped, scratched and cut from the thorns and briers. The man is so exhausted he is having a hard time staying on his feet, they can tell that he has been running in a panic for days.

Jonathan hears his son's thoughts, *"What should we do?"*

"There is nothing we can do, we can not bring attention to ourselves.

Jonathan covers Andrew's mouth with his hand as five men on horse stop directly in front of the two hiding. They are all dressed in black carrying swords, one of the men pulls his back on his bow and arrow and lets it lose.

"I hit him," he yells, **"I hit him in the leg."**

The man running falls to the ground and tries to pull the arrow out. Unable to do so he gets up and starts running again this time dragging his leg. The others get off their horses, they are all fairly large framed men with short dark hair, very dirty, so dirty their smell reaches Jonathan and Andrew.

They quickly catch up to the man and one of them hits him in the face with the back end of his sword knocking him to the ground, they all surround him kicking him until he is motionless.

Andrew hears his fathers thoughts, *"You need to keep quiet no matter what happens."*

One of these men starts slapping the man on in the face until he wakes, "You made us track you for about two weeks, I want you awake for this."

"Please, don't kill me," the man who is now on the ground bleeding cries, "I don't want to die."

"Its not our job to kill you. It's our job to bring you back to the Lord, and when we do you will wish we had killed you." The five men laugh as they roll the man onto his stomach.

"But don't worry, he will kill you and when he does it will take days, maybe weeks for you to die." Another says as he drives his knee into the back of the mans neck pushing his face into the dirt while two more men pull the mans elbows as far as they will go behind his back as another man ties them together, making the elbows almost touch, as they do this the man screams out in pain. They then roll the man over onto his back and pulling his hands as close as they can together in front of him.

The entire time the man is crying begging them to stop. They just laugh as they tie his hands almost breaking his arms.

"Sit him up" the biggest of the men says, this man has an evil smile, he is really enjoying it as they brutalize this man. Two of the other men sit him up, as this big man gets close so they are face to face,

"He will have you live with the pigs for a week or so with your arms tied like this. He likes to watch you fight with the pigs for food before he starts to kill you, and that will be slow and painful." He pushes the man back to the ground by his face, "

This is what happens when you are caught talking badly about him." He grabs a big rock and starts driving it into one of the mans feet and toes, with every hit the man cries out in pain,

"This is so you won't try to run anymore." Another one of these rotten men throws a rope around a branch above them and ties it to the foot that was just smashed with the rock and the five men hoist the man into the air tying the rope at the bottom of the tree.

"You can stay here while we rest for a while and eat." The leader of the men says as they walk back to their horses leaving the man hanging upside down by one foot.

Andrew has tears in his eyes but remains silent while the men eat and rest. After eating and take a short rest they walk back to the man that is hanging, they all laugh as one of the men pushes him as hard as he can so the man is now swinging as another man unties the rope letting it go when the man is high in the air. He falls through the air landing on his back crying out in pain as he hits the ground, the five men continue to laugh as the biggest of the men ties a rope tightly to the rope holding his hands together. The man is dragged and tied to one of the horses.

"Walk or be dragged, I don't care, but you will get back alive." The leader says as he climbs onto his horse. The five men slowly ride away with the man tied to the horse trying to walk behind them dragging his leg. When they are far enough away and Andrew is sure they can't hear them he starts to cry out loud.

"Why didn't we do anything?"

"If those men didn't return to this Lord, others would come looking for them, they may try to kill us."

The two start walking back toward the village. Jonathan has great concern, he knows those men were trackers and had to have noticed the hunting trails. He hopes that they never return. Little is said the rest of the way back to the village.

The moment Andrew sees his mother he runs and puts his arms around her and starts to cry.

Rosemary rubs his head, "Its OK son, its OK." She says looking at Jonathan with a puzzled look as though she was asking what happened.

Shaking his head, feeling sad that his son had seen what he had seen, "We will talk later, but right now just let him cry without asking anything."

Jonathan and Rosemary both know that Andrew did not want his father to see him cry. Rosemary gives her husband a look, he knew it meant to go for a walk letting her talk to her son. After a while of talking Andrew and Rosemary walk out of their home, Jonathan is sitting by the fire warming some meat and vegetables over the fire.

"I'm going for a walk to talk with Rachel," Rosemary says with a look on her face telling him to talk with his son, which he was planning to do anyway.

"I see the look your giving father," Andrew says, "Don't worry I will be fine, I was just a little upset, I've never seen anything so cruel."

Rosemary walks away, leaving the two sitting by the fire to talk.

"There is not much to say about what we've seen. We saw what we saw and can't change that." Jonathan says with a serious look, "People can be horrible to each other." He pauses as he thinks about what to say, "It's OK to cry when your sad, it helps you get it out."

Andrew looks at his father, still with tears in his eyes "I've never seen another man cry here or in our village?"

"You've never seen us cry, that doesn't mean we don't, we just hold it in until nobody is around."

He puts his arm around Andrew's neck pulling him close. "I wanted to cry also, it shows compassion!" Jonathan gives his son a piece of the food he has cooked, "Eat, you must be hungry?"

Andrew takes the food and starts to eat as he tries to get the image of that poor man being beat out of his mind. A short while after Thomas and Michael come over,

"We heard you were home, want to go play?" Thomas asks.

Jonathan stands up, "That sounds like a good idea."

He pulls the rest of the food off the spit and starts walking toward William's home. The three boys run off into the woods to play hide and seek. The next couple of days Andrew has a hard time getting that horrible image out of his head, as the days turn to weeks he is able to forget about it.

He plays with the other children most of the time and does a lot of work around the village keeping himself busy, cutting wood, tending to the garden, and checking the fence around the animals. This village has never kept animals fenced before but Jonathan helped them build it and showed them how to keep animals alive throughout the cold days making fresh meat available even in the harsh storms of winter. Jonathan has also increased the level of Andrews training. He was being trained as though he was a full-grown man and also learning how to throw the small ax with extreme accuracy. The intensity of the training took some of the fun out of their mornings together but he was getting much better, he still liked the time he was spending with his father alone. Every so often Julian and Jacob would come to visit.

This one time they were visiting, Jonathan wanted Andrew to fight all three of them at the same time.

Andrew gives his father a look as though he was crazy, "There's no way I can fight the three of you at the same time!"

"We will refrain from using any bushes and vines," Jonathan says as he steps forward into a fighting stance.

"You will be allowed to." Jonathan says as he moves forward to attack Andrew swinging his stick as the other two men start to surround Andrew. Andrew blocks the stick with his own stepping to the side then uses his stick like a spear driving it into Jacob's chest who is moving forward to attack. The moment he hits Jacob, Julian wraps his arms around Andrew pulling him back. Jacob is getting up and Jonathan is moving forward as Julian tries to throw Andrew to the ground. Andrew drives his stick into the top of Julian's foot causing him to step back into some bushes. He uses the bushes to wrap around Julian's legs and some vines to wrap around his shoulders pulling both of them to the ground.

Julian is stunned momentarily as Andrew uses his legs to roll himself over Julian and springs to his feet to see Jacob rushing at him through the bushes ready to strike.

Andrew rushes toward Jacob as though he was going to fight stick to stick. He swings his stick at Jacobs head as hard as he can, Jacob already thinking about the block and counter strike is surprised to have his stick pulled down by some bushes just low enough letting Andrews stick to get by, Andrew stops the swing inches from Jacobs head. Jacob knowing the full strike to the head would have knocked him unconscious possibly kill him. He gives Andrew a smile and walks to the center of the area and sits down, he is out of the fight. Andrew is still fighting with his father and uncle, blocking both of their strikes as he backs up. Andrew takes several quick steps forward, jumps and rolls between the two, while getting up he uses his stick to push his fathers leg forward causing him to step back catching his balance. Without hesitation Andrew kicks his father in the chest knocking him to the ground. Jonathan tries to quickly get up but is tangled by some bushes, giving Andrew the second he needs to use his stick like a spear stopping it just short of his father's throat.

Jonathan knows that he has lost and is happy to see his son use the bushes to help in battle. He hopes his son will never have to use his gift in a real fight but he wants him ready. Jonathan sits up to watch Andrew and Julian who are still fighting. The two are going back and forth hitting and blocking with their sticks, Andrew is trying to match his uncle's strength with his speed. Andrew has never been able to concentrate enough to block and strike with his stick and attack with vines or bushes at the same time but he watches all the others do it effortlessly. Andrew decides to try again so he steps to the side and blocks Julian's strike, as he does this, a vine jumps out of some bushes striking Julian in the side of the face knocking him to the ground.

Andrew steps back realizing he has hit Julian rather hard in the cheek,

"I'm sorry," Andrew, says with a serious look, "I didn't mean to hit you so hard."

Julian gets up holding his cheek, pulling his hand away making sure there is no blood,

"I would say this fight is over!" his cheek already starting to swell, "Good job, next time try not to kill me! OK."

"I really didn't mean to hit you so hard!" Andrew cries out trying to convince his uncle it was an accident.

"And you didn't mean to hit the top of my foot almost breaking it."

Andrew gives his father a smile then looks back at his uncle who is still holding his cheek, "O No, I meant to do that!" Andrew says in a strong confident voice.

Julian laughs a little, "You do realize I'm the only one that was hit."

"Yes I do," Andrew, says smiling, "Sorry."

Jonathan puts his hand on Andrews back, "I'm ready for some food, I think were done for the day."

The four men start walking back toward the village. Jacob and Andrew are walking a little ahead of the other two.

Andrew hesitates before asking, "Do you ever have dreams about animals running thought the woods, only to wake and realize you were really feeling the animals running through some thick bushes."

Jacob messes up Andrews's hair, "It will take some getting used to," He gives Andrew a strange look, one eyebrow raised, "At least I know I'm not the only crazy person anymore."

Andrew gives him a friendly push with one arm and smiles, "Yes you are!" Jacob looks back at Julian, his eye almost swollen shut, "You really hit him hard didn't you."

Jonathan laughs before saying, "Where in the foot or the eye, both looked painful!"

"I really am sorry, I didn't mean to hit you so hard." Andrew says trying to convince his uncle.

"I know Andrew, its OK," He says rubbing his cheek, and then adds, "You just need to work on your control."

When they arrive back at their home Rosemary has plenty of food waiting for them. The moment she sees Julian's eye she asks what happened?

As they tell her the story she laughs, "That's what you get for the three of you grown men picking on my Andrew."

After they eat Andrew runs off to play with the other children, they have already been there looking for him.

The children do their work around the village together, and then run off into the woods to play various games, as usual young Teresa is tagging along with them. That night while sitting by the fire Julian and Jacob inform Andrew that they will be leaving before he wakes in the morning but they will return before the cold days arrive and travel to Sarah's village with them. Every time her name is mentioned Andrew gets a big smile. Most of the people from the village have joined them by the fire to see Julian and Jacob off, all laughing as they drink. Andrew says his goodbyes to his uncle and Jacob before going to sleep for the night.

The rest of the warm days pass with little change, Andrew is still woken by animals running through the bushes, sometimes he sees them in dreams before he wakes.

One morning while Andrew and his father are training Andrew hears Julian's thoughts, *"Jacob and I are leaving this morning, and we will see you in a few days"*

Andrew replies, *"Can't wait to see you."*

He looks at his father, "Julian and Jacob are on their way."

"I know" Jonathan says.

The two finish training for the day and head back to the village. The rest of the day is spent the same as any other. That night while Andrew sleeps he has a dream of a herd of animals walking through the bushes but quickly falls back to sleep, he is woken in the morning by the same dream. His body fills with terror when he realizes its not animals, its about fifty men walking toward their village less than a mile away.

Andrew closes his eyes and calls for Jacob, *"Are you awake!"*

He really tries to concentrate on calling to Jacob, *"Please wake up and answer me!"*

"What's wrong?" Jacob answers, *"I just woke."*

"I think there are men, many of them less than a mile away!"

Jacob sits up and looks into the woods for a moment.

Andrew hears Jacobs thoughts again, *"Wake your father now and tell him, Julian and I are on the way!"*

Andrew runs into his father's room, **"Wake up father! Wake up!"**

Jonathan startled, still opening his eyes, "What's wrong Andrew?"

"There are men approaching the village, many of them!"

Jonathan jumps up and wakes Rosemary, "Wake everybody in the village, tell them we need to leave now. Men are coming!"

Julian and Jacob have already started to run as fast as possible but they are a full days travel away. Rosemary starts running into homes waking people telling them to take nothing just get ready to leave quickly. Jonathan and Andrew are standing in the center of the village looking into the thick forest.

"How far away are they now?" Jonathan asks his son.

"Its too late, they are here," Andrew says with tears in his eyes, "They are at the villages edge and surrounding the outer perimeter. They know we are here,"

Andrews face turns white with fear when he sees several men emerge out of the woods into the village. Andrew recognizes the man in the middle, it's the same man he had seen beat and drag the man in the forest. This man had a cold stare as he looked into Jonathan's eyes, who stood strong in the center of the village looking back at the man; there was a long silence.

"I told you there was a village in this part of the woods," The man says to another at his side as he pulls his sword from his sheath.

Jonathan takes a quick look around seeing many men step out of the bushes, all holding bows and arrows at the ready.

Andrew hears his father's thoughts, *"I will try to talk to these men, any indication of trouble you run, run as fast as you can toward Julian and Jacob!"*

"Father I can stay to fight!"

"There are too many of them, you must run!"

Jonathan looks at the man standing about twenty feet in front of him, "We want no trouble." He says in a strong voice.

This man turns to the men standing on each side of him then turns back toward Jonathan with an evil smile says, "Trouble has found you!"

"You are welcome to anything you want, just leave us alone!"

"You have nothing we want!"

The man raises his sword high in the air, "You have been living on the Lords land without giving half your food and belongings, your punishment is death!"

The man lowers his sword, as he does this the men at the villages edge are about to let their arrows fly, before they do the bushes around entangle them pulling most of them to the ground, some of the arrows do fly striking some of the villagers. The moment this happens young Teresa runs toward Andrew and Jonathan crying, both her parents were hit by arrows and lie motionless on the ground. More of the Lord's men emerge from the woods, some shooting arrows others striking people down with swords. One of the men catches up to Teresa and hits her in the back of the head with the back end of his sword. As she lie on the ground the man raises his sword to kill her.

Jonathan already started to fight sees this, takes his small ax from his side and throws it as hard as he can hitting the man in the back of his head.

Andrew hears his father yell, **"Run Andrew! Run as fast as you can!"**

Andrew is frozen with fear for a moment, he look around and sees his friends Thomas and Michael lie dead on the ground, both with arrows in them. His fear turns to tears as he sees his mother and Uncle William both being cut down by swords. Jonathan is in the middle of the village fighting with several of the men, he is also using the bushes and vines grabbing, pulling, and choking some of the other men. Andrew starts running toward the men that had just struck down his mother when he hears his father's thoughts,

"There are too many of them. Run, I will hold them back as long as I can, just get out of here!"

Andrew stops and turns to run. He sees young Teresa lying on the ground crying, the back of her head bleeding badly, he runs to her and throws her over his shoulder. He pulls the ax out of the mans head that had tried to kill her, takes one last look at his father fighting surrounded by ten or more men and still has others tangled in bushes and vines at the village edge.

Jonathan hears his sons thoughts as he runs into the woods, *"I love you father."*

"I love you to son, just remember, death is the start of a new life."

Andrew runs into the forest opening a path in front of him and closing it behind him, he has four men chasing him. Jonathan has now fought his way into the bushes and has picked up one of the men's swords. He takes three steps forward using his stick in front of him to push off and flip himself over the men, three run at him. The others stand back stunned by the way he is using the bushes in the fight.

As the three men get close he tangles their legs with the bushes and with a big swing from the sword he is now carrying he takes one of the mans head off. Without hesitation he slams his stick down on the foot of another man trying to step back causing him to stumble, in the same motion forward he plunges the sword into the mans chest. He takes a big step to the side pulling the sword out of the man's chest and swings it at another man who is charging him from the side. The man tries to block the swing putting his sword up to block his head. Jonathan angles the swing down at his leg hitting him above the knee almost going all the way through, he spins around swinging the sword at the mans other leg hitting him below the knee just above the ankle going clean though.

The man lie on the ground screaming as Jonathan turns to the men who have killed his wife. He thinks of his son,

Andrew hears his father's thoughts, *"Are you still running?"*

"Yes, but there are four men chasing me."

"These men are not trained very well, remember you're training if they catch you."

Andrew turns and runs toward their training area, if he has to fight these men that are chasing him that's where he wants to do it.

Jonathan is now chasing the three men who have killed his wife, others are chasing him but he closes the path behind him with thick thorns and bushes making it hard for the others to catch him. The three men in front of him are franticly running for their lives, they have seen Jonathan fight and know they are no match for him. As they run under some low vines Jonathan uses one to wrap around one of the mans neck pulling his feet off the ground, the man struggles to get free unable to breath gasping for air.

As Jonathan runs past the man he hears a snapping sound as he slowly tightens the vine. The other two are still running for their lives through the thorns, both men crying out for help as their skin is being torn from the thick thorns and briers. The path is opening for Jonathan making it easy to catch them. He swings his stick at the legs of one of the men knocking him to the ground, and in a big over the head swing he hits the other man still running on the top of his shoulder with the sword almost taking his arm off.

The man lie on the ground holding his arm in place, Jonathan's eyes fill with rage as he pushes the sword deep into the mans stomach. He then walks to the other man who is trying to crawl away into some bushes, his leg broken from the impact of Jonathan's stick. Jonathan drags the man out of the bushes by his leg as the man screams out in pain. Knowing this man had no mercy for his wife or anybody in the village, he now lies on the ground begging for his life. Jonathan just looks at the man for a moment, having no pity steps forward swinging his stick as hard as he can hitting him in the side of the head killing him instantly. He then turns to face the thirty or more men approaching him, he uses some bushes to hide himself as they pass. He then rushes them from behind hitting one in the head with his stick and swinging the sword into another's side taking his hand off just above the wrist. The man turns to see Jonathan and before he can scream Jonathan hits him in the throat with the sword killing him.

The men in front don't realize he is behind them until several of them are pulled into the trees by their necks with vines and others are pulled to the ground by bushes. Jonathan runs to the men tangled in bushes and quickly kills them with the sword, the others scramble to surround him, several others are pulled into air with vines tangled around their necks. Four more rush at him, one swings his sword at him which he blocks with his stick and in the same motion hits another in the head knocking him to the ground. He steps back using his stick like a spear hitting a man trying to attack from behind in the throat killing him.

He turns to stand off with another man when an arrow hits him in the stomach, then another in the chest. He drops the sword he is carrying, pulls the arrows out and hits another one of the men in the face with his stick. Several more arrows hit him in the back dropping him to his knees.

The first man that entered the village steps forward, the leader, the man who ordered the villagers killed. He looks at Jonathan with the same evil smile and raises his sword as though he was going to take Jonathan's head.

Jonathan holding his stomach where the first arrow has hit him then quickly pulls his small knife from his side and grabs the mans leg as though he was hugging it. Several of the other men pull Jonathan away from the man but as they do Jonathan pulls his knife across the inside of the mans leg. Jonathan now lying on his back looking up at the man. "I said I wanted no trouble, now you will die with me." Jonathan's eyes close as he dies.

The leader of the men looks down at his leg to see blood pulsing out at a steady flow. His evil smile goes away, he realizes he will soon be dead.

Andrew is still running, hears the four men behind him, they are getting closer. He now knows he will have to fight them or leave Teresa behind to die which he refuses to do. Andrew finds a big tree to set Teresa down behind and steps forward to face the men that are pushing through the thick bushes into the small clearing. Andrew is standing in a strong fighting stance waiting for the men, there are only three of them, the fourth man has fallen behind in the chase. As they push their way into the clearing and see Andrew one of the men says,

"Look at the boy, he wants to fight like a man."

There is a long pause as the three starts to surround Andrew.

"Let me kill him," One of the men says as he pulls his sword from his sheath.

The man steps forward swinging his sword at Andrew, who steps to the side avoiding the strike. As he steps to the side he uses his stick to knock the back of the man's foot out from behind him and swings his stick around hitting the man in the face, driving his head to the ground. As the man lie on his back and before he can react Andrew lifts his stick and uses it like a spear into the mans throat, he pushes off the stick and rolls forward at another one of the men. He leaves his stick behind and comes up swinging his fathers small ax into the shin of the man causing him to fall. As Andrew gets up he hits the man in the back of the head with the ax as he holds his shin in pain.

The third man leaps forward trying to stab Andrew with his sword, Andrew steps to the side tripping him and in the same motion he grabs the mans arm holding the sword causing the man to fall on his own sword, as he falls the sword pierces through his stomach. Andrew turns quickly as he hears the forth man running. As he turns a large rock strikes the side of his face knocking him unconscious for a moment.

He is then woken by the man slapping him in the face.

"Those men you just killed were my friends boy!" He says as he kicks Andrew in the stomach.

Andrew's vision blurred, his ears ringing, he puts his hand to the side of his face to feel a large gaping wound that is bleeding badly, his eyes close until the man slaps him again.

"Stay awake boy! I want you to see this." The man pulls Teresa by the hair and drags her so she lies at Andrew's feet crying.

"The last thing I want you to see is your little friend here die before I kill you!"

Andrew trying to concentrate, his vision blurred, his head spinning so bad he wants to throw up.

He sits up against a tree Teresa now crying hysterically on the ground, begging the man not to kill her. The man raises his sword high in the air but before he can bring it down a vine wraps around his arm, then another; the bushes around the area start to wrap around his body squeezing him until he drops the sword. Andrew stands up, very dizzy almost falling a few times, he picks up Teresa and sets her behind the tree. He stumbles back to the man who is tangled so tightly with vines and bushes he is having a hard time breathing. Andrew starts to cry knowing his mother and father are dead. Looking at the man he picks up his fathers small ax and slowly walks toward him.

"What are you doing boy? I wasn't really going to kill you!"

Andrew wipes his tears away as his body fills with rage.

"Please boy! Don't kill me; I don't want to die!" Andrew looks at the man, the vision of his mother lifeless body lying on the ground after being cut down by swords fill his mind.

"Neither did my mother!" Andrew yells as he takes three big steps forward swinging the ax as hard as he can hitting the man between the eyes killing him.

Andrew walks around the tree, picks Teresa up and walks a little further. He finds an area with many bushes and thorns and covers them making a very small shelter that nobody would ever see if they walk by. Andrew holds Teresa and they both cry until they fall to sleep.

Chapter Nineteen

Julian and Jacob finally reach the village to see most of the homes burning as they crouch in the bushes watching the Lord's men walking around laughing.

Jacob hears Julian's thoughts, *"I am unable to contact Jonathan or Andrew."* Both men look around in horror as the see Rosemary and William's body lying on the ground along with the rest of the villagers. Julian now glaring at Jacob, his eyes filled with tears of hate,

"These men must die!" he says as a cold look takes over his face.

"We only kill if we are left no choice." Jacob replies.

"I have no choice!" Julian says with rage in his voice knowing his brother and nephew are probably dead.

Jacob puts his hand on Julian's shoulder, "There are many of them, I count twenty five maybe thirty with five more on horse. Do not let your hate cloud your fighting, remember your training and stay focused.

They sit at the village edge watching the men, waiting for the perfect time to attack, this fight will be two men against about thirty, they need every advantage they can get.

While they watch and wait Jacob contacts Joseph back at their village and tells him what has happened. Joseph walks toward the village edge with a somber look on his face, several of the men he passes ask what's wrong but he says nothing just keeps walking. Nathaniel and Terrance are now walking behind him, they have never seen such a troubled look on his face.

When they pass Daniels home he stops splitting wood and walks up to Joseph, "What's wrong?"

Joseph stops for a moment, knowing Jonathan is his best friend, "Follow me to the villages edge." Joseph says and continues walking.

Daniel joins the walk asking Terrance and Nathaniel what's wrong, they both tell him they don't know. When they reach the villages edge, Joseph stares into the forest for a long moment. He finally turns to the men,

"Rosemary's village has been attacked, and it is believed that all are dead." He says with tears in his eyes.

Daniel asks with sorrow in his voice, "Are you sure?"

"I have tried to contact Jonathan and Andrew, they do not answer." Joseph says, he pauses for a long moment then adds, "Julian and Jacob have seen Rosemary's body."

"They are there?" Terrance asks.

Joseph looks deep into the woods then turns to the three men, "They are about to attack the men who have done this."

Daniel cries out with a sharp tone in his voice, "We must leave now to help!" Joseph puts his hand on Daniels shoulder, looks him in the eyes, "Its two days travel if we run, when we arrive, if Julian and Jacob are still alive we will be there just to help bury the dead."

Daniel says in a strong voice, "That's what we will do then, I'm leaving now!" Terrance steps forward, "I will go with you."

Joseph looks at the two, "I will gather some men and follow, if you arrive and there is a fight to be had, wait for the rest of us."

Daniel shakes hands with Joseph and starts running with Terrance toward the village.

Julian and Jacob still sit watching, they want to cause some sort of confusion before they attack.

They watch as three men light the last of the homes on fire, it is soon engulfed in flames. They stand at the ready as Julian has some roots pull out of the dirt wrapping around the feet of the three men who have set the last of the homes on fire and are now standing above the bodies of some of the villagers laughing. They are pulled to the ground and pushed toward the burning home, at the same time Jacob uses some bushes and thorns to wrap around anybody standing close to the village's edge.

The men being pushed toward the fire are screaming for help. The men tangled in thorns are franticly trying to cut themselves free as the bushes entangle them wrapping around their throats pulling them to the ground, some of their necks break others are just strangled to death. About ten men run to help the three men screaming, being pushed toward the fire, that's when Julian and Jacob run out of the woods confronting them.

The men trying to help the three stop when they see Julian and Jacob ready to fight and watch as their friends are pushed into the burning home by the roots. They are held there until the screaming stops. The roots slowly creep out and submerge back into the earth.

Julian shows no hesitation rushing at the ten men while Jacob runs around their backside. The five men on horse take off running into the woods with about fifteen or so men following behind them. They have seen what Jonathan could do and have no desire to fight these two men.

One of the men still fighting lunges at Jacob trying to spear him with his sword. Jacob steps to the side and slides his forearm under the man's elbow holding the sword. He takes his other hand and grabs the wrist turning his palm upright pulling down with the hand holding the wrist and pushing up with his forearm, his arm breaks at the elbow. As the man stumbles foreword dropping his sword Jacob drives his walking stick into the knee, which is fully extended causing it to fold backwards dropping him to the ground.

Jacob spins quickly using his stick to hit the back legs of another man trying to stab him, his legs come off the ground causing him to land on his back. As he is falling Jacob hits him in the face with his stick, the moment he hits the ground Jacob drops his knee on his throat crushing it. Julian has rushed at three men all with their swords drawn he uses his stick behind him to push off toward the man in the middle. With one foot he kicks the sword to the side and the other foot lands on his chest knocking him to the ground. Julian follows through with his stick, driving it into the man's face several times as he stands above him.

He takes a big step back as another man tries to attack him with a knife. Julian steps to the inside of the man blocking the knife with his stick. He then drives the palm of his hand into the man's nose as he stumbles back Julian wraps his stick around the back of the mans neck. Grabbing the stick with both hands he pulls the man's face into his knee, the man steps back holding his face as he falls. Before he hits the ground Julian swings his stick as hard as he can into the side of the man's head killing him. The five remaining men are now standing between Julian and Jacob. Knowing they are no match they try to rush them all at the same time, two attack Jacob, and the other three rush at

Julian. As the first raises his sword, Jacob drives his stick into his chin snapping his head back. With his other hand he pushes his small knife into the center of his throat dropping him to the ground. Without stopping he spins around crushing another mans ribs with his stick. As the man holds his chest Jacob grabs his head and steps around his backside breaking his neck. Jacob moves toward Julian who has already killed one of the men charging him, blocking the sword and spinning to the inside of the man raking his small knife across the mans throat.

The two men that are left fighting with Julian do not realize that Jacob is now behind them. He takes a big step forward swinging his stick over his head striking one of the men on the top of the head making a loud cracking sound dropping him to the ground. The last of the men is now in a panic, pointing his sword back and fourth standing between Julian and Jacob. Both men feel bad for this man, his face white with fear, shaking so hard he can just about hold his sword, until they see the bodies of young Thomas and Michael lying amongst the rest of the villagers. The man with the sword looks at Julian, there is a pause before he lunges forward with the sword trying to spear Julian who blocks the sword to the side and in the same motion steps forward and jams his stick under his chin with all his might. At the same time Jacob spears him in the back of the neck, they both hear his spine snap as he falls to the ground.

They look at each other for a moment, and then look in the direction the other men have run. A path opens up in the bushes as they start chasing they want to catch them all, even the men on horse. They run for about twenty minutes on a clear path while the Lord's men struggle through the bushes making it easy to catch the slowest of the bunch.

Now closing in on the four men at the back of the pack that are running close together, Julian uses a bush to tangle around the legs of the man in front causing him to fall. The other three tumble over him landing in the bushes, they struggle and pull themselves free to face Julian and Jacob.

One of the men starts running again, the other three stand to fight, Julian runs at the first man who is standing with his sword drawn. Jacob stands in front of the other two who are now ready to fight. The first man slashes his sword at Julian who uses his stick to block the strike hitting the man directly on the hands causing him to drop his sword. He takes another step forward and jams his stick into the man's chest, then spins his stick end over end landing it on the top of the mans head. Before the man hits the ground he takes a step back and swings his stick into the side of the man's head knocking his metal helmet deep into the bushes. Julian then picks up the man's sword in a spinning motion throws it at the man running, hitting him in the back of the legs just below the back knocking him to the ground with deep wounds. Julian then turns to help Jacob who has knocked one of the men he is fighting into the bushes, the man is slowly getting up with blood pouring from his nose and the side of his head.

The last of the four men steps forward, trying to stab Jacob who steps to the side and grabs the man's hand holding the sword. He turns his palm to the sky causing him to drop the sword, Jacob then turns his back to the man now holding the mans arm with both hands he pulls down as hard as he can driving the mans elbow onto his shoulder. The man screams in pain as the bone breaks, Jacob still holding the arm turns around and stomps an the mans knee bending it backwards to the ground.

The other man who is bleeding from the head and nose tries to attack Jacob again. Julian steps between the two knocking the sword to the side and drives his knife into the stomach of the man lifting him off the ground throwing him back into the bushes. Julian and Jacob look at each other and without saying a word start running after the others.

As they pass the man Julian has thrown the sword at, he is bleeding from the legs trying to crawl into some bushes. Jacob strikes him in the head with his stick killing him.

They run for about another fifteen minutes and Julian stops.

"What's wrong?" Jacob asks as he stops and looks at Julian.

"I heard Andrews thoughts in my head but only for a moment and he won't answer my calls."

Jacob stares back toward the village, "I feel no movement and there is no answer to my calls."

He looks at Julian, "If you think you heard him we should go back."

Julian takes a long moment looking toward the village trying to contact Andrew, with tears in his eyes he says,

"I was just hoping I heard him. How far are we from the rest of the men."

"I think the men on horse are too fast but there are about ten more running, they are running into a part of the forest full of vines, briers and thick thorn bushes."

The bushes and thorns pull away as a path opens up letting the men run freely.

Andrew had woken up briefly only long enough to call for Julian before going back to sleep. The Lord's men in the distance are cutting through the thick woods using their swords to slash at the bushes, trying to move forward. It seems as though the more they push forward the thicker the bushes are becoming, this part of the forest is so overgrown it's overpowering them. The men stop trying to move forward when they realize there is a path behind them, no bushes, just Julian and Jacob standing there ready to fight.

The biggest of the men looks at the others, "There are only two of them, if we all charge we can take them!"

The man standing to his side, a fairly small man, he looked to be the youngest of the group, with fear in his voice says, "Please don't kill us! We were only doing what we were told to do."

These words enrage Jacob, he looks at Julian who has a blank look on his face, he turns back to the man speaking,

"You killed women and children because you were told to!" He takes a step forward, "Now I'm telling these vines and thorns to kill you."

As he says this the path around the ten men slowly closes around them until they are completely engulfed by thorns and brier bushes. The men try to cut their way through with little success, the bushes wrap around their bodies, thorns pulling across their flesh and vines wrapping around their limbs, pulling and stretching them. The ten men franticly slash at the vines, screaming as the briers and thorns cut their skin away and vines squeeze and crush then.

It's not long before the screaming stops, Julian and Jacob start walking back toward the village. Not much is said as the anguish of what has happened slowly sets in.

As the two men travel back to the village they know all there is left to do is bury the bodies of friends and family. They both have a look of sorrow on their faces.

Julian stops when he hears Andrew's thoughts. *"I need your help,*

I'm hurt!" Julian looks at Jacob with a half smile, "Andrew is alive!"

Both men start running. As they approach the village the two men stop,

"Where are you?" Julian asks Andrew.

"I don't know? I have a deep wound on my face and my head spins every time I open my eyes. Young Teresa is with me and she is also hurt, she is still unconscious."

"Don't worry, we will find you."

Julian looks at Jacob; "He's hurt and has no idea where he is."

Andrew hears Jacob's thoughts, *"Reach out your hand and shake some bushes."* Andrew with his eyes closed holding his face reaches out and grabs hold of some bushes and shakes them back and forth but only for a moment, he quickly puts his hand back on his head.

"I know where he is, let's go!" The two men start running, Jacob leading the way.

Andrew hears Jacob, *"I know where you are, just rest we will be there shortly."*

The two men run past the village, which is still burning toward their training area. They stop for a moment and look around as they see the four men Andrew has killed.

"It looks like quite a fight has happened." Julian says and they continue walking into some thick bushes. They stop at a small dome shaped shelter just big enough for two children. Julian looks at it and a small opening opens up just big enough to fit his head in. He sees Andrew And Teresa huddled together. Andrew is awake, his eyes closed one hand holding the wound on his face and the other arm around Teresa.

"I'm here." Julian says looking at Andrew's stick and small ax by his side, ready to use, "You can rest now, they won't be coming back today, Jacob and I made sure of that."

Andrew lets himself fall to sleep, Julian and Jacob quietly untangle the small shelter making it big enough so the two men can enter and rest themselves, its been a long day. Before they do they make sure the bleeding has stopped on Andrew and Teresa and treat the wounds then close their eyes to rest.

Jacob wakes after about an hour has passed, the other three are still sleeping. He quietly slips out through the small entrance, makes a small fire pit and gathers some wood. After he gets a fire going he walks into the woods to gather some food, the sun is getting low in the sky and Jacob knows the others will be hungry when they wake. He easily catches two rabbits and gathers some berries, on the way back he contacts Joseph and Daniel telling what has happened and that Andrew is alive, hurt but alive. Daniel tells him that he will be there mid morning with Terrance. They will only stop for a few hours to rest and start moving again, he also let's him know that others are close behind to help.

When Jacob arrives back at the shelter Julian is sitting by the fire.

Jacob puts the rabbits down and asks, "What would you rather do, clean the rabbit or gather some water?"

"I will cook the rabbit, I want to stay close to Andrew."

Julian hands Jacob his water pouch, "I will get Andrew's." he says as he gets up and crawls into the shelter.

As he pulls Andrew's water pouch from his side Andrew opens his eyes,

"I'm awake my head hurts."

"Try to rest, I will bring you some food and water when it's ready."

Andrew sits up a little putting his hand on his cheek feeling the deep wound, "My mother is dead, everybody is dead. All I did was run." He says as he starts crying.

Julian hugs Andrew trying to hold back his own tears, "If you had stayed to fight you would be dead also."

He stops hugging Andrew and puts both hand on his shoulders and looks into his eyes, then looks at Teresa, "You did not run, you saved this young girl, she would be dead if you stayed to fight," he hugs Andrew again,

"You are a strong boy and I'm very proud of you."

Andrew lies back down, "My father is dead, is he not?" He wipes his tears away with his arm.

"I can not answer that, I've tried to contact him with no response."

Andrew sits up again as tears once again fill his dark brown eyes, "I think he is dead, he was fighting many men when I started to run."

"I will look for him tomorrow and we will bury the dead, remember when you die its just a new beginning."

"I know. I will just miss him." Andrew wipes the tears from his eyes,

"I want them buried in the training area it's a special place to me and will mean a lot."

Julian looks at Andrew and sees how serious he is, "That's what we will do."

Andrew looks at Teresa, "We should bury her parents first so she can say goodbye," He looks back at Julian, "She does not understand." He says with a sad look and sorrow in his voice.

Andrew lies back down and closes his eyes. Julian crawls out of the shelter, hands Jacob Andrews water pouch and starts to clean the rabbits. Jacob walks toward some vines he knows he can twist a lot of water from. It takes about half an hour to fill the three pouches, as he walks back he stops and stares in the direction the five men on horse have fled. There is a look of anger on his face, he can still feel them running through the forest. He knows that them getting away can only mean trouble in the future, he turns in the direction of Daniel and Terrance to see how far away they are. They will arrive about mid morning. He starts walking back and tears fill his eyes as he thinks about the day's events. Julian has the rabbit's mostly cooked when Jacob gets back.

Jacob looks at Julian, "We should wake the children, they need food and water." Julian goes to the shelter, "Andrew you should get up and eat something," He hands Andrew his water pouch through the opening, "Make sure you both drink some."

Andrew takes the pouch and takes a big gulp. "I will wake Teresa and we will be out shortly."

Julian walks back to the fire, sits down and turns the spit the rabbits are cooking on.

Shortly after Andrew walks to the fire carrying Teresa, her arms and legs wrapped tightly around him. He puts her down and sits next to her. The moment he sits she grabs his arm with both her hands and pulls him close. Andrew takes a piece of meat with his free hand and starts eating.

Julian hands Teresa a small piece, "You should eat something."

She buries her face into Andrew's side. Andrew takes the meat from Julian, puts it in her hand.

"You need to eat Teresa." Andrew says as he rubs her back trying to sooth her, "Only if it's a little."

She looks down at the meat Andrew has put in her hand and slowly takes some small bites. Julian takes a good look at Andrew's cheek, his eye is swollen shut with a long deep wound from the bottom of his cheek to the top of his ear.

"How are you feeling?" Julian asks with a look of concern.

"My head hurts, and I'm a little dizzy," he pauses before saying, "I will be fine after some sleep."

Julian looks at Teresa, who is still taking small bites of the meat, "How are you feeling? How is your head?"

She looks up at him with a blank look on her face, she looks back down without saying a word and starts to cry. Andrew puts his arm around her pulling her close to him letting her cry on his arm.

Jacob stands up, "I will go gather the leaves we need to tend to the wounds." he walks into the woods.

Julian puts some more wood on the fire and gets the heat lamps going in the shelter so they will be warm. Jacob comes back with the leaves he needs and some berries, he gives the berries to Andrew and Teresa to eat while he crushes the leaves on a stone and mixes in some water making the pasty mix.

Julian hands Andrew his water pouch, "Try to clean your wound the best you can."

Andrew tilts his head back and pours some water on the injury and rubs it gently with his hand, then pours more water on it, he does this several times. Julian takes his knife, puts some of the pasty mix on its edge and smears the mix into the gash, Andrew bites down on a piece of wood as he does this. After the mix is covering the wound Julian cuts a piece of his overcoat, just big enough to cover the wound and holds it in place with some thinly sliced vines wrapping them around Andrews head.

"It's in a bad spot to cover but this should work while you sleep."

Julian then turns to Teresa, "Your next, I have to clean your injury."

As he steps close to her she starts pushing him away and crying hysterically.

Julian steps back and looks at her, "This has to be done."

"Let me do it," Andrew says, hoping Teresa lets him tend to the wound.

Julian hears Andrews thoughts, *"She has not spoken a word yet."*

"Just let her be, when she is ready to speak you will be the one she wants there."

Andrew moves to the back of Teresa and looks at the wound, using his small knife he carefully cuts some of her hair away.

"It's not so bad, there is a lot of swelling but the open skin is not deep."

He pours some water on it and gently cleans it with his hand making sure there is no dirt in it before putting the pasty mix on. Shortly after Andrew carries Teresa into the shelter and they go to sleep. Julian and Jacob sit by the fire for a short time, they are also extremely tired so they cover the fire with dirt and crawl into the shelter for the night.

They are woken early to Teresa sobbing in her sleep, Andrew rolls over and cuddles her until she stops. Both Julian and Jacob get up and gather some wood for the fire and hunt for some food. It was going to be a long day carrying all the bodies to the place where Andrew wants them buried, they will need a big morning meal and a lot of water. When Andrew wakes there is a large deer cleaned cooking over the fire with some nuts and berries to eat.

"How are you feeling?" Julian asks looking at Andrews eye still swollen shut.

"My head has stopped spinning, but it still hurts." He looks at Julian with tears in his eyes, "I feel sad."

Julian, now with tears in his eyes also hugs Andrew, "I feel sad also," He squeezes Andrew tight as tears stream down his face, "Its OK to cry."

They both hold each other letting their tears out.

Julian puts his hands on Andrews shoulders and looks him in the eyes, "You have to be strong for Teresa, you're the only one she has or trusts now."

"I know and I'm worried about her, she doesn't seem the same."

"Give her some time but for now all you can do is be there for her."

"I will do my best." A sad look comes over Andrews face as he steps back,

"Try to find my fathers body, I want him to rest next to my mother."

Once again tears fill Julian's eyes, "I want the same, I promise I will find him!" After eating Julian and Jacob walk back to the village, some of the homes are still smoldering filling the air with a hazy smoke. The first bodies they bring back to be buried are Teresa's parents. Andrew brings her to the burial spot letting her say goodbye, she cries the entire way back to the shelter with Andrew carrying her then sitting down next to the fire letting her hug him as she cry.

Julian and Jacob bury the bodies of Thomas and Michael next, they plan to bury their parents next to them. They bring the bodies of Rosemary and William but wait to bury them, they want to find Jonathan's body first.

Daniel and Terrance have now arrived and are bringing the rest of the bodies back to the burial area while Julian and Jacob look for

Jonathan's body. They walk through the woods for about half an hour following the broken branches and the bodies of the Lords men along the way. When they find Jonathan's body he is still holding his small knife in his hand, several bodies lie around him including the leader of the Lords men, his hand still covering the deep wound on his leg. Julian carries the body of his brother back to the burial area. When they arrive Joseph is there with Nathaniel and most of the other men from the village to help.

Andrew is still sitting with Teresa when he hears Julian's thoughts, *"I've brought back your fathers body, its time to say goodbye."*

Andrew stands up and looks at Teresa, "You can stay and wait or you can come with me, I have to say goodbye to my parents."

She stands up without saying a word and takes hold of his hand. When they arrive Joseph walks up to Andrew, says nothing just puts his hand on his shoulder and the two walk over to the bodies of his parents laying in a hole dug for them. Andrew drops to his knees holding his tears back as he says goodbye, he is thinking to himself that it will be a long time before he comes back to see this area, but someday he will. He gets up and walks back to Teresa with Joseph at his side.

Joseph puts his hand on Teresa's head, "You will come live with us now."

She looks at him as she grabs Andrews arm tightly. With all the men helping all the bodies are buried. As they walk away thorns, briers, vines and bushes overtake the area making it impossible for anybody to pass through.

Chapter Twenty

Before heading back home a few men walk to the village that was destroyed making sure all the fires are out. They leave the bodies of the men who have done this lying on the ground for the animals. Little is said on the walk back to the village, they all have a look of anguish on their faces. After they walk for several hours, Andrew carrying Teresa the entire way starts to struggle a little, his head hurts and his legs are extremely tired.

Julian sees this and walks over to them, "Teresa, Andrew is hurt and fatigued, he needs a rest." She turns her head and looks at him.

He puts his arms out, "I can carry you or you can walk."

She reaches out and Julian takes hold of her. She wraps her arms and legs around him and they continue to walk, Julian carries her the rest of the day staying close to Andrew. The next day she walks along side of them holding Andrews hand. She has still not spoken.

They move at a quick steady pace, when they arrive at the village Daniel's wife is waiting along with several other women to help with Andrew and Teresa. They clean Andrew's wound thoroughly with some cloths and water. Andrew is now able to see from his eye and his head has completely stopped spinning. The swelling has gone down on Teresa's head and the wound looks to be OK, it will be watched closely until it's healed.

Andrew and Teresa both sleep in Daniels home for a short while, when Andrew wakes he walks to the fire and sits. In the far distance he can see his home through the trees, he knows his parents will never come home, he start to cry for a moment. He wipes his tears away when he hears footsteps behind him. He turns to see Teresa, she sits down next to him and looks around. Daniel walks up and gives them some bread, cheese and water then walks away without saying a word letting them be alone. He knows Teresa needs some time to adjust to their way of life. They both eat the food, Andrew looks at Teresa, she has a blank yet sad look on her face.

"Lets take a walk," Andrew says as he stands up, "We can walk to the animals, I like playing with them when I feel lonely."

He takes her hand and they walk down the stream toward the animals. Andrew does not look at his home as he passes. While walking down the stream Teresa is looking around, trying to take in all that she sees. She admires the bridges over the stream, the fish traps along the way, but mostly is in awe at the way the homes are made from the live vines and bushes, and the numerous amounts of colorful flowers through out the village.

When they reach the animals Andrew starts petting one of the goats, a lamb walks up to Teresa and rubs against her leg, she smiles as she starts petting it. They stay for a while playing with the animals, Teresa has laughed a little watching two goats play, one jumping off a rock driving its head into the other goats head, but she still has not spoken.

Before leaving Andrew gives her some water as they sit watching the animals.

"You must have a lot of questions about our way of life?" She just looks at him so he continues, "Our people have a gift, we can feel the life in plants, we can also use the energy to move things like bushes and vines."

He looks at her, still looking at him, "You will see this here, I thought I should tell you first before it frightens you."

They get up and start walking toward Daniels home. As they pass Julian's home he calls them over.

"How are you holding up?" He asks.

"I do not like seeing my home, the sight of it makes me sad."

"I thought you might feel that way," Julian says also with sadness in his voice.

"You are welcome to stay here if you want."

Andrew looks at him with a somewhat of a smile, "Are you sure its no trouble?"

"Trouble! You are my family, it will be my pleasure. I've already discussed it with Daniel and Sandra, they will bring your belongings over if you want them to." Andrew looks at Teresa then his uncle.

Before he can say a word Julian says, "Teresa is welcome to stay wherever she feels comfortable."

Julian looks at Andrew, "Does she know about our gift yet?"

"I have told her about it but she has not yet seen anybody use their power and I don't think she noticed the path on the walk to our village."

Julian looks at Teresa and gives her a wink then turns to his home. As he looks at it roots pull from the ground, bushes intertwine and vines tightly wrap with each other forming a room on the backside of his home.

Julian gives Teresa a half smile trying not to look sad, "You can sleep with Andrew, when you are ready for your own room let me know and it will be done.

Teresa looks at him with an astonished look on her face then smiles, "Thank you for being so nice." She says then looks at the ground.

Julian hears Andrews thoughts, *"That's the first time she has spoken since it happened."*

"Let her come around on her own time, she will speak when she's ready."

Julian stands up, "I will help gather your belongings from your home and bring them here.

Julian starts walking away, as he reaches the path near the stream he hears Andrews's thoughts, *"She has nothing but the clothes she is wearing."*

"I've already talked with the two women who have girls her age, they are gathering a few things for her, we will make her feel welcome, like she is family."

Andrew looks into the fire, his eyes fill with tears as he realizes he will probably never see Sarah again.

While Julian is gone the two women he mentioned leave some clothes for Teresa, one of the girls her age asks if she wants to play.

Teresa looks at her with a half smile and says, "I want to stay here for now." She looks back into the fire.

The girl about eight years of age with very light brown hair and eyes, a little taller then Teresa, a little on the chunky side and a carefree look on her face with a big smile.

She points down and across the stream, "I live over there if you want to play, my name is Joslyn"

The two quietly walk away, Andrew puts the clothes in the room Julian has made for the two and starts splitting some wood.

When Julian returns Daniel is with him, they are both carrying Andrews belongings.

Julian sees Andrew splitting wood, "What are you doing? You still need your rest!"

Andrew puts the ax down, "I was just trying to help."

"I want you to rest so you can get better."

"When can I start training again?"

"When your wound is fully healed." Andrew puts another log on the fire and sits back down next to Teresa.

Daniel sits next to them and Jacob also joins them for a while talking while they drink some ale. When the sun starts to set Jacob and Daniel head for their homes. The three sit by the fire for a while talking as they eat some soup Julian has warmed, they mostly talk about their way of life, so Teresa will know what to expect.

She says very little but is talking, more important she has eaten a lot of soup and bread. She falls to sleep leaning against Andrew shortly after the sunsets. Andrew carries her to the bed Julian has made from vines and bushes woven together tightly covered with several layers of thick animal skins and wool. Andrew walks back outside and sits by the fire and looks at Julian.

Andrew hesitates before asking, "Those men, they will come looking for us, won't they?"

"I hope they don't," Julian looks into the fire for a short moment then turns back toward Andrew, "They may come looking."

"I heard you talking to my father about them, you said there are hundreds of them and they like to kill. What will we do if they come looking?"

"That is something Joseph will discuss with all the warriors of our village."

"When he has this talk and you know what we will do, please let me know."

"I won't have to let you know, we will wait until your fully healed then have this discussion while we are all training."

He looks at Andrew with a proud look on his face, "You have proven yourself to be a strong warrior and deserve to be treated as one."

They sit by the fire for a while longer, before Andrew goes to bed he makes sure Teresa is covered and lights the heat lamp before going to sleep.

The next morning when Andrew wakes Teresa is already sitting by the fire with Julian eating some soup and bread. Julian smiles when he sees Andrews face; his eye is fully open,

"Most of the swelling is gone and the wound is healing well, you must still keep it clean."

"After I eat some soup I was going to walk to the stream and wash it."

"I think it would be a good idea to take Teresa with you and walk around the village. Let her see how we live and show her some of the amazing things you can do with vines and bushes."

Julian smiles at Andrew who hears his thoughts, *"It will take both your minds off what has happened."*

Julian takes his stick and starts walking up the stream toward the training area.

Many miles away the five men that escaped the fight on horse are telling the man they call the Lord of the land the story of the three men that have killed at least fifty of his men. This man stands at least six feet tall with a very large frame with huge arms and hands to match, short dark hair with a scar going across his eye from the top of his eyebrow to his chin. The color is gone from the eye leaving only the white with a small black pupil, but he can still see from the eye. His other eye is a greenish brown color.

He has another scare going down the side of his chin into the middle of his throat and another under his nose going across both lips, showing he has been in many fights. Men standing next to him feel the presence of evil and all fear him. The words of his fifty men being killed by only three men infuriate him. He turns to a man chained to the wall by the wrists, both arms spread apart, the man's body has cuts and burns all over it. His wrist bleeding from the shackles around his wrists digging into the skin when he grew too tired from standing or slept.

The Lord of the land grabs this man by the throat with one arm lifting him off the ground, the man kicks his legs as he struggles for air while this evil man is holding him off the ground.

"When the cold days end, you will take all of our warriors find and kill every one of these men and their family's, they will no longer exist when you are done!!" As he says this, he tightens his grip around the man's neck crushing the bones, making a horrible cracking sound. He turns back to the five men standing there and yells,

"What are you waiting for? Leave now and tell the others after the cold days they travel, find and kill them!"

This evil man enters another room, as the five men exit his home they hear the screams of another man being tortured and the laughter of this evil man doing it.

Back at the village Andrew has finished eating, he smiles at Teresa,

"Are you ready for a walk?" He is trying to hide the heartache he is feeling from the loss of his parents.

She quietly says back, "Yes."

The two walk to the stream, she watches as he cleans his wound. He then checks her head making sure it is still clean, its fairly cold out so he will wait until they are near the fire to clean her injury. They walk along the stream until they reach the animals.

"I like it here, the animals are fun to play with." She says as she pets some of the animals while Andrew feeds them.

After filling their trough he walks over to her and watches her petting a lamb, she giggles as the lamb licks her hand. Andrew watches for a while, she is having fun so he waits for her to walk over to him.

"Are you ready?" he asks.

"Yes. Can we come back here tomorrow?"

"We can come here anytime you want."

She smiles and takes his hand as they walk the stream on the opposite side. They walk past one of the homes and a young girl runs out, the same girl that brought the clothes to Teresa with her mother.

She stands in front of Teresa, "What's your name?" she asks.

Teresa shyly looks at Andrew then Joslyn, "My name is Teresa."

"Can I walk with you?" Joslyn asks.

Teresa looks at Andrew, she's not used to having children her age around. Andrew tells Joslyn that see needs to check with her mother first, if it's OK with her its OK with him. Joslyn runs back to her home, shortly after comes back with her mother. Joslyn's mother also a little on the heavy side with long dark hair starting to turn white with age, her eyes a dark green color and a pointy nose, her name is Helen.

"If she's any trouble bring her home." Helen says as she looks at her daughter.

The three walk the up the streams edge, Joslyn talking enough for all of them. Andrew walks behind them listing to Joslyn as she talks to Teresa. His eyes get a little watery as his mind drifts to his parents and how he misses them, he quickly wipes his tears away not wanting Teresa to see him cry. They spend most of the day walking around the village introducing Teresa to all the people they pass.

The next two weeks are spent mostly the same way, Teresa is playing with the other children. She still cries at night but seems to have fun during the day. When she is crying Andrew cuddles her until she falls to sleep. Andrew still won't look at his old home as he passes.

The days are cold now so they do their eating inside. One morning while they are eating Andrew looks up and gives his uncle a strong confident look.

"I'm ready to start training again." Julian walks up to him and takes a good look at his wound that is mostly healed.

"You can start training tomorrow but you start easy, don't over do it."

"Start easy, that means I will training at your pace."

Julian lowers his head and raises his eyebrows, looking at Andrew he smiles as he says, "Another remark like that and you will get some training right now!"

Andrew laughs a little before standing up to get another bowl of soup and some bread. After eating Andrew gets up and grabs his stick, looks at Teresa who is still eating then turns to Julian

With sadness in his eyes he says, "There is something I have to do."

"Would you like me to go with you?"

"No, this is something I need to do alone."

Andrew looks at Teresa, "Stay here with Julian, I will be back shortly."

Andrew walks out the opening and heads toward his old home, when he gets there he just stands for a while looking at it, remembering all the memories he has had there and how he will miss his parents. Tears stream down his face as he enters and sits at the table where they spent a lot of their time talking. The table was hand carved from wood but the chairs were made from roots and bushes tangled together, just about everything in their home was formed from the life around them. He sits for about twenty minutes crying, remembering all the good times he has had there and how much he loved them.

He finally lets out a big breath and walks out the opening. As he walks past the outside fire pit he turns and looks back at the home, he stands and watches as all the vines, roots and bushes untangle and unravel moving back into the surroundings leaving nothing but the table, the stone fire place with metal pots hanging from it and several cups and bowls lying on the ground.

Andrew wipes his tears away with his arm and slowly walks down the stream toward his new home. He will never forget the happy times he spent with his parents. Daniel has seen what Andrew has done and lets Julian know.

When Andrew gets back, Julian looks at him, "Are you alright?"

Andrew answers back with a sad look on his face, "I will be fine, I just need a little time. This is my home now."

He turns to Teresa, "This is our home now." He says rubbing her shoulder with his hand. The rest of the day is spent sitting by the fire, he is eager to start training again.

The next morning when Andrew wakes he is ready, he picks up his stick and walks into the large room of the home where Julian is already awake eating bread.

"Are you sure your ready?" Julian asks.

"Yes Julian, I'm ready."

"What of Teresa, will she be OK without you? She stays very close to you."

"I've checked with Joslyn's mother, she will watch her while we train making sure she's all right."

"You'd better go wake her then, we don't want to be late."

Andrew walks back into the room and wakes Teresa, she rubs her eyes as she sits up,

"Its early," she says.

Andrew smiles as he pushes the hair from her face with his hand, "We talked about this yesterday, your going to play with Joslyn in the morning while I go with the men."

"I know," she says rubbing her eyes again, "But it's still early."

Teresa gets out of bed and walks to the table to eat. Julian has some warm bread, cheese and water waiting for her. She eats it, still half a sleep then they start walking toward Joslyn's home.

When they arrive Teresa looks at Andrew, "Do you have to go?"

He puts his knee on the ground in front of her, now looking her in the eyes, "Don't worry, I'm not going far and I won't be gone for long. Stay here and play with Joslyn, before you know it I will return."

She looks at him with sad eyes, then a small smile, "I will be waiting, if you take too long I will come looking." She turns and walks toward Joslyn.

Andrew starts walking toward the training area accompanied by Joslyn's father Stephen. He is a tall heavyset man with his beard well past his neck and keeps his hair about shoulder length. His weight makes him a little clumsy but he makes up for it in strength.

When they arrive most men are surprised to see Andrew. They have all seen and talked with him around the village and are happy to see him ready to train. They all move to the center of the training area.

Joseph grabs Andrew placing him so he will start with him, "You will begin with me, I want to make sure your ready."

All the men line up, when Joseph yells fight, that's what they do. Andrew knows Joseph is going easy on him and appreciates it. He knows the next person he faces will not. They train like true warriors, if you're ready to train, your ready to fight. That's the way it has always been and will always be.

Andrew notices the intensity of Julian and Jacob. They are working harder then any man there. As they finish they're training for the day and line up to bow to each other Joseph steps forward, with a stern voice he yells,

"You all need to stay, we have something to discuss!"

All the men have been waiting for this. They all know what has happened and wonder what they will do if others come looking, they stand and wait to hear what Joseph has to say.

Joseph puts his hand on Andrew's shoulder, "I wanted Andrew here for this talk. His loss was great and deserves to be treated like a man!" He pauses, as he looks at Andrew, then all the men who have their attention on him,

"The men who killed our friends and burned their village are many. Jonathan fought and killed many before his life was taken." He pulls

Andrew close to his side as he says this, Andrew's eyes fill with tears.

He hears Joseph's thoughts, *"It's OK if tears fall, no man here will think any less of you."* A few tears roll down Andrew's cheek before he wipes his eyes with his forearm.

Joseph turns to Julian and Jacob who are standing by his side, "Julian and Jacob fought with the rest of them killing most before they could flee, only a few escaped on horse."

He takes a long look at the men standing listing to him. "We are now faced with a decision to make, if they come looking for us there will be more than five hundred men, maybe more. They won't stop until they find and kill us, along with our women and children. We will we let them chase us down or will we stand and fight giving our women and children a chance to escape. This is our home and they may never come looking, if they do we have to be ready, knowing what we are going to do!"

He takes a long look at the men, "There will be no shame if you want to leave with the women and children and flee toward the city of our ancestors. I will stay and fight, any other man who will stay with me step forward! If you chose to flee that's fine, the women and children need someone to provide shelter and hunt for them."

There is little hesitation, all the men step forward,

One man yells, **"This is my home and I will fight for it!"**

Another yells, **"I would rather die than be pushed away!"**

Within moments all the men are yelling things of that nature. Joseph raises his stick high in the air, all the men quiet down to listen.

"If they come to fight with all their men and you stay to fight there is little chance of surviving. If any man wants to flee they are not bound to fight, but the longer we can hold them the better chance our women and children have to survive. With our gift and fighting ability we will stand strong!

He looks at all the men looking back at him and yells, **"We will make them pay for what they have done and want to do!!"**

All the men start cheering at these words. After Joseph is done talking with them they stand around talking for a while and one by one start heading for their homes.

Most of the men have now left the training area except Joseph, Andrew and their closest friends, they are by one of the fires talking.

Joseph turns to his brother and Terrance, "Tomorrow we will look for a good spot to fight if they come."

He turns to Jacob and Andrew, "We will need to be warned if they are coming. I know you two have a great ability. How far away can you feel a man move through the bushes Jacob?"

Jacob stares deep into the woods for a moment before saying, "Usually about two days away, but if they send as many men as I think, it may be more."

Joseph puts his hand on Jacobs shoulder, "That will give anyone fleeing several days of travel before we even start to fight."

Andrew looks at Joseph with a scared look on his face, "How will we fight so many?"

Joseph puts his hand on Andrews shoulder, looking him in the eyes, "You will be with the women and children helping them, they will need a path and shelter."

Andrew steps back, "No, I will stay and fight!"

Julian interrupts, "Joseph is right, they will need someone who can hunt and quickly build a shelter if a storm comes rolling through."

Andrew has nothing to say, he knows his uncle is right.

Joseph looks at Julian, "I'm glad you feel that way, you will be with him, along with Jacob."

Julian now has a surprised look on his face, "I will fight with you!"

"Think about what you have said to Andrew, there will be about thirty women and seven children, that is too many for Andrew to look after all by himself. He will need help. You and Jacob have traveled the most and are also the youngest of the men."

Julian has nothing more to say. He knows Joseph is right.

Jacob, who has said nothing, just listens and looks at Julian, "If they send all their men it will be a great battle, they may be unable to hold them very long, we will need to move quickly."

Joseph looks at all the men standing there, "Maybe they won't come and we won't have to fight at all." He takes a deep breath, "I'm hungry, lets go."

The men all walk back toward Josephs home, checking several fish traps along the way. When they stop for Teresa the men stand watching her play with Joslyn.

Terrance says, "She has adapted well to our way of life well."

Andrew looks at him with a sad look, "I still have to hold her while she cries at night."

Andrew walks over to her and takes her hand. As they walk back to Josephs home she asks, "Can I go back and play with Joslyn after?"

Andrew smiles, "That will be fine."

When they arrive at Josephs home he gets the fire going and starts warming some soup he has made the day prior. Terrance and Nathaniel quickly clean and cut the fish into small pieces, they place them on a square platter Joseph has forged from metal. He has placed it on two big rocks at the fires edge, close enough to the fire so it gets hot enough to cook fish and other meats.

After they eat the older men sit by the fire talking, Andrew walks to the animals with Teresa to feed them and then back to Joslyn's letting her play. Andrew sits at the streams edge watching it flow, throwing some stones into it and watching some fish swim by. He hopes he will not have to leave this place, it is his home.

Joslyn's mother walks over and sits by his side, she looks as though she has been crying, "My husband has told me of the decision you men have made," she pauses and takes a deep breath, "I know he must stay and fight if those men come." Another pause as she looks into the stream then back at Andrew, "I'm sad he will stay and fight, yet I'm happy that you will be with us along with your uncle and Jacob,"

She wipes the tears from her eyes, "We will need protection from anything that might come our way and help with hunting and shelter.

She sits with Andrew for a while just looking into the stream, when they walk back to her home there are several other children playing with Teresa and Joslyn, all running and laughing.

Helen smiles as she looks at Andrew, "I know you have become a busy young man, anytime you want me to watch Teresa she is welcome."

Andrew thanks her and walks down the stream, he has had little time to be alone and wants some time for himself. He walks past the animals into the woods and sits next to a tree. He thinks about all that has happened and what will happen if those men come looking for them, he hopes they do not. Somehow he knows they will!

Chapter Twenty-One

When Andrew wakes in the morning there is a crisp chill to the air. Julian has the inside fire going along with two heat lamps. He has also made sure Teresa and Andrew both have plenty of animal skins lined with wool to cover them while they slept.

"I'm not used to having children around."

"You are doing fine." Andrew notices that Julian has cut some animal skins to different sizes and has them soaking in the same oil they use on their walking sticks.

Julian places a large skin to the top part of his leg and starts cutting it to that size. After it is cut he stands up and wraps it around his leg. It almost covers the entire part of his upper leg. He then sits down and starts pushing some holes through it with a sharp metal poker. Andrew has never seen this tool before nor has he ever seen anybody cut animal skins in this manor.

"What are you doing?" he asks.

Andrew hears Julian's thoughts, *"Its best if I tell you when Teresa is not around."* Andrew now knows it has something to do with the battle they may be facing. Teresa has already helped herself to a bowl of soup and is now sitting, eating it with a piece of bread.

"Don't forget to wash after you finish eating." Andrew says looking at her.

Andrew has only been training in the morning and when he does so he leaves Teresa with Joslyn's mother. All the other men have been training both morning and night and the intensity of their training has reached a new level.

Julian and Andrew only have some bread and water, they will eat more when they return from training. They leave Teresa with Helen and start walking toward the training area.

"Can you tell me what you are soaking those animal skins for now that Teresa is not here?"

Julian looks at Andrew with a serious face, "I'm making battle armor to wear if those men come to fight."

Andrew with a confused look, "Battle armor?" He has never heard of it.

"We use thin pieces of animal skins to fit our body, we cut them where our body moves. After soaking them in the oil we use on our sticks just long enough so we can bend them to fit the part of the body we want protected and then tie them together with thin slices of skins. Soaking it in the oil makes it very hard for a sword or arrow to pierce through yet it is very light so it won't slow us down in battle.

"I hope you never have to wear it."

"That's what we are all hoping for." Julian says as they continue to walk to the training area. They are quiet the rest of the walk, as they enter the training area the other men are already there warming up, both fires are going and they quickly move into a fast hard workout. Lately a lot more time has been spent on full contact fighting, they don't hurt each other but they fight as though it was a real fight.

The next couple of weeks Andrew spends a lot of time gathering wood, he is expecting snow to arrive soon. Sometimes Teresa walks with him as he gathers wood but most of the time she spends playing with Joslyn and the other children. When the first snow arrives there is plenty of wood to burn for warmth, and has he expected the winter is cold with a lot of snow. Andrew is happy when the days start to grow longer and warmer but he also knows that if the Lords men are going to come it will be when the warm days arrive.

That night while eating Andrew asks Julian, "If those men come and we flee why do you and Jacob need battle armor?"

Julian puts down the food he is eating and looks at Andrew, with a serious tone he says, "We can not be certain they won't follow us." He looks at the two looking back at him, "Even if they do chase after us we should be able to stay far ahead of them, we just need to be ready for anything."

Andrew takes a long pause, he looks at Teresa and then back at Julian.

"I should make some for myself. If these men catch us I will have no choice but fight." A long pause before Andrew ads, "I have already fought with these men, I know they will think nothing of killing women and children."

Julian looks at Andrew with sad eyes, "I have already made it for you." He pauses before saying, "I have made it very light so you can run but it will also help stop a sword or arrow if need be."

"Why have you not told me?"

"I did not want you to think about it, if I told you that I've made you battle armor you would have thought about it over and over."

"You're right, I would have thought about it all winter, thank you for waiting." After eating Julian and Andrew walk to the training area. Andrew is now training twice a day with the other men. Teresa stays back at their home while they train, she has no problem staying by herself now.

As the next couple of weeks pass the days grow warm, every day more birds can be heard and the trees grow full of green leaves. One morning after training Joseph asks all the men to come back to the training area after they eat. On the way home Andrew and Julian walk with Joseph, Andrew asks what he wanted to talk about.

"We will walk to the place that I think will give use a good advantage in the fight and to discuss our battle plan. If they come there, we must be ready!"

"I will come with you."

Joseph turns to Andrew then Julian and Jacob, "The three of you can stay back if you want, there is no need for you to come with us today."

Julian puts his hand on Joseph's shoulder, the two stop walking, "If you are going to fight letting us lead the women and children away, I want to see and hear where and how it will be done."

Joseph tilts his head down and closes his eyes for a moment before saying,

"I can respect that and the three of you are all welcome to walk with us." They all start walking again.

Joseph smiles at Julian, "What are you cooking for our morning meal?"

"Soup and your more than welcome to join us."

When they arrive at Julian's home, Teresa runs up to Jacob and gives him a big hug, he always seems to make her laugh somehow. Teresa already has the soup warm and bread cut and ready to eat, she helps as much as she can without being asked. They finish eating and bring Teresa to Joslyn's home where Helen will watch her as the rest of the men meet at the training area.

Once inside the training area all the men are there waiting, including Andrew there are forty-four men. They all line up side by side and start running at a slow steady pace with Joseph leading the way. They travel for about an hour stopping at the place that they gather the metal they use to forge their pots, pans and heat lamps.

Joseph looks at all the men standing around sipping water catching their breaths, "On the other side of these hills is the perfect spot for us to fight.

They take a short time to rest before walking to the top of this high steep hill. When they reach the top they look down into the huge valley on the other side. Most have been here before and are surprised that they have not noticed the shape of the hills, they are shaped like an enormous half moon. Looking down into a vast valley as far as the eye can see, it is overgrown with trees, vines, briers, thorn bushes and all sorts of green life. If they look to each side of them there are hills and peaks, which look down into the valley. Most are too steep to climb but the ledge in the area they stand stretching for about half a mile is also very steep but they will be able to run down it to fight.

Joseph turns to the men looking down into the valley, "We will know they are coming and lead them here," he looks at Terrance and Daniel,

"The two of you are the best at moving the plant life," he points to two high peaks far in the distance on each side that overlook the valley,

"You will each take a man with you to watch your backs as you use the vines and bushes to divide an confuse them as we fight."

Joseph looks down into the valley, "I have already left a path for their trackers leading them this way, all we have to do is keep some fires going with some smoke to lead them into the valley." He looks at all the men standing looking back at him, "We will be sit ready to attack if need be."

Every man agrees that if they must fight this will be the best spot to do it.

The man they call Lord of the land has already sent his best trackers and a legion of men. They are four wide and two hundred deep, moving through the woods with orders to kill all they find and not to go back until they do.

Before Joseph and the rest of the men walk back down the hill and head back to the village, Daniel asks Andrew to stay behind. He would like to have some words with him. Andrew tells Julian that he will walk with Daniel. Julian nods his head at Daniel in a strange way, puts his hand on his shoulder,

"Take all the time you need." He says before walking down the hill with the rest of the men. Andrew and Daniel sit for a short while looking down into the valley.

Andrew turns to Daniel, "What would you like to talk about?"

Daniel looks at the ground, then Andrew, "You are like family to me, your father was my best friend, we grew up together, we played together and our minds were opened around the same time." Daniel's eyes fill with water and a single tear runs down his cheek, "What I'm trying to say is that your father was more like a brother than a friend."

Andrew now with tears in his eyes, "I know the two of you were very close, you don't have to tell me that."

"I know you know how close we were, I'm not trying to tell you that, I'm trying to ask you for something."

"I will do anything for you, anything you want."

Daniel looks down into the valley, "If we have to fight, they will send most of their men. All of us fighting them will probably be killed. We have trained like worriers our entire lives and all that fight will except that." He takes a long pause looking into the valley, then turns toward Andrew with a very serious look on his face.

"My wife is with child, it is very early but we are sure."

With tears in his eyes Andrew says, "You must flee with us, you can't stay to fight!"

"My place will be here giving you the time you need to safely get away," he pauses again before saying, "What I'm asking of you is a great responsibility, I want my child to know me as a good man. Boy or girl I want you to open its mind to nature, using your memories letting them see me and how I was. Your father has many memories of me and I'm sure most are good."

Andrew takes Daniels hand with both of his, "It will be my honor to do so." He then asks, "I have never heard of a girls mind being opened, is it possible?"

"Generations of not exercising the gift has lost the ability to move plants or communicate the way we do but they can receive memories, its done the same way."

"I will treat your child as though it was my brother or sister. I will always do my best to protect your wife and child!"

Daniel smiles, "I have no doubt about that, I see the way you treat

Teresa, you are a good man." He gives Andrew a serious look, "Like your father."

The two start walking back toward the village.

As the next week or so passes there is little change, everybody goes about their business. One night Andrew wakes from a deep sleep, he is not sure why, he just knows something is wrong. He lies in bed concentrating deep into the forest making sure no one approaches. He feels nothing, it takes some time but eventually falls back to sleep.

The next morning when he wakes the first thing he does is concentrate deep into the woods. He is horrified when he feels ten horses walking side by side, he knows they are horses by the way they walk. If they are walking side by side he knows men must be on them.

Andrew jumps out of bed and runs to Julian who has already awake.

Before Andrew can say a word, "I have already been told by Jacob," he looks at Andrew, "Eat we have a long day ahead of us."

Teresa walks into the room rubbing her eyes, Andrew hears Julian's thoughts,

"Try not to scare her, she's been through a lot."

Andrew and Julian both know this is one of the last meals they will spend together in this home, they quietly eat. After eating all the men gather in the training area. Jacob is standing with Andrew concentrating deep into the woods. They are now able to feel the massive amount of men heading their way.

Andrew turns to Jacob with great concern, "How many are there?"

Jacob looks at Andrew, "Too many to count."

The two walk back to the others, and stop near Julian, Jacob says, "We have to inform the women and children and let them know we must leave now!"

The group of men walk down the stream, stopping at every home telling the women they have little time, they must flee. Most of the women have tears in their eyes and all the children are crying as they say goodbye to their fathers. Andrew has already told all the men with children that he will protect them with his life and will always be there to help them in any way. Andrew walks up to Joseph, Julian and Jacob both behind him. He gives Joseph a hug.

"You will win this fight." Andrew says.

Joseph nods at him, "When you arrive at the city of our ancestors safely with the women and children, that's when I have won this fight!"

Andrew steps back and takes Josephs hand, "I will never forget you."

As Andrew says this Teresa runs up crying and gives Joseph a big hug.

He picks her up and wipes her tears, "Don't cry, you are traveling to a great city in a wall where no one can hurt you."

He puts her down and Andrew takes her hand. Joseph looks at the three men leading the women and children,

"You must leave now, move as quickly as you can."

Andrew, Julian and Jacob all put on their battle armor making sure they are ready to fight whatever crosses their path as they travel. They start walking into the thick forest leading about thirty women and seven children, all carrying only what they need to survive. As they pass the animals the fence made from bushes unravels letting them run free. The men start to get ready for battle, sharpening knifes and putting on their battle armor and start to walk side by side to the place that they will make their stand. They move quickly to the ridge where they want the fight to be and look down into the valley. They make small fire pits along the top ridge, they want to be found and are ready to fight!

The rest of the day passes with no sign of any men. About mid morning the next day Joseph watches as the ten men on horse ride into the valley. He tells the men to be seen but act as though they don't know they are being watched. He observes as the men on horse watch them for a short while then turn and ride fast into the distance.

Joseph turns to his brother, "Tell all the men to eat well, we will be fighting today!"

Daniel and Terrance both chose another man to follow them as they run off to the peaks on each side of the valley, there they will sit and wait.

Hours pass, all looking into the distance watching and waiting for any signs of men. When the Lords men finally come into sight, Joseph and the others stand at the top of the ridge letting themselves be seen. They are standing spread apart along the top edge looking down ready to fight. Several men lead the Lord's men on horse as all the other men spread themselves apart forming four separate lines. The men on horse are leading the first line with about fifty men all carrying swords. A few hundred yards back stand hundreds more all carrying swords, behind them is another line of men spreading across the valley all with bows and arrows. Even further back is another line of hundreds of men with both bows and arrows and swords. The ten men on horse who were the trackers are not to be seen, they probably will not be fighting and won't enter the valley.

Joseph looks at the formation the men have taken, he then looks at his men all standing, waiting to fight.

Daniel hears Joseph's thoughts, *"At the first sign of battle tangle the men with bows and arrows. The men in the back will try to go around and attack from the back, make it hard for them."*

Terrance hears Joseph, *"When the fighting begins tangle and separate the two front lines, cause as much confusion and kill as many as you can. You will receive no mercy so show none!"*

Joseph steps on a rock and yells to the men standing on the ledge,

"I will go talk, if we can avoid a fight we all win." He takes a long pause looking at all his men looking back at him, "But I'm afraid we will have no choice but fight, the moment I think there is no talking to be had I will attack. When I do move down the hill and start dividing them using the bushes, keep them chasing you and kill as many as possible. The longer the battle lasts the longer the women and children have to escape, **we will let them know we are worriers! We will stand strong as long as we can! We will make them regret trying to kill our kind!"**

The men all raise their sticks in the air and start cheering at the same time. They quickly quiet down as Joseph starts walking down the hill toward the three men on horse.

When the men see him approaching they move forward with about ten men walking behind them all dressed in black with metal helmets and chest plates, with their swords at the ready. When they meet Joseph he stands in front of the middleman on horse. This man has many scares on his face and looks to be a large man. He has a cold stare as he looks at Joseph and is telling the others what to do. Joseph thinks that he is the leader of the men. Joseph is holding his walking stick firmly in front of him as the two men stare at each other for a long moment.

"We do not wish to fight with you, we just want to be left alone!"

The man Joseph is talking to turns to the man on his side laughing then says, "They just want to be left alone."

The laughing stops as he turns back toward Joseph, "You and all your men will die here today!"

Joseph steps back, "Not one of my men plans on leaving this battle and many of your men will die as well!"

Joseph takes another step back with his eyebrows lowered and a serious look on his face, "I promise you one thing, if you do not take your men and leave now you will be dead before the battle begins!"

The man laughs out loud and turns to the men behind him, "Kill him!"

Daniel and Terrance both hear Josephs thoughts, *"We have no choice but fight!"*

As the man turns back toward Joseph, bushes wrap around the horses front legs pulling them backwards, throwing the man forward. Before the man hits the ground Joseph steps forward driving his stick under the man's chin spinning him backwards so he lands on the back of his head. Joseph takes another step forward crushing his face with his stick making sure he is dead. As this happens Terrance and Daniel both do what they have been told to, Daniel using bushes and vines to pull the bows and arrows to the ground. The men on the ridge all rush down the hill to battle while Terrance and a man named Robert use the roots, thorns and bushes to divide and confuse them. Some being choked others having skin torn from thorns and briers wrapping around their limbs, they are all in a panic. The other men on horse ride away from Joseph as the ten men start to surround him.

The men from his village have reached the bottom and separate as they run into the thick thorns and trees allowing them to hide as bushes and vines are used to divide the Lords men into small pockets trying to fight through the thick bushes to regroup. That's when the men of the village attack allowing them to fight ten to fifteen men at a time before disappearing back into the thick green life of the valley. About twenty men, hesitant on attacking, now surround Joseph. He stands with his stick held with both hands ready to fight.

Another man named Christopher comes to his aid, he is a tall skinny man with a very short beard and one of the only men in the village to keep his hair short. Christopher grabs one of the men surrounding Joseph by the back of the head and pulls his small knife across the man's throat killing him. Before the man hits the ground Christopher steps to the side swinging his stick into the face of another man turning to see what has happened. The man drops his sword and puts his hands to his face. Christopher kicks his feet out from under him, the man fall backwards landing on his back. Christopher lands on top of him with his knee on his neck making a loud snapping sound.

Another man rushes Christopher swinging his sword, which is blocked by Christopher's stick. He then does a forward roll bringing himself to his feet, as he springs up he plunges his knife into the mans stomach, lifting him off the ground and throwing him back.

As this is happening Joseph turns to the man behind him and pulls out the small ax he carries on his side. He takes a large step forward throwing it at the man who is now in front of him landing it right between the eyes. As the mans body hits the ground Joseph pulls the ax from the mans head while moving to the side he hits another man in the back of the neck with the ax, quickly turning to face two more men rushing him with their swords.

He steps to the side hitting one of the men in the side of the head with his stick, causing him to stumble into the other man making them both fall to the ground. Joseph slams his stick into one of the mans chest crushing his ribs, pushing himself into the air landing with both feet on the back of the other man's head and neck.

He turns to see Christopher fighting with about five men with many more approaching. He grabs one of the five from behind and pushes his knife through his spine, then hits another on the top of the head with his stick knocking him to the ground.

The rest back off for a moment letting the others join the fight, Joseph and Christopher are now standing side by side.

Christopher hears Joseph's thoughts, *"We must run and take cover, we will use the thick woods to separate them."*

Both men turn and run into the thickness of the valley closing the path behind them.

The Lords men are startled, realizing that two men have killed so many so quickly, they chase them with caution.

Another man named Tyler and average sized man with hair down to his shoulders keeping his face clean of hair has already killed about ten men and now has about twenty or more chasing him as he looks for a good spot to confront them. He stops when he walks trough an area with many trees that have many vines hanging from them, so many they block out the light.

He hides behind a tree as he uses his gift to lower the vines, the men chasing him now have to push through the thick vines hanging down from the trees. As they do so one of the men stops he looks around and says,

"Something doesn't feel right, these vines give me the creeps, I don't think we should be here!"

Tyler steps out from behind the tree, "You are right, you should not be here, you should have left us alone." He looks at the man who has just said that the vines give him the creeps with a cold stare. "And now you will die here!"

As he says this, vines start to entangle the twenty men, wrapping around their bodies as though they were in a pit full of snakes. Some try to run, others try to slice at the vines with their swords, all are screaming in fear. The screams of fear are turned to screams of pain as some are crushed to death while others are pulled apart by the vines.

Tyler walks a little further and encounters another group of men, about forty of them. He knows there is no chance of surviving so he uses the bushes to kill as many as possible and fights as hard as he can until a sword in the back takes him to the ground. As he lie there another sword is driven through his battle armor pushing through his heart killing him.

Another man named Charles has had no desire to hide, he has sought out as many men as he possibly could and fought. He has done this all day and has killed about a hundred men. He has finally become to exhausted to fight with efficiency any longer. He is still swinging his stick and a sword he has picked up in battle when an arrow hits him in the center of the chest knocking him to the ground. As he lie there breathing his last breaths one of the Lords men raises a sword in the air above him to finish him off. As he does this Charles rolls over driving his elbow onto the man's knee knocking him to the ground and rolls on top of him pushing his small knife into the center of the man's throat. He is quickly stabbed in the back by several men and killed.

Daniel and Terrance have used vines and bushes to control how many of the Lord's men that can gather together. They have a good vantage point both looking down into the valley seeing the men through the trees. They do their best trying to keep large groups from forming. Terrance has all the bushes moving around in what looks to be a frantic pace keeping the Lords men in a panic trying to figure out what's happening.

If Terrance sees a group of men assembling through the trees, he uses vines and bushes trying to crush the life from them. This is hard to do from such a distance but every time Terrance is able to tangle a group of men he does. Some are pulled to the ground with roots wrapping around their bodies squeezing the breath from them, others are pulled into the air by their necks left kicking and pulling at the vines as they tighten around them. Some are tossed high into the air by their limbs landing to their deaths.

Daniel has spent most of the day using the green life of the valley doing the same with the Lords men in the back of the valley. He has also been keeping the men with bows and arrows stuck in a clearing, not letting them join the fight.

If they try to move forward the thorns and brier bushes start to move creating a wall that entangles any man trying to pass through ripping the flesh from the body. If they try to back up they encounter a wall of briers and thorns even thicker than the one in front of them, they are stuck in a part of the valley with little green life.

The group of men in the back of the valley has been trying all day to move around the hills with little success. Daniel watches them, cutting off any path using vines and thorn bushes to entangle so tight it's impossible to pass through. They have tried with no progress, many of the men have been pulled into the thick wall of vines and thorns.

Each time this happens the Lord's men back off as the man pulled into the thickness of the bushes screams in pain as the thorns rip the flesh off the bones and vines pull the mans limbs from the body. Most of the Lord's men are in a panic, wishing they had left these men alone.

Another man named Brandon, he is the smallest man in the village, only standing about five and a half feet tall has been seeking out small groups of men all day. He uses the trees to hide himself, as they pass he attacks from behind, he has killed about fifty men this way. He lets a small group of about ten men pass. Terrance spots him from the peak he is sitting.

Brandon hears Terrance's thoughts, *"There are men all around you, try to hide yourself!"*

Brandon replies, *"We are here to fight, divide them the best you can. I will make them regret coming our way to kill us."*

Brandon chases down the men who have just passed, they barely have a chance to turn before Brandon swings his stick into the head of one of the men. As that man falls he takes a quick step back now holding his stick in his hands shoulder length apart, his front hand over the stick, with the hand that is closest to the body wrapped underneath the stick.

With the look of anger on his face he lunges forward using his stick like a spear driving it under the chin of another man following through until the mans head hits the ground. With no hesitation he steps back and to the side lifting the stick off the man's throat and spins himself around hitting another man in the face dropping him. As he turns two more men are rushing him with their swords held high. As the two men rush Brandon used vines to tangle their arms, causing them to drop their swords. With the two men still trying to get free from the vines Brandon spines to the side cutting the throat of one of them and continues his spin driving the knife into the back of the other man's neck killing him. Another man lunges forward trying to stab Brandon who kicks the sword to the side, as his foot hits ground he steps forward holding his knife firmly. He moves it from the hip pushing the knife under his enemies chin snapping his head back, as the man's head snaps back Brandon stomps on the mans knee folding it backwards.

The rest of the men start running away with Brandon chasing them, he catches one the men running with a swing of his stick to the side of the head. He confronts a group of about twenty or more while chasing the men running. He kills about ten more men before he is overwhelmed and killed.

Joseph and Christopher have battled several more times killing many.

Joseph looks up at the sun, "It's going to be dark soon, we should find a good spot for cover we will need some rest."

They move into some thick bushes making a small shelter, just big enough for then to sit in without being seen. Joseph tells Christopher to sleep for a short while, he will stay awake and be alert.

Joseph sits listening to his surroundings, he tries to contact his men, only seventeen respond and all very tired. The Lords men are scared, he does not think they will look for them in the dark so he tells the other men to find a safe place to rest for a while. All the men move into the thickest bushes they can find making small shelters they can rest in.

Many miles away Julian, Jacob and Andrew are still walking at a rapid pace.

Andrew sees the sun falling behind the trees, "We should start gathering some food and make shelters."

They walk a little further finding a good spot to stop for the night.

It's not long before several small shelters are formed from bushes and vines. The three men walk into the thick woods to gather food while some of the women gather wood and others make several small fire pits for cooking and warmth. Few are talking, there is a heavy feeling in their hearts. They all know that the other men from the village are fighting a loosing battle to give them time to escape. They are all terrified and exhausted.

"We should go to sleep soon, we will start traveling early." Julian says in a somber tone.

Most go to sleep shortly after the sunsets, Julian and Jacob sit by one of the small fires along with Andrew and several of the women.

Julian turns to Jacob, "Are you able to feel what's going on with the fight?"

"It's very far away and the bushes have been moving so much that all I can feel is a fight, a big fight!"

Andrew looks at the women, then his uncle and Jacob, "We should all get some sleep. Joseph has told me that he will win the battle when we arrive safely at the city of our ancestors. He feels his life is worth giving for our safety." He pauses looking at the fire before saying, "We should do our best to get there!"

Little is said after that, they put the fires out and go to sleep.

Julian and Jacob are up before the sun the following morning and already have the fire going with some meat cooking. Andrew is the next to wake, he tells the other two that he will watch the food while they hunt. They should gather as much as they can and cook it all letting them travel all day without stopping to cook or hunt. Julian and Jacob agree and they walk into the woods gathering as much food as possible.

When some of the women wake Andrew asks them to get another fire going and to be ready to cook the food when the two get back letting them get an early start.

Back in the valley where the battle is going on all the remaining men have little if no sleep and the Lord's men are once again trying to regroup so they can fight in numbers. In the cover of night some of the Lord's men have escaped through the thick bushes and are circling around the backside of the hills moving their way toward Terrance and Robert. When Robert realizes this he informs Terrance and the two men rush down toward the twenty or so men to battle.

Joseph hears Terrance's thoughts, *"We have been found, I will be unable to assist you any further."*

As they rush down the hill to battle both men hear Josephs thoughts, *"Fight strong!"*

Now rushing down the hill, Terrance leaps off a large rock above the approaching men kicking one in the face, landing and spinning at the same time, now standing behind most of them. As they turn to face Terrance, Robert holding his stick across his body drives it into the back of two of the men's necks snapping their heads backwards and their bodies forward. They land towards Terrance who swings his stick into one of the men, keeping his stick moving he hit's the other man in the back of the legs causing him to fall back. As the man hits the ground Terrance leaps in the air landing on the man one knee in the throat and with his other hand he pushes his small knife deep into the mans stomach.

Robert steps past Terrance swinging his stick over his head landing it on the top of another mans head hard enough to crack his skull.

Without stopping he moves forward driving his stick like a spear into the face of another man. As Robert turns to hit another, a sword pushes into his side. Terrance hits the arm of the man holding the sword knocking it to the ground and quickly brings the stick back up hitting the man in the chin. As the mans head snaps back Terrance steps past the him grabbing his hair and brings him to the ground using his knee in the back of the man's neck to stop the fall and pushes his knife into the mans chest making sure he is dead.

Terrance jumps up to see Robert take another sword in the back, as Robert falls to the ground another sword hits him in the head killing him. As Terrance turns to fight another man he is hit in the back by an arrow, before he hits the ground he throws his ax hitting one of the men in the head. As he lies on the ground several swords push through his battle armor into his chest killing him.

Daniel hears Josephs thoughts, *"Terrance has been found and there are too many to hold back much longer. I want you and Joshua to move past the opening of the valley and kill as many of their trackers as you can. While you are doing that the few of us that are left will rush their back line, they will think we are fighting out of desperation giving you time to kill most of their trackers. That will be the best we can do for the women and children now."*

Daniel and Joshua start running toward the valleys opening, the men on horse are the men they want. They move as quickly as they can trying to avoid being seen.

Joseph contacts all the men left in the fight, he is able to reach only twelve, he lets them know what they will do, they all hide and wait to hear from Daniel. When Daniel and Joshua are close to the trackers Joseph will give the word to attack. That's when the last of them will charge the hundreds of men that are regrouping, now that there is little movement in the bushes. Daniel and Joshua move quickly yet quietly along the top ridge of the hills making sure they are not seen while they try to locate the men on horse.

They spend about an hour moving toward the back opening of the valley. They past all the men grouped in pairs of fifty or more, each group close to the others. Daniel can see that they are trying to form one massive force to move through the valley and kill all in their path.

Daniel and Joshua search the woods past the opening of the valley for a while moving all the way back to a large stream. They are now about a mile past the valley, they stop when they hear some men talking and quietly creep up to get a better look, they see that it's the men they are looking for. Daniel looks at the surroundings then Joshua, they are ready to attack the ten men who are sitting by a fire with their horses off to the side.

Joseph hears Daniels thoughts, *"We have found the trackers and will attack any moment."*

Joseph replies, *"Fight hard and strong, if you kill all their trackers they will have a hard time following the women an children giving them the time they need to reach their destination."*

Daniel turns to Joshua, "We attack now!"

Joseph has already contacted all the men left and they are ready to make their final stand. Daniel and Joshua both stand up and charge at the ten men, as they do vines and thorns form a wall between the men and their horses leaving them no choice but fight.

At the same time in the valley where the Lord's men have now gathered into one massive force, they all stand at the ready as they watch tunnel like paths open in the thick bushes all around them. The thorns and briers they are standing in start to move and tangle their legs. A panic comes over the massive group of men as they slash at the bushes wrapping around their legs and watch the tunnel paths waiting to see how many men come rushing through.

All the Lords' men are turning back and forth looking at the paths in fear as they cut and push the roots and bushes that are creeping up their legs. Many of the men are now on the ground trying to pull the brier bushes off their necks with no luck. The others watch, as these men are choked to death, unable to help as they are trying to keep themselves from being pulled to the ground.

Daniel and Joshua have moved apart separating the men. Joshua slams his stick on the top of one of the men's foot then stomps on his knee folding it backwards, dropping the man to the ground screaming. Joshua turns to the side, hitting another in the chest with his stick knocking him back then drives his stick into the side of his head, without stopping he steps back thrusting his stick back into another mans throat trying to attack with his sword held high. Before he can turn to face another man he is struck by a sword pushed deep into his side, when he turns to hit the man another strikes him in the back of the head cutting it open, when he falls to the ground another sword is pushed through his back killing him.

Daniel has already killed three men, as the others attack he backs up knocking one of the swords from a man's hand and hits another in the head with his stick dropping him to the ground. He steps forward driving his stick into another mans chest and quickly moves it up to the throat. As Daniel turns to the side he is hit in the head with a sword cutting him deep, dropping him to his knees. He jumps back up holding the wound on his head and lunges forward pushing his small knife into the stomach of the man who has hit him, lifting him off the ground throwing him back.

As he turns to face the last man standing who is already charging foreword. His sword pushing it deep into Daniels shoulder, almost all the way through. The man pulls the sword out and as he passes Daniel he takes a large swing slashing the back of Daniels legs badly. As Daniel stands there looking at the man he drops to his knees, the man slowly walks up to him and smiles as he raises his sword as though he was going to take Daniels head. As the mans hands are high in the air a vine hits the man in the face knocking him back, as this happens Daniel jumps up driving his knife into the mans heart killing him.

Daniel takes a step back and one of the men on the ground, the man who has had his knee bent back drives a knife into the lower part of Daniels leg, cutting it from his knee to his ankle causing him to fall. As the man tries to stab him again Daniel blocks the knife using his forearm, the knife sinks deep into his arm. He turns his arm pulling the knife from the man's hands and puts a knee on the man's shoulder. With both hands he grabs hold of the man's head and twists it around snapping his neck.

While this was going on the Lord's men in the valley are still trying to pull the bushes away from their bodies as they watch the tunnel like paths ready to fight.

All the green life in the area starts to move at a rapid and frantic pace, thorns cutting the skin and vines wrap around body parts. Limbs are being pulled in different directions ripping away from bodies, men are tossed high in the air by vines as others are hoisted into the air by their necks. The Lords men who are not entangled try to slash away at the vines wrapped around the others, panic and confusion has overcome the Lord's men.

The last of the men led by Joseph now rush through the tunnel like paths with a high level of energy. They want to kill as many of these men as possible, they want to put fear in their hearts, making them wish they had not come this way to kill them and hope they will not pursue the others.

Nathaniel is the first to reach, striking one in the face with his stick. Picking up the man's sword as he falls to the ground he moves forward, spins around taking another mans head off. In the same swing he turns the sword down hitting another man on the top of the leg cutting all the way through. He steps over that man as he falls to the ground and pushes the sword deep into the belly of another man pulling it out quickly and driving it under his chin. He turns to the side blocking a sword swinging at his head with his stick and takes the man's arm off with a swing from the sword. He kicks his feet out from under him, as the man hits the ground he drives his stick into the man's face then throat.

Joseph and the last of his men are all mixed in this massive force of hundreds using their sticks and swords to kill as many as possible. Joseph has fought his way almost to the center of the men using the vines and bushes to assist him in the fight. Christopher is on the other side and the rest of the men are scattered all about fighting with all their energy.

This battle goes on for several hours, the Lords men feel as though they are fighting hundreds of men, but there is only a handful. Eventually the numbers overwhelm the few men that have fought so strong.

Joseph is the last standing, surrounded by hundreds, he smiles when he sees the fear in the eyes of the Lord's men.

He kills about fifteen more as they rush him and is finally killed by a sword in the back and several more are pushed through his armor as he lies on the ground.

The Lord's men spend most of the day gathering there wounded and regrouping. As they regroup one of the men has taken charge, he is a strong man with fairly long hair. Its tied back keeping it out of his eyes, he has many scars on his face and arms and is feared almost as much as the Lord himself. This man talks with the Lord often, he knows the Lord will be disappointed that they did not find the women and children, someone or many of his men will pay for this.

After they have all regroup there are still about three hundred with minimal wounds and about a two hundred more severe. Their loses have totaled about three hundred or more. This man who has put himself in charge talks it over with the best and most skilled of their men. They decide to divide the group into two packs, the least skilled and weakest of the bunch will help the wounded back and explain to the Lord what has happened.

The other group with their best trackers will chase the women and children until the catch and kill every last one of them. But know they would move back to where their best trackers are waiting for the battle to end. They will rest for the night before separating into different directions.

It takes some time to move back out of the valley to where the trackers are, when they arrive there this man in charge who is infuriated to see that all the best trackers have been killed. He tells his men to search the area for any signs of men or any trail to follow. He realizes that the men they had fought had no intentions of surviving the battle and he will follow, catch and kill the rest of them and their families or die doing so.

They thoroughly search the area with no sign of anybody or anything. Before resting for the night they look for any of his men with good tracking skills. The man who has put himself in charge is a very skilled tracker, there are about twenty more men with these skills. They now have about twenty men who can track, he picks the ten strongest men and tells them to wake early. He wants them take the horses and start tracking but to leave a trail for them to follow, he will lead the rest of the men in that direction, about one hundred and fifty of them.

Daniel has used the fire to stop the bleeding and has made it to the stream letting himself float for several miles in the water before crawling out. He gathers some berries and the leaves he needs to tend to his wounds. He quickly makes the mix that will keep infection out but he is very weak and needs some rest before crossing the wetlands. He knows he will have to keep moving for a while to avoid being caught, so he slowly stagers through the bushes using what little energy he has left, he tries to leave little or no trail for the Lords men to follow.

He travels well into the night before collapsing from exhaustion. He wakes very early the next morning wet, cold, hungry and feeling very sore and ill. He knows he must keep moving before resting anymore so he pushes himself forward toward the wetland. He travels most of the day stopping only for short rests, eat some berries and clean his injuries that are extremely extensive and need a lot of attention. When dusk starts to set in he stops for the night and makes a small shelter.

He thinks he has traveled far enough putting a lot of distance between himself and the Lord's men letting him light a small fire in the shelter without them smelling the smoke. He knows without heat and food he will die so he makes a small fire in the shelter and starts cooking a rabbit he has caught and killed along the way. After eating he falls to sleep by the warmth of the fire.

He wakes late into the next day still feeling ill, he eats some more of the rabbit before walking out to twist some water from some vines. He fills his pouch, while doing this he listens deep into the forest for any signs of the men. There is none so he decides to thoroughly clean and wrap his wounds resting for the day, he will start traveling the next morning. He knows if he has any chance of surviving he must travel through the wetlands and make his way to Aaron's village for help. He also knows that it is many miles away and will probably die trying but it is the only chance he has.

Andrew is walking with Teresa, holding her hand with Julian at his side behind the group, Jacob is in front leading the way. They have been traveling for several days without talking very much. Julian has been doing his best to hide any signs of the path they are traveling which is very hard. Being such a large group some small branches are being broke but he knows if the Lords men are chasing them they have a good lead. With their ability to move through the bushes with ease it will help them stay in front of them. Both Julian and Jacob have been making sure the path behind them is extremely full and will be hard to travel through without their gift.

As they are walking and dusk is setting in Julian notices some of the children and women starting to have a hard time, staggering as they walk and breathing heavy.

"I think we should stop and rest for the night." Julian says.

"There is still plenty of light left." Jacob answers.

Jacob hears Julian's Thoughts, *"Some are very tired and are having a hard time walking."*

Jacob stops and looks at all the women and children, they all look very sad, hungry and exhausted. "You are right, we should stop and rest for the night."

They all stop walking and the three men look around into the bushes, as they do many small huts start to form all in a big circle around them. There is enough room in the center to make several small fire pits.

Julian says to Andrew, "Make some small fire pits while Jacob and I catch some food, tonight we eat well."

Jacob looks at the women, "Make sure all the children have a comfortable place to sleep, they all look very tired."

Julian and Jacob walk into the thick woods to gather food while Andrew gets the fires going. After about half an hour Julian and Jacob come back with several small animals to eat.

Julian looks at Andrew, "Have some of the women help you cook these and feed the children, make sure they eat well, we will go gather some more."

The two walk back into the forest. About another half an hour passes before the two come back with some more food, all of the children have eaten and most are sleeping already. They cook the rest of the food, after eating most of the women go to sleep. There is little to talk about, all are very sad knowing their friends and family that has stayed to fight are probably dead by now.

After most of the women go to sleep the three men are sitting by the fire with only a few of the women.

Jacob has been staring into the woods for a while, "I can not feel anybody following us but I will keep checking." He looks at the rest sitting by the fire, "I think we should slow down, the children grow more tired every day."

Andrew looks at him, "Once we get past the great ravine we will be safe."

Julian turns to Andrew, "What are you talking about?"

"There is a spot where two raging rivers meet and fall into a great gorge."

Jacob with a shocked look, "How do you know this?"

"I saw it when my mind was opened."

Julian surprised Andrew has seen this, it is something he did not know about himself asks, "Do you see how to get across?"

"They used the vines and roots to form a bridge at the falls edge." He then looks at his uncle, "What do we do if the Lords men start to catch us?"

Julian looks at Jacob and then Andrew, "Jacob and I have already talked about this possibility, you and Jacob will be able to tell if they are getting close. We want to stay far enough ahead of them, but if they start to close on us Jacob and I will lead them in a different direction letting the women and children get away."

Andrew looks at his uncle with tears in his eyes, "I don't want to lose you!"

"I said we would lead them away, I didn't say fight. The two of us will be able to stay far ahead of them, they won't be able to catch us."

"Well let's hope that we can stay together the entire way." Andrew says.

They sit by the fire for a while longer before going to sleep all knowing the Lords men may be chasing them but if they are they are far back. They must keep moving toward the city of their ancestors to ensure safety.

The old man telling his story looks at his grandchildren. Marcus is staring at him in awe, young Andrew is sobbing quietly. They have sat and listened to his story all day, only eating the little food they have brought with them. The old man looks at the sun, its getting low in the sky,

"We should start back, your grandmother will have our evening meal ready."

Marcus looks at him, "We can't leave now, I want to hear more of your story!"

Young Andrew asks, "Can I move bushes like you? Am I a worrier?"

The old man stands up holding his side. He has also been sitting all day, "Lets start walking, it will be dark before we get back."

As they walk back Marcus Jr. asks, "Will you tell us more of our story tomorrow?"

The old man smiles at his grandson, "I will continue telling you the story the next time you come to visit. I don't see you very often so I will tell you some of my story every time you come to visit."

Andrew Jr. asks, "Will you teach me how to move the bushes and vines and teach me how to fight like a worrier."

The old man looks at his grandson, "That's up to your father, I have taught him all that I know, he may be a better fighter than I am."

Marcus Jr. asks, "Why has father kept our gift a secret?"

"That is something I cannot answer, you will have to ask him that."

The rest of the walk back the two children ask all sorts of questions. When they arrive back at the home their grandmother has a large meal waiting for them.

As they sit down to eat Marcus Jr. asks his father, "Why have you kept our gift a secret from us?"

"I have not kept it a secret, I was waiting until you were old enough to keep it a secret, we have a gift that others are threatens by." He looks at his sons with sad eyes,

"If the people in the villages find out who we are, they may give us a hard time. We have a special gift that others do not understand."

Marcus Jr. looks at his father, "I want to learn our ways, I want to train like a worrier!"

His father smiles back at him, "I will teach you all I know. When I think you are ready I will open your mind to nature." He looks at his boys "You must keep this secret," he gives young Andrew a stern stare,

"You can not tell anybody, people will think we are different, they will be scared."

Young Andrew looks back at his father, "I will not tell anybody."

Marcus Sr. looks at both his sons, "When we are back home I will start training you, but now eat, it's been a long day.

After eating they all go to bed. They spend a little more than a week at their grandparents before heading home. Both Andrew and Marcus can't wait until they start training. Even more important they both can't wait until they go back to their grandfathers, they want to hear more of his life's story!

StrongStand takes the reader on a journey led by a young warrior as he matures from a boy to a man. He tells his story to his grandchildren, detailing his younger years of heartache and heroism. As he tells his story to his grandchildren, they will be introduced to their ability to move nature and communicate telepathically. For years these people have lived in seclusion, keeping their small village away from persecution. These years of peace are broken when an evil leader known as the Lord of the Land and his legion of followers mark these territories and scorn to their way of life. The book builds up to an enormous climax: many outnumber them, but their ability to move nature with their minds equals the odds. Through Andrew's story, meet a unique group of people and learn their way of life as they live through serene moments and battle for survival.

Matthew James Mendoza was born June 4, 1971. Since high school he's had an underlying desire to write a book. At age thirty-six, he bought some notepads and started writing, realizing it was something he really enjoys. He now spends any extra time he has writing, hoping all who read his work take pleasure in it.

www.PublishAmerica.com

"my book of happy memories"

By JOAN ELLIS GETCHELL COLE
12/25/1907 to 12/19/1943

Compiled by her daughter
JOAN COLE PENDERGAST